The Cats of Seroster

Cam didn't want the knife the blacksmith gave him – and when the blacksmith crumbled to dust before his eyes he was even more reluctant to take it, even though it did have an uncanny ability to find its mark. He didn't want to take the blacksmith's letter across marsh and desert to the Seroster, either.

Cam solved problems. A letter written here, a town drain sorted out there – the young student was happy to wander about earning what he could. The blacksmith's message, and his weapon, didn't suit Cam at all. But however hard he tried, he couldn't rid himself of either. Miserably conscious of compulsion, he finally reached the Seroster's town – and the great golden cats were waiting for him.

It was the cats, the Miw, who had rescued the boy Duke when his father was murdered. They were utterly opposed to Little Paul, the cunning, evil usurper, and his henchmen. From the most ancient times they had owed allegiance to the Seroster, the legendary hero and leader who appeared when the city was in trouble.

When Cam found the Seroster and, horrified and reluctant, realised the magnitude of the task that lay before him, it was the Miw – Amon, his friend and guide, Sehtek, who led the Miw, wise Smerdis, who saved his life, and all their brethren – who gave him the help and comfort and courage that he needed.

The Cats of Seroster

Cam didn't want the knife the blacksmith gave him, and when the blacksmith crumbled to dust before his eyes, he was even more desperate to get rid of it. But though [illegible] his place [illegible] didn't want to take the messages [illegible] across [illegible] which sent [illegible] the [illegible].

Cam [illegible] problems [illegible] a horse [illegible] down [illegible] the young [illegible] was [illegible] to [illegible] about [illegible] what [illegible]. The [illegible] riders [illegible] and his weapon [illegible] Cam [illegible] however hard he tried. [illegible] Without [illegible] companion, he finally reached Seroster's [illegible] – and the great [illegible] waiting for him.

[illegible] the Cats [illegible] who had [illegible] the [illegible] Duke when his [illegible] was murdered [illegible] opposed to [illegible] the [illegible] and the [illegible]. For in the [illegible] the [illegible] had sworn allegiance to the Seroster, the legendary hero and leader who appeared when the city was in trouble.

When Cam found the Seroster and [illegible] the magnitude of the task that lay before him, it was the [illegible] who [illegible] guide, Seroster who led [illegible] who [illegible] – who gave him help and comfort and courage [illegible].

The Cats of Seroster

ROBERT WESTALL

"For I will consider my cat Jeoffry
For he is the servant of the living God
For he keeps the Lord's watch in the night
Against the adversary,
For he counteracts the powers of darkness
  by his electrical skin and glaring eyes.
For he counteracts the Devil, who is death,
  by brisking about the life.
For in his morning orisons he loves the sun
  and the sun loves him.
For he is of the tribe of the tiger
For the Cherub Cat is a term of the Angel Tiger."
Part of 'My Cat Jeoffry' by Christopher Smart (1722–1771)

Unless the Lord build the house
They labour in vain who build it
Unless the Lord keep the city
The watchman waketh but in vain.
Psalm 127 verses 1–2

Piccolo Books
in association with Macmillan

First published 1984 by Macmillan Children's Books
This Piccolo edition published 1986 by Pan Books Ltd,
Cavaye Place, London SW10 9PG
9 8 7 6 5 4 3 2

ISBN 0 330 29239 0
Reproduced, printed and bound in Great Britain by
Hazell Watson & Viney Limited,
Member of the BPCC Group,
Aylesbury, Bucks

Note

I owe a literary debt. This whole book grew from a passage in the travel-diary kept by Mrs Lindy McKinnel in the South of France in 1971.

"We arrived latish in the afternoon when it was again possible to look at the sun through the soft veil of cloud that shrouded it and rendered it pinky-red and harmless. The low scrub-covered hills of the Alpilles are of white miocene limestone. This gives the region a patched and scarred look. I knew nothing of Les Baux's turbulent history as we drove up the narrow valley with towering crags on either side. Far above, on the highest point of the highest hill, stood the castle of Les Baux. The barons of Les Baux, in the eleventh century, ruled over seventy-two towns and boroughs.

"From below it appeared a jumble of white ruins and white rocks, inextricably mixed. When we walked up the narrow winding cobbled street, with its tiny old stone houses and larger mansions of the wealthy, a sense of history, a will-o'-the-wisp began, for me, to become apparent. Permeating the ruins was a feeling of what I can only describe as 'bloody trouble'. I could feel in my bones, feuds, war, murder, conspiracies and the lust for power. I could almost hear the shouts of the lookouts on the bastions and the roars of the inhabitants as they rained down death and destruction. I should not have liked to be alone in the place at night.

"The impression I had gained from below was completely justified – it was impossible to tell where the ruins ended and the rocks began; just one huge jumble of terraces and pits, walls, steps and towers. Those rocks were a dazzling white, pitted and weathered into the most fantastic shapes like honeycombs. They looked as soft as butter, but I rubbed them with my fingers, and only a little chalky dust was apparent.

"'A good place to do yourself in,' commented an American tourist as we peered gingerly over the brink to see the cliff dropping away vertically for hundreds of feet. Provence was spread out before us – little fields filled with rows of olive trees, aged and gnarled, the soil reddish in places, the flat plain stretching as far as the eye could see towards the Camargue and the Mediterranean.

"The place was full of cats. They did not obtrude on one's consciousness – cats seldom do – black cats, white cats, tabby cats, tortoiseshell cats, ginger cats and even tiny kittens peering terrified but transfixed under the bottom of a heavy studded door watching the world of legs and feet, boots and shoes tramping and stamping past. When I tried to stroke them, they turned tail and fled. The grown cats sat, erect or curled up, immutable, disinterested, in corners and on windowsills enjoying the sunshine but somehow embodying Les Baux's past spirit of independence and cloaked malevolence."

Robert Westall
October 1983

For Marni and Di, who sowed,
and Felicity, who reaped

I

It was night in the Palace.

The boy was eating with his father the Duke. It wasn't cheerful. The black stone walls were hung with tapestries that swayed in the draughts, so that the woven figures seemed alive as the boy watched them out of the corner of his eye. They had cruel stupid faces, twisted noses, piggy eyes and jaws like wolves.

When the boy was happy, he could see the faces weren't really cruel. The weaver had just been a rotten artist. But tonight they looked diabolical. So much killing and dying. The boar twisting under the hunter's spear, shedding drops of blood as big as pears. The slain warrior, forever falling, grimacing. Even the tiny peasants who filled the corners glanced over their shoulders from their ploughing with sly hating looks.

The boy sat at the bottom of the table, far away from his father. Father didn't talk much these days; brought great leather books to meals and pored over them, mumbling about money, money, always money. Eating so clumsily that the boy watched stain after stain spattering his once-fine robe.

The boy would rather have eaten anywhere else. In the guard-room, where the soldiers told increasingly filthy stories, shouting betweentimes that they were not fit for royal ears. In the kitchens, where there was always a cold chicken-leg and a turnspit-stool by the enormous fire. Even with the ageing ladies-in-waiting who would now wait for ever, talking incessantly of the good old days when the Duchess was alive, and making incessant stealthy trips to the wine-bottles on the side-tables. Until, in the end, they would clutch the boy's head to their ample or skinny bosoms (so he could smell stale clothing and winey breath) and call him 'poor child'.

But now he was twelve, he must eat in state, fumbling with knobbly gold knives and spoons that seemed made for giants. Besides, all the good warm friendly places in the Palace had gone cold recently. When he entered the guardroom, the soldiers fell silent. The cooks still gave him chicken-legs, but they gave him odd unreadable glances as well. When a lady-in-waiting called him 'poor child' now, the others silenced her with slight shakes of the head. And the people he met in corridors bobbed abruptly and hurried past.

Just like when Mother was dying.

Everything cried out danger. Dukes should sense danger *before* other men; that's how Dukes survived. But Father, at the far end of the table, slurped and mumbled on, sensing no danger at all . . .

There were two other living creatures in the room. The royal bouteiller carving the joint, and Sehtek, the royal cat. Sehtek, friendlier than any human. When he felt rotten, he would bury his face in her fur. She smelt of dust and clean washing and deep inside, like the sea far off, he could hear her purr. She was golden, with golden eyes, and far too big to pick up.

She looked bigger than ever tonight, sitting by the fire. Hunched, fur all standing up on end with the firelight glowing through it. He could tell she wasn't purring, just by looking at her. She'd sat thus, the night his mother died. It always meant something terrible; it made the boy's stomach curl up, so he could hardly eat. What danger was coming? Was it coming across the red plain below the city walls? Already inside the city, in the alleys between the tall stone houses? In the Palace itself? So much *whispering* . . .

He listened; heard nothing. The black walls were too thick. Far, far away, his father muttered, and crossed out a whole line in the leather ledger. The bouteiller went on carving meat.

Then the bouteiller stretched both arms above his head, as if his shoulders ached, both hands clenched around the long carving-knife. The boy pursed his lips at such ill-manners, but the Duke did not notice.

Then the bouteiller's arms descended, plunging the carving-knife, still dripping fat, deep into the Duke's neck.

The Duke fell forward without a word. Only knocking over a goblet that rolled down the table, spilling wine, and fell with a clang on the floor.

The bouteiller pulled out the knife with a sucking noise, and walked down the table towards the boy.

The boy couldn't move; just sat.

But Sehtek moved; streaked like flowing gold between the bouteiller's legs, so he crashed full-length and his knife went skittering away across the floor-slabs. The boy leapt up and away round the table. The bouteiller got up slowly, retrieved his knife and came after him again.

The boy's legs stopped working. He stared at the bloody, greasy knife hanging above him and shut his eyes, waiting for pain to thrust down into his heart.

Instead, the bouteiller screamed.

The boy opened his eyes. Why was the bouteiller wearing a great fur hat, with straps down over his eyes?

Then the hat moved, and fine red lines drew themselves across the bouteiller's cheeks. The hat was Sehtek, ears flat against her skull, golden eyes glaring wild.

Blindly, the bouteiller lunged upwards with his knife. Now there was blood on the golden fur too.

At last, the boy could move. His father's death was unreal, a nightmare; his own death too. But Sehtek's hurt was real. He grabbed the first thing his hand found on the table and jabbed with all his strength; a two-pronged carving fork. He didn't expect it to go through the bouteiller's leather, but it did. The bouteiller squealed, pulled away and reeled down the table, knocking over chair after chair, Sehtek still riding his head. Then he fell again, with a massive splintering of wood.

Sehtek sniffed the bouteiller's face carefully. When she walked away, the boy knew the man was dead.

His father dead; the bouteiller dead; it was all too queer to bear. He looked at his own hands; sticky red gloves holding the two-tined carving-fork . . .

Hammering on the door; shouting. The bouteiller must have bolted it beforehand, so he wouldn't be disturbed. The boy tottered across to unbolt it and let them in . . .

Then Sehtek called, warningly. And he realised the voices outside were shouting the wrong sort of thing. They weren't asking if the Duke was all right. They were asking the bouteiller if he was all right, and if the job was done. They weren't nice voices.

Somebody shouted for an axe to break down the door. An axe was brought. The tip of its blade appeared through the door-panel with the first booming stroke.

Sehtek called again, urgently; standing by the open window, urging him to come. He ran to her, and looked down. The Palace was built on the edge of a cliff; below a narrow ledge was a sheer drop into the dark.

Sehtek jumped out on to that narrow ledge, urging him to follow. But even with the axe behind, he didn't dare.

She leapt back on to the windowsill, and stared at him. The pupils of her eyes got bigger and bigger, till they filled the whole world. Then she took his mind and he was no longer a boy, but her kitten.

He looked back into the room, and saw it with kitten-eyes, Sehtek's eyes. Everything was grey, except those things that were red. The rivulet of blood, winding down the table from the dead Duke, making islands of the golden dishes. The spreading stain where the bouteiller lay. The pear-shapes of blood on the tapestry, around the dying boar. Red, red, red. Redder than red. And the smell of blood and roasted meat were a quivering excitement. And the tapestries moving in the draughts were a wild enchantment. And the shining axe-tip, appearing and disappearing through the door . . . and the white chips of wood, bouncing and rolling . . . catch . . . pounce.

But Sehtek called again, and this time he followed her. The ledge seemed wider now, and the drop into the dark nothing. He leapt. And since he was small and nimble, landed safely. And he followed Sehtek along the catwalks. Along the tops of walls they went; down vines and trellises, clinging to the sides of houses. Through drains and over the moon-dreaming rooftops, among the very spires. Sehtek had so taken his mind that the catwalk seemed the only sensible road. And the streets below were lamplit canyons, where alien giants walked upright. Like any cat, he had no fear of falling.

Back at the Palace, the door collapsed. The bouteiller's friends burst in. They looked nervously at the Duke, but he didn't leap up and curse them. The rest of the room seemed empty. They called the bouteiller's name, while the candles flickered. Then they found him, a splintered gilded chair-leg jutting upwards through his back. They turned him over, and saw what Sehtek had done to his face. At last one said, "The cats knew . . . "

And even they crossed themselves. Even Little Paul, their leader . . .

For the cats of that city were an old legend.

No man could have noticed Sehtek, as she led the boy to the Mausoleum in the depths of the city. She went softer than black velvet falling in darkness; softer than cobwebs blowing in the night-wind. She could have hidden in a goblet of shadow.

But the whole city, unwitting, felt the vibrations of her rage and shock. Men by their firesides crossed and recrossed their legs, stretched and yawned and rubbed their shoulders, unable to get comfortable. Then went to fetch a drink. Their wives snapped at them for leaving the door open. But when they'd fetched wine, they left it at their elbows, undrunk. Wives fussed with fires already burning comfortably, blackening them with unneeded coals; picked up embroideries and threw them down again, complaining that the rushlight strained their eyes. Happily-married couples quarrelled suddenly, about nothing. Apologised, saying that the wind was in the wrong quarter. Then quarrelled again.

The ordinary cats prowled the rooms, miaowing to be let out, and immediately miaowing to be let back in; clawed the draperies and got thrown out for good. Outside, they wandered in black, back-twitching misery; not even knowing what was wrong. Meeting on rooftops they bickered so hideously that people flung open windows and drenched them with water.

Only a few, the brightest, were drawn to the Mausoleum.

But the Miw knew what was wrong. Nobody ever mistook a Miw for an ordinary cat. They were twice the size. Just to stroke a Miw (and they weren't averse to being stroked) was to know the difference. Their bones were brutally heavy, and their muscles thick as cream. When they chose to sit on people's knees, people were glad when they got off again. Too heavy for comfortable breathing; they lay heavy on the soul too; men felt less the masters of their own fate.

All Miw were golden. Even the black Miw, the Matagots whose constant fight against the dark powers had stained them black from ear to tail, were gold beneath their black guard-hairs. Miw were forbidden to mate with other cats. Mating with Wildcats in the Former Days had produced the tabbies, blacks and greys – the Weaker Brethren who took so much looking after.

Miw never foraged for rotten fishskin in the middens. They sat on men's tables, eating the choicest morsels offered. They belonged to no household, came and went as they chose. But they were welcome, even if they left the best cushions thick with golden hair. A bracelet of plaited Miw-hair brought good luck and easy childbirth. A contented Miw kept the whole house happy. Wives became sweet-tongued and quick to bed. Children were thoroughly washed, but never beaten . . . Besides, Miw were courteous – never clawed hangings or fouled the rushes or outstayed their welcome.

The moment Sehtek began to transmit her rage, every Miw knew who was sending. Where she was; where she was going. They were summoned; none thought of disobeying. For she would not stop that nerve-twitching agony until every living Miw was with her.

Mostly, they just went to the door, and courteously asked to be out. Some, alas, were caught in empty rooms. One leapt to the top of the bed-hangings and clawed his way out through the ceiling. Others climbed the intricate warrens of chimneys, sending down sooty swarms of squawking starlings that terrified families sitting at supper. Two ascended chimneys in which fires were actually burning. One died, halfway up; his massive bones were brought down by the chimney sweep's brush the following spring. Others leapt through windows of horn, oiled parchment and glass, ignoring their cuts and bruises. One she-Miw, spreading her plumed legs and tail, fell seventy feet to the rocky slope below the city wall. Then got back into the city up a stinking privy-outlet, terrifying the straining man squatting on the privy. She was not the last to arrive. Later, mere men swore that all these happenings were portents of the death of the Duke.

None knew why Sehtek was summoning; there was just the feeling of a golden thunderstorm with claws for lightning. And the endless repetition of the lament from the Former Days.

> "You have lain too long by the winter fires,
> You have basked too long in the arms of the sun."

Amon met his half-brother Smerdis, as they crossed the grass-grown top of a triumphal arch that spanned the street. They touched noses, but didn't sniff backsides. Smerdis was two years heavier and more solemn than Amon.

"Again?" sent Amon, as another burst of Sehtek-rage hit them. He was afraid his back-muscles might twitch, and his brother notice.

"Goddess in-her," sent Smerdis, reprovingly

"She-goddess, goddess, all this cold weather!"

"Miw not-listen her. Miw turn-backs. Now, great-evil." Smerdis's sending-images were as small and neat as ever, but nearly overwhelmed by the Sehtek-storm.

They trotted in single file along a sagging lead gutter, and looked in through a shattered window of the Mausoleum.

It was the funeral-place of the Dukes. Built by a grateful people, regardless of expense. An architect had come from Italy; built a thick-walled octagon with vast copper dome, and doors twelve feet high, to admit the black-and-gold hearse with its plumed horses and black-and-gold footmen balanced precariously on top.

Inside, black marble columns stretched from floor to ceiling. The black marble coffins were stacked six-high, each telling, in fine Roman lettering, its Duke's ferocity in war, magnanimity in peace, loving fatherhood, mercy on orphans, thirst for justice . . . Each coffin sang the praises of its occupant more fully than the last. The lettering got smaller and smaller, to the point of illegibility.

The domed ceiling was painted with the puffy white clouds and pink cherubs of Heaven. The floor was tiled with great glowing patterns by a dark man from Muslim lands. The Mausoleum was thrown open every day to the people, so they could pay their respects, and see what they paid their taxes for.

Few came. It was dark inside, and nobody could read Latin. Eventually, when the last coffin-shelf was filled, the custodians got tired of the sound of dust gathering; one could make more money selling cloth in the market . . . The bronze doors were fastened with an iron chain and padlock. The padlock rusted. When some city historian finally wanted it opened, the key would not turn. No man had been inside since.

Such pomp, wealth and death gathered in one place grew oppressive. Nobody wanted to live next door. The houses on each side fell vacant; vacancy spread like dry rot. The whole street fell empty. Small boys dared each other to run along it after dark. To prove they'd done so, they scribbled on the bronze doors and broke windows; mice and beetles, birds and bats moved in.

Eventually, a young and wandering Miw discovered it. Eyed with horror the mice and beetles, the cracked ceiling of Heaven where the bats hung in rows. There was no *respect*! For several of the Dukes really *had* been great warriors and catfriend.

The Miw began meeting in that place, on rainy days in winter, to hold their parliaments. That was the end of the mice and beetles. And the Miw invited the owls, who are wing-Miw and catfriend, to nest there respectfully, without owl-pellets and droppings. That was the end of the birds and bats. The place suffered no further insult, except that damp lifted the tiles and young Miw, in their unfu-time, played mad games swerving round and round the octagon, sending the floor-tiles skittering to break in fragments against the black marble walls. But they were punished, if they were caught.

The Miw liked pomp and power and death. They worshipped daily the dead Dukes who had been catfriend. Miw are not afraid of death; it is shown them as kittens, immediately after they are shown birth. No Miw minded dying providing it was timely or fruitful and he had a safe dark place to die, with one friend to lick him comfort. Many of the greatest Miw, especially Matagots, were permitted to die in the Mausoleum, on the higher shelves. Their crouched dried-up presence was a comfort; the living Miw felt blessed by their hollow, shadowed eyes . . .

Most of the Miw were already gathered. From high up, sitting in their radiating pattern, they looked like the gold beads of the Mother's necklace. Sehtek sat in the centre, still occasionally sending, but tending her wounded shoulder with a pink tongue betweentimes. The rest crouched low, ears back, resentfully bearing at close range her incessant battering.

There were a few Brethren in one corner. Nibblefur and her grandsons. The grandsons were notorious; huge, for Brethren; huge enough to make even a Miw steady his nerves and his ears as he walked past. Black, with the tattered ears of many an unjust quarrel. Their coats shone greasily from the best of chicken-offal. They lived on the fat of the gutter, terrorising other Brethren out of what they'd found.

They were difficult to tell apart, but not impossible. Ripfur showed the brownness of middle-age round nose and paws; in sunlight, his fur looked all brown, with the ghosts of tabby stripes showing. Tornear was true black, except for five white hairs under his chin, which he held his head down to conceal. Gristletongue was fattest by far; the fool of the family, but the dirtiest fighter.

Their mother, Nibblefur, also had an evil reputation, but only for her thoughts. She had moused-out some unpleasantness about every cat in the city, and shared her knowledge generously. From the follies of her youth she had descendants in every part, though most had settled in the surrounding villages to escape her wise-sendings. She spent most of her life in slow journeys round those villages. She too had been black, but age had silvered her nose and ears.

There had been a brisk exchange of sendings between Sehtek and Nibblefur. Nibblefur was reduced to a fit of nervous coughing; crouching close to the floor with her neck outstretched, she sounded as if she was trying to blow the contents of her stomach out through her lungs. But she held her ground, leaning against Ripfur for support.

But the strangest thing lay in another corner. To the human eye, the boy would have borne a grotesque resemblance to a cat. He crouched on his elbows, legs drawn up beneath him, hands clenched to resemble paws. Head down, eyes closed, he seemed to doze.

But to the Miw, he was all too human.

"Why-bring man here? Unfu!"

"Unfu! Unfu! Unfu!"

Sehtek shifted uncomfortably. "Not-man; only small-minnen."

"Minnen also forbidden."

Twitching at the disharmony, Amon and Smerdis dropped down inside, leaping from one dusty-bellied, trumpet-blowing statue to another.

Sehtek glared balefully. "Last-come. Now . . ." And she fed into their assembled minds the murder of the Duke. The Miw kept perfectly still. Only the flicking of their eyes, a sudden tensing of a paw showed their excitement as the Duke fell forward again and the blood flowed red, red, down the table. The boy showed the same eye-and-paw movements, watching his father's death with the same passionless fascination.

Finally, the bouteiller staggered and died.

"Well-moused!" sent the Miw, cool breath sighing from a thousand nostrils. Some asked to have the scene again. Sehtek refused.

Silence and stillness for fifty breaths.

"Well?" asked Sehtek. "WELL?"

Smerdis rose, twisting his tail into a question-mark. "Not our quarrel. This Duke was not-catfriend." Little dartings of agreement from the Miw.

"NOT-CATFRIEND?" Sehtek's rage blasted every ear in the Mausoleum flat. "I will show you not-catfriend."

She built a vision of another walled city, within the loop of a river. Towers and unknown pennants flapping in the sunlight. Out from the gate wound a procession. Halberdiers in red, then choirboys singing sweet and shrill; priests, swinging censers of scented smoke at the crowds lining the route. Then men carrying torches that sent ragged towers of smoke into the clean morning air. Then the chief magistrate, also in robes of red, red. Lastly, twelve men carrying strong baskets.

In the baskets were Brethren. Some poked out desperate paws, at the hands of the men carrying the baskets; but the men wore thick leather gloves. Others gnawed without hope at the thick wood of their cages. Others lay still, as if already dead.

The procession wound at last, after many hymns, to a great iron basket on an iron stake. Beneath, logs had been piled. A ladder was set up . . .

Now, even those Brethren who had lain still began to struggle. Uselessly. One by one they were passed up and put into the iron basket; where they lay heaped on each other, and yet still in harmony.

After a priest had said a prayer, the magistrate stepped forward, and took a torch. When the cats saw the flames, they began to struggle and step on each other; but still they did not hurt each other. Then, with a fine flourish, and a roar from the crowd, he thrust his torch down among the logs.

Flames rose. At last the Brethren began to fight, and claw each other hideously to escape the flames. The crowd roared again, to see the Devil revealed in them, in all his hate and rage . . .

It was a long time before the last paw ceased to move, and the merciful flames hid all.

"It is a great pity the Mother made men," sent Smerdis.

"Where is that city?" asked the Miw; a sending so awful the very stones seemed to crack.

"Mainz, in High Germany," sent Sehtek. "The Bishop of Mainz was not catfriend. My sister of Germany sent him a gift of rats, and he died of the swelling-sickness. They not so merry in Mainz now."

But that did not satisfy the Miw. Red roses of rage blossomed in their minds . . . memories of the Former Days . . . Brethren whipped to death for sport; walled up in the foundations of houses for luck; thrown from the tops of newly-built towers to make them impregnable; garlanded with flowers and ploughed into the fields to nourish the corn.

"There is a little lost-magic left in the Brethren," sent Smerdis. "Men squeeze it from them, like wine from grapes."

Sehtek drew herself up. "*Now* say this Duke was not-catfriend!"

There was a blessed darkness, and a great shuddering stillness.

"Kill," sent the Miw. "Kill, kill, kill." Their sendings were dull with misery.

"There is a better-way." Sehtek built another vision. Inside a grey cathedral, other choristers sang evensong by the light of clustered, melting candles. Far above, in the shadowed galleries, a golden Miw leapt from pinnacle to pinnacle. Then climbed down a steepled gilded throne, on to the knee of a cardinal who sat there massive, ponderous of jowl. She coiled round on his scarlet lap, then settled, purring, nose inside tail. The choristers burst into a new tune.

"Do they sing the Magnifi-cat?" asked Smerdis. There was the faintest flicker of amusement from the Miw.

The song ended; the choristers departed. The Cardinal picked up his Miw and carried it to another room. They ate from the same rich table, the Miw taking pieces from the man's very lips.

Till a red-bearded man burst in. Stood astride, hands on hips. Asked to sit, he would not; he strode about, stared out of the window, whistled a tune, roared with rage one minute and laughed the next, and the laughing was worst.

"Unfu!" sent the Miw, backs rising. "Unfu!"

"Wait."

The Cardinal took the Miw in his arms, stroking her from head to flicking tail-tip with long movements of his ring-clustered hand. And the Miw soothed the Cardinal, and the Cardinal's slow words soothed the wild man, and again there was harmony of sorts.

"That is my sister of England. The unfu is Henry and the red-priest, Wolsey. They do not burn Brethren in England. Miw rules man through man. And *we* have the next Duke . . ."

The Miw looked afresh at the minnen dozing in the corner. He opened his eyes, took one terrified look round and burst into chaotic grief.

Dreadful. Even at her worst, Sehtek never lost *control* of her mind; it still fitted into the minds of the other Miw, though it strained them to bursting. But this minnen's grief was like wolf-jaw and swords and tombs sinking into swamps and dying not one death but many, over and over. Never had the Miw so suffered. Every ear was skull-flattened; backs twitched like a sackful of rats.

It was not to be borne. One by one the Miw walked across to the writhing minnen, lying first beside him, then on top till he seemed covered with a great golden robe. His sobs ceased, his limbs stopped twitching and he slept, far from any pain. There was even a small smile on lips nearly buried in fur. They had taken his mind; for good.

"Keep-safe, here?"

"Teach kitwise?"

"Feed mice-beetles-birds?"

Decided, the Miw rose and stretched to go.

"One-thing remaining," sent Sehtek. Her mind was fading from weariness and the pain in her shoulder. Again, her pink tongue explored it. But she was still Royal Miw. The others resettled.

"Horse must be told!"

A cold shock of horror filled the Mausoleum. "Horse? Surely it has not come to *that*?"

"Not-speak Horse in our memory."

"Not in many-memories." Pink roses of questions bloomed everywhere. There was something terrible, irrevocable in horse having to be told.

"Horse has forgotten us." All the minds pushed against Sehtek. She began to rock, wearily; but she held them.

"Horse must be told."

"Why?"

"Old-custom. Horse ancient-catfriend. Horse is entitled . . . we may need . . . "

"Horse may have gone . . . no longer where he ran."

"Horse *is*. Can-feel. Who will go?"

Silence fell. Horse lived unthinkably far . . . outside the city walls. Horse was a tale to frighten kittens with, by winterfires. The silence deepened. All except in Amon's mind. He was busy asking Smerdis what all the fuss was about. He had lived all winter with a horse. Warm. Drystraw. Too late, Amon realised he alone was sending, and stopped.

"Who will tell Horse?"

Miw at the edge of the group began drifting out on to the catwalks. Those in the middle, imperceptibly, without unseemly haste, began to follow.

"Wait!" But the drift continued.

"Let Amon go," sent someone, "since he knows so much about horses." And in the glimmer of a whisker, Amon and Sehtek found themselves alone.

Except for Nibblefur and grandsons in the corner. "Why yellowcat go tell horse? Why always yellowcat? Us good-as yellowcat."

Sehtek turned the remnants of her glare on Nibblefur. It was as well she was fading. Her glare, when the goddess was in-her, had been known to make a she-Miw drop her litter of kittens prematurely.

The four black cats, hunched together, spat defiantly. Nibblefur developed another coughing-fit. But they didn't flee. "Brethren good-as yellowcat," repeated Nibblefur faintly. "Has this yellowcat ever been outside city? Not-know how get-back home. Not-know enough to come in out of rain. We been outside city. Many times."

Sehtek closed her eyes in contempt. "You too-old catch-mice."

"Ripfur go. Tornear go. Tell yellowcat when come in out of rain."

Sehtek's eyes remained closed. But from the stirrings in her mind, like mice among straw, Amon could tell she was considering. Finally, she blinked agreement. "Ripfur meet Amon city-gate, next Re-rising."

Ripfur and Tornear rose and stretched with pleasure, extending claws and dislodging several loose tiles. Their arrogant purring filled the place.

"Hard luck, fat-brother!"

"Fat-brother stay here, keep eye on city." Both black toms thought this an enormous joke. But Gristletongue didn't see it; he was taking them seriously, already casting a proprietorial eye round the Mausoleum.

"Where horse?" sent Nibblefur.

"No-tell you. Amon will know. Go!"

Purring insufferably, the black cats went. Sehtek turned to Amon, sending very softly. He had to put his jowl against hers to receive at all.

"When leave, keep Re on your left-ear. In your eyes at noon. On your right-ear at Re-setting. Six days Miw-walk. *Walk* – not run. Hunt at dusk – not get hungry. Clean between pads – not get sore-paw. Be nimble – Horse is faster than dream. Listen with your paws and see with your ears. Quick-dodge. If Horse is running, he will not heed – will kill. Hide till Horse eats, then Horse will heed. Horse quick-run – slow-think – quick-frighten. But not unfu. Tell Horse all.

"What if two horses? Which tell?"

There was a quivering in Sehtek's mind that might have been laughter in a lesser Miw. "Each Miw separate. Horse is one. Now go sleep."

Her eyes closed. Amon left, with a last look at the dreaming, smiling Duke.

Re's disc was already rising as he left the Mausoleum; rising behind spire and dome, melting them with its brilliance into black cages. Coating every roof-slab with a light like blood.

The cobbles below were new-washed with dew. Fine smells rose from the city's gardens: lavender and valerian, catmint and stale water in vases. But for once, Amon couldn't enjoy them.

Smerdis was waiting, crouched, filling in time praying to Re. Smerdis prayed a lot, even in the Mausoleum for the dead Dukes who had been catfriend.

Amon just stood; he'd never felt less like praying for men, living or dead. His strong gold limbs still trembled from the memory of Mainz.

Smerdis finally opened his eyes and unfolded his legs. "Why not-pray Re?"

"Men," sent Amon, bitterly.

"Must pray for men, or *all* go unfu!"

"What wrong with men?"

Smerdis blinked thoughtfully. "I think – is way men walk."

"Walk?"

"Miw walk on hindlegs sometimes – to fight – see over walls. Man walk on hindlegs all-times. Man's back hurt all-times; make him angry all-times. Man's spine grows stiff – cannot see behind himself – nor lick own back. Man's head too far from earth – cannot smell properly – hear properly. Cannot see what he is walking on – at night cannot see at all.

"So man live in his mind. Thinks mind can change all-things. If Re shines, man wants rain. If it rains, he wants Re-shine. If night, he wants day. If day, he wants night. Man thinks other-time, other-place always better. Each man wants whole world. Only one world so . . . unfu."

Smerdis sighed deeply through his nostrils, so that his cool breath stirred Amon's fur.

Amon sent, "City happy – men not unfu-here."

"Miw-here. Now Duke dead – happy how-long?"

Amon closed his eyes in anguish. Smerdis nosed him gently.

"Not-worry – Re shine now – be-happy. Tomorrow – go tell horse."

But for all his wise-sending, Smerdis walked away with his own tail drooping.

Back in the Mausoleum, Sehtek seemed to doze; but tiny ear-movements showed she was still awake. In her mind was the image of a pair of golden scales; in these she weighed everything that had happened, against the feather of Maat, the feather of truth. Why hadn't she stopped them killing the Duke?

Suddenly, her eyes shot open, and her ears flew every-which-way. Into the darkness of her mind, a sending had flamed like a shooting-star. Only for an instant, then gone. She searched back to trace it. It had been sent by a Matagot; Matagot-sends were quite different. It had been sent from very far away. And it had been a send of pure glee. Some Matagot had found something he had been looking for for a long, long time. She felt out delicately, to her furthest limits, trying to locate the Matagot. But he was no longer sending. Or else only his first moment of glee had been strong enough to get through . . .

Sehtek closed her eyes again.

Her last thought was that the send had come from the south.

2

Far south, Cam shouldered his pack and disembarked.

He avoided the waterfront taverns. Fishermen could mend their own gear. Even if they needed your help, they always tried to pay you in fish.

He walked up the cobbled hill. More like a cobbled tunnel; the wooden houses leaned together overhead, leaving only a long blue rag of sky. Signs hung above the shops. The gilt balls of the moneylenders, the great gilt scissors of the tailors, the red-and-white poles of the barbers, signifying blood and bandages. The wooden boot of the cordwainers, the shields of the armourers . . .

Not much lacking in this town.

Cam eyed the open sewer running down the middle of the street, reflecting the blue rag of sky among floating islands of the town's filth. There could be profit in sewers . . . Like the new one at Marseilles that dumped every turd in town on the Mayor's doorstep whenever it rained. It only needed deepening in one place and then worked perfectly. But it had taken Cam to spot that, and he'd walked away with three gold pieces. Cam lived off other men's stupidity. There was plenty of it about . . .

But the people of Marseilles had called him young wizard. He hadn't liked that. The Church had a quick fiery end for wizards; and the man who accused the wizard got the three gold pieces . . . Cam left Marseilles quick; even left the Mayor's fine supper lying on his table.

He *wasn't* a wizard. He simply understood how the world fitted together; how axe joined handle, stream flowed from hill, rock broke wave.

Anyone could do that, who wasn't stupid.

Anyway, this town's sewer was flowing nicely. Dumping dead dogs and rotting oranges into the harbour with every shower of rain.

As he climbed uphill he felt like a salmon, swimming against a torrent of men's shoulders, and eyes. The shoulders pushed you outwards towards the sewer. Everybody wanted to walk next to the houses. Because chambermaids emptied chamberpots straight into the sewer from the upstairs windows. The more courteous shouted 'gardez loo' first, but most didn't bother.

But people's eyes were worse; every eye scanned him because he was a stranger, always a stranger. One day people's eyes would wear him away to a ghost. Seaports weren't as bad as inland towns but . . . He was glad of his big boots and black leather jerkin. The boots made a reassuring clumping. The jerkin, set with metal plates like pennies, clinked cheerfully and made him look broader than he was. A soldier's jerkin; payment of a debt. It made him look a fighting man, which he wasn't. More trouble . . . but he kept it.

The taverns of the climbing street were useless. Clay floors strewn with rushes under which lay fossilised layers of ancient beer, grease, bones, spittle, excrement of cat and dog. Rooms full of eyes, sharper than the eyes of the street. In one door a girl stood. As Cam passed she let her rags slip, revealing a shallow white breast already wrinkled with hunger.

You'd lose money, not make it, in a place like that.

But, at the top of the street, the Fleur-de-Lys looked better. The green bush over the door was unwithered. The stone flags carried muddy footprints, but only today's.

His kind of place. Velvet knees rubbing against brown scarred ones. Furred shoulders rubbing leather. Gesturing hands wearing gold rings . . . The prospering men of the town, pretending to be still one with the common people. Keeping their ears to the ground.

The problems of the rich interested Cam. Gold.

He ordered the smallest measure of wine and paid in coppers. Never show gold in public. Then he slumped down in a corner, glowering at the toes of his boots, the perfect picture of a youth crossed in love; only an idiot accosts a youth crossed in love. . . .

Cam attracted company when he smiled. He didn't want company now; he was listening.

His glower worked; a formidable glower. He had dark skin, long greasy hair, black eyebrows peaked like tents and the promising ghost of a moustache. Glowering, he looked twenty. Hair washed, blue eyes smiling, he looked a child and the landlord would have thrown him out. He was eighteen; tall but not yet broad.

Head down, he let his ears rove the room. Who had a problem? A cart that wouldn't run straight? A spotty daughter? A dry farm, needing a new well? (He smiled slightly, remembering the twitch of the divining-rod between his hands.) He could solve anything. But if he looked too young, nobody took him seriously . . .

Two men on his right, grumbling about the price of leather. Cam knew leather was cheap round Bézieres; too many cattle had died in the hard winter. But Bézieres was too far away; nobody would pay for that news.

The group on his left was sniggering wearily about nuns . . .

At that point he became aware of being watched; felt eyes rest on him, run up and down his jerkin, boots and hair.

Only when the eyes moved away did he turn and look.

A barrel-chested man with arms thick as horses' legs, hairy, veined and rippling. Soot in every pore of his face, every wrinkle of his forehead. Hairy nostrils like charcoal-pits and thumbs burnt blue.

A blacksmith; but no ordinary blacksmith. Thick scarred gold ring on his right hand; he must wear it while he worked. He could afford to ruin a big gold ring. Boots of fine leather, also marred by his trade. Some blacksmith! His table was covered with wine-bottles and he wasn't drunk at all.

Important man, for a blacksmith. When he made a loud-voiced joke, people laughed to the far corners of the room. They kept an ear cocked for his voice, even when they were talking among themselves.

The smith, on the other hand, kept his eye cocked on the door. Hailed everybody he knew; seemed to know everyone except Cam. The people he hailed came across, had a drink. The blacksmith gripped their shoulders with his iron grip; slapped them painfully on the back. People winced, but kept smiling. The blacksmith agreed to shoe horses, temper swords. Tomorrow, next week. Never today. So how did he earn the kind of money he was spending on wine?

Was he trying to buy friendship? But he was popular. People were flattered to drink with him. At least, they kept smiling . . .

The smith asked every newcomer the same questions. Where'd he been? Who'd he seen? In Roquevair and Brignolles, Avignon and Nimes?

But no sooner were these questions answered than the blacksmith was pushing his guest back on his feet with that huge hand. Couldn't get rid of him quick enough. And always with his eyes on the door, especially for younger men . . .

The smith oppressed Cam. Why was he so restless? He looked like he feared neither man nor beast; but he had the whole tavern in a twitch. Cam couldn't hear half the things people were saying; and had a sudden gloomy conviction that no rich man's problem would come his way that night. Would he have to sing for his supper? He had a voice and good new songs. But after he sang, things happened. Trouble with the landlord's wife, if he stayed the night; trouble with men outside if he didn't.

Cam's glower became real. What a pointless life he led, walking round the world wearing out boots. Living hand-to-mouth. Writing letters for idiots who couldn't write to send to idiots who couldn't read. What was he looking *for*?

He'd go home to England; but they'd make him marry. He'd go back to the university of Paris; but monks smelled like old women under their black skirts; and sooner or later he'd ask some question, pull some trick that would get him called wizard again.

He wasn't really looking for anything. It was just that if he stopped more than a week anywhere, he got *bored* . . .

He must have brooded a long time. A growing silence broke in on him finally. The young drinkers had remembered a better inn; the older ones their wives and supper. They were all jamming in the doorway, swearing eternal winy friendship. Night showed in at the windows. The fire grew brighter as shadows filled the room. A girl brought two candles and began clearing pots off tables. Sloosh and rattle of washing-up from the kitchen.

It was too late even to sing for his supper. Should he spend one of his last pennies for a sleeping-place among the rushes, or walk out under the new stars?

He looked towards the middle of the room.

The blacksmith was still there; silent now. Hunched; the firelight running red down one side of his pitted face, making him look like a new moon.

The smith had been silent some time. Was that why the inn had emptied?

Don't be stupid.

But there was a deep-breathing contentment in the blacksmith's stillness. Like a spider that's caught its fly.

Stupid . . .

But unease seized Cam. He snatched up his pack, intending to leave with the tail-end of the revellers.

The smith turned and looked at him. Now the firelight ran thinly down each side of the smith's head, outlining his ears, but leaving his face blank.

"Wine?" asked the smith courteously. He was between Cam and the door, and his arms looked long enough to reach the corners of the room.

The voices from the kitchen were very distant.

Cam willed himself to walk towards the man. At the last moment he would refuse the wine and be past. He could run faster; the man was heavy. Cam's eyes picked out the quickest path to the door, through the clutter of benches . . .

But before he even reached the smith, the man leaned out and took him by the wrist and forced him down to the table; at the same time pouring wine steadily with the other hand.

Now Cam knew who the blacksmith had been looking for . . .

"Supper, landlord!" The way the landlord came running, Cam could tell he was the blacksmith's man. That this scene had been played out before, many times.

Supper was a bowl of roasted chestnuts, smelling delicious.

"Drink up," said the smith. He released Cam's arm and drew a knife. Placed the first chestnut on the table; cracked it with the knife's hilt and handed it to Cam.

Cam chewed and drank somehow, watching the knife rise and fall. The smith also chewed, with noisy gusto.

"Want to see the knife?" He offered the hilt politely.

Cam took it. The smith waited expectantly.

At the same moment Cam felt, with the back of his neck, that someone else had come in through the night-filled open door and was also watching expectantly.

But when he looked, there was no one there; only a small dense shadow under the benches.

Cam ran his thumb gently down the blade. It removed a thin bloodless paring of skin; must be perilously sharp. Cam smelt the blade, careful not to twitch his nose.

"Spanish steel – Toledo," he said, proud of his calm.

"So are half the knives in the world."

Cam felt someone else come into the room; but again there was nothing but two small shadows under the benches. "A well-honed blade – nearly at the end of its life."

"Any child could tell me that!"

Now a third small shadow was watching, under the benches.

"The cross-guard is older than the blade." Cam felt the notches where sword-blows had been parried. "Many battles."

"Many battles," agreed the smith, sighing with boredom.

"The hilt is bound with silver wire – good grip when you're sweating."

The smith simply yawned. But the room was full of watching shadows.

Cam stared at the knife desperately. He wouldn't be beaten. He'd show the bastard. He smelt the hilt itself; the part the blacksmith had cracked nuts with. "Bronze – like no bronze I've smelt before . . . oldest of all?"

The smith waited in silence. Cam stared at the end of the hilt. It was neither round nor square. A battered shape, from cracking so many nuts . . . hard to make out in the firelight's flicker.

"Like . . . a cat's head . . . ears back . . . an angry cat."

He had gone too far, made a fool of himself. The smith was laughing openly.

"Or an angry lioness?" asked the smith.

"I have never seen a lioness," said Cam stiffly.

"Neither have I," said the smith. "But see how she hunts." He took the knife and flicked. The knife shot down the room, a streak of red firelight, and embedded itself in the mantelpiece. The smith laughed again, pleased. "See how she hunts! Try for yourself."

Cam walked down the room on trembling legs; tugged at the knife. It was embedded deep in the oak. If the mantelpiece had been a man, the man would be dead. Cam got the knife out at last, twisting it up and down. Walked back.

"Go on, try it!"

"Never thrown a knife in my life."

"Try!"

Cam had awful visions of the knife flying wild; breaking a window or scuttering feebly along the sawdust on the floor. The man was still trying to make him look a fool. Desperately he tried to work out how the trick was done.

But as he hesitantly drew back his hand, it seemed to flick of its own accord. Again the knife flew down the room like a streak of fire and embedded itself in the mantel.

"Well done. You've got the trick. Must be near my own mark. Go and see."

Cam went. The knife was embedded as deeply as before; but he couldn't see the blacksmith's mark.

"It's gone back into your mark," said Cam. "How bloody stupid."

"Throwing indeed . . ."

"Mug's luck."

"Try again."

Six times Cam threw, and six times the knife returned to the same mark. It drove Cam to a frenzy. He tried spinning round and throwing it too quickly. Turned his back, bent over and threw between his legs. Every time the knife flew true.

Cam threw once more, willing it to fly wild.

It pinned the emerging landlord to his own kitchen door through his own dirty apron.

The landlord wiped his brow with his apron, when Cam released him. "Is there anything more you need, gentles?"

"Go to bed," said the smith. "While you still have all of yourself."

The landlord didn't need telling twice.

Cam threw at a thin black cobweb trailing from the ceiling.

The knife pinned the cobweb.

Then Cam realised he couldn't reach the knife to get it down.

It immediately dropped at his feet, quivering gently in the floorboards.

"How much you want for it?" asked Cam. He had five gold coins nailed up in the heel of each boot, and he was ready to lever off both heels there and then.

"Leave your heels on your boots," said the smith. "You'll need them for walking. You can earn it by going on a journey for me."

"No," said Cam. Suddenly a lot of things came together in his mind. The watching shadows, the knife that always found its mark, this man who smelt of soot and burning . . . Cam crossed himself, for the first time since he had left home three years ago.

The smith laughed, but not unkindly. "Come now – who do you think I am? I've lived in this town for years. Ask the landlord – he'll tell you."

"Lived here *all the time*?"

"Coming and going. Here and there."

"Never long in one place?"

"Come," said the smith, "it is simply a matter of a good man and a good knife. You deserve each other . . ."

Cam picked up his bundle and made for the door.

The blacksmith didn't make the slightest attempt to stop him . . .

Cam looked up thankfully at the stars. Began walking. Met no one, except a few cats coming up the hill in the opposite direction. This whole town was thick with cats, more than he'd ever seen in one place. He remembered them earlier. Sitting on the quayside, scrounging fish. Trying to snatch the meat from the market-stalls and only being shooed gently away . . .

The further he walked, the duller the world seemed. And the more wonderful the knife. The most wonderful thing he'd ever come across, and he'd run away from it.

By the time he'd reached the quay, the thought of the chance he'd missed was unbearable. He ran all the way back, knowing the smith and the knife would be gone.

They were still there, exactly where he'd left them.

"Where's this place I've got to go?"

"A city. I want a letter delivered."

"Why don't you go yourself?"

The smith sighed. "I am too old, and in that city I would not be welcome." There was sadness in his voice. And indeed, as he got to his feet for the first time, he seemed older and more bent than he had sitting down. Firelight was tricky . . .

"Why wouldn't you be welcome?" asked Cam stubbornly. But he knew he would go.

"Come," said the smith. "There's not much time."

As they walked out, the shadows under the benches were quite empty.

They walked up through the sleeping town. At the doors of the bigger houses, black stumps of torches flickered. But the only living thing was an old black-and-grey cat, that limped past them in an alley, terrified, crouching close to the wall, but oddly determined to overtake them.

The blacksmith was limping too; leaning his weight on Cam's arm. Heavier and heavier, till Cam doubted they'd ever make the top of the hill.

The last few poor houses dropped away.

Before them lay an ooze of black water, spanned by a bridge that swayed uneasily as they set foot. From the hump of the bridge, they looked out on a sea of reeds that sighed their endless fronded heads in the night wind; and mazed the eye under the full moon.

Channels of black water led crookedly away. There was a path on the far side of the bridge, but it was hard to see in the moonlight.

"What is this place?"

"Look further," said the smith. He was gasping with the effort of the climb; lungs wheezing like old bellows. The sweet smell of old age filled Cam's nostrils. Was this the loud-voiced man who had filled the inn with laughter? But his hand still held Cam's arm in an iron grip.

"Look further," said the smith.

Cam strained his eyes in the moonlight. Mountains, far away? White mountains like rows of teeth, rising ridge on ridge? With a broad valley between, overhung with marble crags? A narrow path seemed to lead up, up, till, on the last row of teeth, there was a long squareness, white also under the moon. So far away . . . *Could* you see that far by moonlight?

"There is the city. The path goes all the way. Stick to the path. Here is the knife. And the letter."

The letter was vellum, very greasy and bent from the blacksmith's pocket. Folded twice and sealed with a blob of wax that looked black under the moon. On the other side was written, in a crude blacksmith hand, 'To the Seroster'.

"Who? Where . . . ?" asked Cam.

The blacksmith made such a long gasping that Cam thought he was dying. But it turned out just to be laughing.

"There is not a child in that city that hasn't heard of the Seroster," said the smith at last. "Farewell." He let go of Cam's arm, and Cam heard his footsteps go, slow and limping off the rotten bridge.

Cam looked again, across the black water.

All he could see were reeds, fading away under the moon.

"Hey," he said to himself; or to the letter he held in his hand. The wax seal seemed loose. He picked at it. The wax parted from the vellum.

In the moonlight, the page was a total blank.

Cam turned it over again. All the other side said was, 'To the Seroster'.

"Hey," yelled Cam again, turning so violently the whole bridge swayed. He saw the smith's crooked figure forcing itself between the first of the hovels with agonising slowness. As Cam watched, he vanished round the corner.

Cam ran after him so fast, he felt the rotten bridge was going. He too ran among the hovels and turned the corner.

The black figure was still ahead, crawling now on hands and knees like a half-squashed insect. It turned a desperate white face in Cam's direction, as Cam shouted a third time. "Hey, here's your knife. I won't take your stinking letter!"

The figure moaned, began crawling into a corner among a clutter of broken barrels. Just as Cam caught up, it vanished under the shadowed overhang of splayed barrel-staves. Cam heard it call out, "Mother . . . servant . . . depart in peace."

"Come on, out of there!"

Silence.

Cam reached in brutally, grabbing for a shoulder. His hand met fraying cloth and cold bone. As he snatched his hand away, a long bundle fell with it, rustling dryly.

A skeleton stared up at him, bare-armed in a sooty jerkin.

"Here's your letter," screeched Cam, absurdly thrusting it between two shining ribs, and the knife in after it.

The wind blew.

The skeleton seemed to fall in on itself; and then there were just piles of black-and-white dust. Blowing in a long fan past his feet down the sandy alley.

As Cam watched, the rest of the blacksmith blew away into nothingness. Leaving in the sand the knife, the letter and a heap of gold coins.

Blackness overwhelmed him.

3

When he opened his eyes it was dawn. A lot of people were staring down at him.

"What . . . what?"

"You dropped these, mate," said one man, bending over him. He handed Cam something. Cam took it, before he realised it was the letter.

The man helped him to his feet. "These is yours, too," he said, sticking the knife in Cam's belt and stuffing the gold coins into his belt-pouch.

"They're not mine."

"They were lying aside you," said the man. "They don't belong to anybody else. Not here."

"But . . . but . . . "

"On your way, mate. You're late already." The man indicated the way to the rotting bridge, with a nod of his head.

"I'm not going over there."

"Well, you're not coming back into this town. Not with that knife."

"All *right*!" shouted Cam. And threw the knife as hard as he could, over the rooftops, in the direction of the sea of reeds.

One of the crowd went to look round the corner and came back saying, "It stuck in the bridge."

"All *right*!" shouted Cam again, running round the corner in a frenzy and on to the bridge. He pulled the knife out of the boards and threw it again, far into the reeds. "See?"

But the crowd had gathered behind, blocking his way off the bridge. He tried to push through, but they resisted, pushing him back so hard he fell.

"On your way, mate."

Somebody threw something large, that landed beside him. His pack.

"Now look . . . " said Cam.

Somebody else threw something, that hit him in the face. Suddenly everybody was throwing things. Mud, stones, a dead black cat, its neck pitifully askew.

He picked up his bundle and ran; over the bridge, round the first bend in the track and out of range.

The knife lay waiting for him, upright in the earth.

He ignored it, lay low for an hour.

When he peeped again, the people were still gathered round the bridge. Far more now; half the town. Some were carrying nasty-looking poles. They had set up a straggle of wooden crosses, blocking the bridge-end. From one cross, the dead cat hung, crucified.

He waited till nightfall.

At nightfall they set fire to the bridge.

There was no chance of swimming across the black water unseen, even if he'd dared enter it. And if he reached the other side, he knew they'd spot him in the light of the flames, and push him down into the black depths with the ends of their long poles . . .

Then the first reeds caught alight, from the bridge. Choking smoke drove him back even from the water's edge.

Ah, well, this path must fork somewhere. He could work round back to the coast, somewhere near Aigues Mortes.

He considered the knife. Picked it up reluctantly. It was the only weapon he had, and the reeds might hold anything.

Another dawn. He lay dazed, staring up at the pink sky with small friendly clouds like sheep. Trying hard to throw off an awful dream; a blacksmith clutching, withering, turning to bone and blowing to dust . . .

Then he realised all his left side was soaking wet; heard the dawn breeze hissing in the reeds, saw their fronded tops blowing above him and knew it hadn't been a dream at all.

He remembered. He hadn't walked far last night; only far enough to clear the fire. Found the driest spot he could and built a nest of reeds to lie on. It had seemed high enough then; during the night it had dissolved to a mushy mass. The old cloak he'd slept under was glistening with dew and cobwebs.

He built himself a new dry nest, sat and considered. This was a wretched place. Reeds towered everywhere, except where there was black open water. The track was a winding alley, floored with black mud. Well-used. Hoofmarks on hoofmarks on hoofmarks.

Well, there'd be no horsemen this morning, with the bridge burnt down.

Why had they burnt their own bridge? He stood up on his nest and peered south. Smoke still hung in the air. What a mess! God, they must have felt nasty, burning their own bridge! He tasted their hatred again, like sourness in his mouth. A whole town . . .

It was the knife. He'd walked into the trap like a greedy mouse sniffing cheese. How well the smith had understood him . . . his need to be clever . . . his nosiness . . . everything that got him called young wizard . . .

Now he knew who the wizard was . . . When he caught up with that wizard . . .

His mind gave a jerk, like the cogs slipping in a petard.

The blacksmith was dead. Dead and dust.

He kept on trying to swallow that; the cogs in his brain kept slipping over and over again.

The blacksmith had wanted to die. Desperately crawled towards death. Pleaded for it.

"Mother . . . servant . . . depart in peace."

What Mother?

And the way the blacksmith died. Middle-aged strength to dust in half an hour. *How*? Cam bent his head in his hands, trying to remember the smallest detail.

It had started when he accepted the knife. The more he'd played with it, the more the man had aged. If he'd given the knife back, the smith could not have died. Released from the knife, the man had returned to his natural state.

Dust.

How old had be been?

How old is dust?

The knife, oh no, dear God, the knife, must confer eternal life. I am now immortal, thought Cam wildly. What all men desire, I have. Rubbish! *Rubbish*! It's sleeping out in the marsh that's done this. I'm feverish . . . marsh-fever. He stared round at the reeds, as if they would tell him the answer. They just went on whispering. He buried his face in his hands again, trying to shut out all thought. But thought kept seeping in like the marsh-water. The blacksmith had eternal life, plenty of gold, friends . . . well, men who smiled at him, anyway . . . a knife that would fly at will, kill any enemy. Everything the heart could desire . . .

But he'd only wanted to die. Cam remembered his restlessness; his hopeless hope as he watched the inn-door. A prisoner aching for release.

Now he, Cam, was the prisoner.

Rubbish. You cannot be in prison in the open air, with the sun shining. Not if you don't want to be. I am Cam. The same Cam as yesterday. Bugger the knife!

He pulled it out, and flung it into the reeds again, with all his strength.

Sort that one out, knife! Get out of the mud and chase me! He sniggered, found the letter, screwed it into a ball and flung it away too. It didn't go far. Stuck between two dry spear-like leaves across a belt of ooze. Chase me, letter. Roll after me! Get nice and wet doing it!

There remained the blacksmith's money. Over a hundred gold coins when he counted them. They annoyed him, weighed him down, bulging his belt-pouch to breaking-point. He was on the point of throwing them away too, when he remembered. The blacksmith hadn't given them; the townspeople had. They weren't part of the wizard's bargain, just a mistake. Except, when had poor men ever given away gold? *Mad*!

Mad to cleanse themselves of every trace of the blacksmith; who had seemed so popular . . .

Stop *thinking*!

But the sight of the gold cheered him, as he buttoned up his pouch. He hung his soaking cloak on the back of his pack to dry and set off whistling. As well as you can whistle, with the early-morning shivers.

A hundred yards on round the bend, he stopped.

The knife was waiting, right in the middle of the path.

That wasn't the direction he'd thrown it, surely? He checked with the rising sun. Couldn't be sure.

He walked straight past. Grow legs and follow me, knife!

The path forked. He chose the right fork, towards Aigues Mortes and the rising sun.

Curve, fork, curve, fork.

The knife lay waiting, exactly where he'd left it. The letter still hung between two dry, spear-like leaves. He'd walked in a circle. Stupid! Stupid! Stupid! Aim for the rising sun!

But the sun had moved up the sky.

He walked all day, desperately trying to judge his course, as the sun swung overhead and declined west. Eleven times he strode past the knife. Each time it got harder to pass.

He came on it again, his mind crazed with intersecting tracks, as the sun lowered itself on to its bed of sharp, black reed-tops. He knelt beside the knife and wept from sheer weariness. Two more days like this, and he'd be dead. Already his legs were wobbling; his throat like dust.

Better alive with the knife than dead beside it.

He picked it up, then remembered the letter. Perhaps Seroster was another wizard, who could release him? At least you could *argue* with a wizard, unlike mute steel and bronze.

There was no way of reaching the letter, except by wading . . .

The mud came up to his mouth; he couldn't reach high enough . . . shook the reeds frantically . . . felt the black bottom give way under him, sending up masses of stinking black bubbles.

When he got back to solid ground, he was moaning out loud.

After that, things got a bit better.

The main path became perfectly obvious, even by moonlight. But he could see his own stupid footprints leading off, now left, now right, into the meaningless maze.

After a mile, he came to a wider place. There, for a little while, the water ran clear. Clear enough for *his* kind of thirst. Clear enough to wash most of the stinking mud off.

Then he noticed it was a place where travellers camped; heaps of their rubbish lay all round the clearing. Amongst which he found two bruised apples and a lump of grey soggy bread.

It was the first food he'd eaten since the blacksmith's chestnuts.

4

He walked till noon next day, with only the flitting of reed-buntings for company, and the fat quack of moorhens out of their watery strongholds. The reeds were endless; only the muddy track told him anything.

Hooves, crossing and recrossing. Always galloping, throwing up clots of mud that hung and dried on the reeds around. Why were the horsemen always galloping? Nasty to meet one in a narrow place . . .

But he met no one.

In some places, the hoofprints had been blurred by a mass of smaller paws. Foxes? Never so many foxes in one place . . . cats? . . . he remembered the thieving cats of the fishing-port . . . the dead cat hung from the wooden cross . . . He shook his head and pressed on. Wild thoughts bred in this swamp like mosquitoes. Once on the open road, they'd vanish.

But when he finally came to the open road, he was reluctant to venture out. Starve-faced, still streaked with mud, he looked a beggar. A beggar with a hundred gold coins in his pouch, fraying the buckle. An uneasy mixture. He slid back and sat among the reeds.

This road ran straight and knew where it was going. Its mud carried cart-tracks; and the hoofprints were walking, not galloping. He waited to see who would come past.

Two laden ox-carts. Drivers walking alongside, flicking habitual goads at the oxen's mud-caked flanks. Habitually goading each other, too, about some fly-blown side of bacon.

Cam wasn't tempted.

Then two black monks, walking one behind the other. The first carried a big rough cross, and his habit was peeled forward off his shoulders. The second carried a whip of knotted thongs, with which he beat at his companion spasmodically, a look of total boredom on his face. The companion's back was covered with tiny whip-scars; the skin between wrinkled and stretched like bad vellum. But no blood was being drawn this morning; the blows would hardly swat a fly. Fifty yards down the track the pair stopped and changed places. Then went on, singing a lamentable dirge in which Cam could make out a few words of mangled Latin.

Again, he wasn't tempted.

Then, after a long, fly-buzzing time, three horsemen. Or rather (as he peered between the reeds) two horsemen and a girl. Their voices sounded harmless through the still, hot air.

The girl rode astride, in spite of her velvet dress, which was far too good for riding and already badly spattered. Cam was shocked by the view of her booted legs and feet. Feet which never stopped wriggling in the stirrups. She glanced around a lot (Cam wriggled his bottom deeper into the reeds), talked a lot, waved her arms a lot and looked very sure she was welcome in the world. She had glossy brown pigtails and the habit, when she thought no one was watching, of popping her left pigtail into her mouth and chewing the end.

Her father wore a black gown and flat black hat, with a pilgrim's badge from Compostela. Silver, not lead. He had black-and-silver hair, a nibbled moustache, and a mouth that turned down meanly at the corners. He wasn't listening to the girl; answered with grunts till she made him lose his temper, then carped on and on. She paid no more attention to him than he had to her.

The last rider was a red-faced cocky fool, who played constantly with his sword as if he'd never handled one before. Nervous . . .

As they drew alongside, they halted so abruptly that their horses blundered into each other. Then sat, as if frozen.

Had they spotted him?

But they were staring ahead, down the track. The older man said, "Is it . . . ?"

The fool hauled round his horse so fast, it reared. Then he was off, the horse's hooves throwing up great shapeless clouts of mud.

The girl tried to follow, but the old man grabbed her bridle.

"Too late . . ."

Cam craned his neck desperately. Through a thinner patch of reed, he saw men riding up the track, filling it from side to side.

Soldiers? Their armour was too rusty; nothing seemed to fit. Their fine big horses were ragged-coated, didn't hold up their heads like horses should. There was too much hauling on bridles and hurting mouths for no reason.

They didn't ride like soldiers; straggled and quarrelled, carried drawn swords with which they pricked each other's horses, and tried to knock off each other's helmets. Some rode wildly through the reeds, smashing them down in great swathes, exulting in the destruction. Drear though the marsh was, they left it looking like a gnawed carcase.

Cam grew afraid. Felt his crouching legs grow tight as winched crossbows. Heard a low panting from his own mouth, which grew dry and foul. There was a fluttering under his belt . . . He put a hand down to still it. His hand closed over the blacksmith's knife. It almost seemed as if the knife had a life of its own, fluttering like a bird that wanted to fly . . .

The man and girl sat their horses like pale statues. Only the horses' necks quivered, against the flies.

The human wolfpack straggled to a halt. Their bickering dwindled into intent silence, as their leader rode forward. He had a hugeness that bred despair. His stallion seemed crushed donkey-like beneath him. He wore no helmet. His whole head seemed a helmet of bone, from which tiny eyes peered. Cam felt that if you tried to push a knife into his flesh, the knife-point would break. He had pale ginger hair, short as fur.

Cam edged even deeper into the reeds. Nobody noticed. Every eye was on the man and the girl.

The leader held out his hand silently. His fingers were long and thick.

The old man fumbled with the pouch at his belt. Nearly dropped it, then reached forward trembling and put it into the leader's hand. The leader weighed it, put it in his saddlebag. Then held out his hand again, with tiny coaxing movements of the huge fingers.

The old man took off his rings, with difficulty, and his silver pilgrim's badge, and put them into the coaxing hand.

The hand put these, too, into the saddlebag; then gestured towards the girl. White-faced, she took off her rings and gave them to her father, who put them in the great hand . . .

The hand pointed down to the muddy ground.

Man and girl dismounted.

The leader galloped on down the track, knocking them flat as he went.

They were still picking themselves up as the rest of the men, excited, closed round them.

There was nothing Cam could do, against so many. He turned

his back and crawled deeper into the reeds. Curled himself into a tight ball, eyes shut and hands over his ears so he could see nothing, hear nothing. He felt a sharp prick on his cheek. He was still clutching the blacksmith's knife, drawn now. Both the knife and his hand were quivering as if they had some life of their own.

He did not know how long he lay, before a thudding through the ground told him the men were riding away. He crept back to the track, his whole face screwed up against what he might see.

Nothing dreadful; yet. The old man and girl were still standing, naked now, apart from their shifts. The old man's legs were knotted, but the girl's were white and beautiful. Their eyes were dazed, vacant. Their horses were gone.

Two men remained, busy stuffing the father's black gown and the girl's blue dress into their saddlebags. One was dark, little and quick like a dancer. The other was gawky with an absurdly large chin, made larger by a straggle of beard. They were looking at the girl and giggling. In no hurry, they fastened their saddlebags and moved towards her.

Cam suddenly belched; bile welled up in his throat. They might have heard, but they were too intent on the girl. Cam could hardly stand; no strength in him . . .

Yes, there was. His right hand, holding the knife, felt solid, warm and strong. Even as he realised, the warmth and strength swept up through his wrist, into his arm, across his shoulders.

From the knife.

Back on the track, the father had thrust himself between the men and his daughter. Shouting something about more money . . .

"What, more money?" jeered the tall one, pointing at the old man's shift and bare legs. They tried to push him aside, but he resisted. And his daughter clung on behind, so that they were only pushed knee-deep into the swamp.

"Kill him," said the tall one. "No – maim him – let him watch."

The small one drew a knife.

The warmth in Cam's shoulders spread to his chest; he took the first decent breath for a long time. But at the same moment he felt his whole body turning, of its own volition. Until his left shoulder pointed straight at the small man.

The position for throwing the knife.

I can't kill somebody, thought Cam. I've never, I can't, I can't.

The small one stood right up against the old man; put an arm lovingly round his neck. Bent both his knees for an upward thrust . . .

"Careful," said the tall one. "Don't *kill* him . . ." And giggled again.

I can't, I can't, oh God I can't.

The backs of the small man's legs tensed, muscles standing out like rope under his ragged hose.

Cam groaned, shut his eyes and let go the knife.

When he opened them again, the little man was lying on the ground quite still.

"What?" shouted the tall one. "What? What? What?" Then he saw the handle of the knife sticking out of his mate's back.

Cam hoped he'd run away then. But he only ran behind his horse, leaving the old man and the girl staring.

Nobody moved for a long time.

Then the man behind the horse shouted, "Come out, sneak. I know there's only one of you."

Cam didn't stir.

"Come out, dirty sneak, or I'll kill them both."

Still Cam didn't stir.

The gawky one came from behind his horse with a blundering rush, pushed the old man aside and gathered the girl to him as a shield, holding a knife to her long bare throat. "Come *out*, dirty sneak!" His knife-hand moved; a thin line of blood ran down the girl's neck and spread in a pink rose across her shift.

Cam stepped out.

The man's eyes flicked to Cam's hands, saw they were empty. "A brat. A filthy sneaking brat." He threw the girl aside, and walked steadily towards Cam.

Cam would have died then, if a memory hadn't saved him. A memory of playing with his brother in the harvest-field. He snatched up a bundle of broken reeds and thrust them in the man's face.

The man tried to push through. Then cried out and gave back, blood running from the soft skin below one eye. He walked back to his horse, and again Cam hoped he was going away.

But he took down a sword, and a heavy wooden kite-shield painted with a faded pink chevron. A ridiculous old thing; a thing to hang on the wall . . . But the man carefully fitted the shield-handles over his forearm, got a good grip on the sword as if it was a hammer, and came for Cam again.

It was absurd. Cam snatched up armful after armful of reeds, and the man simply chopped them to bits. Cam tried leading him away into the swamp, leaping from tussock to tussock while his enemy ploughed heavily behind. If only he could run round and get back to the knife . . . But the man wasn't that much of a fool. Every time Cam went too far into the swamp, the man retreated back to menace the girl.

He was a blunderer; got plastered with mud from head to foot; hewed down whole young trees with his wild swings. He was cross-eyed, and as he got out of breath, his threats turned into a babble of slaver.

But unless Cam could reach the knife, there was only one end. Sooner or later, he'd pick the wrong tussock and go sprawling . . . He kept panting and giggling. It was so unbelievable . . .

Then they were actually circling round the helpless pair. Cam clinging on to them for handholds, swinging them round and round, like children playing tag. While they stood like dummies . . .

Then Cam saw the girl glance sideways, stick her pigtail in her mouth and shove out her foot to trip the gawky one.

He fell with a great whoosh of breath. Cam, gathering all his remaining strength, leapt clean over him.

He crouched over the corpse, groping for the knife, not looking at the face. The knife came out with a slither, and grating of bone.

He straightened, and shouted to the gawk, "Get away, get *away*! Go *now*!"

The gawk, back on his feet, laughed. Totally misunderstanding why Cam was afraid. Very sure of the protection of his shield, he came straight on.

Cam whimpered, and flicked. Then crouched in the path and was violently sick. So he only heard the gasp, the falling clatter. They seemed far away. It was more important not to be sick on the corpse; the first corpse.

Small firm hands took Cam's head and lifted it. Cam stared straight down her shift at her small round warm breasts. It would be awful to be sick down *there* . . . he managed not to be.

The girl's green eyes were strangely shining. He couldn't bear to look at them. He felt filthy; and not from wallowing in the swamp.

"Have you a wound?"

He shook his head.

The girl bustled across to the dead men's horses, pulled clothing from the saddlebags and dressed first herself, then her father. It was soothing to watch.

When the old man was dressed, he seemed to recover. "All our things gone . . . our horses. It's the Duke's duty to keep his roads . . . he takes our toll-tax quick enough . . ."

"*These* are good horses," said the girl sharply. "Better than ours – except for their poor mouths . . ."

"All our money . . . a lifetime's labour . . ."

"Have you looked in those saddlebags . . . ?"

The old man looted the saddlebags vigorously; seemed quite enlivened by what he found. Metal clinked. Then he went to loot the corpses with equal eagerness, though he never stopped moaning, "Mere trifles . . . knick-knacks."

"You old fool . . . you never had such wealth in your life. Look at it. *Look* at it."

"All the bother of melting it down . . ."

"Shut up." The girl came back to Cam, still sitting with his head between his knees. "Can I help?"

"Could you fetch my knife?"

He'd rather have left it where it was. But if he did, somehow he'd be forced to walk back to these two dreadful things lying on the track. And after dark, it would be worse . . .

He heard her pull out the knife, and wash it briskly in the swamp. Then she came back, drying it on the folds of her dress. It didn't seem to leave any stain, just water.

"All these chattels," the girl gestured round, "belong to you, by right of combat. Even my dress." She said it with stilted formality, as if she'd been taught to say it as a child. But she enjoyed saying it, nonetheless.

"Keep them," said Cam, still staring at his boots.

"Sir, you are a true knight!"

There was a sudden thudding of hooves. Cam hauled himself blindly to his feet to face them, the knife curling back in his hand. He had no resistance to it at all now.

But the knife remained motionless. It was only the red-faced fool. As he opened his mouth to speak, the old man tried to pull him bodily from the saddle.

"Call yourself a guide? You only came back to loot our bodies. Get off my horse!" He beat at the fool's booted legs.

"But sir . . ."

"Get off, I say."

Eventually, the fool dismounted. The old man grasped the bridle as if it was the fount of life itself.

"Get out of my sight!"

"But sir, my wages . . . "

"Wages? I've lost all my living because of you."

The fool shrugged and walked away, shouting back over his shoulder, "You'll get lost . . . "

"I'd rather be three times lost than ride with you. What about all my food you've eaten? Who's going to pay for that, hey? Hey?" He turned to Cam. "Lead us to the city, quickly, boy. You may ride this horse. If those villains return I will lose all my wealth. I ought not to have to carry such riches at my age. Unwise, most unwise!" He patted the dead men's saddlebags as if they were his dearest children. Then sprang into the saddle with amazing spindle-shanked agility and trotted on, scarcely pausing to berate the guide again.

The guide stuck up two fingers.

"Can you manage?" asked the girl. She helped Cam tie his pack to the saddle. Helped him get one foot into a stirrup.

Cam had to guide his horse's hooves carefully past the dead men. Their faces looked like melting marble in the heat; already the flies were buzzing. The gawky one still had one cross-eye on Cam; the other stared at Heaven with a look of surprise. His brown straggle of beard stirred in the wind, meaningless as grass.

He left them to their friends, or to the birds. The girl didn't even give them a second glance. The fool put up two fingers as they passed. The girl chattered on about everything, waving her arms and looking about her as if she was very sure of her welcome in the world . . . The old man began grumbling about the increased toll-tax they would have to pay in the city . . .

Everyone acting as if nothing had happened . . . He had to stop to be sick again.

"I'm worried about you," said the girl. "You *are* a questing-knight, aren't you? In disguise I mean? You *were* acting as my *champion* back there?"

"Well, no."

The girl frowned. "I was starting to wonder. What are you, then?"

"I mend things . . . "

"Oh . . . " said the girl, gloomily. "A . . . tinker. That makes things very awkward for me, you know. I can hardly give my heart and maidenhood to a tinker." She rode on staring straight ahead, very put out.

Cam rode on dizzily. The old man's babble went through and through his head. Taxes, villains, the outrageous price of shoeing a horse. Above all, his own dire poverty.

Finally, Cam could bear no more. He rode alongside the old man, stopped him with a hand on his rein, opened his purse (the old man's jaw dropped to see the contents) and pushed ten gold pieces into the old man's hand.

"Now shut *up*!"

Then he dismounted, pulled his pack from the saddle and walked away down a narrow path back into the swamp.

"Wait!" called the girl, worried.

"Wait!" called the old man. "That gold . . . I can get you a better bargain . . . "

The reeds closed in, shutting off their cries until they sounded no more than marsh-birds.

5

Amon was at the closed city-gate before Re-rise; sitting on a windowsill, pretending to wash. Women all round him; women who brought greenfood to the city in rustling sweet-smelling baskets. They had lodged in the city overnight, were anxious to start home. Their baskets were empty and money jingled in their skirts, like metal mice. They were impatient, hammered on the door where the gateguard slept; was he dead or drunk?

The guard shouted angrily back through the door. But it all happened every morning. Nobody here was unfu. Nobody wanted to kill cats. Amon was sure. *Nearly* sure. Would these people ever flock to watch Brethren burn?

Yet in spite of his doubts, the city was sweet this morning. Leaving it sharpened his eyes to every whorl of wood in the great gate; to the twist of rag on a nail, fluttering in the morning-wind . . .

The gateguard emerged, scratching an armpit. He grabbed at one of the women. She twisted away from the smell of his breath. The other women were laughing; other guards calling from the fusty darkness of the guardroom. They seemed as harmless as kittens . . .

The guard pulled down the gate-bar with a squeak of overnight rust, swung the gate wide. The women bundled through, shouting final rudenesses. Now they had gone, the gateway was filled with the wide blue view, stretching endlessly down the valley. A view Amon loved to watch from the walls on sunny afternoons. Roads thin as threads and wagons crawling along them, small as ants. And the slow creep of harvesting in the summer fields.

But this morning, the countryside was not a toy to watch between his paws. He had to walk out into it. The ant-like carts would become as big as houses; the roads would stretch to make his legs day-weary. Quivering in every nerve, he thrust himself through the gate into the wide blue gap.

He hadn't gone ten yards before there was a yell. Amon half-crouched, looked back over his shoulder. The gateguard was waving his arms wildly. But he hadn't gone unfu. He was trying to call Amon back; there were tears in his eyes.

Baffled, Amon trotted on. All the guards were calling now; one was waving a piece of cold meat near the ground. He caught the distress in their minds. They saw his leaving as an ill-omen. No Miw had left in living memory . . . tonight, their gossip would be all over the city. Amon tried to send the idea that he was coming back. But their minds were much too noisy. They were worse than five-week kittens. He trotted on.

As the height of the city walls receded, he grew tenser. Oh, the flatness of the world; nothing to climb, nowhere to hide . . .

What would dare attack a Miw?

Then he caught faint flickers of sending from the city. Mother-blessings far-off as echoes, fading, fading. The Miw bidding him farewell. It made the flat emptiness worse.

So he sensed, with relief, two flickers of gleeful malice ahead, well-hidden behind a pair of gateposts. Bubbling with excitement, waiting to leap out on him as he passed.

As he drew level with the gateposts, as the glee reached a crescendo, he swayed a step backwards instead of forwards.

Ripfur leapt from the right and Tornear from the left. In the absence of Amon they landed on top of each other and rolled off down the road, a cartwheel of slashing claws and flying fur. Amon padded silently after them.

Finally, realising their error, they fell apart. Ripfur got to his feet first. Amon, judging the distance to perfection, hit him a clout on the jowl that sent him straight into the ditch. Tornear, dazed and blinking, received the same treatment. Amon stood, appalled by his own ruthlessness.

They picked themselves up, looking very put out.

"You knew we here?" sent Ripfur.

"He more use than we thought," sent Tornear.

"He stronger than we thought," sent Ripfur again, scraping cow-dung off one ear with the back of his paw.

They could both do with a thorough wash. Amon got a pungent hint of how they'd left the city without using the gate. It was not a way he would ever have chosen himself. Still, they seemed to bear remarkably little malice. He walked on feeling much better. They fell in behind.

"Not-walk behind," sent Amon. "Two-cat-walk is wonder, three-cat-walk is magic to ignorant-men."

"Catsarse!" sent Tornear. It was an image peculiar to him; the rear view of a fat black cat walking away, tail high in the air, leaving nothing to the imagination. It was his unique way of being unharmonious.

The two blacks plunged away into the bushes on the right. He could still feel their minds. They were hunting and catching; having fun. It made him feel hungry, boring and oddly old . . . had they already forgotten the fiery basket at Mainz?

"Fine-fat-hen," sent Ripfur. "You want share?"

"Do not steal; farm-people are catfriend."

"Catsarse!"

Their images of the hen made Amon drool. He shook his head in resentment, spattering saliva over the dusty road.

He passed through a village, a little nervous, tensed to run. He needn't have bothered. Villagers stopped and stared; children were brought to see; babies held up from cottage windows. Someone came out with a dish of milk for the lucky golden cat, the first ever to grace their village. Amon drank it gratefully, but refused a pressing invitation to stay.

"Good-milk," he sent to the others. "You miss." But it didn't seem much to set against the hen.

"You-wait! You-see!" sent Ripfur enigmatically.

Amon saw soon enough, when the road passed the yard of an isolated farm. Two children followed him. Shouted. Waved their arms and finally threw stones at the strange, bold, unfrightened creature. Outraged, he turned. They fled, screaming that the giant cat was attacking them. Next thing he knew, there was a whizzing in the air, and a crossbow-bolt sticking in the ground between his legs. He departed swiftly, but with dignity. From watching the city-men shooting, he knew to the nearest breath how long it took to rewind a crossbow.

"Farmers-catfriend?" sent Ripfur. "Not in your-city now, yellercat."

Tornear sent his usual vision; only now it was the rear-end of a Miw, with its tail between its legs.

They were both very, very trying. Knew this countryside like their own pawmarks. Dallied, hunted, stole, lay about, hovering just on the edge of his sending-power and holding up the journey horribly. Re-knew what Sehtek would say. But there was no feel of

Sehtek; she had turned her mind to other worries. Or was already out of range. It again grew unbearably lonely, though he had no more trouble from men. Gave their dwellings a wide berth; slipped through a hedge when he saw one coming.

Towards the middle of Re's voyage, when it was hottest, he felt the Brethren closing up. Another ambush?

But there was worry in their minds now, which grew steadily. It made him anxious, till he realised. They had come to the edge of the country they knew; the country that could be raided between dusk and dawn, even in the dark of winter. The journey was now as strange for them as it was for him. At least *he* knew where he was going . . .

He quickened his pace; they quickened theirs. There was a low protest from Ripfur . . . tired. Tornear was too tired even to make catsarse. Amon pressed on harder. Now they would know who was in charge! Now they would make up for wasted time!

At Re-set, he had mercy; led them into a scrub of silver-barked trees that struggled to prosper in red soil already turning arid. They hunched into resentful heaps, their eyes alternately closing in weariness and opening to glower. Their no-sending was oppressive.

But at least if they were weary they were full of meat. Amon had had nothing all day but the bowl of milk.

"Go hunt?" sent Ripfur sarcastically. Amon was outfaced. He'd never hunted in his life; men had always given food.

A large black-beetle crawled past his paws. He clawed it in and crunched it hungrily. Not pleasant; its wing-cases were sharp and brittle in his mouth.

"Now we know what yellercat eat," sent Ripfur. "Yellercat beetle-eater!"

"Mother was hedgehog?" asked Tornear.

Amon closed his eyes and decided to go hungry.

Then he felt something gentle approaching; twitching and soft and nervous. He opened his eyes.

A hare was limping into the clearing; fooled by the utter exhausted stillness of the cats. As Amon opened his eyes, the hare fled.

That flight set Amon's muscles afire. Before he knew it, he was after it as it twisted and jinked through the trees. And somehow his muscles and his eyes came together, in a way he had never known before. He knew every twist and turn the hare would make before it made them. He cut corners, catching up with amazing ease. Came up on its right-hand quarter and leapt, his left paw, the stronger, digging into its back.

The hare's back legs collapsed; the rest of its body began to roll. Amon's neck arched; his jaw opened for the hare's neck.

But as his teeth were about to close, he saw the dark, terrified eye of the hare right against his own. Saw in it the memory of quiet pools and grass, and the black terror of ceasing . . .

He weighed that terror against his hunger, as the soul is weighed against the feather of Maat. His jaws didn't close. He spun off the hare, rolling over and over in a cloud of dust. Felt the hare's soul hesitate at the dark door of death. Then it was up and running again, with only the claw-wounds in its hindquarters to remember him by. Before it passed beyond the range of his mind, its soul was wiped clean of the fear of death, of the memory of cat. It was just running and feeling pain. It would live.

He got up and licked his shoulder; less to ease the shock of his fall than the shock of grasping his own true savage nature. He trotted back.

"Fine-night for run?" enquired Ripfur. "Not-tired?"

"Strong-leg – weak-jaw," added Tornear. "Some fine-beetles pass. Not too hard kill."

He ignored their thoughts. Neither of them could even have caught up with the hare. Rejoicing in the higher nature of Miw, which transcends that of Brethren, he set about eating beetles.

They tormented him about the hare all next morning, padding south. In spite of sore-paw, they made good time. The Brethren hunted, but not excessively. There were no longer rich farms to tempt them, only a succession of tiny rodents they could eat on the march. Amon didn't bother trying to feed; Miw could go weeks without food . . . he'd be back in the city by then . . . the skin of roast duck . . . he controlled his thoughts firmly.

At Re-high, he called a rest, settling among the black sticks of a patch of burnt gorse that threw black shadows across his red-gold fur; it blended in so well with the dry red soil; from three paces he was invisible to the half-blind eye of man, at least . . .

As his body rested, with many a gentle easing of the legs, and the odd lick to fur, he let his mind wander in delight. It was so much more *alive* out here, away from the clatter and bumble of men. He could sense the timid scurry of fieldmice, torn endlessly between hunger and terror. Stare-eye, ear-twitch, nose-twitch. How unpleasant to be born a fieldmouse! And the dry ticking fearless life of insects that had no soul. Or had they? Out here, even the little trees seemed to have souls – slow contented souls, a slow searching of root for damp-dark, a pleasant shimmer of wind through leaves, punctuating the never-ending warm life of Re, which was what he was feeling too. The oneness of Re filled Amon's soul; he purred.

Ripfur and Tornear were restfully distant; still seeking fill-belly; tormenting each other now.

"Not-eat *that*? Moon-dead!"

"Maggots – tasty."

"Gutter-rat."

Then terror. Sudden as rain falling out of sunlight. Terror from Ripfur, terror from Tornear. And a confusion of shrieking frustration, a slavering unfu that could only be dogs. And worse, the unfu amusement of men.

Dreamer! Dozer in the sun! Amon's long limbs thrust him towards the wild barking that came faintly through the hot air.

He saw it all in one eyeful. The leafless tree, so long dead the bark had peeled off, leaving it naked and polished by the wind. Ripfur and Tornear, crouched in the highest branches. Two shaggy hounds leaping up the trunk, scrabbling with blunt claws then falling back. Two horsemen, gaily clad in fringed blue leather, with long feathers in their hats. One held a hawk that flapped wildly at the excitement invisible to its hooded eyes, but flooding in its ears, and through the trembling arm of the man who held it.

The other man was winding a crossbow. The click of its ratchet came clearly.

There was no time; the crossbow was almost bent. In a moment, the man would straighten. At that range, even the most stupid couldn't miss . . .

The old civilised city-mind of Amon despaired.

But the hunter new-born in him knew the one, exact thing to do. Man stiff-spine; cannot look behind. Gathering every ounce of pace, Amon leapt on the haunches of the crossbowman's horse. He regretted hurting the horse, as his claws dug into the smooth rump.

The horse bolted. The crossbow triggered off, sending the bolt high, high in the air.

The man tried to turn, lash out backwards with the bow. Then the horse stumbled, and the bow went flying. The man, snatching at the reins, missed them, and clung desperately to the horse's neck.

Amon renewed the hold of his claws, deeper. The horse whinnied, high and shrill, galloped faster. Amon became aware of the other man, galloping up behind to the rescue. But the other man was afraid to gallop fast; the ground was rough here.

Far behind, Amon felt the minds of the hounds change from insane rage to doubt, as their masters galloped off, abandoning them. Amon knew they dropped to the ground, stared round, whined. That was the black cats' chance . . .

They took it; dropping like vengeful meteors on the hounds' backs. Now the hounds were running in terror too, in different directions.

The two riders were yelling at each other. Idiots! Their mutual amusement had fallen apart into hate and contempt. What poor friends men were! The man behind tried to reach forward and grab Amon, but the fluttering hawk impeded him. Then the leading horse fell, rolling, kicking its legs in the air. Amon fell on his feet. The man fell on his head and lay still. The horse, after a moment's panic, discovered it still had four legs and galloped on. The second rider blundered past and returned, full of caution and care for his own skin. Very terrible Amon seemed then, twice his real size, for the man had never seen Miw before.

Then the fallen man groaned; tried to sit up. Time to go. Amon vanished silently into the scrub.

The blood of action pounded in his head; fogged the grasp of his mind. He could not sense Ripfur and Tornear. Headed back for the dead tree.

"You-ride horse fine. We-ride dog better!" Ripfur was sitting under the tree, casually licking blood from between the extended claws of his right paw.

"Where Tornear?"

"Gone unfu. Want dog for noon-meal. Back soon. Dog run too fast."

And Tornear came swaggering back, a long piece of grey dog-hair trailing unnecessarily from his mouth.

"Boaster!" sent Ripfur.

Tornear dropped the dog-hair reluctantly. "Make good-nest for kittens. Dog not-need it."

"Boaster!" Then Ripfur turned to Amon. "You-hunt hare ill, horse well. My life in your-paw . . ."

"Amon want piece of dog-hair?" asked Tornear, with gratitude of a sort. Better than catsarse.

He would have no more bother from either of them; not for a bit. His mind was clearing. He sensed the two men still raging at each other; each telling the other what he should have done, and yelling angrily for the dogs betweentimes.

The dogs could hear them, but for once were refusing to come to heel.

The horses were sympathising with each other.

The hawk was vainly trying to unruffle its feathers . . .

No danger left; but time to move.

"Come!" The black cats took up station, thirty yards behind and thirty yards apart.

That evening, as they settled for the night, Ripfur left a dead rat at Amon's feet, and stalked off stiffly without a send.

Twenty miles away, the two sportsmen, still quarrelling, were regaling the inn-keeper with the tale of a savage gold lion, twice the size of a man . . .

6

Cam walked and walked. He knew now why the blacksmith wanted to die. Those stupid old stories . . . geese laying golden eggs . . . King Arthur's magic sword . . .

You didn't own the goose or sword; they owned you. The goose laid eggs for its own sake; just needed you to fetch the corn. Excalibur killed its own foes, not King Arthur's. When it had used him up, it went back to its lake and left him to die. That fool Geoffrey of Monmouth got Arthur all wrong. Unless Geoffrey owned a magic quill that wrote its own lies and just needed Geoffrey to fetch the ink, till his hand dropped off with weariness. Whereupon the quill would find another lucky owner . . .

Hard luck, knife! I shall walk right into the middle of this swamp, where there are no men for you to kill, and no one to find you when *I* die. When broad paths lead to narrow, and narrow into ooze, I shall drop you to the bottom, where you can't even float back to the surface on my bloated body . . .

He deliberately chose the narrowest paths, daring them to dwindle to nothing. But there was always somehow a way through.

He kept walking.

But, his mind made up, there was quietness in him. He enjoyed every detail. The sharp diamonds the setting sun carved out of the reeds; every hoofprint on the path. The galloping horsemen were back. Twice he crossed the track of the fleeing cats, travelling north. He came to love the small things of the swamp, the new tiny frogs, the flocks of finches that retreated endlessly before him. He held his foot as a green watersnake crossed, with bright oval eye and harmless darting tongue.

Dusk. The moon came up.

There was a horse in the middle of the path, white, but black up to its belly with mud. Poor horse, you lost too? He wanted to lead it out of this filth, to grass and clean water. Till he perceived the cunning of the knife . . . Where there was grass and clean water, there'd be men to kill. Then he'd have to start back into the swamp all over again, and mightn't have the courage.

Still, he called to the horse, softly.

It pricked its ears, but didn't come.

He lost patience; shooed it out of the way, waving his arms like windmills.

It remained still as marble. It was he who finally paused, doubtful.

No bridle. Under the bright moon, no mark of curry-comb or shears; no place where its coat was worn bare with a saddle. Mane long, tangled. A wild horse, standing like a king.

He shouted and waved his arms again . . . wild horses were timid, shy . . . But the horse stood, only nodding its head violently now, blowing softly through its nostrils.

Cam knew it was he who shouldn't be there.

It came straight for him, at a gallop. The swamp shook.

Not knowing which way to dodge, he simply closed his eyes. At the last moment, as he smelt its grassy breath, it swerved. Its shoulder brushed him; the rounded bulk of its belly swiped him sideways into the reeds.

As he scrambled up, he heard it whinny and turn. Again the earth shook. Again he dared not move. Again it bellied him, head-over-heels.

When it turned a third time there was another horse running with it. They blocked the whole track, leaving themselves no room to swerve. He ran himself, now . . .

They passed like the wind, leaving him sprawling.

Now the earth shook and shook; the air was full of snorting and the pathways full of horses. Over and over he went; over and over again, into the mud. And still he ran. He thought they didn't *mean* to kill him. They only ran for the sake of running; heedless, like the waves of the sea.

And then, in a little clearing where three tracks met (and he no longer wondered who the galloping horsemen of the marsh had been) he laughed out loud.

It was the knife again, up to its old tricks. Using the wild horses to drive him where it wanted him to go. But the knife couldn't afford him dead . . .

He sat down calmly in the middle of the clearing, head resting on his arms. Here he would stay; till it was over.

It was over quickly. More horses came galloping. Some leapt

over his head, showering him with clods. Others pulled up, legs splayed, blowing hard. Then they simply gathered in a circle; dark eyes shining black in white faces, under the white moon. Horses of the moon. They sniffed him, blew softly, soaking him with their warm drool. Latecomers pushed through . . .

So many came, he grew weary. So he simply curled up with his pack under his head. Dragged out his old cloak and pulled it over him. There wasn't much room between the muddy legs and questing nostrils.

He fell asleep, to the sound of tearing and munching.

In the morning, they were gone. Only the reed-tops, stripped bare as far as the eye could see, proved it hadn't been a dream.

Well, knife? What now, knife? So you cannot force me, knife? He patted it, as if it was a barking dog outfaced.

The knife lay still in his hand; just a knife. He pulled down a reed, and used the knife to slice it. In spite of the swamp-mists, the blade had kept its edge. The nails of his boots might be red with rust; and his belt-buckle. But not the knife.

It was a warning . . .

But he certainly no longer wished he was dead. He wished something small and pleasant would happen. Like meeting the girl again; watching her hands tightening saddle-girths, popping her pigtail in her mouth.

Or breakfast . . . His inside was a cavern; his kneebones looked sharper than he remembered. He counted his ribs through his jerkin, wondered idly how long he'd survive, if he didn't eat. Stood upright with an effort that made his head swim, so he had to put one hand back on the ground. When the dizzy bout passed, he straightened and saw, through the bare stems of the reeds, a house.

House . . . breakfast. But where there was a house there'd be men . . . But where else was there to go but mud and reeds? He headed towards it, warily.

When he saw it was an empty ruin, he didn't know whether to laugh or cry.

It stood on an island in the marsh, that nowhere rose more than twenty feet above the water. But it was covered with blessed green grass, and the river surrounding it ran fresh and clear.

It had been the smallest kind of house a gentleman might own. A hall, with three lancet windows and a lancet door. At one end, an octagonal watchtower with a turret; but the battlements were gone;

the tower sat on a heap of its own fallen stone, like a bird on the nest. The hall roof had fallen in. Only the great wall-chimney stood guard against the sky, its golden stone rimmed with soot.

A bridge led across; but fallen in the middle, a gap too wide to leap. But the river had shrunk in the hot weather to half its normal size. On either bank lay a stretch of silken mud that popped bubbles under the sun. The mud was embroidered with the arrowed tracks of birds, the zigzag of watersnakes. But no print of horse or man, even on the margins, where the mud was dry and cracked.

Nobody had been here for months. He walked all round, just to make sure. No stir among the ruins, no drift of morning-smoke.

Very well, knife, I'll cross. He watched carefully for deeper pockets in the mud. Looked back over his shoulder at the glaring evidence of his own footprints.

Halfway, a plaintive miaow reached his ears. A she-cat sitting on the far bank. A white face from which dark eyes looked enquiringly. Otherwise she was black-and-ginger, and her tail curled over her back like a little dog's.

All the way across she kept up her querulous complaint. Trotted round to meet him as he landed, rubbing against his legs in ecstasy. He picked her up. She was large, plump, spotlessly clean and obviously lonely. How many days had she passed just catching mice and lying in the sun, washing herself from boredom? Had she come from the fishing-port too? Very much the mistress of her island, and keen to make him master . . .

Never had he known a ruin so happy. Was it the golden lichened stone, where lizards sunned themselves, scurrying away when his cold shadow fell across them? Was it the total absence of roofs, so that the sunlight had scoured away every shadowy corner and human memory? Was it the upper breeze, blowing high and clean above the ooze and filth, bringing the smell of healthy growing things? He felt at home.

The floor of the hall was buried in shattered roofing-slabs, with the dry grey wood of rafters sticking out in jagged clumps, ready to burn. When he looked up inside the great chimney, he could see a blue flag of sky above the towering soot. All he needed was an axe . . .

There was an axe.

A shattered battle-axe, spikes bent and haft broken halfway. As he reached into the deep cranny where it lay, a sudden suspicion crawled up his back . . . Oh, you don't catch me that way again, knife . . .

But the axe-blade was grained with rust; nobody had even chopped wood with it for a long, long time.

There were two sacks in the fireplace; full of dusty oats for horses. That was what the whole place was full of, the memory of travellers, arriving weary, chopping wood, sleeping safe and departing in the morning.

The she-cat summoned him on. Through a mossy ruined orchard where the apple-trees grew huge and wild and sag-branched, laden with good-sized crabs. To an ancient kitchen-garden where cabbages grew five feet tall, laden with yellow flowers.

Nobody; nothing; nowhere. It pleased his soul exceedingly.

When she led him up the spiral stair of the watchtower, he could see the blue edge of the swamp, far off. And a distant valley, bordered by white crags, faint as clouds. The valley he'd seen, impossibly, from the rotting bridge.

Oh, *there* you are, knife!

But the knife lay quite still in the palm of his hand. He put it in a crevice of the fallen battlements, and left it.

Someday, knife! Perhaps!

Then he ran down the stairs to chop wood, and light a fire with his flint-and-steel in the old fireplace.

For the first time in days, he was happy.

7

Amon climbed another slope of loose red soil; flattened himself as he reached the crest. Poised for flight, he peered through a cleft. Better than sticking your whole head suddenly above the skyline, where even a man might notice. He didn't show his whole head; only nose, eyes, ears protruded flatly. He looked no more than a drift of red-gold soil, sifted by the wind between two boulders.

In four days, he'd learnt about men. The further you went, the worse they got. They didn't just kill for food. Or from fear, like rats. They didn't even kill for fun, like the worst of the Brethren. Just killed for the sake of killing. Lucky they were so wrapped up in their quarrelling, and counting gold inside their heads. If Re vanished from the sky, some men wouldn't notice till they tripped over a rock in the dark . . .

Beyond the cleft, he saw only another small empty valley, rising to another white crest. He'd crossed so many . . .

But a new thing was drawing near. A hissing in the air that, angle his ears as he might, he couldn't locate. A huge smell, like the water in vases, but less pleasant.

He closed his eyes, felt outwards with his mind. No cats for miles, except the two behind, monotonously bickering. No men, except a scattered line, miles east, on the road. But nearer, something huge, restless. Horse? Better be. Sehtek said walk six-day, and this was the seventh. He was sore-paw, in spite of washing.

He wearily summoned the black toms, slipped down the valley and up the next crest.

The world beyond was unfu. His nose gave nothing but the smell of black water, and things rotting forever. Who could smell enemy inside *that*? Ears gave nothing but hiss, hiss, hiss with every breeze. Eyes gave only a tormenting sea of movement that mazed his brain. Sehtek could not mean *this*! No sane Miw . . .

Sehtek wasn't sane; goddess in-her.

He told the toms to stay, and walked . . . He was Miw.

Close to, the pale stems that waved so far above seemed impassable. Grew only inches apart, out of black water. He investigated left; right. Came to a place where the stems had been mashed flat into the water, making a place where it was *possible* to walk. Into the unfu.

It smelt of Horse. Walk in. What else? Wrinkling his nose, stopping frequently to shake the foul black water off his paws. No-chance see enemy right or left. Nor in front or behind; the track curved. He could only sense the all-over twitter of insect, bird and frog, and the hugeness of horse, lying like a black cloud over all. Near panic, he ran in jagged spurts, close to the ground, aghast at his own unfu.

Then the mud beneath his paws began to quiver.

Sehtek said listen with your paws.

A low rumbling, all round.

Sehtek said see with your ears. Quick-dodge. Horse kill-you, not see-you.

Desperately he forced his body between the unyielding stems at the side of the track. The black water squelched up between his pads.

Then the whole world was a thunderstorm. They passed within inches of his astounded nose. Huge, white as clouds. Hooves throwing up fountains that soaked him from nose to tail.

"Goodrunrunrun. Runwind. Runrunrunwind. Windmane good. Windtailgood. Goodmane runtailwind."

He awaited death with dignity. But eventually, the ground ceased to shake. He crawled out more dead than alive; rejoined Ripfur and Tornear.

"Find-horse? Or been-swim?"

Tornear was delighted. He sent a picture of a horsearse, travelling at speed.

They laid up for the night, far inside the tall-stems, finding a place a little drier than the rest. Ripfur reported an abundance of newts and slimy delights; Amon abstained. His mind roamed the wet blackness, moving among Horse. They slept on their feet. (Amon, shifting uncomfortably as the damp seeped up through his fur, thought that very sensible.) A few, here and there, were always awake and on guard; though they feared little, except some large grey-creature with pointed ears, and they weren't very afraid of that. It was only a danger to the sick and young, and only when it came in packs. Horse knew how to deal with it; thunder in the narrow places, flashing hooves. Then the grey-creature was fleeing, or was-not. Grey-creature disliked the Wetness; only came desperate in winter, when the Wetness was rock-hard-cold.

Amon envied Horse his size and fearlessness.

At Re-rising, he told the toms to stay put. Drowsy after a night's fill-belly, they didn't argue. He set off up the narrow way cautiously.

But this morning, Horse was placid. Good-graze, munch-belly. Scattered all round him, the ones in poorgraze drifting across to the ones in goodgraze.

Amon picked out one grazing by itself. He let it see him clearly; not wishing to be mistaken for a grey-creature. Horse stopped its grazing momentarily; diagnosed him as point-ear, but not grey-creature. Golden, alone, larger than usual . . . It sent these tidings to the rest of Horse. They weren't very interested, except in his size and aloneness. Why-only-one? Where were the rest?

Baffled, Amon sat down. *Were* there other cats about? In *this* abomination? He let his mind rove wider. There was a hint of cat faint and weak and sickly. Maybe a nest of ailing kittens in a farm the far side of the wet-place.

He started sending to Horse, very softly. "Miw-Horsefriend. Horse-Miwfriend." Over and over, getting slowly louder. He didn't want to start a thunder-and-lightning . . .

The nearest part of Horse raised its head again; seesawed it violently, splayed its ears, even stopped munching, a bunch of drooly fronds hanging comically from its mouth. It advanced, blowing softly, turning its head to watch him with one eye. Something new, it sent. Something *new*!

Immediately, all of Horse was moving in. Slowly at first, then quicker. Their own speed excited them . . . mane-lift . . . tail-blow . . .

The ground began shaking again; Amon slunk back quickly in the reeds.

It lasted a long time. Amon sat hunched, unsending. To attract their notice was certain death. He hoped Ripfur was far away; didn't even dare ask him.

Finally, the thunder ceased. Good-run. Now, good-graze. Where Horsefriend gone? When they were nicely settled, and the sound of munching once more filled the air, tail-swish, rumble-belly, Amon tried again.

"Miw-Horsefriend . . ." They packed round him, denser than midges in midsummer. Too packed to run, thank-Re. He moved among them; they sniffed and blew in a friendly way.

"Miw," they sent, as their slow minds stirred with ancient memories. "Miw-Horsefriend. Long-ago. How-many cold-rock-winters?" This also took time; and he could sense the run-urge starting to build up in their muscles again. Better start giving his message. He sent everything, slowly and simply, as to a three-week kitten. It seemed to take forever. But they were interested, even worried. Disorder in the city was linked in their mind with men coming with ropes and nets. He got a vision of his own city as a dreary prison of broken spirits, heavy loads and nowhere to run. Pain-mouth . . . lost . . . no-wind. Finally, they made up their mind. "Miw ask – we-come." There was a lot of that, too, getting louder and louder. Finally, to rid their mind of the memory of that dreadful place where ropes were placed round your neck and metal in your mouth, they took off at a furious gallop. He was glad to see them go; felt utterly drained by their big slow mind. But a last send came back.

"Man near – Horsefriend. Miwfriend?" There was a blurred vision of a low green island.

"You-finished?" sent Ripfur, nearby.

And a horsearse.

"Keep-watch." Amon closed his eyes and sent his mind out further than it had ever been. After Horse it was restful to travel far-out where things were faint. He felt Ripfur and Tornear move in on each side of him, lending him the closeness of their bodies. It made him feel so safe he ventured out further still. So far it amazed him. He thought he caught a trace of Sehtek in the city; another furious rage; *more* trouble. He tried sending to her about horse, but she didn't notice. Goddess in-her, she didn't notice what any Miw sent, even under her very nose.

Westwards, he got a baffling jumble. A trace of a man, happy, not-unfu. And a fuzzy haze of cat, with great sadness in it. But almost blotting out both, something strange, more exciting than the smell of valerian, that drew him irresistibly.

That was the way to go.

Cam leaned on the battlements of his tower, and sighed. Such a lovely evening. Such a lovely six days. He'd done so many things.

Found a war-axe, and chopped wood.

Found a shining war-helm, and turned it into a blackened cooking-pot.

Found a spear, curiously unrusted, and turned it into a roasting-spit.

You don't catch me that way, knife!

He'd found carrots, turnips and onions growing wild in the ruined garden. Made some fine stews with what the cat brought in. She'd been slow to understand that mice wouldn't do; had mewed and looked pathetically baffled when he returned her offerings with a shake of the head. Finally, she got it right. A fresh young rabbit every morning, with dew on its fur. He'd try roasting one tonight . . .

He'd slept inside the great fireplace; built a wall across to keep out draughts. Floored it with rushes. The cat shared his bed till dawn, more soothing than any wife. Snug. His kneebones no longer stuck out.

But the evenings were darkening into autumn. Soon, the plants in the garden would wither, the young rabbits grow too big and clever for the cat. Winter would come and the mistral blow, and his summer palace would become a draught-chinked, cheerless hovel.

The cat would manage; he would not.

And as his strength returned, the swamp-edge, seen from the tower, seemed to draw nearer. This evening, it seemed only a stroll away; the whole swamp little more than a fringe of reeds, scarcely hiding him from the road and the endless travelling-men.

Not only the road seemed nearer. So did the red valley with its high white cliffs. He could almost imagine, if he shaded his eyes, he could see the city.

He took the knife from its niche. It had stayed there so harmlessly; only sometimes, as he walked his domain, the cat hunting before him through the brambles, he would look back at the tower and see the rustless knife glinting red in the rays of the setting sun . . .

Had it really killed two men? He tried to remember their melting marble faces. But they had faded, like relics in a glass case, dusted over with time. The knife lay so quiet in his hand, he was suddenly bored. He would see if it would still fly true and hit a target. No harm in *that*!

He ran down the steps whistling. Mended the fire. Put the rabbit on the spit to roast slowly, and went off for some target-practice among the trees.

For once the cat didn't follow; she was sitting on the broken bridge, washing herself.

The attraction of the green island grew as they walked. The black toms kept increasing their pace. Amon's whiskers twitched a warning. The place was *too* attractive. Unfu. Like when a Miw-kit sniffs too long at his first piece of valerian, and gets mazed, and is found hours later, still sniffing and rocking and purring in a daze. He called out to stop the toms, but they were too far ahead, and didn't respond. All he could do was follow, fast.

They reached the island when Re was low, and cooling among clouds. Insects danced flickering in Re's long arms. The island had welcome sheltering man-walls, but Amon felt the unfu power in the very marrow of his bones.

The mud of a river; manprints going across and not returning. Drift of smoke, smell of roasting meat. A white-and-ginger sister washing herself on the broken bridge.

"Come – meat," sent Ripfur, plunging across the mud with Tornear in hot pursuit.

Amon turned all his rage on them; saw them freeze, cower on the cracked mud. My-sending stronger, he thought, surprised. Like Sehtek's. He felt ahead, trying to pierce the unfu attraction that hung over the island like a storm about to break. Felt for the white sister's mind. Found nothing but simple contentment. Full-belly, lie-sun, lick-fur. The sister, feeling the touch of his mind, gave a startled prook, stopped washing and stared across the river with dark eyes.

"You-well?" he sent. "What man like?"

"Man," she sent. "Man!" Then a mass of blind adoration and something about catching rabbits. Her mind was simple, even for a sister; she was not of the city. He felt out for the man himself. Still no unfu, only minnen-glee. The man was doing something he enjoyed, right across the island.

Reluctantly, he released the toms. They shook his hold off their minds with a vigour that made their ears rattle. Chased each other on a swerving course across the mud, splashed through the shallow water and greeted the sister, tails aloft. Backsides were sniffed with gusto. Amon followed, circumspectly, touched noses with the sister, trying to get more facts about the man. She gave a weak, shimmering image of the man throwing a knife.

Amon shook; it was the knife that was unfu; dreadfully, joint-crackingly unfu. His mind reeled . . .

But Ripfur and Tornear were off again, their nostrils splaying after the roast meat. At the same instant, Amon knew that the man had finished his game and was returning.

Trouble, with those two thieves ahead. Amon ran wildly in among the buildings.

The knife still flew true; split the smallest twigs.

Time for rabbit, for cat, for sleep. He ambled back, contentedly.

Something was after the rabbit; reaching up over the fire, trying to knock it down. Two . . . black . . . thieving . . . cats.

The knife flew from his hand in a spurt of rage. Right down the space between the ruined walls, like a streak of flame in the sunset.

Cam's mouth gaped in horror. Oh, God, no more deaths . . .

But it was the roast rabbit that was pierced. Lifted clean off the fire, it thudded against the fireplace wall. The black thieves took to their heels.

Sighing with relief, he turned and saw the Miw.

It did not run away. On the contrary, it sat and stared at him. Fascinated. Staring back, he was caught up in the great golden eyes.

The sky flashed black.

Then the Miw seemed to him to be sitting on a red rock. By a dusty road in mountain country. The mountains had flat tops and one, far off, trailed smoke from its crest, under the high glaring sun.

There were men behind him, waiting in a patient column. Strange soldiers without armour, save for leopard-spotted shields, broad bronze collars and leaf-bladed spears. Their hair was long and black, held back from their foreheads by bronze bands. Their chests were brown, glistening with sweat, above short kilts, and their broad muscled feet were bare. When they saw him look at them, they beat spear on shield and shouted, "Sesostris! Sesostris!" And he thought they did it for love, not fear.

He looked again at the cat on the rock; the cat looked back fearlessly and, he thought, laughing, A cat can look at a king . . .

He was pleased with the cat, and the cat was pleased with him. It raised a paw, as if reaching out to pull him closer. He raised his own arm in return; warriors saluting each other.

They touched noses, delicately.

Then other golden cats came leaping down the red rocks. Each greeted a warrior. There was mirth and wonder, but also respect, on both sides.

As he walked back to his men, the first cat walked stately before him; not at his heels like a dog.

"Sesostris! Sesostris!"

They marched towards the smoking mountain, and the cats marched with them. Hot spirals of wind blew whirling dust-devils down the road, and the cats pounced on them with glee. And the warriors laughed, and began their marching-song, in an outlandish tongue.

Cam blinked.

Marching men and leaping cats were nowhere to be seen. Neither road, rocks nor dust-devils. It wasn't hot; the evening breeze was sighing the reeds. The sun was no longer white overhead, but red, and low in the sky.

And the foul taste of wizardry was back in his mouth. He shook his head to clear it of the sound of singing men. Oddly enough the golden cat shook its head too, blinked, set its ears askew in a baffled way. Then began to wash the base of its tail violently.

Not the cat's doing . . . the knife's. Cam glowered at it, still stuck in the dead rabbit. The moment he touched the hated thing . . .

But nothing else happened, except the black thieves returned, still drawn by the smell of rabbit. And his own cat with them. Great rubbing of furry cheeks and stately pacing to and fro.

In spite of the sorcery, he liked the golden cat better than anything he'd met in his life.

Later, he lay under his cloak, sweetly weary, watching the black toms scrambling round the ruins, pawing sleepily at each other's tails. The ruins glowed with the memory of sun. The blue of the sky deepened; but, high above, the swifts still wheeled and screamed.

He must have dozed, for he was startled by a soft thump and the sense of something passing over him. Dust fell on his face. He looked up to see the gold cat sitting on his wall, facing west. More red than gold, with the last of the sun's light glinting on its tufted ear-tips. The sun shone through its ears, making them a pink transparency with a network of tiny veins. Its eyes were bottomless pools, drinking in the sun. It began to purr softly; the purrs got louder, till its whole body was swaying with them. Massive claws extended, in, out, in, out, scraping into the stone wall.

Then the cat flung its tail aloft in a flame of welcome . . .

Greeting *who*? Cam shot up in a panic; every shadow within the walls seemed a person, then dissolved back to a shadow.

The cat was only greeting the red disc of the sun, as it finally touched the dead branches of the swamp-trees.

Only the sun . . . but the cat shook more and more in its ecstasy of greeting. Irritated, he reached up to touch it, break its weird mood.

He might as well have touched a rocking, purring statue. He felt offended, half-disgusted. What business had cats with the sun, where mere men were irrelevant? He felt like pushing the cat off the wall . . .

But he was sleepy . . .

Sometime in sleep he felt the cat jump down and tread its way delicately to sleep on a corner of his cloak.

He wakened from the best sleep he could remember. The cat was alternately rubbing its face and swishing its tail against his cheek, as it pounded back and forth across the cloak in a sentry-go of morning greeting. He stroked it sleepily, letting it pass under his hand from the massive round butt of its head to the flick of its tail.

Cam glanced jealously at the sun; but it was only a bright light in the sky that the cat was ignoring.

It was a morning even better than the night before. Every bird sang, the river's waters sang. Kingfishers darted in swerving sparks of blue. A breeze kept down the clouds of insects. The swamp today seemed a blessed place.

The toms had caught something black and revolting in the reeds and were squabbling violently over it; but even their snarls were part of the morning.

He shared the remains of the rabbit; the cat sat on the edge of his cloak, a frozen study in politeness, only betraying hunger by the slightest alternate flexing of its forefeet. When Cam tore a piece of meat off the bone, it took it gently, tilting its head to avoid biting his fingers. It got far more meat than Cam; yet Cam felt the gainer. Like feasting some shy young caliph . . .

When they'd finished, the cat ran towards the north end of the island. Looked back with a silent miaow. Cam somehow knew it was an invitation to a journey. An offer he could never resist. He stuffed his cloak into his pack, splashed two handfuls of water on his face, wiped it off again with his sleeve, picked up the knife from the fireplace and was ready to walk.

Meanwhile, Amon had touched-noses with the sister.

"Us-go. You-come?"

"Peaceful here."

"Farewell."

"Lonely without man."

"Will send brother. Have many-kitten. Be-happy."

Then Amon led Cam away north, into the reeds; waiting at every corner of the twisting track.

Cam felt sad leaving the white-faced cat. But she'd been here before he came. Meanwhile, it was merry weather. Cloudless sky; the reed-tops whispering like girls. His legs felt eager. He could hear the toms racing and darting in the reeds around.

So where was the sadness slowly seeping in from? The loss and desolation that slowly grew as he walked north? His own stupid moodiness? No. Ahead, that golden tail also drooped. The toms closed up behind and padded on, heads down and backs twitching, too miserable even to squabble. At last, they came to a clearing where the sun's light seemed blotted out. Everywhere, cats lay on their sides, panting in the morning heat. Their eyes swivelled on to Cam; they started up as if to flee, but dropped back immediately into dull indifference. Only the eyes went on watching. He could have kicked a dozen to death and the rest would scarcely have moved. Their mouths hung open. They hardly twitched their ears at the flies and mosquitoes that hung in clouds. They were caked with mud from head to foot. Here, a bunch of kittens sucked at their near-skeleton of a mother with frantic pounding paws; but sucked in vain. Some cats lay totally flat, breathing shallowly through caked nostrils. And there was at least one, a small tabby, eyes and nose a mass of crawling blue flies, that would never breathe again.

Cam recognised the old female, marbled black-and-grey. These were the cats from the fishing-port. They had fled in vain; nothing could save them now.

The golden cat ran from one to another, sniffing noses. It hit one sleeping cat lightly on the head with a tentative paw, over and over again. That cat hardly stirred. The golden one grew more frantic, running here and there, trying to rouse them. Then it turned to Cam, one paw slightly lifted. It was a plea for help.

Cam raised his hands helplessly. He could have carried half-a-dozen. But there were *hundreds*.

The gold cat seemed to realise. It turned its head and looked three times north; the way they had been going so cheerfully.

It gave a miaow of dismissal, quite unmistakable.

Cam went with a heavy heart.

8

Amon felt his heart would break. He lifted his head to the blazing disc of the sun, the slits of his eyes thin as knives.

"Father, Re, Horus of the Horizon, behold *your* – children. Behold *your* – kittens that you-made! This *must* not be! Ever since Nun and Naunet first appeared in the Island of Flame . . . Father!"

His rage and pain ascended to the sun's disc for many moments, until his soul was empty. Till he could feel only the silence, and the sunbeams like tiny paws of Re touching the tips of his fur. Then, into the silence, dropping like the smallest feather of the smallest bird, like the feather of Maat, came a single thought.

"You!"

"Me? What can four-paws do?"

"You."

He came out of his sun-blinded dreaming with a jolt, seeing nothing at first but tiny black sun-discs that danced over everything.

Then he saw all the doomed cats staring at him. But with a difference. They stared with interest now. Nearly all were on their feet . . .

"What changed?" he asked Ripfur.

"You." Ripfur sent back a vision of a golden cat transfigured, ten feet tall, bristling with what Sehtek bristled with . . . goddess in-her. Amon was shocked to recognise himself.

"Tell them what to do," sent Ripfur urgently. Some of the standing cats were already beginning to sag back to the ground.

"Get up, filthies," sent Amon with all his might. "Get up . . . wash . . . wash between paws . . . drink much . . . drink *good*-water . . . catch food . . . give kittens. We have far to go. When I come back . . . we *all* go."

But where? He only knew that for these cats the swamp was death. Go they must, and soon. But which way?

He had to do something. So he followed the way the man had gone. He hoped he wasn't just running away. The man couldn't help . . . He came to the end of the swamp, the edge of the reeds. And realised why the doomed cats had got stuck.

Mile after mile stretched the dry red plain. It must have been farmland once; walls of white limestone, now thrown down and trodden; irrigation-ditches choked with blown soil, full of dead brambles. Larger heaps of stone where farmhouses had stood. Black stumps of trees, vineyards and whole orchards, stuck lifeless out of the ground. Here and there, round some remaining well, a house still stood, with wretched patched roof and a few scratched fields where limp crops hung pale. But few and far between.

A healthy Miw could've crossed that plain in hours, unseen, loping behind walls. But these cats were not Miw, not healthy, and there were hundreds. Amon pictured a pack of dogs getting among them on the open plain . . . Brethren could run fast, but not far. They escaped enemies by leaping and climbing; needed high-place, walls and trees.

But the plain wasn't the worst. The road cut across it, straight as a sword towards the city. Although it was not yet midmorning, the road was already busy. Carts, men on horseback with hounds passed constantly, seldom a spear-throw apart. Sometimes they came in endless long straggles.

And the road felt more evil than the swamp. Amon felt men's hatred coming from the road; their pointless never-ending rage. The same sickness was in the dogs, running wildly in circles, barking themselves hoarse and dry for no reason at all. Oh, dog, dog, once you were free! Till you sold your soul for bones and caught man's unfu. What are your lives now? Slavery for yourselves and death to all other creatures. He felt the dog-sends, slavish, whimpering, savage, cowering, and he despaired.

If the lost cats stayed in the swamp, they would die slowly with some dignity. If they left the swamp, they would die quickly, with none. Oh, Father Re . . .

"Look further!"

He looked further, and saw beyond the plain, faint as clouds, the white cliffs, patched with blue shadows that moved with the sun and clouds. Somehow he knew that in those cliffs water trickled clean. Small furry prey moved through the shadowed caves and gullies. Places to leap and hide, and man never came. Safe.

"How?" he asked again, thinking of that terrible road.

Then came the thought of Father Re at midday. Heat. Men lying by the roadside resting their heads against their saddles, drinking wine and belching. Dogs dozing helpless, tongues hanging out . . .

That was the time to cross the road. He *saw* the cats crossing in formation, like an army.

That was how it could be done. He quivered with excitement. Then forced himself to be still. Forefeet together and tail curled round, he gave thanks to Father Re.

Then he trotted back.

Things were lively back in the swamp. Every cat was on its feet and busy. Queens slunk through the reeds, catching with low careful leaps the horde of white butterflies that now fluttered everywhere, the gift of Re. A huddle of old cats and kittens were gathered in a group, steadily eating what the queens brought; not only butterflies but beetles, newts and frogs. Even a dead watersnake that five kittens dragged to and fro vigorously. Ripfur and Tornear were everywhere, keeping things moving with a heavy paw.

"All drink clean-water," sent Ripfur. "Go soon?"

"Would rather have crossed road at night."

"Go soon," sent Ripfur, "or more die." He looked at the dead unmoving tabby, then at the old marbled black-and-grey, who had managed to prop herself up on her forefeet, and was mouthing feebly at a worm; but kept lapsing, with drooping eyes and gaping mouth. Other she-cats sat round, touching her gently to keep off the flies, and occasionally giving her a half-hearted lick.

Amon stared at her with deep sorrow; until he became aware that every other cat had stopped and was watching him. A fresh desolation swept in from them . . .

"I have found a hole," sent Ripfur urgently. "Send dead on journey." He turned to the tabby corpse, set his teeth gently into the slack of its pitiful neck, and dragged it towards a culvert that carried the track over the stream. Two stones had fallen out of the culvert, leaving a gaping black hole. All the cats watched as he painfully dragged the corpse into it.

"Food for journey?" asked Ripfur, panting slightly. A she-cat brought a frog and dropped it down. Two butterflies followed, into the black hole.

"Talk to Father Re!" sent Ripfur, his mind fierce as claws. Amon came out of his sorrow with a start, and turned to the incandescent disc of the sun.

"O Father Re, we-bring sister to you, that she may behold your great-beauty . . . "

There was great silence while he prayed. Then a stirring in the circle of cats; a stirring of appalled horror. Amon looked down, his eyes near-blinded with sun-discs.

The old marbled female was dragging herself through the circle, heading for the black hole. Only three of her legs were working; one hindleg dragged.

"Wait!" she sent, and lowered herself with agonising slowness down into the dark. Then, "Talk Father Re!" A cat started forward with more journey-food, but the old female sent, "Enough, both for friend and I."

Amon returned his eyes to the sun. "O Father Re, we-bring sisters to you, that they may behold your great-beauty . . . "

When he had finished, the old she-cat sent, "Scratch earth."

Ripfur hesitated, then turned his back on her lowered head and began to fling mud off the track with great kicks of his hindlegs; till the hole was completely filled, and her head was covered. She sent, out of the depths of the earth, "Farewell. Remember me," and then was silent.

All the cats looked at Amon.

"Show them city," sent Ripfur urgently.

So Amon sent his longest send. A picture of the city where all cats walked free and in honour. A picture of the cliffs where cool water trickled and small prey scuttled. A picture of lines of cats moving across the red plain; and what every cat had to do.

It seemed to all that the living cat beneath the earth heard and was glad.

"Move," sent Ripfur savagely. And they were moving.

They lay at the very edge of the reeds, a great company, panting. As Re climbed higher, a breeze blew off the marsh on to the hotter plain, and Amon was afraid the dogs would scent them. Indeed, one black dog did come bounding across to the first low reeds. There it stopped, knowing the cats were there, but frightened because it sensed so many. It would not enter, but ran to and fro, barking itself frantic.

"Kill?" sent Ripfur.

"Wait," sent Amon.

Finally, the dog's owner spurred over, shouting, sweating, and lashed the dog with his riding-whip until it followed him, tail between legs. The quivering in the cats, on the verge of panic, stopped. Instead, there was nervous mirth, and gladness not to be dog. Amon followed the dog's misery a long way, till it merged into the moving line of the road. How can they bear it . . . he thought.

As Father Re achieved his full height, the line of travellers slackened to a dribble, broke into gaps and finally stopped. Amon pushed his head out, close to the ground, looked left and right.

Left, there was a great huddle of men and beasts, about four spearthrows' distant; no more than a dark unmoving huddle, shimmering in the hot air on the red of the land.

To the right there was nothing, except a solitary dozing horse tied to a bush.

The horse worried Amon. It was nearer and a tied horse meant a man . . .

He waited, but the man did not appear.

"Move?" sent Ripfur urgently. Amon did not need to be told; he could feel renewed waverings of panic, running like little waves through the cat-host. In a moment, their nerve would break.

"Move!" sent Amon with all his might. And held the pattern of all of them in his mind, willing them forward towards the road in their set order.

For a long moment, nothing happened. Then the old toms of the host were moving past him, line abreast, two lines deep to give each other comfort in that terrible red flatness that made every back twitch. Behind them, gaining courage from their scent and footmarks, came the rest. They reached the road, began to cross, and still Amon watched the tethered horse.

And, at the point when half were across, a man came staggering out of the swamp. He wore fine clothes, and was fumbling with the belt of his yellow breeches. His scent blew down to Amon; wine, urine and vomit. The man held his head wearily. Perhaps he was too blind to see the cats, crossing almost at his feet . . .

He reached the horse, and tried three times to mount, each time falling back on his shaky legs and supporting himself on the horse's bridle. Amon felt the mouth-pain in the horse's mind, as the man pulled too heavily on the bit. The horse backed away, pulling the man further from the cats.

The cat-host was nearly across.

But, at his fourth attempt, the man mounted, swung the horse round and *saw*. His foolish blue eyes grew wide; his slack mouth dropped. He pointed to the cats and shouted to the men up the road. But they were too far and too hot to pay heed.

Amon felt for the man's mind; found it full of stupid wonder.

The man spurred his horse forward towards the lines of cats.

Amon felt the cat-lines falter. The young females on that side were looking over their shoulders, crouching closer to the ground, laying their ears back.

"Walk," insisted Amon with every bit of his strength.

The lines held, though the whole host was breaking into a nervous trot.

The man on the horse paused at the first cats. There was no kill-hate in his mind. Just . . .

The man opened his slack mouth, filled his lungs and yelled, high-pitched like a woman.

Again the lines wavered, nearly broke. Again, Amon summoned up all his will . . .

The man took off his hat and waved it violently over his head, still screaming at the top of his voice. Still the lines held. Then he rode straight through the cat-ranks – cats would have died if the horse hadn't leapt to clear them – and out the far side.

The man turned and came through them again. Still the cats held their course, though now *very* low to the ground. Much more and they would scatter all over the plain, prey to every enemy that moved.

"Kill?" sent Ripfur.

"Wait," sent Amon. There was another way. He trotted straight to the man, who had drawn rein in their midst and still gawped about him. Amon made quite sure the man had seen him. He and the man stared each other full in the eyes. Amon searched the man's mind for the foolish old French legend of the Matagot; the magic cat which, if caught and imprisoned in a chest and fed on chicken, will drop a fresh-minted gold coin every day . . . Yes, the legend was there, though old and feeble, a childhood memory. Amon fostered it lovingly, till the man remembered and his mind filled with gold-lust. Then Amon began to walk slowly away, limping in one forefoot, in the opposite direction to the host.

The drunk followed. Amon limped more pathetically, hardly moving. The man dismounted and came after him, making wheedling pussy-noises. Amon led him far, far. Once, he let the drunk almost lay hands on him, the hardest thing he had ever done in his life. And all the time he felt the cat-host safely receding.

When the host was far enough away, Amon sniffed around for an old snofru's lair. Carefully, for it would be unfortunate to meet a living snofru halfway down. He found one stale enough in the end, and vanished down it . . . and came out the other end safely, to see the fine sight of the man's backside in the air and his head down the hole . . . and slipped silently away, red-gold fur lost against the red earth and shimmering sunlight.

He looked back once. The man was still kneeling by the lair, pleading, imploring the lovely Matagot to emerge. Didn't the fool even know that all snofru's lairs have two entrances?

Later still, he saw the man catch his horse and make for the other men dozing by the road . . . felt the flick of men's mirth and irritation at the fool's arrival with the ridiculous old story of the Matagot.

Now, he must hurry. He'd been away from the host too long. They were growing faint in his sensing. What if another enemy struck? Worse things on the red plain than drunken fools . . .

Red cat, desert-cat, lengthened his flowing stride.

He found them moving steadily, still in their lines. Old toms to the front, under their original leader, a shrewd grey called Splayfoot. Old toms that could only move slowly, but were slowest to panic, too. Who hadn't the breath to run, but certainly had the breath to fight. Wise, enduring, hard to kill, with tattered ears and the odd eye missing. Splayfoot himself had lost an eye, but kept his wits. Amon was careful to give him proper greeting, cheek-to-cheek. Splayfoot might grow jealous . . .

But that was not Splayfoot's way.

"Glad you-here," he sent, respectful in his turn. "Tried best – am too old."

"Did well," sent Amon, as they inspected each other's backsides, while the other toms watched and the whole host rested.

"How-far?" asked Splayfoot.

Amon eyed the white cliffs, nearly as far away as ever.

"Nearly halfway."

Neither believed it. But when they continued, the old toms were heartened by the respect paid to their leader Splayfoot.

Amon took up his place in the middle of the host. There the kittens walked, tended by their mothers and other old queens, stiff in the joints but still able to carry a small kitten for hours on end. And the old queens had a soothing effect on the older kittens who, having survived so far and got used to walking on the plain, were starting to have wild ambitions like hunting down men-on-horseback.

Here also were the youngest and wildest toms, under the baleful eye of Ripfur, who soon quelled their impulse to rush everywhere, looking for fame.

Behind came the rearguard, under the strict paw of Tornear. Toms of middle years, not likely to panic unduly, who didn't forget to look over their shoulders as they walked.

On each flank, comforted by the scent of the toms, young females hunted and foraged. Amon had told them to eat what they caught, without stopping their march. So that by evening, well-fed, they could hunt for others . . . Still, they occasionally brought the kittens insects to keep their spirits up. And if they caught anything too big, like a young rabbit, they would drop back and give it to Tornear's toms, who could munch half-a-rabbit without slowing down.

They were all still nervous; missing their walls. Backs twitched too often. But their strict order was a wall of sorts; nothing had killed them yet, and they admired the way Amon had disposed of the man. And Ripfur and Tornear kept up a flow of insults about drooping tails and spindly walks, and whenever a cat dawdled, a clip across the rump got it moving again.

But it was more than that. The town-cats liked the feel of dry soil underpaw, after the swamp; liked the dry wind that blew away the swarming insects. For all cats in the beginning were desert-cats. Felis Libyca, the cat of the Libyan desert.

Amon dropped to the rear. Tornear was walking smugly, the two largest, fiercest and most-favoured of his new followers on either side of him; the weaker Brethren sidling in as near as they dared. Amon could tell Tornear was enjoying his lordship; not being younger-brother for a change.

They touched noses. "Goes well?"

Tornear sent back a picture of a hundred catsarses, all on the move together, tails waving high. The other toms fell back respectfully, and Amon and Tornear walked together. Amon noted the smell, as they passed a multitude of hastily-scrabbled holes, marked by damper patches on the surface of the earth . . .

"They drink too much bad-water," sent Tornear. "Eat too many slimies in-swamp." But that didn't account for all of the smell. The leading toms were marking every rock within reach, though the marks were growing fainter as the hot wind began to dry up their body-juices.

"Bad," sent Amon. "Stop them. Even man could follow this trail."

"No," sent Tornear. "Enemies follow anyway. Smell keeps cheerful."

Amon trotted back towards the vanguard. For in spite of all his will, the cat-host was twisting slowly left, to where some shattered white walls loomed above the low mounds of the desert.

Bad-place, thought Amon. No men, but . . .

Next second, the red claws of battle bloomed in his mind. From the front; from among the white walls. Twenty cats blinked as the violent kick of Amon's hindlegs showered their faces with desert-dust.

A savage fight was in progress. Splayfoot, crouched in a gaping window, was lashing wildly backwards at a snofru that was leaping and scrabbling up the wall, trying to catch hold of his tail and drag him down into its slavering jaws. Amon saw clear the deep red coat of the snofru, its pointed muzzle, huge red ears and bristling brush of tail. Other toms were watching helplessly at a distance. The snofru had beads of bright blood on its nose, where a lucky blow of Splayfoot's had gone home. The snofru's mind was confused; by prey who fought back painfully; by other prey who watched and did not run away . . . it did not sense Amon coming till too late.

Fifteen feet short of the snofru, Amon took off, arching six feet up into the air. Descending, thirty pounds of desert-cat hit the snofru behind the neck. Its wiry body collapsed against the base of the wall. Amon heard the thud and gasp as the air exploded from its lungs. His own head turned sideways, unbidden, reaching for the snofru's throat. But the ruff of hair round that throat was thick; Amon only tore out a mouthful. And the snofru wriggled like rope and bone beneath him, then was free and away. Amon turned as quickly and went after it. Hit it again in the middle of the back; again felt its hindlegs collapse in a deeply satisfying way. Both animals spun in a confusion of dust; but the snofru was quicker on its feet, swerving and jinking now like a hunted hare. Once more Amon hit it, then watched it make off. Snofru was danger-mouth, hardly worth eating. Enough to teach it a lesson; snofru talked to snofru . . .

A wave of approval like a zephyr of wind tickled the hair on Amon's rump. Looking back he saw that every window and pinnacle of that ruined place had its perching purring cat. Every eye watched him with gladness. They had found their beloved walls.

"Re-reigns?" suggested Ripfur hopefully. "Re-rest?"

Amon squinted up at the sun's disc. Father Re was still at his hottest. The white cliffs were now no further off than the blue blur of the swamp. Ripfur's request seemed reasonable. The tiny streets of the ruined village were empty of prints of man or dog. Only the zigzags of sandsnake, the prints of snofru.

But it still felt bad-place. No water. Not enough high safe-perches.

"Short-rest. Keep-watch," sent Amon.

9

But it didn't seem so bad-place when he was stretched out on the topmost warm stone of the watchtower, which the other cats had left for him. And the tiny warm paws of Father Re touched his fur-tips. He closed his eyes and stretched his mind out further and further. He could feel the stirring of grasshoppers; the flight of winged insects high, high on the warm-air currents. The frantic swervings of the swifts who scythed in pursuit. Small-brains of swifts like fire-sparks, turning, turning in their circular world . . . pleasant to rest, and fly with the swifts . . .

The death hit him like a black fist, from far out on his left. He knew it had been a small sister, straying too far from the safety of the watch-ring, trembling with excitement at the prospect of prey. Now she was-not, and her last agony of unbeing was a ripping gash in his mind.

He leapt to the ground direct from the tower, hit the dust with a grunt and raced towards the last place she had been.

Had she just died? Heart-fail?

But when he reached the spot, there was no body. Only a dribble of blood and a few tufts of brown fur blowing about beneath a white rock. And a smell . . .

"Dog," he sent to Ripfur, who came pounding up with twenty others. But why hadn't he sensed the dog? Too busy sensing the flight of swifts . . . He licked at his shoulder violently, to ease his soul of the shame of that small black death. Or had the dog been lying asleep? Then he would not have sensed it anyway . . .

"Not-dog," sent Ripfur. He was right. This smelt like dog, except that dog smelt of man; grease and firesmoke.

The faint smell of not-dog led away into a vast huddle of broken rock. Amon knew better than to follow into that many-cornered, many-shadowed place.

"We-move," sent Amon. Then "*We-move!*" more fiercely. Most of the cats did not know what had happened. He sent them a picture of the black fist of death, and *that* got them moving.

Amon moved in their midst, jumpy. He made the other young toms walk ahead of him, so he could simply follow. His mind was so far out, searching for not-dog, that he couldn't pay attention to where he was going, and would otherwise have stumbled into rocks.

He didn't even know the *feel* of not-dog; but guessed it was big; one small sister wouldn't satisfy its hunger. It would return, using the cat-host as a slow-moving larder. Amon was afraid.

The black claws of pain bloomed, away on the right, ahead. Another small sister, hunting too far out from the ring. Not dead yet, but death-fearing. Amon ran like the wind, and Ripfur and thirty more ran after him.

He saw the she-cat on top of a high rock. She had her head down and was trying to back away from something; something small and dark that hung from her throat and wriggled too fast for the eye to follow. Amon leapt on to the rock. The terrified she-cat backed down towards him . . .

Ripfur swept past and hit the dark thing with both paws together. It fell from the sister's throat, and slithered down the face of the rock. Then recovered itself and wriggled back up again, a long low short-legged bundle of brown lightning that attached itself to Ripfur's throat in turn. Ripfur dropped flat on his belly, as if in submission. Then placed a huge black paw across the wriggling creature and heaved his body upright again. The wriggling thing detached, with a large tuft of Ripfur's hair in its mouth, and a red spot of flesh with it.

Before it could wriggle free again, Ripfur bent and bit off its pointed head. He crunched cheerfully, while the body under his paw still quivered.

"Mirfu," sent Ripfur with great satisfaction. "Small-brain, big-heart, good-eat."

"You-eat too many mirfu," sent Tornear coming up. "You-turn small-brain yourself!"

"But big-heart," sent Ripfur cheerfully. "Amon send picture how to kill mirfu!"

Amon, rather shakily, sent everybody a picture of how a mirfu should be killed. There was a lot of interest, especially among the sisters; and a demand from the kittens that they be allowed to hunt mirfu immediately.

Amon walked across and touched noses with the stricken sister.

She was drooping with the weariness that follows terror, and there was a ruff of drying blood-spikes round her throat, but she was not dying. Amon sent her into the middle to join the kittens . . .

"Take it, small-heart," sent Ripfur spitefully.

Amon turned to see the rest of the mirfu vanish down Tornear's gullet.

"Now lick my throat," sent Ripfur.

Tornear turned his pink tongue with equal vigour on to his brother's wound. "You-taste better than mirfu."

It was as well that Amon had sent the picture of how to kill mirfu. The place was swarming with them. Tiny excitement and alarm signals from the females plagued Amon's mind as he searched and searched for not-dog. At first the females, now hunting in pairs, coped clumsily. One would chew a mirfu nearly in half while it still hung on to the other sister's throat. But eventually they learned the trick, without anyone getting killed. The first she-cat to kill solo carried her mirfu into the middle of the host and presented it to the kittens; holding her head proudly high to stop the mirfu trailing on the ground, and lashing her tail with passion. The mirfu caused a near-riot among the kittens that stopped the whole host. But it put them all in such a good mood that Amon waited patiently; until he ended the kitten-quarrel by eating the mirfu himself. Tasted good; better than rat.

But all the time his mind ranged, searching for not-dog.

Yet when not-dog came, its feel was so strange that it was a long moment before Amon sprang into action. Where was the wild hysteria of dog? The bark-one-minute, cower-the-next? Even as Amon leapt forward, another sister died. The agony of that black unmaking quivered down Amon's spine as he ran, to the very tip of his tail; nearly blinding him so he stumbled. Then he was running down a deepening gully full of small white stones. At the bottom, not-dog stood, with a small tabby shape drooping lifeless from its jaws.

Not-dog indeed. Huge. The wrong colour; a pale grey. Head too big for dog, ears too big and pointed, body too slim and forelegs far too long. And the eyes blue, not dog-brown. Cold as snow.

"Big-brain," sent Ripfur warningly. "Blunt-claw, big-tooth."

But Amon was beyond taking advice. The sight of the limp body of the sister blew away his calm, his sense, even his battle-prayer to

Father Re. The only thing that screamed through his mind like a storm was, "Cat is not-prey, not-prey, not-prey."

But he could sense the flurry of bafflement in not-dog's mind. With its mouth full of prey, it saw another juicy lump of prey running straight for it . . .

At the last moment, as Amon changed his stride to spring, not-dog let its victim drop softly to the rock, and opened its mouth as far as it would go. Amon found himself heading straight down the most massive jaws he had ever beheld.

Too late to check his attack. He would simply end up a tumbled heap under those very jaws. All he could do was leap harder, higher.

He leapt. The jaws yawned nearer and nearer, the rank bloody breath . . .

His forepaws hit the top of not-dog's nose. His hindpaws hit the top of not-dog's skull and he pushed upwards again, turned a somersault, fell off down not-dog's tail and tumbled in confusion on the ground behind.

The not-dog turned in its own length like a tightly-coiled spring. Its nose pouring blood, one ear flapping in ruin, but its jaws closing round Amon's very head . . .

Ripfur, ten yards behind, launched his own leaping attack. The black landed on not-dog's haunches, lost his balance and fell off backwards, his claws too drawing blood. Again, not-dog turned like a coiled spring. But before it could bite Ripfur in half, a third cat launched its leaping attack from the side, hit and fell, claws dragging. And a fourth and a fifth and a sixth. The ground was littered with writhing cats, the air was full of leaping cats, as even the smallest launched itself into the fray. Amon was lord, Amon was always right, Amon knew the way . . . And in the midst of them not-dog spun and spun, wilder and wilder, like a young dog chasing its tail.

Amon, on his feet again, did not know what to do next. But he could feel the panic rising in the not-dog's mind; the confusion, the trying-to-make sense. "Rabbit-flying? Rabbit thorn-foot? Rabbit no-fear?"

Just as the last cat leapt, and hit the not-dog on its already lacerated ear, not-dog's mind collapsed into chaos. At the moment when every cat was baffled, ready to flee, not-dog turned and ran. Not seriously hurt; but its world had fallen apart, its mind was in ruins.

A madness seized Amon when he saw the fleeing rump. He pursued, launching his spring as if not-dog was no more than a snofru. He hit not-dog's back, felt not-dog's legs give way just as the snofru's had done. But where snofru's helpless neck would have been, there were the dreadful jaws again. Amon let go and fell off.

The not-dog recovered its feet and went on running. Now every cat was after it . . .

Amon called them back with every ounce of his power. In another fifty yards there would just be thirty winded cats and a massacre . . .

He watched not-dog continue on its way in a tireless lope; it looked back every so often, to make sure it wasn't being followed. Amon could see the lolling tongue, the great fangs, the torn ear. And the tail, tucked right between the legs.

It was a picture worth sending to the cat-host.

They dragged the dead sister into a crevice among the rocks and sent her soul to Father Re. There was not even a beetle to give her for her journey; but Ripfur scrabbled a few loose stones down on her. Soon the birds would come, and snofru, to claim her . . .

It did not bear thinking about; but they had done their best. They followed the host, miserable. Just as they caught up the rearguard, Ripfur sent, "I have think!"

Tornear sent a catsarse.

"We have great-new-claw," went on Ripfur, unabashed. Then he sent his first big wavering send. An image of an armoured horseman, and cats waiting among rocks and up trees. And as the horsemen passed, the cats launched themselves at horse and rider, not all together, but one after the other. Until the horse reared and the rider fell to the ground and . . .

"Enough," sent Amon. "Unfu. No-think. We-go cliffs."

"Very good great-new-claw," persisted Ripfur. "What call? In old-time-word?"

Amon sighed. "Heb-Miw. Thirty-cat." Just to shut him up.

"Heb-Miw," mused Ripfur dreamily. "Heb-Miw." He rolled the idea round his black furry mind as if it was a fresh-caught mouse in his paws.

Nobody guessed how feared the heb-Miw would become.

"Have other-think," sent Ripfur.

Amon took a deep breath and let it out in exasperation.
"What is old-time-word for great-warrior?"
"Calisirian," sent Amon wearily.
"Hail Amon, Calisirian," sent Ripfur.
Tornear sent his usual vision. But it afterwards became the habit to refer to Amon by that name.
It was no comfort to him now; he was in deep distress. All he wanted was to lie down and sleep. He felt as if life had drained out of his body through a great wound. But when he sniffed himself here and there, he found no harm from the not-dog, except a great patch on his back sticky from not-dog's drool. Yet still he wished to crawl into a dark hole to die.
He could sense nothing with his mind; nothing but the weariness of putting one paw in front of the other. If he closed his eyes, blocking out the fuzzy shapes of cats moving round him, he might have been alone in a great desolation. He could not sense the cat he was bumping into, let alone an approaching snofru, or another not-dog. At any moment, another not-dog might attack . . .
Some cat was walking alongside him, guiding him away from boulders he would otherwise have stumbled over. It was a comfort. He opened his eyes. It was Splayfoot, regarding him as if he was a very foolish kitten.
"*We* do fighting," sent Splayfoot. "You-stay in middle with kittens. You can command – you can feel-far-off. *We* do fighting."
Amon made a stir of protest. But Splayfoot was not to be silenced.
"If me-killed . . . " Splayfoot turned his ears down, as if it was nothing. "But if you-killed . . . all die."
Amon was too tired to argue. He just concentrated on putting one paw in front of the other.

Slowly, his powers returned; a ghostly sense of the host moving about him, still faithfully in their lines; though the old toms ahead were very slow now, and the females had given up hunting and were plodding along in groups. The most dangerous time, now, as their strength waned. How many could still run at all?
But, no danger. No mirfu, snofru, not-dog. This land was utterly empty. Not a flicker of nervousness among the cats, only a growing hope as the cliffs towered higher, and the cliffs' shadow moved out to greet them, as Father Re sank and became Re-Harakhti, the Hawk of the Horizon. It was time for prayer; but

there was no time for prayer. Keep moving. Keep putting one foot in front of the other.

"Any cat still run?" asked Amon.

A few young toms answered cheerfully.

"Go cliff," sent Amon feebly. "Find water." As they departed, with the fresh-springing energy of the very young, he sent, "Keep together – still danger." He hoped they heard.

The host crossed another field, and another. The field-walls were less broken here, and the fields were wider, near the cliff. There came a faint jubilant flicker from ahead. Water, shadow . . .

But something was pressing into Amon's deadened mind like an arrowhead. High in the sky, coming from the left. He made an effort to reach the mind of whatever it was; got a picture of cliffs and fields seen from far above.

Bird? But he only got the view from the bird's eyes. No impression of its brain at all; not even small-brain. Only a feeling of pride, arrogance, infinite sureness, moving in huge circles. Feeling nothing, pitying nothing, above all-things.

Amon stared upwards, eyes slitted like blades of grass. He saw the bird circling the dark top of the cliff. Black against the sky with wings like the fingers of a hand, and a tail like a black shield. New. Bigger than bird; too big to *be* a bird.

Its shadow swept across the moving cats. Every cat ducked, stayed pressed to the ground, unable to move. Amon sent with all his remaining power, to force the cats on. But his force was spent; the cats lay as if caught in traps.

Now other arrowheads were pressing on Amon's mind, other views of field and cliff, circling and recrossing each other till Amon's head spun. He looked up again, and now there were ten shapes circling against the sky; ten shadows crossing and recrossing the frozen lines of cats. Every cat's ears were flattened in terror.

What were these circling shapes, terrible, like gods? Gods circling in the sunset? Sunset . . . the time of Re-Harakhti, when Father Re became Horus, the Hawk of the Horizon. These were hawks, the manifestation of Father Re himself . . .

Be still, he sent to the silent ranks. Show respect. These are the messengers of Father Re, welcoming you, his children.

The cats wriggled on their bellies uneasily; swallowed with dry throats; but did not scatter in panic.

Then the first arrowhead pressed down, down, down. Through its eyes, Amon could see the unmoving lines of cats, smaller than beetles. Could see himself, tiny and yellow, in the centre of them.

Then the hawk's eyes moved off him; focused on the body of a white she-cat with her kittens pressed close against her flanks. Nearer and nearer.

There was a rush in the air, a whistle of feathers.

Amon felt death coming.

The gods demand sacrifice . . . He closed his eyes and his mind.

Then a heavy shape ran past him; a black shape that sent she-cat and kittens scattering. A black shape that rolled over on its back and was snatched up instantly by a pair of huge talons, beneath mighty beating wings that scattered leaves and dust and twigs with their wind.

In a second, Tornear, his good friend Tornear, was far above him in the claws of an eagle.

Amon waited wincing for the dark of Tornear's death. But it didn't come. Instead, red waves of Tornear's fury. And, for the first time, the brain of the greathawk. It *was* small-brain after all; nearly as small as mirfu. "Wing-weak? Wing-weak? Earth-near! Earth-near! Heavy, heavy!"

The greathawk flew aimlessly back and forth, trying to gain height with desperate beatings of its sail-like wings. It hadn't meant to catch anything as big as Tornear. And Tornear was not already dead, but squirming with all his strength. And his black claws were busy.

But the greathawk couldn't think of anything new to do; it was small-brain. Sameway, always sameway!

It gained a little height. It was halfway up the cliff when a bunch of feathers exploded from its throat. Amon was sitting up by that time, watching. So were all the other cats. So were the other greathawks, for they made no attempt to attack.

Amon could feel Tornear's pain; the iron talons squeezing his ribs; sharp rows of points needling into his fat back-muscles, searching out his life.

Then a leap of red triumph . . .

Another cloud of feathers exploded. And another, and another. The greathawk's brain was weak like a grasshopper's now; a grasshopper helpless under a paw. Wing-weak! Earth-near! Sky-dark!

It let go of Tornear.

Amon watched his friend falling through the air backwards;

starting to turn his body. Then, face-down, spreading his legs far apart so that black folds of loose skin were almost like wings. Then Tornear vanished behind rocks, and a monstrous spray of green liquid shot up into the air.

Death?

No, a violent picture of a catsarse.

But there was a death. Sky-dark. Wing-dark. Heavy, heavy. The sadness of the dying came to Amon, as when anything died.

Above, the greathawk's wings twisted unnaturally backwards in the stream of its passing. Then it was falling, like a rustling sack of feathers bursting open. It hit the ground with a whistling thud, narrowly missing the kittens that had been its intended prey.

Its neck stretched bloody; its eye blinked wildly once, then closed forever. Its yellow wings would have covered a hundred cats, like a bony blanket. From under them, kittens scrambled to escape in all directions.

While all the cats still stared, the image of a catsarse strengthened rapidly. And there was Tornear not black, but green with slime from head to tail, smelling and dripping most evilly. And with blood seeping red from the wounds in his back and mingling with the green slime.

He and Amon touched noses.

"*God*?" asked Tornear scornfully. "Horus of the Horizon? Gods should have thicker neck-feathers." He took a healthy lick at the greathawk's throat. "Prey. Tasty."

The assembled cats closed in. Even the kittens snatched a feather and ran off with it in triumph. The rock where the greathawk lay became a mass of chewing furry bodies.

"Good," sent Tornear. "Not god – prey. Eat heart – great-heart. Not eat brain – small-brain." He sat back and watched, making a feeble attempt to lick his wounds.

Amon wasn't sure it was as simple as that. If the bird was not really Horus, it might still have been a messenger . . . a sacred servant of Horus.

But it was hardly the time to say so.

All he could do was lead the cats, with all the dignity he could muster, to their new refuge in the cliffs.

The other greatbirds departed also. It was impossible to guess if they had understood anything at all . . .

* * *

Amon sat on the topmost pinnacle of rock and filled his round black eyes with the moon.

Who was Mother Bastet.

Who had brought them safely where they ought to be.

All around, safely tucked on to lower pinnacle and ledge, into deep cave and gully, the cat-host too bathed their eyes in the moon. Waves of pleasure ascended to Mother Bastet; pleasure of full-belly and clean-water; pleasure at groomed fur and still-licking tongues. Pleasure at Mother Bastet sailing high, touching the soft luminous clouds with her paw as they passed.

Pleasure at the complaint of the old she-cats about their aching joints; pleasure at the riotous quarrelling of kittens who had found a worm; pleasure at the valour of Tornear, who was still being groomed, free, by six other cats, of the ill-tasting slime of the cliff-foot ooze that had saved his falling bones.

Tornear was purrily telling how to kill a greatbird.

"Follow its shadow *on the ground*. Do not look up or it will spoil your leap. When the greatbird strikes, it *meets* its own shadow on the ground. Catch the shadow and you catch the bird . . ."

A wavering of doubt came from the host.

"Amon think bird is god . . . Amon tell . . ."

Then Tornear's burst of loyalty. "How else he keep you still? How else give me room pounce? Who suffer because Amon tell you bird is god?"

Mother Bastet keep Tornear her kitten forever . . .

Amon still wished he could have told the cat-host the truth; that he had been mistaken. But Tornear had been adamant. "You tell truth . . . they lose faith . . . all die." Tornear was right; but Amon felt lonely just the same. To lie was to claw at Mother Bastet; but the same lie saved lives precious to Bastet . . . a mystery . . .

Bastet had kept them all within her paw.

But Horus had not kept the greatbird; Anubis had not fought for snofru and not-dog. While the unknown god of rat and mirfu . . . perhaps rat and mirfu had no god. Perhaps their god was the unspeakable Seth, who ate his own children. Rat and mirfu were death to all . . .

Amon hated death. Death of cat and greathawk. Death of rabbit and hare, of mouse and shrew who harmed none. At home in the city, he lived on kitchen-scraps . . . could never get used to kill. His whole body ached with kill, more than the long walk. Still, he could have eaten a nice fresh mirfu . . .

A cat came walking to him, along the narrow ledge. A young black sister, tail high and neck held proudly high too, because she was carrying something. She laid it carefully at the base of his pinnacle with a flicker of mirth. The smell of fresh-killed mirfu came up to his nostrils. The sister made off, tail held even higher.

Amon sighed with all his lungs. Were none of his thoughts private now? He sent at the retreating tail, "Will eat mirfu-heart. Leave mirfu-head for you, small-brain!"

The black's departing tail flicked indignantly. *That* would show her. Miw did not mate with sisters ever. She need not hope when her time came . . .

A flicker of mirth ascended from all the cat-host . . .

At least they had forgiven him the mistake about the greathawk.

As he settled to the mirfu, there was a silent sweep of white wings overhead, but Amon did not crouch. He had spoken with owl already. Owl was catfriend. More, owl was cat-with-wings, big-eye, night-fly, mouse-hunt. All the centuries, cat slept at the foot of owl's perch, to keep rats off owl's nest. Owl watched over kittens, when cat went hunting.

Owl showed, again, surprised pleasure at the presence of so many cats. The pink rose of question blossomed tinily; then owl sent a picture of the white cliffs speeding, curving past.

Amon felt sad for a moment; why had Mother Bastet chosen only some cats to fly?

Then he thanked owl; for the quick loan of his eyes.

He enjoyed the mirfu.

Owl passed again.

10

Sehtek sat on the city-wall, staring down at men moving smaller than mice. Re was warm on her back, but the fur between her ears was furrowed. Every so often her tail lashed, sending down showers of crumbling stone from the wall-top. Any Miw would have given her a very wide berth.

Odd things were happening in the south. She shouldn't be able to sense things so far away. There was a creature down there whose sendings were stronger than her own.

Nothing should be stronger! She was Royal Miw. And the strange sendings were chaotic; rage, delight, agony, without discipline. Coming at any hour, without warning. Worse than having kittens in your belly. When she sent angry questions, she got no answer.

It wasn't horse; she'd sensed horse faintly, when horse got the news. So that kitling Amon had got that far; he might have noticed something. But he was seven Re-voyages overdue . . . Even the southern Matagots were silent.

Absurdly, she couldn't help pinning hopes on these new chaotic sendings; sniffing at them as if they were the first thin pale leaves of spring. Because here in the city, all was bitter as winter. In spite of all her watchfulness, things were getting worse.

Brethren and Miw had been warned away from the Palace; had obeyed at first. But the usurpers didn't stay in the Palace. They swaggered the streets as if they owned the place. And in every alley they met Miw who *knew* they owned the place. The usurpers stared at the Miw, remembering the death of the bouteiller. The Miw stared back, remembering the death of the Duke. Some starings lasted a long time; but the usurpers' eyes always dropped first.

One usurper, late at night and drunk, picked up a stone and threw it at a staring Miw. The Miw began to follow him; he ran all the way back to the Palace, with the Miw padding behind. By the time he got there, he was gibbering.

But the hangers-on were worse. They'd flooded into the city after the Duke's death, like germs into a wound. Looking for pickings. Mountebanks, jugglers, rainmakers, fortune-tellers who pointed two fingers at you if you turned them away from your door. They were always picking up things that were lying about and asking who they belonged to, offering to tidy them away. Even when they were told to put them down, the things vanished soon after.

The hangers-on camped near the Palace in ragged tents, surrounded by their starve-ribbed animals. Made the place filthy. Worse, they just threw down unwanted scraps of food. And the Brethren drifted back . . .

One day, two hangers-on had an argument whether a cat dropped upside-down always landed on its feet. They dropped old Mizzletrumper over the cliff to see. He broke his legs and lay a week dying on the rocks, with four cats to lick him comfort.

Then Pouncefoot vanished, in the arms of a hanger-on witch, and was never seen again. But since he'd been black from head to tail, and a cat's bones, boiled white, were found on the Palace midden . . .

Smerdis, scouting the Palace gardens after dark, found Miffwhisker caught in a stout wooden trap, where he'd been lured by a piece of stinking fish. Smerdis had a nasty ten minutes chewing the cage apart. He found seven similar cages, and dragged them one by one over the cliff . . .

Yet still the trodden food on the cobbles drew the Brethren.

Sehtek decided to call another meeting.

Nibblefur was there. And Gristletongue, still keeping his eye on the city, as his brothers had said. Nibblefur washed between her hindlegs in front of everybody; the Mausoleum might have been some hell's-kitchen in the alleys . . .

Sehtek, controlling herself because harmony must prevail, insisted that something be done. But what? The Miw sat long in unpurring silence.

Then Gristletongue sent, "Kill 'em."

The Miw sighed, deeply. Silence continued. Gristletongue scratched his ear so violently that wisps of black hair floated off the end of it. "I not-afraid kill 'em."

"Not your *courage* we-doubt . . ."

Gristletongue belaboured his other ear. Both were nearly bald from so much thought. "Four-us kill-man sure."

"One Miw kill-man. Then?"

"Kill another!"

"Usurpers sit, be-killed one by one?"

"Not know it us?"

"Who else kill-claw? Maybe they-think rat *nibble* them dead?"

It was not enough to make a Miw laugh.

"Rats," sent Nibblefur. "Rats is answer. Finis felicorum, initium, murorum, finis urbis."

Every Miw present arched and spat. Every Miw knew the old saying that foretold the end. The end of cats is the beginning of rats, is the end of the city. Ill-luck to send it. Even men knew better than to say it. The very *idea* of rat . . . no rat in the city since the Beginning.

Every Miw braced itself for Sehtek's blast.

But Sehtek's mind was seething like ferrets in a sack. Black rat . . . big-ear, long-tail, yellow-tooth . . . nibbling the hooves of horses as they stood in the stable . . . biting the faces of sleeping children. Worse, rat crawling out into the open, sneezing, dying. Men sneezing, falling. Stinking sores, unbearable writhing. Yellow crosses on the doors. Carts coming, sticks rattling. Men with yellow hoods over their heads, wearing yellow gloves, thrusting bodies stiffly on to carts. Wailing, smashed windows, unhinged doors, roofs rotting and breaking . . .

"Miw not-die rat-death," sent Nibblefur, ingratiatingly.

Then every Miw was sending, remembering men who were catfriend, warm fires, soft cushions.

"Will use dead-rats," soothed Sehtek. "Dead-rat not-bring sickness. But will warn city-men . . . they-blame usurpers . . ."

"Men still know what rat looks like?" asked Gristletongue.

Nobody bothered to answer. Turmoil.

"Where find rats?" No Miw knew. Maddeningly, Nibblefur did.

"Barns above Harcourt!" Many of her descendants had fled to Harcourt to avoid her wise-sendings. It hadn't saved them. She licked her chest grandly. "Us-go – get pair of rats."

"Cannot have plague of rats with only pair."

"Miw do better? Us-catch more in one-night than Miw in year. At my age . . . should not go-out after-dark – ingratitude."

In the deepening silence, they awaited Sehtek's explosion. Only Gristletongue ran nervously on. "Live-rats better . . . bring live-rats, chase, kill . . . city-men grateful to Miw . . . hate Palace-creatures. Every-cat catch live-rat . . . "

The Miw stared him into silence at last. Trouble was, no Miw could think up anything better.

"When?" asked Sehtek, finally.

"Michaelmass Fair," sent Nibblefur, with maddening logic.

Michaelmass Fair dawned bright and cool. The usurpers were early on the battlements. The Fair was important; half their revenue would come from the merchants who paid to set up their booths in the marketplace in spring, summer and autumn. Fairs had been held for a thousand years, because there were no rats to nibble the cheeses and soil the bread. Great ladies came to buy furs, because there was no risk of plague or something nasty running up their skirts.

Had the merchants heard of the Duke's death? Would they still come? Anxiously the usurpers watched north and south, east and west. They needn't have worried; though nervous, having only just heard of the Duke's death on the road, the merchants had their stalls up and busy by ten.

The usurpers stayed up on the battlements (drawing many a speculative glance). They sent down Glumbach to make the merchants comfortable, for he was a known man of the city. Pity he was also a fat fool. The respected men of the city would not touch the usurpers; yet.

Glumbach made up the rules of his job as he went along; smiling his greasy smiles, rubbing his greasy hands together, pumping the hand of anyone who offered it. Obviously he must sample every kind of food offered for sale, to make sure it wasn't poisonous . . . Kept sticking his thumb in people's gravy and sucking it. Once he drooped his long furry dirty sleeve in somebody's punch, and wandered up and down absentmindedly sucking that. The cheese-wives clasped their cheeses to their bosoms as he passed. Unwise, because Glumbach had an interest in bosoms, too.

One newcomer offered Glumbach a bribe for a well-placed stall. Glumbach couldn't resist, though every other merchant had been coming for years and knew his rightful place. Glumbach kept on making people pack up their booths and move elsewhere, unless they slipped him a coin. The merchants got angrier, Glumbach richer, till he clinked as he walked. Then he thought he'd spend some of his new money; began hanging round the booths of the goldsmiths, hinting about bargains.

"Don't mind this lot killing their Duke," muttered one merchant. "Pity they didn't kill Glumbach as well."

Meanwhile, all round, Miw crouched on roof- and wall-top, each with a wriggling rat underpaw. It had been agreed harmoniously that all rats would be released when the great clock struck eleven. Then Gristletongue had become worried that some Miw might not be able to count to eleven. He would personally sit on top of the great clock and give the signal by sneezing twice, and wiping his nose with his paw. The Miw, after long thought, could not see how Gristletongue could do any harm . . .

Unfortunately, Gristletongue's rat seemed to have met with a nasty accident. He poked it hopefully with an encouraging paw, but it didn't stir. He poked it harder. It shot forward over the edge of the clock and fell from a great height into a simmering cauldron of soup. A rain of soup showered passers-by.

"*That* looks an interesting brew," said Glumbach tolerantly, wiping his face with his sleeve, then licking the sleeve appreciatively. He reached forward and stuck his thumb in the soup and pulled out the rat and began to chew on it blissfully. "Most interesting!"

The soup-seller looked at the dripping object in his hand. "Rats!" she screamed.

"Unfu," sent Sehtek.

"Unfu yourself," sent back Gristletongue. He peered so far over the ledge to see where his rat had gone that he lost his footing and sailed down into the cauldron himself, landing at great speed and emerging even faster, for the soup was just coming to the boil. He landed next in the middle of a goldsmith's stall, and emerged with a King's Ransom in emeralds dangling round his neck.

"Pretty as the sacred crocodile of Sebek!" sent Smerdis.

Gristletongue's next scalded leap landed him in the arms of a fat fishwife, who fainted, knocking over a whole line of booths.

"A one-cat army," sent Smerdis. "Who needs Miw?"

But the clock struck eleven. All round the square, Miw released their rats. A hundred rats ran everywhere. Women screamed at other women's screaming and merchants beat at the rats with sword and sausage. Gristletongue, still dripping soup and emeralds, covered himself with glory trying to kill everyone else's rats.

It resulted in five head-on collisions and [illegible]
away. Then he tried to kill Smerdis's rat. An ear-tingling [illegible] him into the midst of a furrier's stall, inextricably jammed between bear- and wolf-pelts, till a potential buyer felt his tail appreciatively . . . At that point he escaped, blinded by a wolf-pelt that had become wrapped round his head. Tales are still told of the quaint legless wolf that ran round in circles that day.

Smerdis's rat ran up a damsel's skirt for refuge. Smerdis, though normally the most courteous of Miw, believed in doing his duty . . . He would never discuss it afterwards, but three months later the damsel was known to have bidden the world farewell and entered a nunnery . . .

In five minutes, it was all over. Every rat lay dead, and the Fair was in ruins. The merchants began to pack up what remained of their stock, and demand their money back from Glumbach. Some of them got it back twice, by rejoining the end of the queue. When he could no longer pay, they stripped him of purse and presents, knife and gown, and left him shivering in his shift. In vain, all soup and shift, he tried to persuade them to stay. They walked straight through him, many vowing never to return. Many quoted the old saying, "Finis felicorum, initium murorum, finis urbis."

The usurpers still stood on the ramparts, helpless and furious.

11

Meanwhile, Castlemew was dozing by the fire in the late Duke's chamber. She knew she shouldn't be there. Since the untimely end of Pouncefoot, all right-thinking Brethren had shunned the Palace. But Castlemew was no longer right-thinking. She was old, her white patches turning yellow and her black patches fading and going bald through too much nervous licking. Many Brethren said that a sister of such wretched appearance could be no true cat of the city. So she went her own way, uncaring, and seldom touched-noses . . .

She had taken up with one Sir Henri, whom she thought not so much bad as sad. He had been a hero in the Wars, and was still a dangerous sword. But since the lady whose glove he had always worn in his helm had married another, it seemed to Sir Henri that the world had gone to pot and he might as well go with it. He'd turned up after the death of the Duke; stayed to drink the cellars dry, and because usurping seemed the most dangerous thing going. He seemed to Castlemew to live only for drink and danger; he looked like an ageing wolf, with greying hair worn long in the style of twenty years ago, and a sad grey moustache. His face was deeply lined from drink, and thinking about his lost love.

"Her hair was so long," he would say to Castlemew, "that even braided it fell below her waist." Castlemew would purr, and beam her green eyes at him, not understanding a word. But pictures of the lost love came to her from Henri's mind, and never in the world had she known anything so beautifully romantic. *She* had always found Brethren-toms rough, swift and ruthless . . .

"Her feet in their damask slippers were so small . . . " continued Henri. Castlemew had heard it all before, but she didn't mind. Each time, the images got better, the hair longer, the feet smaller . . .

Someone was knocking at the door, very gently. No more than

the tapping of a fingernail. Sir Henri swore, and threw an empty wine-jar at the door. Fragments flew all over the rushes.

In response, a small figure sidled in; Little Paul. Sir Henri loathed him, Castlemew was terrified of him. He had a sheet of vellum in his hand torn from a book.

"Henri, there is still the matter of the arrests . . . " Henri thought Little Paul had a mind like a bent nail in a shoe, that keeps sticking up and hurting, no matter how much you hammer it down . . .

"Can't you see I'm *busy*?" said Sir Henri.

Little Paul looked from cat to wine-jar and smiled like vinegar. Sat down neatly, and smoothed the vellum on his tiny girlish knees. "The priest must be taken. He has preached on the text 'They have slain the Lord's Anointed'."

"I never go to church," said Sir Henri, as if that settled the matter.

"I do. I go everywhere."

"We can deal with the priest when the time comes. He's not bothering us now . . . "

"Bother taken today is bother saved tomorrow." Little Paul produced his portable inkwell, dipped his quill and wrote down the priest's name. Castlemew stirred uneasily. She disliked the pictures coming from Little Paul's mind.

"Then there's the matter of the grocer . . . "

"He been preachin' too?" asked Henri. "What's the world comin' to, when grocers start preachin'? We'll have priests sellin' rotten eggs next."

"Ha *ha*!" Little Paul made a noise like a gate creaking in the wind. "The grocer has too many friends . . . "

"Envious?"

Little Paul gave Henri a look that said he would like to have added his name to the list, if he dared. Instead, he wrote the grocer's name.

Castlemew became agitated. The grocer had often given her bacon-rind, in the winter-hard.

The distant clock struck eleven. Distant uproar sounded from the marketplace. Little Paul turned pale.

"Trouble!" Sir Henri buckled on his sword, looking suddenly cheerful. They ran out together, the little man laying his vellum carefully on the table by the door. As ever, Sir Henri locked the door behind him, to keep the varlets from the wine.

Alone, Castlemew thought deeply. Then picked up the rolled vellum, settled it comfortably in her mouth, and leapt from the open window on to the narrow ledge beneath. The sheer drop didn't trouble her, only the wind worrying at the vellum.

When she got to the grocer's, she dropped the vellum, damp from her mouth, on to his stall-board. The grocer, busy discussing the new plague of rats, picked it up absently.

Read his own death-sentence. He stared at it a long time; but when he read the other names, he knew what to do. He ran for the priest's house, and Castlemew ran limpingly with him.

She saw each condemned man snatch up the thing dearest to him. The grocer his moneybags, the priest his Bible. Old Geoffrey the soldier took down his rusted sword, and the Mayor his chain of office. Now they stood in an alleyway, shouting frantically.

"... flee the town ..."

"My wife ..."

Then the curfew-bell tolled from the Palace, though it was not yet midday. Within a minute, the town-gate would be shut and barred.

Only Castlemew knew what to do; though the panic in the men made her head ache. Sehtek had taken the young Duke to the Mausoleum; she would take her people there too. She mewed sharply, ran to the corner and looked back.

The men followed without hesitation; they'd been taught since childhood it was lucky to follow a cat that called. It might lead you to a gold piece in the gutter, or a tool you'd mislaid, or a hole starting in your roof. Only fools and strangers ignored a cat ...

Castlemew led them, by quiet alleys, through the broken window into the Mausoleum. Inside, at first, there was only the dark of the lichened window-glass, the sound of their own frightened breathing. Then, as their eyes got used to the dark, they saw the Miw sitting in their rows; watching.

Now some Miw had only come to boast, modestly, about their exploits with rats. Others had come in anger, sensing Castlemew's plan. But to the men, the Miw seemed a great gathering, all of one mind, who had summoned them for some mighty, magic purpose. Each man had learnt at his grandmother's knee the legend of the Parliament of Cats. And the fact that the Miw were sending great waves of rage against Castlemew did nothing to make the atmosphere less awesome ...

"What do they *want*?" asked the priest, and crossed himself.

At that moment, a weak cry sounded from the corner. A cat bigger than all the rest crawled slowly towards them. At least, it mewed like a cat, moved like a cat, thin and filthy, with blood and feathers stuck round its mouth.

"Great God," cried the Mayor. "It is . . ."

The Miw released their hold, and the Duke cried once more like a human child. The Mayor, fear forgotten in pity, picked him up.

Everybody had assumed him dead; no one had dared ask . . . Now, to find him safe among the tombs of his ancestors . . .

"They have given us back our Duke!" The Mayor looked wondering at the Miw.

"What do they mean us to do?" asked old Geoffrey, throat dry.

"We are the Chosen," announced the Mayor, proudly.

"Chosen for *what*?" asked the priest, sharply.

"To put the Duke back on the throne of his fathers!" Grandeur came readily to the Mayor's lips, even when he was scared to death.

"Why . . . us?" asked old Geoffrey. Still, he straightened himself a little.

"God knows," said the priest, with more fervour than usual.

There was a faint splaying of ears among the Miw; for once, it was enough to make a cat laugh. Castlemew would be forgiven; eventually.

But, as Smerdis asked, if you could feed a small boy on rats and birds, what could you feed four grown men on?

Meanwhile, Castlemew was hurrying back to her beloved. She had just got back enough breath to purr by the dying fire when the key turned and Sir Henri burst in, unbuckled his sword-belt and threw it on the table; his mind afire with leaping cats and squealing rats and booths collapsing. He banged Paul on the back. Which Paul hated.

"What a mêlée! Admit it – the liveliest thing you've seen in years! That black devil – all emeralds and porridge . . ."

"Soup!" snarled Paul.

"A black paladin after my own heart!"

"A *costly* paladin . . . all the booth-rents lost . . . and they won't come back next spring."

"After you closed the gates on them and charged them gate-tax to leave? I wouldn't come back myself . . ."

"We can't rule without taxes . . ."

"Oh, fuss, fuss, fuss! Stop whingeing like a ruptured farrier. Have a drink." Sir Henri poured wine, swung his earthy boots up on to the table a foot from Paul's nose.

Paul's nose wrinkled. "This city has not *seen* taxes yet . . . "

"They won't pay – not if they're men."

"They'll pay, when they see a few hang . . . *where is my list?*"

"How should I know? Drink up – steady your nerves!"

"I left my list on *your* table." Little Paul fidgeted into every corner of the room, turning over Henry's scattered belongings with nose-wrinkling distaste.

"Must be somewhere," boomed Henri, from the depths of his goblet. "Locked the door – I've got the only key."

"Yes," said Little Paul meaningfully, turning over all Henri's belongings with a spiteful foot again; even giving Castlemew a searching look. Castlemew hunched herself tighter; the feeling in the chamber was getting very bad. Henri's red joy was darkening to rage. And the visions issuing from Little Paul . . . who returned to the table, cracking the joints of his fingers one by one, with venomous precision.

"You objected to me making that list . . . "

"I tell you I've never seen your wretched list. Are you calling me a liar?" Sir Henri had gone alarmingly pale; his mind was full of red knives.

"Yes!"

Paul started backing towards the door; Sir Henri's hand tightened round his goblet. Then he threw.

Paul leapt frantically in the air, to avoid a shattered shin. Henri's rage changed back to red joy, as he threw everything he could lay his hands on . . .

Little Paul fell through the doorway, pursued by roars of knightly laughter, and a shower of broken glass.

"Good riddance to bad cess," said Sir Henri, picking up dented goblets, quite restored.

Castlemew wasn't. Why did her master judge men only by their skill with the sword?

Little Paul's mind was full of dark bottles . . .

Sehtek sat all afternoon on a high chimneystack, savouring the foolishness of men, as if it was a choice piece of roast duck.

She sensed Little Paul, rewriting his death-list with trembling fingers. Giving it to the Captain of the Guard.

The Captain returning in half-an-hour, saying all the birds had flown . . .

Little Paul tore his list into tinier and tinier fragments.

"They were *warned* . . ."

He rapidly scribbled a new list, while the Captain watched, appalled, over his shoulder. For the new list made no sense. Priest, Mayor, old soldier might have been dangerous. But now Paul wrote down the names of anybody who'd annoyed him. Including the Captain's wife's mother, who had complained about the state of the sewers. The Captain disliked his wife's mother, but he didn't see why she should be hanged. So he went to warn her first, before turning out the guard.

She had a gift of reading lists upside-down, having worked for the grocer in her youth. After the Captain had gone, she ran to warn everyone else.

So the guard, turned out, arrested nobody.

The Captain, realising too late what had happened, kept silent for his life.

"Black sorcery, sir! Someone knows your thoughts afore you knows them yourself!"

An honest man would've arrested the Captain on the spot. But Little Paul had often taken a potion of his own making, to journey out of his body and try to read the minds of others . . . he was quite sure it could be done. He was also fairly certain who was doing it . . .

All this Sehtek savoured in her heart, merely twitching her ears to keep the passing insects moving on their way. Men who wove nets for others tangled their own legs. It was the simple-hearted ones she feared. Like Sir Henri . . .

12

Long before Cam reached the city, it made him uneasy.

He liked towns you could drift into, starting with a straggle of hovels, an old man sitting in the sun. So you could say "How do?", get talking, learn the gossip. So by the time you reached the middle, where things might happen, you weren't a total stranger.

But this city rose straight from the red plain. Bastion after bastion of cliff topped by cunning white walls that took advantage of every ravine and overhang. Where the cliffs were high, the walls were low. Where the cliffs were shallow and broken, the walls soared, covered with cleverly-placed arrowslits and murder-holes. Cam felt the weight of the brain that made those walls; thought, That man was as clever as me. It depressed him.

No drifting into this city. One gate and one road leading steeply up, curving back and forth so that the battlements could study you at leisure before they let you in. The broken stone of the road hurt his feet even through his boots; he felt like a lonely fly crawling up a white tablecloth, where giants sat, waiting to swat him.

One thing gave comfort. People had been letting things slip. Trees, a veritable young forest, had been allowed to flourish too near the gate. A small army could hide, rush the gate when the yawning guard opened it in the morning. And young trees growing out of the walls themselves . . . footholds. Cam saw the grapnel-ropes coiling upwards, the scaling-ladders being carried forward in the dark before dawn . . .

He shook himself. Why am I thinking like this? I'm not a soldier . . . He glanced down at the knife suspiciously . . .

He arrived at the gatehouse panting and sweaty. The main gates were shut, only the little postern open. *Two* guards on duty. Trouble.

One was a typical guard, fat with leaning against too many walls and sending for too many flagons of ale to while away hot afternoons. His sword-belt, on its last notch, was still nipping his paunch; he looked resentful, as if somebody was making him wear it.

The other wasn't typical. A slinky, ferrety ginger man whose feet never stopped moving, and whose eyes were everywhere. Not a man to take a drink as a bribe; or he'd take your drink and report you afterwards.

Ferret was in charge. "What you want?"

"To come in."

"What *for*?"

"A bed for the night."

"There are beds in the villages."

"Village beds are full of fleas."

"So are the beds here." Ferret scratched himself to prove it.

"I need work."

"Isn't enough work for those who live here." Ferret was really enjoying himself. "What work do you do?"

"I mend things . . ."

"Such as . . ."

"Carts," said Cam, getting nettled. The man took out a dirty sheet of parchment, already scribbled on both sides with hardly a space. Wrote, with a stub of charcoal, 'Runaway apprentice blacksmith.'

"I'm not a runaway apprentice."

"Oh, you can read, can you? Upside-down, too. You a runaway monk or something?"

"Like you?" Cam could have bitten his tongue off; he'd just made an enemy for life. "I am a scholar, of the universities of Cambridge and Paris."

"A *penniless* wanderer in search of truth?" Ferret's eyes moved over Cam's torn and muddy clothes.

"I can pay for my lodging . . ."

"Show me!"

Cam turned out his belt-pouch; glad that by now it only held coppers.

"At least you can pay the gate-tax," said Ferret, taking all the money and putting it into his own pouch. "What's your name?"

"Cam." The ferret wrote 'Cam of Cumbria'. There were many ways of spelling Cambridge but . . . Cam's lip curled. Ferret looked up and caught it curling. "Present yourself to me here in the morning. If you haven't found enough work to feed yourself, I'll have you thrown out of the city."

"Hey . . ."

"This way or that, friend," Ferret indicated the postern-gate, or the road winding back downhill.

Cam went in.

He stayed ill-tempered till he reached the Bleeding Wolf. Trying to find an unobserved place to get his smallest gold coin out of his pack hadn't been easy. The streets were curiously empty, even at midday; no crowds to get lost in. But Cam sensed plenty of eyes watching behind half-closed shutters. And unpleasant little groups of armed men wandering about, asking you over and over who you were and where you were going, and taking a never-failing interest in the emptiness of your purse.

Finally, he found a house with totally-closed shutters and a cobweb spun across its front door. Nipped up its entry, hopped over its garden wall, pulled down his breeches and squatted in the corner, till he was quite sure no one was watching. Only then had he taken out his gold coin, and buried the rest under a prised-up slab in the outhouse.

All of which left him feeling very uneasy.

The Bleeding Wolf was better. An evening-fire lit, bright flames darting between thick dry logs. An old grey cat hunched in the doorway, forcing every newcomer to step over her carefully. Walls hung with brass plates polished wafer-thin over the years. There was also a clumsy arrangement of crossed swords over the mantel-piece, hung on new nails that had split the panelling. A rushed job, and no decoration; the landlord was expecting trouble.

And he looked ready to deal with it, as he laid massive arms on the counter, and his massive belly on his arms. A fool would have thought him fat; but he would heave a man around as easily as one of his barrels. His hair, so black it shone blue, was cropped, soldier-fashion, where a helmet would fit close. It revealed folds of flesh round his neck that gave him the look of a bulldog. He had a way of opening his blue eyes wide in mock-innocence . . .

Nevertheless, Cam thought him honest.

The landlord changed the gold coin in payment for a drink, though he pursed his lips and whistled.

"Got any more like that, son?"

Cam showed his empty pouch.

"Just as well," said the landlord. "Where'd you get that kind of money?"

"Writing letters . . ."
"Some letters . . ."
"Love-letters."
The landlord raised his thick eyebrows, as if he'd seen every human folly. His wife brought cold beef and new-baked bread. The bread reminded Cam so much of home; he could've wept. The inn-wife took his jerkin to brush, returned it nicely dubbined with all the studs shining. Took the liberty of hauling off his boots to do the same. Offered to take his breeches . . . Cam blushed.
"Lay off, missus," said the landlord, "he's eighteen years, not eighteen months."
Cam sat in his evil-smelling socks and ate. The landlord's talk was curiously empty. How early the birds had departed . . . The winter had been so cold the very chamberpots had frozen under the beds . . . How few swallows had returned this spring . . . A good harvest hoped-for, and a better vintage . . .
Not a word of gossip. He might have been a lonely hill-shepherd, instead of a busy inn-keeper. What was *wrong* with this place?
After a long time, in which things got no better, Cam asked, as casually as he could, "Know someone called Seroster?"
The landlord dropped the glass he was polishing. When he'd picked up every single fragment, thoroughly, he straightened and said, "What makes you ask that, son?" His eyes were needle-sharp; he was trembling, his hands clenched on his counter. Cam felt he was on trial for some dreadful unknown crime. It was hard to keep his own voice off-hand.
"Oh, I met a man on the road . . . said this place was famous for a man called Seroster . . . no wandering scholar should miss him . . . casts horoscopes, he said . . ." His voice dwindled.
"This man who told you," asked the landlord suspiciously. "What did he look like?"
Cam invented desperately. "Oh . . . thin . . . scuffed green jerkin . . . bushy grey hair . . . called Raoul . . ."
The landlord frowned. "Wonder who that could've been?" He pondered. "In my trade, I know all who live here, *and* all who pass through. Never heard tell of a man like your Raoul . . ."
He was silent so unbearably long that Cam burst in, "Well, is there a man called Seroster, or not? Raoul said any child in this city could tell me . . ."
Suddenly, all tension left the landlord. He smiled, pityingly. "He was pulling your leg, son. Every child does know. The

Seroster's a tale we tell them round the fire on winter's nights. Be good, or the Seroster will come for you!"

Cam stared, dazed. "A bogeyman? A hobgoblin?"

"No son, more than that. They reckon he built this city from a scatter of white stones, in the beginning. By magic. An' they say he lies buried under this very cliff, and will come again, if the city's in danger. Though I reckon he's leaving it a bit late, this time . . . a tale, son, a tale." The landlord smiled wanly, like a disappointed child.

"Just a legend?" said Cam, trying to give a casual grimace.

"Mebbe he really lived; a thousand years ago!"

A breeze blew round Cam's legs. The inn-door had opened. The landlord's voice changed back to normal heartiness.

"Aye, we expect a fine vintage this year sir!" Then it changed again. "Oh, it's only you, Thomas!"

Thomas was very tall, with a long dark face set in permanent gloom. He sipped the wine set before him, then relaxed, as if it had confirmed his worst fears.

"Have you heard the news? Ironhand is done for!"

"What have you heard?" asked the landlord, cautiously.

"Ironhand caught this Flemish prince and his daughter in the Great Mire. Stripped them naked, left them for his swine . . . Then this questing-knight appeared and killed ten o' them, single-handed!"

"I heard it was only four . . . "

"Ironhand ran for his life, an' the questing-knight gave the prince fine horses and clothes an' a whole sack o' gold."

"I heard your Flemish prince was a nail pedlar, an' he got his own clothes back an' a bit o' money . . . "

"They're saying the questing-knight killed by knife-throw. You don't think it might be . . . ?"

"No I *don't*!" said the landlord, flicking his eyes warningly in Cam's direction. Cam dropped a bit of bread on the floor and bent to pick it up, meanwhile desperately stuffing the telltale knife down his breeches under his jerkin.

"Rollo has made up a song about it," said Thomas. "Sat up all night, and comes here to sing it presently."

"Rollo should have more sense. More sense o' rhyme, and more sense for his own skin."

"I warned him, but he wouldn't heed."

Cam ordered more beef and bread. After the news about Seroster, only filling his belly made any sense; and the warmth of the fire and the inn's kindness. He ate steadily, while the inn-wife fetched his boots back shining, and stood with arms folded, admiring the appetite of the young.

The inn filled up; a friendly lot. A few spoke to Cam (having received a nod from the landlord that he was harmless). They told about returning swallows and chamberpots that froze even while in use . . . They were all the same type: young, greasy leathers, bare muscular arms. Masons with stone-dust in the folds of their jerkins; wheelwrights with curled shavings still in their hair. Hard lads. Cam doubted any could read or write. All their talk was of how things worked. And siege-warfare. Could a mangonel throw a stone further than a trebuchet? But all their knowledge was second-hand; derived from Georges the landlord who had veritably served at the Siege of Calais . . . And had once built models of mangonel and trebuchet, and bombarded Thomas's house with rotten oranges to settle the argument. Happier days . . . at present, they were having a contest to grow the longest moustache. Georges made great play with a steel clothyard under their noses.

Finally, Rollo arrived, a vague and shambling youth with long fair hair, a stubble of beard, and bits of parchment hanging from every pocket. He spent a long time pinging away at a wretched lute, while people bought him drink and urged him to get on with it.

"True art cannot be hurried," said Rollo, pinging harder than ever.

"What's true art got to do with it?"

"He's forgotten the words!"

"Good!" cried several. Finally, Rollo struck a dreadful discord and began. He had two separate voices, one deep and rumbly and one painfully high-pitched, and he could no more join them together than a man could join Afric and Europe. So his song migrated from one to the other, like the infamous swallows, but without their sense of time and season.

"Dusk was deep-falling, o'er the dread Mire . . . "

"It happened in broad daylight!" shouted somebody.

"Dusk was deep-falling," screeched Rollo defiantly, "o'er the dread Mire

When weary came rambling, upon horses ambling
The prince and his daughter . . . "

"He was only a nail-pedlar . . ."

"Skies were a-lowering
Thunder was rumbling . . ."

"We haven't had a drop of rain in weeks . . ."

"Thunder was rumbling
Earnest for shelter
The Prince and his daughter . . ."

"Nail pedlar . . ."

"Down came the Ironhand
With his fell minions
Ruthless as wolven
Taloned like eagles
Heartless as vultures
On the Prince and his daughter.
Stripped them of all things
Stripped them of hope of life
Stripped them of hope of death
The prince and his daughter . . ."

"Not bad, that last bit," said somebody grudgingly, taking a deep draught of ale, and wiping his mouth on the back of his hand.

"Bloody the swords they swung
Bloody the daggers hung
Over the daughter
When over shaking-reed
O'er the dread Mire
Riding on hooves like wings
Came the lord-questing.
Smote he the wolven brood
Smote he through helm and hood
Gleaming his golden hair

Rippled broad shoulders bare . . ."

"What – no armour?"
"Wouldn't rhyme," shouted Rollo defiantly.

"Rippled his shoulders bare
Red now his arms and hair
With blood of the wolven.
Fled they in sorry plight
Fled they to left and right
Crying for dark of night
Fled were the wolven.
Twenty he slew that day,
Thirty without delay
Brought back the light of day
Did the lord-questing.
Fled he so far away
Fled he for many a day
Fled he until this day
Ironhand weeping . . . "

"That bastard – *weep*?"
"It only happened last week!"
"Let the lad finish," said Georges.
Rollo took a very deep breath. A far deeper breath than seemed warranted by the song he'd sung so far.

"When dies the Ironhand
And all his bloody band
Where shall he go then
Go the lord-questing?
Shall he come here again
Knowing our deadly pain
Shall we be freed again
By the lord-questing?"

A terrible hush fell over the inn. The sound of several goblets being dropped.
"Oh my God, he's done it now," said Georges. "Run, Rollo, run, lad. Don't stop running this side of Morville!"
Rollo looked round dazed, as if he had amazed himself. Then ran into the back premises. There was a commotion by the front door, shouts of "Stop him! Get the little rat!" Armed men came thrusting through, but people got in their way. Eventually they reached the back premises, but returned shouting that the back door was open, and the rat flown.

"We'll take somebody," shouted the hard-faced sergeant. He looked round. The crowd had broken into two halves; one round Georges who was brandishing his steelyard and handing out empty bottles. The rest moved towards the mantelpiece where swords were being swiftly pulled from the wall and surreptitiously passed from hand to hand.

Sweat formed on the sergeant's lip. He glanced round again, desperately, and his eyes fell on Cam, standing alone, still gaping with amazement.

"He'll do. Take him!"

And in a moment, Cam was bundled outside.

13

They bundled him roughly through the night. He saved his breath. Never argue with small-minded idiots. Save your breath for the bigger idiots they always took you to.

Twisting alleys, a cobbled square, the huge bulk of a domed building, torches flaring between pillars. Through double-doors, across a hall with filthy black-and-white tiles, and into a room full of people.

The feel of this place alarmed him. Too many people shouting, giving orders, and nobody obeying. Much worse than the cold high tyranny; in this kind of place you could get killed by accident . . .

But at one end of the room there was order; a pool of quiet fear. A group of very large, very ugly men, playing with their sword-hilts and watching each other. Cam didn't understand. They were all afraid, but of what? A vicious court without a king. No place for that young boy, with his huge violet eyes, snub nose and pouting girlish lips, who sat on the absurdly-large gilded throne, playing with the gilded knobs. Somebody's son? These men were all too ugly to have sired him. He looked so *bored*, fiddling. Let him go and play . . .

Cam nearly cast him a look of sympathy; just in time noticed the bitter wrinkles round the boy's eyes and mouth; the intent watching of the violet eyes.

It wasn't a boy; but the source of all fear. After that, Cam kept his own eyes fixed on those violet ones; ignored everybody else in the room.

A tiny glint of pleasure warmed the cold violet. The boy gave the slightest perceptible nod of the head, as if Cam had passed a test . . .

"Yes?" The boy had a fatal girlish lisp.

"We have caught a traitor, sire. Singing a treasonable song against the city."

"What have you got to say, traitor?" A bored question; a very final sort of question. The flick of notice you give a fly before you squash it . . . Cam knew he had two breaths in which to save his life.

"Can't be a traitor – don't belong here. Only arrived today."

The violet eyes came awake with cruelty. "Prove it!"

Cam looked round desperately. His eyes fell on Ferret, who was just trying to slide away behind the gilded throne.

"*He* let me in. Wrote my name down. Cam of Cambridge – runaway apprentice blacksmith. Charged me gate-tax . . . "

"Gate-tax list!" said the boy, holding out a languid hand. "Gate-list *now*!" Ferret put it into his hand, reluctantly.

"I suppose that dirty mark could be read as 'Cam of Cambridge'. Why don't you learn to write, Ferret? Even unfrocked Benedictines can *write*! How much gate-tax charged?"

"Fifteen pennies – all I had."

"Illegal – the gate-tax is three pence. *Money*?" Again he held out a languid hand. Ferret put twelve pennies into it. The money immediately vanished inside the folds of the fur mantle, which the boy wore and stroked even in the heat of summer. "The illegal gate-tax is hereby confiscated by this court."

"But . . . " said Cam.

The violet eyes stared him into silence. "You come as a guest to our city and within the day are singing treasonable songs. *What* song?"

Cam was as near death as ever. Again he stared round desperately. His eye fell on one of the guards who had taken him; an especially stupid-looking guard, staring into vacancy.

"Hey, mate," said Cam. "That song the fair-haired lad was singing – the lad with the straggly beard – what was it about?"

"A questing-knight," said the guard, coming to with a start, "questing-knights and freedom."

The grim sergeant felled him with one blow. He lay dazedly at the boy's feet, spitting out teeth. The boy kicked him away, with tiny spitefulness, and looked at Cam again. "Why did they arrest *you*, then?"

"The other lad got away."

The boy nodded wearily. Then his eyes sharpened once more. "If they took all your money at the gate, what were you doing in an inn?"

"I sold my cook-pot."

"What money have you left?"

Cam reluctantly turned out his belt-pouch again. Paul counted the money and said, "The prisoner is found guilty of being present at the singing of a treasonable song. Fined twenty-seven pence." Again, the money vanished inside the mantle. Then he said, "Where *have* you come from?"

"Up the road from the sea-port."

"Did you see any sign of a questing-knight?"

"What do they look like?"

"What is the main inn of the sea-port?"

The change of tack threw Cam off balance; it was meant to. He had a bad moment before he remembered the Fleur-de-Lys.

"Hmmm. And what do you *really* do for a living?"

Cam had never endured a scrutiny like those violet eyes gave him. He was shaking all over. It was a relief to tell the truth.

"I solve problems." He told about the sewer at Marseilles.

The boy waved everybody else away. Leaning forward he grasped Cam's knee, pulled him down to the step of the throne. "You are not without wit. You have just saved your life, and added thirty-nine pence to the coffers of this city. I have a problem of the sort you mention . . . "

It took a long time telling, and Cam was in a daze already. He came out of it when the boy said, sharply, "So you can see our dilemma. We broke down the door, found the royal bouteiller stabbed to death, the late Duke stabbed to death and the son fled. What other conclusion can we draw?"

"None," said Cam cravenly, his courage exhausted.

"So . . . I want you to find this father-slayer, so we can put him away quietly . . . "

"But if his father is dead, he's the new Duke . . . "

"Can a father-slayer profit from his dreadful crime?" asked the boy dreamily.

The room suddenly felt dangerous again.

"I'll try," said Cam.

"Fetch your belongings *now* – there are plenty of empty rooms here. You won't be . . . popular, down in the town. Once they know you're working for *me*." Then he added, "You may call me Paul."

Cam fled.

He went back to the Bleeding Wolf. Georges reached his pack down, from the top of a very dusty cupboard. "I looked inside, to see if I could find out . . . we didn't expect to see you again . . . But you'll find everything inside as you left it. We're honest, here."

Cam was glad the letter to the Seroster was inside his shirt.

"What happened?" asked Georges casually, wiping a table.

"Proved myself innocent."

"You didn't blab on Rollo?"

"Didn't mention his name."

"So what now? Back where you came from? Don't blame you . . ."

"I'm working . . . up there."

All the drinkers turned to stare.

"Doin' what?"

"They've got their sewers in a mess . . ." Even that lie didn't go down too well.

"Well, if you want to get covered with filth . . ." Georges didn't mean the sewers.

Cam picked up his pack and left quickly.

"Best of luck," said one drinker. And they all sniggered.

The inn-door slammed behind.

He'd never felt so lonely in his life.

He had to bribe the doorkeeper to let him back in; hadn't even a penny to bribe him with. Had to turn out his pack on the doorstep, and offer a little inkwell he valued.

"Ever play dice?" asked Cam, as the door finally swung open.

"Yes, I'll take your money off you, son. When you've got some."

Cam would get his inkwell back, with interest; he had dice he never used with decent men . . .

Upstairs, he wandered littered corridors, by moonlight trickling through broken windows. Trying doors to see if they were locked, listening to the groans, snores or babbling within. The Palace didn't seem a happy place to sleep. Behind one unlocked door, he saw a fat naked woman, in bed with three black dogs and a monkey. She beckoned . . .

But in the end, high in the roof, he found an empty chamber with the key still in the lock. It smelt no worse than musty; no one had eased themselves in the fireplace. All it contained was a huge bare bed. As he was closing the door, a slim girlish shape swam through the gloom, whispered to share his bed. Her hood dropped away, and in a glimmer of moonlight he saw a moustache . . .

He slammed and locked the door. Sat on the bed, sweating and listening to pig-like sounds next door, and screams far below. It was long before he slept.

In the morning, he found no food being served in the half-wrecked hall. People seemed to buy or steal down in the city and walk about eating it with their fingers. A lot of trodden food in the corridors; the dogs were busy, but not a cat in sight. He found a man camping in the Palace kitchens, who claimed to be Little Paul's cook. At least he had a fire going, and unwashed pans around him. And he needed writing done . . . Recipes, he called them; they involved wolves' legs and boiled babies. Cam did his writing, in return for some greasy apples, which seemed safe enough.

He decided to furnish his room; there was plenty of stuff lying about, in rooms once fine. Now, there were nails knocked into the giltwork, to take a horseman's gear; ceilings had fallen into piles of urine-reeking plaster. Cam took too much stuff, for he pitied the gilded chairs raked with spurs, the tapestries someone had pulled down to make a bed, then abandoned to the hairy sleep of dogs. In an hour, without being challenged, he had a room fit for a prince.

Then he pocketed his key and went down into the city. He felt uneasy about searching for the father-slayer. But no harm in getting his bearings . . . he'd have to have *something* to report to Little Paul . . . He revisited his gold-hoard, changed another coin at the Seven Stars which was as far from the Bleeding Wolf as he could get; but still the drinkers fell silent, stared, till he drank up and left.

Miserable. But he had one merry encounter. In a totally-abandoned street, where grass grew and children had scrawled on walls, he discovered a curious octagonal building with rusty pad-locked doors . . . He was just trying to work out what it might be, when a couple of golden cats caught his eye. Remembering his old friend of the Mire, he watched with interest. They were having a difference of opinion; fought superbly, leaping yards in the air, throwing each other down with soul-searing grunts, rolling over on their backs to use all four paws in combat. It was a running battle; they used every doorstep and windowsill as a fortress or ambush. He followed their swift progress. They seemed to be fighting more for sport than rage, for no blood was drawn.

By the time he had followed the fight to its conclusion, and one cat had chased the other clear away over the rooftops, he found himself in quite another part of the city, among fruitsellers' stalls.

He quite forgot about the octagonal building . . .

He went to bed early, tired by the city's hostility. He'd found some fascinating books in the Duke's library. Pity their bindings had been torn off, by somebody after the gold in the titles . . . but he was snug by the glow of two rushlights.

Soft tapping, with a thumbnail, on the door. When he unlocked it, Paul sidled in. "Well . . . ?"

"Well what?"

"What have you found out?"

"This city's like a rabbit-warren! Rome wasn't built in a day!"

"Rome was *destroyed* in a day." Paul stared round. "You *have* made yourself comfortable."

"People were chopping them up for firewood . . ."

"Where did you get money to buy rushlights?"

"Writing letters for people . . . "

"Yes, I *heard* you could write." Paul held out a languid hand. Raging inwardly, Cam passed over seven pennies, and watched them slide into their usual destination.

"Tomorrow – you hunt for the father-slayer. Don't waste my time writing letters. Did you find out *anything*?"

"Awful lot of cats about . . . "

Paul shuddered. "Don't you know the old name for this place? Citie Deschats? The city of cats? I shall put an end to *that* soon. The cat is evil." He took Cam cruelly by the elbow, drew him close. "Cats not only infect with their brains, but also by their hair, their breath and their gaze. Their breath is infected by tabithic poison. I cannot breathe if a cat as much as enters a room . . . "

This man's a Tom-o-bedlam, thought Cam, caught up in the violet eyes.

"A haruscopist told me I shall come to my end by means of a black-and-white cat. So do not tell me there are cats in this city. I never forget it, night and day."

He wandered about the room, picking at Cam's belongings. (Cam would have leapt out of bed, if he'd been wearing more than a shirt.) "What else have you found out?"

"I tell you I must get the *feel* of the place first! It's not going to be easy, with all these empty houses . . . "

"*What* empty houses?"

"The shuttered ones."

"They all shutter their windows at night."

"These are shuttered at midday. With spiderwebs spun across their front doors. Not today's webs, either."

"What, are people leaving?"
"The city's half-empty."
"Why didn't they tell me? That lying Captain. Get dressed, I shall confront him with you . . . "
"No!"
Paul stood very still; looked at Cam in the glow from the rushlights. Was it just their flicker, or was his face working like a bed of maggots? Cam felt his own feet starting to sweat. He blurted, "If you face the Captain with me, he'll think I'm your sneak!"
"You are my sneak!"
"But if people know it, how can I hear their gossip?"
Paul smiled. "You are like me in many ways." Then, abruptly, "I shall pass a law forbidding anybody to leave the city!"
"That's stupid. Most don't want to leave – nowhere else to go. But if you forbid them, they'll *want* to!"
Paul smiled at him again. "You are *less* like me than I thought."

The rest of the night, the Palace was in uproar. In the morning Cam found everywhere, nailed to doors, wildly-lettered proclamations that no one was to leave the city, on pain of imprisonment.
Within a week, the prison was full. People were caught lowering ladders down the walls at midnight; smuggling out their children under the turnips in a farmer's cart.
Others got clean away.
The prisons got so full, Paul had to start letting people out again. But only on payment of an exceedingly large fine.
Cam began to see there was method in Little Paul's madness.
The Captain of the Guard began giving Cam some very funny looks.
More people left.
All this, and other things, Sehtek sensed with her mind. She spent most of her time now, high up in the Mausoleum, among the crouching bodies of the mummified Matagots. She scarcely came down to eat; grew thin with vigilance, as she watched the city like a mousehole, waiting, and pondering the unfu of men . . .
The four heroes in the Mausoleum got very bored. They had enough to eat; Miw mightn't be good ratters, but they were better thieves at kitchen windows. Trouble was, they'd little idea of human tastes. The heroes found it hard going on lard and raw bacon.

Worse, having resolved to give their lives for the cause, they couldn't think what to do. Just sat, cooped up, talking and staring at the tombs of dead Dukes.

Finally, old Geoffrey could stand it no longer; slipped out for a walk one night, after curfew. One of Little Paul's patrols tried to arrest him. They were a bit half-hearted, because they were cold and bored and only doing what they'd been told.

Geoffrey, with a hangman's noose dangling before him, was neither bored nor half-hearted. He drew his beloved sword, forgot his age and got in a lucky first blow.

Besides, he'd been followed at a distance by several worried Miw, including Smerdis.

It's hard to fight with a Miw on your back . . .

In two minutes, Geoffrey found himself standing breathless, with two men groaning at his feet and four more running for their lives. Finding that he wasn't past it went to his head. He gave chase, shouting wild things about the young Duke.

"Duke William forever! Death to the usurpers!" Being an old soldier, he had to shout something; he shouted the first things that came into his head. The high stone houses picked up and echoed his shouts.

"William! William!"

It seemed to the patrol there was far more than one man after them. And the Miw ran along the wall-tops, looking twice the size in the pale moonlight, and yowling like fiends out of the pit.

Far above, windows flew open, and elderly ladies without their fat-lensed spectacles leaned out and saw what they expected to see; dozens of men and hundreds of Miw.

The patrol hammered on the Palace door, screaming to be let in. The door was opened by a doorkeeper dragged out of sleep, and slammed again quickly. Geoffrey, still drunk with success, ran in under the arch and thundered on the door with his rusty sword-hilt.

"Open in the name of Duke William!"

It would have gone hard with him if they had. But there wasn't one cool soldier behind that door; just twenty cold, yawning terrified men who thought two of their mates were dead and four more reduced to gibbering idiots.

A sentry peered down from the battlements; all he could see were waves of Miw streaking across the square; mostly out of curiosity, but they looked like an army . . . He rang the great alarm-bell, which shocked everyone in the Palace out of their skins.

After two minutes, Geoffrey and the Miw came to their senses and slunk away. By the time Sir Henri, frantic for a fight, had felled two varlets and forced the door open, there was nothing in sight.

Next morning, the city was agog. People remembered old Geoffrey had been a great sword, who had charged the last charge with Richard Crookback, at the Battle of Bosworth Field. They forgot that thirty years had passed; were in a mood for miracles.

And the young Duke was alive! Had led the attack in person! The Miw were for him! People forgot the Duke's youth, like they forgot Geoffrey's age.

Next night saw another miracle. The priest slipped out to try to get enough wine to say Mass. He was seen by a terrified mother. Her baby, she said, was dying in agony; it must have the last rites. The priest went with her, thinking he was going to certain death. He picked up the screaming child in front of a whole crowd of neighbours. Almost dropped it, his hands were shaking so much; made a frantic grab to recover his hold. The baby, which only had extremely persistent wind and a very silly mother, gave a tremendous burp, sighed and fell into peaceful sleep.

White mother and neighbours were giving thanks for a blessed miracle, the priest slipped away.

By the next morning it was being said that the child was not only dead but nigh buried, before the priest brought it back to life. The Pope should be written to; the priest should be made a saint, or at least a Bishop.

Other people, narked at being left out, joined in by inventing brave things the grocer had done. The Mayor's peevish grumbles became a noble stand against tyranny.

Scrawls about Duke William began to appear on all the walls.

All this Sehtek noted, and more. But far more troubling was the strong sendings coming from the south. Nearer now, more disciplined, but still a pain and trouble to her.

And she sensed the knife was back in the city; felt the claws in it, the kill-fury. The knife was awake, and hungry. Between the sendings and the knife, she felt distressed, like a cat in labour. Within the city, she sensed the dreaded, the awaited Birth.

Meanwhile, the four heroes watched aghast, as the Duke lay in the bat-droppings of the Mausoleum floor. It seemed to them his mind was gone for ever. Their only hope was that the Miw still fed him . . .

But in fact, the Duke was happy. Not just because, closely pressed in by well-grown Miw-kittens, he was less lonely than humans ever feel. But because the kittens were having a Miw-learning, from Smerdis who was gracefully lounging at the back of the group.

Moving images came from Smerdis's mind; the same as had been passed to him when he was a kitten. Having been passed from Miw to Miw for countless generations, the images were blurred; but very pleasant.

A vast expanse of pale-blue flowing water; the yellow smudge of the further shore. White and brown triangles, moving in opposite directions, graceful as swans.

An avenue of trees, tall as the sky, casting purple shadows and rustling coolly. A gateway, flanked by golden towers covered with carved figures, twice the height of men. Before the gate, a cool green canal. On the gate lounged golden cats, staring at the world with bland, blinking calm, soaking up the sun. Every so often they would drop off the gate, drink at the green canal, retire to the shade under the trees. Happy; they made even Smerdis look like a tattered vagabond.

Then a Miw-kit trotted down the avenue. Two men with white robes and shaven heads immediately followed, carrying rolls on which they recorded each time the kitten sat down to scratch, or turned aside to nose some rubbish. Then they would shake their heads and bicker earnestly, till the kitten trotted on . . .

Passers-by stopped to watch, as if the kitten was a procession all by herself. Brown men in short white kilts. Brown women in gauzy linen dresses that revealed every sway of their elegant limbs . . . The people held up their hands to stop carts from passing, lest their wheels endanger the kitten. The carts waited patiently.

On the kitten ran; to the quayside, her nose working steadily. To where fish lay in baskets. The kitten was in paradise. Some fish she licked and some she bit, and some she pulled from the baskets into the dust. The fishermen didn't yell at her, but waited patiently also.

Then the kitten ran up the gangplank on to a very large boat, high in stem and stern with glittering gold, and sails of linen. The shaven men followed, never taking their eyes off her. A great crowd gathered, with baited breath.

The kitten sat, and began to wash her nose, inspecting her paw from time to time. Then she began to wash her face . . .

The crowd sighed.

Then she began to wash the front of her ears.

The crowd gasped.

Finally, the kitten passed a paw right over her ear . . .

The crowd groaned. Everyone began running. The sailors began taking down the masts and sails of the great boat. A man was hurried ashore, a man with a high, proud face, a flaxen wig and gold cobra on his forehead. The fishermen began carrying their fish to the higher ground. Things were tied down. One of the shaven men picked up the kitten, and bore her off in his arms . . .

The sky darkened; the river grew broken and uneasy. Then came a mighty wind, sudden beyond belief. It tossed the boats on shore, rolled and broke them. Stripped the leaves from the great trees and sent them bundling over and over, down the avenue.

Then the sky was suddenly clear once more, and the wind gone. The river was full of floating baskets and drowned men.

When the man with the high, proud face returned, he worshipped the kitten lying in the priest's arms, as if she were a goddess . . .

The image faded. The Duke lay entranced. But the Miw-kittens yawned. They'd seen it all before; too many times to remember. It was about the importance of how you washed your face and held your tail. Boring. They had tried to introduce a little mouse into the vision, to do comic things, especially in the solemn parts.

But they had learnt the heaviness of Smerdis's paw . . .

14

Amon stood on the cliff, letting the paws of Re caress him. Soon, time for prayer.

He'd never felt so well. Gently moved his feet, delighting in the thick smoothness of muscle. An endless supply of red meat . . .

All the host was the same, glossy-furred, ears that flicked and turned without ceasing. War-wise; mirfu were only food now, food that offered itself unasked and unhunted. Both Ripfur and Tornear, black fur shining with sun and washing instead of guttergrease, had fought-off snofru. Snofru had learnt wisdom, at the expense of lost eyes and tattered ears. When snofru met cat now, snofru looked the other way uneasily, departed quickly.

Not-dog had been harder; would always threaten death. But Amon had learnt to sense his coming far-off. Sisters and kittens withdrew into the crevices, guarded by the flashing claws of toms. Then the heb-Miw went forward to meet not-dog, as he ascended some narrow place, nose to ground . . .

Amon stood back these days. Enough to hurl a hate-sending, that sent not-dog's mind into a whirling chaos, as the heb-Miw dropped from a height. Amon was still ready to lend a claw . . . The last three times he hadn't needed to.

He watched his people, settling for the night. They still wouldn't pray-Re, but liked to listen while Amon did. It ended a contented day.

Men made you beggars, he thought, toys and pets, then turned and tried to kill you.

That young sister, finishing her mirfu; would she ever be content again with herringskin scavenged from a sewer?

Others thought the same. Ripfur and Tornear had come to him, one evening when they had halted in a very pleasant place. They pointed out the clean water, strong bastions of crag and cranny, grassy hollows that kept out the wind and held the sun like a cup.

"Make new city here? We lords now!"

Amon had stared at them with troubled eyes. He had grown massively fond of them. They enjoyed being heroes, instead of hated gutter-bullies, and who could blame them? He asked them if they'd thought of winter-food, winter-shelter. They had, carefully . . .

"Stay then! Be-kings. Be-happy. I must go to my own city."

"No good without-you. Who think? Who pray-Re? Who see not-dog far-off?"

Once, old Splayfoot had sent sadly, "Would like to lay my bones down in place-like-this."

But they went on.

At the tenth sunset, they came across three Matagot, sitting on a tall rock, tails hanging down like black question-marks.

The host gave them grudging greeting. The Matagot too had come from the fishing-port. They were not popular. The first to flee when the blacksmith died, they had only passed on their warning while in full flight. Some cats, young and old, had not heard the warning in time . . .

The Matagot had fared better than the Brethren, in the swamp. Travellers had fed them richly, being led to hope for gold coins. They had survived the perils of the red desert, sensing not-dog far off and taking refuge in deep clefts. But the journey had left them thin and ragged. They'd spent their time running away, and it showed.

Nobody offered them mirfu.

But they were still Matagot. Very terrible their faces, when they sniffed noses with Amon. Black faces, flecked with gold in drifts like stars in a midnight sky. They kept ears and whiskers very still, so no cat could tell what they were thinking.

They sent, all three together, addressing Amon.

"You should not be-here. You should be in-city. You are ten Re-voyages late . . . "

"Have finished my-task. Horse is warned."

"Unfu, you should be in-city." Very terrible is the sending of three Matagot together. Like bone-desert, kitten-death, black-cliffs.

"Why?" Amon's pink rose of question was disrespectfully large, tinged with the red of anger.

"Is *time* for you to be in-city. It is *your* time to be in-city."

"I am unimportant."

The Matagot exchanged slight flickers of what might have been Matagot-mirth. Amon began to shift from foot to foot with annoyance.

"Go. Now!" Again they sent together. Their sending was unbearably heavy.

"What about my-Brethren?" Amon looked round; every face in the host was turned to him, expectantly.

"These are of no-importance . . . "

Amon sent a sending he later regretted. A sending that blasted the Matagots' ears flat to their skulls, almost drove them into the very earth. At the time, he enjoyed it; so did the host.

The Matagot got up and shook themselves, dazedly. Then immediately continued, heavier than ever.

"Go now. Run-all-way. Tomorrow too-late. The courses of the stars are shifting against you. Go, or you will regret to your life's end."

When Matagot mention the courses of the stars . . . A great fear came on Amon, so that his strong gold limbs trembled.

"Why?"

"Must not tell-you. We stay here, guard your people. We no longer matter. Our time is past; soon-die anyway."

"Can you fight not-dog?"

Everyone knew the answer.

"Then you cannot guard my-people." Amon paced back and forth, while the host waited, and the Matagot watched, almost humble. Amon lashed his tail with rage at the riddle he could not solve. He turned to pray-Re . . .

But Re had vanished, while he paced and argued. He sent out his mind further and further, searching for the grief the Matagot foretold.

"You will not find it," sent the Matagot. "Even you cannot reach the stars, Lord Amon."

He did not notice what they called him. He threw a tremendous sending to Sehtek, far off in the city. Caught her. But her reply was so faint, all he got was querulousness at the violence of his sending . . .

And still his people watched.

"I will not go," sent Amon. "I will not leave you."

Since then, the Matagot had followed the host; three ever-present black dots behind Tornear's rearguard. They suffered much from his Matagot-arses, but did not deign to reply. Re-knew what they fed on. They did not try to interfere with Amon again; but they would not go away.

Tornear said they were afraid to leave the protection of the host.

But Amon knew that was not the answer.

Three days passed peaceful and prosperous. The foretold grief did not happen.

15

Smerdis was worried about the blind beggar.

For one thing, despite his hooded cloak, white staff and begging-bowl, he wasn't blind. Smerdis had tried tripping him up. He just stepped over, saying, "Ooops, puss!"

The beggar was searching for something. Went all over the city, whereas most men kept to their regular man-walks. This one was always poking into corners when nobody was watching. While he was being watched, he moved like an old bent man. Otherwise, he was as nimble as a boy. He seldom begged. When somebody put a coin in his bowl unasked, he looked guilty and later gave it to the real blind beggar.

He came past the Mausoleum too often.

Smerdis was much at the Mausoleum for Miw-learnings; afterwards, he often joined the sentries who guarded it. Because he was the Teacher, other Miw expected him to know how to cope with every problem. Unpleasant; even the old learning didn't have all the answers. Many bits had lost all meaning; were only shown to the kittens out of reverence.

And having spent so much time on the old learning, Smerdis was weak at reading minds. Not half as good as Amon. He'd tried reading the blind beggar's mind; got only nothings – no anger, no hate, no violence. The beggar had a quiet mind that noticed too much. Smerdis could have liked him, if he hadn't been so worrying.

It was easy to distract any usurpers who came too near the Mausoleum. They'd turn aside to bet on a well-faked cat-fight (though they kicked at the loser when he lost them money). But the blind beggar was impossible to distract from his counting of house-doors, marking on walls with lumps of chalk. If you rubbed against his leg, or played with a chicken-head, throwing it in the air and catching it, he would simply smile and continue his search.

One evening he stood so long outside the Mausoleum that

Smerdis was panicked into playing his final trick . . . the silly old tale that a Matagot followed, will lead to treasure . . .

The Miw had made this old foolishness come true. If a Miw found a coin in the gutter (late at night, outside inns, was best) it was its duty to carry the coin to an appointed place and bury it in a well scrabbled hole.

Being led to such a hole distracted men wonderfully . . .

The beggar followed Smerdis, groped in the hole and found six pennies and a small gold piece. He pushed back his hood with a whistle (appointed places were usually deserted) and revealed a young face with the ghost of a moustache. His blue eyes shone as he pouched the money. He found an abandoned house and stuffed his staff and bowl away for the day. His carefree thoughts turned to taverns.

Smerdis turned away, well-satisfied.

But Cam was touched; this must be his old friend from the Mire . . .

Smerdis found himself swept off his feet, cradled in strong arms. Outraged at being picked up like a common brother, he began to kick his way to freedom.

Then lay suddenly still.

This was the dangerous foe; the rest were so stupid even Gristle-tongue could cope. To be constantly with this one; know what he was doing . . .

Smerdis even managed a purr. At least the beggar's hands were gentle. He smelt good, and kept up a smooth even pace.

They turned into an inn; the din made Smerdis's tail lash. Cam loosened his claws and put him on the table.

"Landlord . . . wine . . . a whole chicken . . . !" When it came, Cam tore off a leg, and gave it to Smerdis.

"Thanks, cat. Better than rabbit, eh? Better than the rotten Mire!"

Smerdis slowly lowered his tail, accepting the food. Cam offered more; poured him a pool of wine. Smerdis lapped quickly, to soothe his nerves. Cam grew merry; began to sing.

A mistake; a stranger came sidling up. "Got money to throw away on cats, then? We don't like cats here."

"This cat is my *friend*." Cam suddenly wondered why he felt so quarrelsome. Why was his stomach fluttering in that funny far-off way? Must be the wine talking; better close his big mouth. But something drove him on.

"This *cat*, this *friend* of mine, found me the hidden hoard that's paying for this meal."

"Perhaps he could find me some?"

"They only do things for people they *like*!"

"Let me *persuade* him." The stranger drew a knife, tried the edge with his thumb.

"With a knife?" Cam threw back his head and laughed, till everyone was staring. And all the time his stomach kept fluttering. When had it fluttered like that before?

But the haze of wine got in the way.

"They say stupid things about cats in this city," said the stranger. "They say they can understand human speech. Find me money, Sir Cat, or I'll slit you from bowels to gizzard." He slammed the knife into the table between Smerdis's paws.

Smerdis wanted to run; but something held him still; some exciting thing was going to happen . . .

"The cat can't understand a word you say," said Cam. "Neither can I. Which gutter did you crawl out of?"

The man grabbed for his knife; but before he could work it free, Cam's knife was out, curling back . . . Warm strength flowing up his arm . . .

Now he knew why his stomach had been fluttering. Too late, he recognised the man. One of Ironhand's.

He tried to think up soothing words; but, horribly, they came out insulting. "Farewell, *friend*. If I need company I'll talk to the cat."

The man again contemplated recovering his knife; but something seemed to warn him. He blundered out, crashing against tables in his rage.

"And we'll keep your rotten knife! It'll do for the cat to scratch against!" Cam's mouth seemed to have a life of its own . . .

Still, his own knife stopped quivering. He put it away, wiped his brow and ordered more wine.

The man would be waiting outside. If he sat long enough, maybe the man would get tired and go away. Should he spend the night in this inn?

It grew late; the inn emptied. So did the streets outside. Nearly curfew. The landlord began sweeping up, piling stools on tables with loud thumps; snuffing out candles. The sweet dead smoke made Cam feel sick.

"Out," said the landlord coming over, "before I throw you out."

The knife stayed still; it didn't want to kill landlords . . .

Cam got to his feet with what dignity he could muster; draped the Miw across his shoulder. He attempted to bow to the landlord.

"Go on, before you fall down."

"Goo . . . goo . . . goodnight. Goodnight, goodnight, goodnight."

Smerdis had never been in drunken arms. He dug his claws deep into the jerkin, as Cam reeled from side to side of the alley.

"Ouch, mind claws, puss. Goo . . . goo . . . good Sir Puss." He lapsed into a song called 'L'amour, la morte et la vie'. Or at least the first two lines, sung over and over.

Smerdis worried over his own lack of worry. Why was he *expecting* an event as joyous as mousing?

At least they weren't quite alone. It was the Miw's hour for walking. Miw after Miw, as they passed, offered Smerdis astounded greeting. Then a Miw called Mut came walking. As he passed a side-alley, Mut glanced left, arched his back, hurried on. Something was up that alley.

"Evil man?"

"Evil *men*. Need help?" Smerdis sensed him turn and follow, velvet-footed. They approached the alley. Smerdis could hear three sets of quick, shallow, man-breathing, even over Cam's drunken bawling. He gave a warning yowl so dire that even a drunk . . .

Cam stopped, nearly falling over. "What . . . what's up, Sir Puss?"

Smerdis yowled again, staring at the alley.

"Wha?"

Dark figures running; glint of steel. Smerdis launched himself at the first; the kick of his hind-legs knocked Cam flat in the gutter. Mut, already at full gallop, leapt straight over Cam's body at the face of the second man.

The third towered over Cam as he lay helpless. Except . . . he was clutching at something sticking out of his breastbone; making gasping noises . . .

Cam groped stupidly at his belt. But he knew the knife was already flown.

Then the man fell.

Running footsteps, retreating, one voice swearing and one sobbing.

The cats sniffed delicately the handle of the knife, in the chest of the dead man. Began to purr. Looked at Cam, their eyes catching greenly the faint light of the moon.

Shouting, coming nearer. Couldn't be help; Cam had no friends . . .

Suddenly he was running, the cat running with him.

Somehow, the dreadful knife was back in his hand.

He hammered on the Palace door. The grille opened; the bristly face of the doorkeeper was almost like a friend's.

"No cats!"

"This cat's just saved my life!"

"Then save his. Get 'im away from 'ere. 'Is lordship'll do him in for sure."

"He also found me some money." Cam, recovering part of his wits, displayed the small gold coin.

"Why didn' yer say. Come in, come in!"

"What about the cat?"

"What cat? Can't see no cat, on account of that lovely gold blinding me. Give it here, son, so I can keep it safe from thieving rogues."

"Like you," shouted Cam, hauling himself up the chipped marble steps by the battered gilt handrail.

Once inside his room, with the door safely locked, he began to feel very odd again. Ruined his tinderbox lighting a single rush-light. If only the room would stop spinning . . . He made a grab for the bed as it swung past, but it threw him off like a bucking horse. He crawled back and clung to the bedclothes for dear life. Was the place bewitched?

Eventually, the bed quietened. But any moment, as the drink wore off, he might remember the face of the new-dead man. Gaping silent mouth with rotting teeth . . .

He took out the knife. He had plunged it, and his whole arm, into an icy horse-trough in the square. But there was still a stickiness on the silver-bound handle . . .

Smerdis, feeling painfully the tumult in Cam's mind, decided to distract him . . . He leapt on to the table and stared at the candleflame, so close Cam wondered he didn't singe his nose. Purred delightedly, sniffing the hot wax as if it was a rose. And as he stared (and the reflections glinted in his eyes) the flame grew higher and higher, till it was as long as the dagger.

Then it collapsed in smoking ruin, no bigger than a grain of wheat, till Cam feared it might die altogether, and leave him in the dark with the memory of the rotting teeth. Then it went high again, then low; till the cat tired of the sport, and leapt off the table.

I must be drunk, thought Cam. But he was wrong; each Miw has one bit of magic.

There was a red leaf on the floor, blown in by the autumn wind. Smerdis gathered it, flipped it into the air. Then, rearing on his hindquarters, he tapped the leaf from paw to paw, round and round his body, making it live. Making it into a red mouse so that Cam could have sworn he saw mouse-eye, mouse-ear. Finally the leaf shot up in the air out of control, fell to the floor and was only a leaf again.

Cam laughed his old joyous laugh. Smerdis drew a deep sigh of relief. Once you got them to laugh . . .

Next the cat explored, rustling inside cupboards, sniffing everything with equal interest from the water-ewer to a sweaty shirt. Satisfied at last, he returned to the table and washed himself from ear to toe, spreading out paws like fur-gloved hands to get his tongue down the inmost crevices. He seemed to Cam a very perfect little cat-warrior who, having spied out his new fortress, settles to clean his weapons.

The cat had fought more savagely than Cam; left a man screaming. But now, having washed, he was calm and reposed. Ready for sleep. Oh, to be a cat . . .

The cat looked at him, abruptly. Almost as if to ask: Would you really like to be a cat? Kill without thought, without memory?

Outfaced, Cam dropped his eyes. Suddenly he felt he could sleep without fearing dreams. He crawled under his cloak. Dozing off, he felt the cat crawl under too, settle inside the cave made by his arms and legs.

He liked this cat better than anyone he had ever known.

He did dream.

But in his dream he dreamt he was again leading his white-kilted army. The smoking mountains were long past. They stood on the lip of a great valley, that snaked through the midst of the desert like a green cobra, with the blue-and-white river making a zigzag down its back. The smell of water and greenery came up, the warriors beat spear on shield, greeting their home. He took a deep breath of green and walked down into it. And the golden cat walked before him; as if he too was entering into his kingdom.

16

He was wakened by a purring in his ear. Sun was streaming in the windows. He dressed; scrubbed at the stain on his hand. It came off easily; just like mud. Yesterday was fading . . .

Until the hammering on the door.

"Paul wants you. *Now*!"

He went down, heart pounding; after locking his door.

Little Paul was on his throne; alternately picking at the gold leaf and jingling the money inside his mantle. Not looking anywhere but the floor.

Twin towers of rage stood each side of him. Ironhand, blazing like a furnace; Sir Henri, grey as a tower of ice. The room was full of men playing with their sword-hilts. Quarrel hung in the air like smoke.

Worse; at Cam's waist the knife fluttered; hungering for Ironhand. Cam folded his arms tight, shoved his hands right up into his armpits, squeezing them with all his strength. Did the stupid knife expect him to kill everybody else in the room as well?

"There has been . . . debate," said Paul, risking one sly look before returning to his study of the filthy floor-tiles. "Ironhand demands blood-vengeance for the murder of his man. But Sir Henri holds that since the two witnesses were also Ironhand's men, the . . . combat . . . was three-to-one and you are to be applauded for . . . knightly prowess. Especially since you were known to be as drunk as a lord . . .

"But . . . "

Little Paul held up a pale hand. "Furthermore, it has been found that you concealed a cat within these walls, in *express* defiance of my wishes. A cat that attacks men . . . we shall hang it, for an example."

"I have a cat too," said Sir Henri. "Does any man wish to hang *her*?" He looked round hopefully, thumb hooked through his belt by his sword.

Little Paul sighed, as if Sir Henri had made that remark several times before. "Why did you bring in a cat?"

Cam's mind cleared; he thought he saw a way out. "The cat led me to a hoard of money."

Paul's face lit up. "How much?"

"Six pennies and a gold piece."

The languid hand came out. Cam put two pennies into it. Paul looked pained.

"I spent some – on chicken and wine. And I gave the doorkeeper the gold piece to let me in." The last remark gave him great satisfaction; tit-for-tat, sneaky doorkeeper . . .

"Needless expense," said Paul. "Summon the doorkeeper immediately. Meanwhile, I fine you two pence for murdering Cragg . . . in a remarkable feat of drunken chivalry." He stole a glance at Ironhand and Sir Henri; who continued to glower. "Now we shall hang the cat. Bring leather gloves and nets."

Before Cam could draw breath, the whole crowd were flocking upstairs, a look of glee on their faces such as Cam had never seen before and hoped never to see again. He followed desperately, trying to push through to the front; but all he got was elbows in his face. Perhaps from the blows, tears were streaming down his face.

He tried, ridiculously, to send a warning to the cat with his mind; run, run, run!

"Softly," said Paul, as they reached the last flight of stairs. With a scuffle of leather, the mob reached Cam's door.

"Key?" whispered Paul. "I can have you searched, if you'd rather?" Two men gripped Cam by the elbows; he gave up the key reluctantly. Two small men donned helmets and great leather gloves. Others held a net ready.

If only I'd left my window open, thought Cam.

The key turned, the men went in; the net was laid over the door with baited breath. In a moment, that magnificent gold body would be writhing helplessly in its black meshes . . .

A little man came out, took off his helmet and gloves with an air of finality.

"Gone, worshipful sir! Fled!"

"Impossible!" said Paul, his face starting to work like a bowl of maggots.

"See for yourself."

Everyone crowded in. It was perfectly obvious. The window-catch had been pushed up; the window hung wide. A goblet had been knocked over on the windowsill; red wine dribbled down the wall like blood. And, outside the open window, on the inevitable narrow ledge, a trail of wine-dark pawprints led away to where they dried and faded out.

"You didn't say you'd left your window open," screeched Paul.

"I didn't."

"A cat couldn't push that catch up!"

"They're very *strong*." Cam had the joy of seeing Paul wince.

Once the room was finally empty, Cam locked the door and sat wearily on the bed. He would miss the cat.

A plaintive mew came from the canopy of the great four-poster. Looking up, he saw Smerdis looking down.

"You crafty sod!"

Smerdis purred violently, like canvas ripping.

"You took a risk!"

Smerdis distinctly looked to his right. Craning his neck, Cam saw, nearly concealed by the bed-canopy, a black hole in the ceiling. Freshly-clawed; clawmarks quite visible. And the hole led up into the inextricable maze of beams and rafters that held up the Palace roof . . .

"You crafty sod," Cam repeated, lost for words. He sat heavily on the bed. "You had it all worked out, didn't you?"

Purr.

Another thought struck Cam. It took *time* to claw a hole in a ceiling, push up a window-catch, spill wine, make footprints and return dry-footed. Hardly the work of a moment.

"You got my warning, then?"

Purr.

But Cam had only sent his warning when they were halfway up the stairs . . .

"You knew before that . . . you knew all the time?"

Smerdis purred agreeably and jumped down from the bed-top, in a shower of previously-concealed plaster.

Cam's mind reeled; it didn't bear thinking about . . . was he actually having a conversation with a magical beast?

But not even magic is as shocking the second time. Cam shrugged. There was nothing he could do about any of it. He quite suddenly got his appetite back, found himself ravenous. No harm in going down into the town to buy pasties.

But Cam had the last laugh. As Smerdis settled to his share of pasty, Cam strolled across to one whitewashed wall of the room. On it, with charcoal, he had made a huge crude drawing of the city. Now, pasty in one hand and charcoal in the other, he began to muse aloud.

"That house is searched, and empty. Dust thick on the floor – no new footprints." He drew a large black cross through that house. "And *that* house is owned by a widow. Who doesn't buy enough food to feed a sparrow, let alone a boy . . . " He drew another cross. "This city is a rabbit-warren, cat. And a madhouse. I shall be glad to finish my search, take my gold and go . . . we will search *here*, today."

Most of the houses were already crossed out. The dome of the Mausoleum was not crossed out . . .

"Let's go, cat!"

Cam turned; all he saw was a trail of pasty-crumbs on the floor.

It was Smerdis's turn to flee in horror.

17

"Cannot move Duke," sent Sehtek. "No-house safe. Men cannot hold-tongue."

"Cat-tongue smooths; man-tongue makes-crooked," sent Nibblefur piously.

"Smerdis must lead searching-man wrong way!"

"Cannot," sent Smerdis. "Too-wise."

"No man wiser-than Miw!" Indignant sends from all over the Mausoleum.

"This-one is."

Stony horror. Every ear laid back.

"Only one was ever wiser than Miw!"

"Who?" enquired Nibblefur, with great and malicious interest.

But Sehtek ignored her; swung round to a very old Matagot called Notep.

"Is there Wakening?" A shudder ran through the Miw.

"*They* still sleep," sent Notep. "They are dry. Dust." His send was very final.

Then Sehtek and Notep went into an intolerably long sending that no other Miw could fathom; it seemed hidden inside a cloud, though all knew it was very dreadful.

Finally, Notep walked across to Smerdis. A cold fear crept through Smerdis's strong bones. For Notep was awesome beyond all Matagot. So old his black fur was tipped with silver, not gold. He moved very slow and stately, from stiffness of the joints.

"Can you hold the mind of this man?" asked Notep.

"No . . . not all-time . . . Too-strong." It was hard to admit, before all the Miw.

"Has this man sent you a sending?"

"Yes," said Smerdis, remembering Cam's mind-shattering warning, that had come just as he was clawing the hole in the ceiling. "Yes."

Notep's old eyes were terrible, for they watched through a milky cloud that came from being too long in the dark.

"Smerdis," sent Sehtek. "Go with Notep. It is better that you make the Journey now."

Smerdis trembled. Only Notep's family ever made the Journey. Knowledge of the Underwalk passed from father to son. Only Notep could make it. And, when the time came, one other . . .

The thought was unthinkable.

"Not me," sent Smerdis. "Not me . . . Khufu . . . Sehtek . . . Amon . . . "

"*Go with Notep*!"

Smerdis looked desperately round at all his friends. But all his friends drew back.

He followed Notep humbly out of the Mausoleum.

They went a way no man could follow. A lion-head was set in the paving, at the corner of Palace Square. Few men realised it was a lion-head; it was so worn with the feet of centuries. The outlet for a drain. When it rained, water gushed from its mouth.

The two cats entered the drain. Far in, an earthshaking had split it, the year Charlemagne became king of the Franks. The cats descended the fissure, covering their fur with green slime. They gained a cave where flint axes tinkled underfoot and painted animals ran forever round the walls, stained black with the soot of ancient fires. Further on, where the caves had collapsed, they had to drag themselves through a crack so narrow that Smerdis thought he must remain there forever.

Down and down they went, where mice ceased to squeak and dark-lizards ceased to run; where all was black, and the sound of water dripping.

They stopped by a door.

"Is this where They sleep?" asked Smerdis, trembling.

"This is where the First and Second sleep."

"Must we go in?"

"The roof is fallen. They lie beneath a blanket of stone."

They passed, and came to a second door.

"Here?"

"No. Too shrunken, though wonderfully preserved. You would not recognise . . . "

They passed to a third door. Crept under it.

Smerdis stared hard; stood trembling a long time.

"Yes," he said finally.

"Come. You have much to learn, because you have much to teach."

Cam spent a miserable day alone. He knew he was being stupid; what did a cat matter?

But the sky was grey, and it rained. Everything seemed pointless without the cat.

Long before dusk, he crept under his cloak and tried to sleep. Do I really prefer cats to men? he thought, dreamily.

But all was forgotten when, as the town clock struck midnight, there was a scrabbling on stone outside, and a loud purr, and a furry form leapt on to the bed.

The world was whole again.

18

Miw teach without words.

Smerdis went with him everywhere; vanishing through the hole in the ceiling before he unlocked his door in the morning; joining him effortlessly as he mingled with the crowd in Palace Square.

The men of the city began first to nod to him, then greet him warmly, then even invite him into their houses for a leather bottle of ale. Cam couldn't understand it. He never realised it was the cat's doing; ancient memories were awakening. Few men had ever walked through that city with a golden cat as a constant companion . . .

Smerdis taught Cam the meaning of loss; led him through looted houses where the shutters banged and the children's toys lay broken on the floor.

Taught him the past. Led him into the sewers, and the secret ways through the rock. To church crypts where banks of candles flickered before the skulls of dead men who were not forgotten. Where relics of saints were housed in glass-and-gold caskets so thick with dust that you couldn't tell if they held toe- or finger-bones.

Taught him the present; how the city held four villages under its wings. Morville to the south, Harcourt to the north, Beauly to the east and little Hadel to the west. And the great roads running north, south, east, west, full of rich carts and baggage-trains passing within bowshot of the city.

Taught him the future. The churchyard where children chanted strange rhymes while they bounced a ball against the tombstones of the great. Cam found the children's games very strange. Once, a child picked up a striped cat and ran at the other children. The children ran hither and thither screaming enjoyably until the poor cat escaped.

The churchyard became Cam's sanctuary, when his feet grew weary . . .

The church wall kept out the wind; glowed golden in the sun. He put his back against the warm stone of a box-tomb and listened to the quiet; the chirr of grasshoppers among the thin dying grass, that forced its way up between the tombstones and scattered bleached seeds across them as it died. The seeds blew round in tiny circles as the stray breeze caught them . . . like the dust-devils he'd seen the golden cats chasing, in that funny vision in the Mire . . . Strange. He dozed.

And was wakened by the excited giggling of children. Thought at first they were plotting something against him. But when he peered out their attention was all on each other. They hadn't spotted him.

He watched across the tomb-tops, furtively. A crowd of boys round one girl. He wondered whether he ought to interfere . . . but they were only dressing-up. Old bits of curtain hung round their necks for cloaks; wooden swords that were only two bits of stick nailed together.

They broke up; most of the boys came whooping across the tomb-tops and out over the churchyard wall. Leaving the girl and one boy.

The girl had a cloak too; but longer, right down to her feet. And finer, in a tawdry way. Threads of tattered gold glittered in the sun. More startling, she was wearing a parchment mask with slanted eyeholes and big pointed ears, and curling black whiskers crudely drawn.

The boy wore the same sort of cat-mask; but he was stripped to his ragged breeches. Below, his bare shins and feet were blackened with soot. His thin bare chest was blackened too; but little round bare patches of white skin had been left. His wooden sword was twice as long, with *two* pieces nailed across, instead of one. He climbed on to a flat tomb-top; rubbed his bare feet across the green surface, kicking off bits of moss in all directions. Getting a good foothold.

The girl stood against the church wall behind him, well out of the way. Together, they stared down the churchyard, motionless, eyes hidden inside the dark, blank eyeholes of the masks. Eerie, despite their shoddiness. The stillness and the sunlight . . .

The boy suddenly held his sword high above his head and shouted, in a shrill carrying treble, "Wrecks, I gypped us some!"

Immediately, a screaming horde of boys returned, leaping over the wall and charging across the tombs.

It looked a foregone conclusion; but the masked boy whirled his long sword two-handed, round and round his head, round and round his legs. Nobody could touch him. And as his sword touched others, they died instantly and completely, sprawling loose limbs across the tomb-tops, heads hanging over the edge, staring glassily at the sky. One child, thus collapsed, stared straight at Cam; but he didn't move, or even grin. His face stayed absolutely expressionless. He really did look dead; mouth open, flies crawling over his face, and he didn't even twitch his nose . . .

By this time, half the attackers were laid low. The rest fled everywhere, ducking and dodging between the tombs, giggling with glee. The cat-masked boy chased them down, one by one. And as his sword touched them, they lay quite still.

Total stillness. The masked boy turned to Cam, mistaking him for a last foe. When he saw he wasn't, he turned without a word and faced the girl still standing against the church wall.

"Wrecks, I gypped us some!"

She still didn't move.

Then he ripped off his mask, all the dead came back to life, and the churchyard was just full of curtained children carrying sticks.

Who gathered round the girl and stared suspiciously at Cam.

Curiosity drew him across. "What game were you playing?"

Silence.

Cam held up two pennies . . .

The leader grabbed. Cam held them high out of reach.

"What game were you playing?"

The boy looked at the pennies, then at Cam. He licked his lips; he was pathetically thin. In his mind he was already turning the pennies into food. Cam decided to give them the money, whether they spoke up or not.

"Who are you supposed to be?" he coaxed.

"I am the Seroster!"

"And who are all these?"

"Evil-men!"

The evil-men pulled terrible faces at Cam, dragging down their mouths with their fingers, pulling down the skin under their eyes, to show just how evil they were . . .

"And who is she?" The girl was still standing motionless, still wearing her mask. Uneasy, Cam held out the two pennies to her, just to see her move.

She didn't take them; the dark eyeholes stared at Cam, expressionlessly.

"Who is she?"

They all pressed their lips together. Cam tried a new tack.

"Is it an *old* game?"

"We just made it up . . . "

"What's this?" Cam indicated the bare white circles on the boy's chest.

"Soot," said the boy. "Soot and lard."

"No – I mean – what does it *stand* for?"

"Dunno," said the boy. But his eyes flicked at Cam's own chest.

Cam looked down; saw his own jerkin, black with shining steel studs sewn on, big and round as pennies.

"Is it meant to be like my jerkin?"

"Dunno." The boy grabbed the coins from Cam's relaxing hand. "Pasties, lads!"

The gang, waving their swords, made off across the tombstones and down the alley. Cam watched them go, then turned back to the girl.

She was gone.

Cam walked to the wall that looked out over the ramparts to a high blue view. Smerdis walked with him. Cam leaned his arms on the sun-warmed parapet. "This city is a madhouse, cat! I've checked every house and I swear the father-slayer is in none of them. Like trying to find a dead man among the living. What could be harder? Oh, finding a living man among the dead, I suppose. Hey . . . " he smote his hand against his forehead, "why didn't I think . . . where is the Mausoleum where the Duke's family are buried? Must check . . . "

But the day was warm and lazy; more for dreaming than doing. "When I find the father-slayer, cat, I shall go home to England and buy a manor, with a stone tower and a duck-pond. And I shall be lord, and you shall be lord of the rats and mice . . . I shall allow you three wives, no more . . . "

Surprised by the lack of response, he turned.

Smerdis was gone, flying on velvet feet.

"Funny . . . !" But the day was warm, and he went on dreaming.

19

It was ending.

They'd been in sight of the city since dawn. Now they were dropping down the broken slope above Hadel, still keeping their old order of march. Natural as breathing, now.

They weren't the same cats. Twice the weight, after so many days of red meat; tails up, they swaggered. Fed themselves; owed nothing to man. There'd been no more deaths. They'd killed two buzzards who'd tried to help themselves to growing kittens. Tornear's way – follow the shadow, pounce . . .

Soon they'd be scattered throughout the city, forgetting each other, never to be of one mind again.

He didn't want to see them scavenging for bacon-rind in the ginnels; begging at doors in the hard frosts. He *pitied* the Brethren of the city now . . .

He crushed down that impious thought. Halted the host well above the village. As they fell to washing, he sent to Sehtek confidently, right across the valley, "Returned! Bring-you many-children!"

Her reply was surprisingly weak and crotchety. Where had all these Brethren come from? Why had he brought them? Hadn't she enough to care for? Finally, "Come-alone! Be-careful!"

"Why?"

She wouldn't reply.

He refused to enter alone. So many cats together would have made a fine show . . . a little indiscreet, perhaps? Still, he would take Ripfur. And Splayfoot, to show him the promised land.

They loped down the track, Ripfur and Splayfoot dropping back a respectful distance. As they approached the gate, he was surprised to see it shut, with only the little postern open . . .

A group of men gathered before the postern, gabbling, arguing. Then a ginger man picked up a rotten orange, fallen from the vegetable-women's baskets.

If that man eats that orange, he will be very sick, thought Amon.
Then the man threw the orange. It hit the ground at Amon's feet, splashing foul pulp into his face.
With Ripfur watching. And Splayfoot, seeing the promised city for the first time.
Rage seized Amon. After all that long Miw-march . . . he would not have retreated from the gate, if the orange had been a crossbow-bolt. He walked on steadily.
The unfu ginger man had a crossbow, now.
Amon did not hurry. But as the man began to raise the weapon, Amon sent his biggest hate-sending yet.
The man put the crossbow-bolt straight through his own foot; doubled-up screaming; began rolling down the hillside in agony.
Amon walked straight past. The rest stood well aside.
Behind, Ripfur and Splayfoot slunk off; Ripfur knew an easier way . . .
Amon walked on, into his city. How it stank; his nose wrinkled in disgust. How narrow the alleys! The tall houses oppressed him. Was this the vision that had kept so many alive in the wilderness? Suddenly he longed for the wilderness, the dry earth underfoot, the clean breeze, the absence of men. The pressure of men's minds was all round him, an unfu, squabbling, bickering chaos. Why had the Miw allowed such disorder? Amon sent to the men to be silent, as he might have sent to the kittens in the wilderness. The men's minds fell to a confused whimper. Then started up twice as riotously, full of outraged surprise.
Amon made his way up on to the walls, to get a clean breeze and a distant view.
There he met his brother Smerdis walking.
With a man.
His friend from the Mire . . . he leapt forward to greet them.
"Not-now," sent Smerdis sharply. How thin and yellow he looked; even bent a little. There was a flicker of desperation in his mind, of chaos, that had never been there before.
The friend from the Mire strode past, without a glance . . . was *nothing* straight in this city, today? It was as if a dreadful grey mist stood between him and all he loved. As if he, Amon, should not *be* here. Nothing fitted together any more . . .
Then he remembered the star-drifted faces of the three Matagot. Warning . . . warning that the stars were shifting their courses against him.

You will regret, to your life's end . . .

A gut-shrinking terror seized Amon; he turned to run after the two whom he loved. But they had vanished as if into the same grey mist; he could no longer sense them.

Further along the wall, Sehtek called. Wretchedly he shook his ears and trotted on.

Much later, he squeezed his massive shoulders with difficulty out of the privy-pipe. Following Ripfur and Splayfoot, he felt soiled all over. Could have spent a day washing . . .

They trotted back towards Hadel.

"Sorry you cannot-live city," he sent to Splayfoot. "I am forsworn . . ."

Splayfoot splayed his ears philosophically. "Cliffs better than dead. I like-cliffs."

"Till winter . . ."

"Will try winter-cliffs. Deep-cave. Warm-nest. Bird-die. Sheep-die. Much-prey."

Amon searched Splayfoot's mind diligently.

Splayfoot really meant it.

"No-men," Splayfoot added.

Amon could have wept, for the lost friendship of cats and men.

20

Smerdis led Cam to a street by the city-wall, that he hadn't bothered with before. The houses were roofless; only birds lived there, passing in and out of glassless windows. Yellow flowers sprouted from the cobbles; long grasses blew on the wall-tops. Even the children never came, and it was very quiet. The life of the city sounded no louder than the hum of a distant hive.

Smerdis stopped in front of a bricked-up Norman window and a little green door. Cam's heart leapt. The father-slayer?

But the green door hadn't been used in a long time. There was a tit's nest in the round ring of the door-handle.

Cam removed the nest carefully. The handle was so rusty it took all his strength to turn.

Inside had once been a tall house. Now, like the rest, open to the sky. Only damp holes where the rafters had sat. And a blackened fireplace with a coat-of-arms painted faintly on the crumbling plaster; a grinning cat's-head. The motto might have been 'Amie Deschats'.

But Cam couldn't be sure.

The floor was carpeted in moss, spreading from cracks in the stones. Smerdis walked to the far corner and began to scratch at the moss, sending it flying in all directions, rolling like green balls. Then he stood and mewed.

One floor-slab had a ring set in it. Smerdis, standing in the middle of that slab, mewed again.

The ring was so thin with rust Cam feared it might break. As he heaved, it cut his hands. But the slab lifted and a great strange smell swept past Cam's face. Not the smell of damp and decay, mildew and slime, but of dry dust. Very old, very sad, and yet sweet. Dust of leather and flowers and ancient laughter. Cam felt so glad he could have cried, if that hadn't been stupid.

A stair led down. Smerdis vanished into the dark with a twist of tail. Down and down he led, twisting and turning into the heart of the rock. Cam groped from step to step. He might have felt afraid; but the scent of ancient laughter grew stronger, and Smerdis's eyes glimmed green, looking back at every turn.

At last, a trickle of light crawled up the rough walls towards him. And then a glowing fiery cross. Cam caught his breath; then laughed. It was only the forgotten sun, shining through the kind of arrowslit that lets an archer fire up, down, right and left. This must be an old part of the city's defences.

By the arrowslit, another green door; a double-door, with a gap at the bottom and a pair of silver cat-head handles, tied together with silver wire.

Smerdis mewed a third time; demanding he open the door. Cam paused, looking at the cat-head handles. They reminded him of the knife . . . another trap?

But what could be worse than living with that knife? Perhaps, just perhaps, this was the knife's home. He could leave it and be free . . . And still the smell of ancient happiness blew to him from under the door.

Somehow knowing his life would never be the same again, he undid the silver wire. You cannot stand in front of even the strangest door for ever. He took a deep breath and went in.

A spacious room, carved from the rock, with a great glassless window over which ivy trailed and fell to the floor. By the window were two birds, a thrush and a hawk. The thrush turned his eye, chirruped and flew away into the boundless blue that lay beyond the window.

The hawk did not move. Its eye regarded Cam steadfastly, its claws embedded deep in its leather-covered perch. He walked over and touched it. It moved slightly, with a dry rustling, sending up a cloud of golden dust that danced in the sunlight. It was dead; stuffed perhaps. Yet it looked more alive than any stuffed bird he'd ever seen.

His eyes roved the room. A rich room, almost a king's room. The room of a man held in honour. On a table, chessmen carved in black-and-white stone sat, in an unfinished game. Cam could see the next move white should make . . . Alongside, an odd-shaped wine-bottle whose contents had dried to red powder. The walls were hung with banners, and weapons shining and rustless, and an unsheathed two-handed sword lay balanced against a chair as if someone had just put it down.

He put his hands round the handle of the sword. Only then did he see the battered cat-head on the hilt . . . by then he could not remove his hands. Tighter and tighter he clutched the silver-bound hilt. Slowly, as warmth and strength flowed into him, he raised his arms above his head, taking the sword with them until it stood vertical, its point scraping against the high ceiling. His lungs filled, and he shouted, "Seroster! Seroster!"

The echoes of his own voice took so long to die they frightened him.

"Seroster! Seroster! Seroster!" The echoes were all different; some desperate, some triumphant, some pleading. Memories came flooding back; the smoke of burning houses, war-horses neighing.

Memories of things that had never happened to him. An avenue of tall broken trees; a gate with twin flat towers, carved with the figures of men. Behind the gatehouse, a temple burning.

The avenue was littered with dead; many in bronze breastplates and red cloaks, with red-crested helms beside them. But more were brown and naked, save for short white kilts. And among them lay the pitifully-hacked bodies of golden cats; yet they had red stains around claws distended in death.

People ran hither and thither, wailing. The only order was in a thin line of golden cats, many limping, that made their way down towards a quay, where old ships waited, sails already up. Slowly the trail of cats ascended the gangplanks and men with them. Then the ships, high in prow and stern, cast off, and the sky became dark . . .

Cam dropped the sword with a clang, and the memories faded.

The cats rubbed against his legs approvingly. Wanting him to have the sword.

But there was something more to his right.

He did not want to look; but he had to.

In a shadowed alcove, half-hidden by a rich hanging, were three beds.

Something lay on two of them.

He wanted to run away; but his legs took him slowly across.

On two of the beds lay the bodies of men. The first was in chainmail, which had weighed down his body so terribly that chest-bone and hip-bones stood up like rocks from the grey sea of mail. The man's head lay on his helm; dead, but not fearful to look at; neither ghoul nor skull. More like the head of a man who is lean and brown with the sun, whose muscles stand out like rope when he works. Only thinner, more rope-like, more leathery. His eyes were closed; his grey hair cropped like a warrior's. His smile a little grim, a little humorous, and full of peace at duty done.

He had died in honour.

The body of a golden cat lay curled on his chest; and his hands lay gently upon it.

The second man was clad in armour of a later time; intricately engraved plate-armour and velvet surcoat. Another silent cat lay on his chest.

And his face was similar. Calm, shrewd, assessing, with a grim humour. And Cam knew that face somehow, that assessing look.

He turned to the third bed.

It was empty; just leather cross-straps. Waiting. On its foot was carved one word, "Seroster".

And that name was carved on the foot of the other two beds also.

Those faces . . . Where had he seen that shrewd assessing look before? Almost every day, somewhere . . .

He crinkled up his own face in thought. And then he knew. Somehow the faces were his own face; the face he saw every time he looked in a mirror.

The third bed was waiting for him; and for the cat that was even now twining round his legs in ecstasy.

His head was whirling. Suddenly he knew every nook and cranny of the city. Not just the ones the cat had shown him, but others that had lain empty and forgotten for an age.

He had a feeling of changing; of becoming someone other. He snatched the blacksmith's blank letter from his pouch; opened it. It seemed blank still, for a moment, then writing began to swim out at him from the crumpled vellum.

"To the Seroster, greetings. You should be glad . . . "

He was becoming the Seroster. He would lie here dead, mourned and honoured by all. It had all been meant, from the beginning . . .

Then a crying squalling thing leapt in terror within him, as the grey curtains of certain knowledge closed round.

"I am Cam" he shouted. "Cam, Cam, CAM!"

But his voice did not echo now in the chamber. It fell dead like a shot bird. Dead like the dust.

He kicked out at the sword, and sent it spinning. "I am *Cam*. I live in England. I have a father, mother, two brothers and a dog called Maunciple. I am going home, and I shall never leave it again as long as I live. Cam, Cam, CAM!"

And he blundered up the stairs in the dark, leaving behind a cat that looked after him with eyes of sad, deadly regret.

He reached the open air, slammed the trapdoor down viciously. If the cat loved dead men so much, it could spend the rest of its life with them . . . and leave him alone.

The painted cat above the fireplace leered at him. It, too, had once been golden. The motto mocked him: 'Amie Deschats'. The friend of cats.

He ran out of the evil, roofless house, slamming the green door even harder.

A scavenger was passing with his cart. The iron-shod wheels ground on the cobbles. The scavenger was fat, dirty and had black pimples on his nose. But Cam loved him, for he was part of the *real* world.

Cam walked and walked; looked at the children playing and old men scratching; drinking up the ordinariness of everything. The sun was warm on his back and it was good.

But every cat he met looked him full in the face. Not accusing, just . . . expectant.

He shivered. It wasn't just the cats. He was knowing things he shouldn't know; *couldn't* know. That in the house he was passing, a man was writhing with toothache (though he could hear nothing). That up in the Palace, Little Paul was counting again his vast hoard of pennies. That on the far western slope of the city a usurper-patrol was plundering a house, and that the men of the city watched them silently, raging within . . .

And he knew that the golden cat was no longer trapped underground with the dead, but worming its way up into the light, looking for him.

Rubbish! he thought, shaking his head till his long, black, greasy hair fell into his eyes. Yet the knowings, minute by minute, grew realler; more real than that housewife arguing with her fishmonger. The rock below him was not solid, but hollow like a cheese tunnelled by maggots.

And the cat underground still followed.

But if he knew all this, he must also know where the father-slayer was hidden.

It only took a moment's concentration; in that octagonal building, of course. He'd half-known it for days. But that sodding cat had led his mind away, fooled him like a mazeling. Finding him gold . . . cheering him up by playing with a leaf . . . it hadn't been friendship, just trickery.

He didn't owe the cat a thing.

Right. Seize the father-slayer. Up to the Palace with him. Screw the reward out of Paul, grab his own hidden gold and *go*.

He ran to the Mausoleum. In vain the Miw-guard met him. They were in confusion. Some tried still to lure him away with feeble tricks. Others fawned on him. Some even tried to attack him, but he pulled out the knife, and they fell back, more confused than ever.

He leapt for the low roof; ran up it, sending roof-tiles slithering down to crash into the depths; crawled in through the broken window.

He hung on the windowframe, getting his eyes used to the darkness within. And in that darkness Sehtek sensed the peril in him, the confusion, the seeds of disaster. Mastering the Duke, she led him to a window that gave out on to the ledge running round the outside of the city wall. She was still getting the Duke on to the windowsill when Cam saw them.

He scrambled down the high tombs; ran across the broken floor, scattering floor-tiles before him. Reached out for the Duke's leg, as the Duke struggled out of the window. A wild joy leapt through Cam; he'd *done* it; the impossible again; earned the reward . . .

Too late he sensed the other cat behind.

Smerdis's heart was breaking. He loved Cam. He'd been Chosen, as Cam had been Chosen.

But it had all gone wrong. He had done something the wrong way. His mind had been stuffed too full of the old meaningless learning. He didn't understand the minds of men. Why hadn't they chosen Amon?

All over. But one thing left to do. A ruined Seroster was worse than no Seroster. While he lived, no other could come . . .

He launched himself at the ruined Seroster, framed in the window.

Cam never had a chance. He only had a light grip on the windowframe as he groped for the Duke with his other hand. Thirty pounds of flying cat carried him out through the window, and he was falling, falling . . .

In midair, he grasped the cat to him, as he had so often done on waking in the mornings. And the cat relaxed its claws; even a slight purr.

Smerdis watched the clouds, turning, turning. Then something was beating at him; the sound of tearing branches . . .

Then suddenly he was in the prow of a boat, thrusting across pale water. Behind, the morning-wind sighed in the great-bellied sail; the boat's prow dipped, and the blue water chuckled beneath it. And the disc of Re was shining in his face, bathing his eyes with light.

They drew to shore; towers, shady trees.

And under the trees, a great company of Miw gathered; more than Smerdis had ever seen together in one place.

It was his own old sending of the Former Days; but not blurred now. Every detail clear, every ripple on the water, every flicker of leaf in the morning-breeze. Even the fur blowing into rings, on the flanks of the Miw. And Meni his dead mother was there, and old Sebi his grandfather.

I dream, thought Smerdis.

As the boat touched land, the assembled Miw raised a paw in greeting.

Welcome, Smerdis! Hail Smerdis, hero!

But I have *failed* . . . thought Smerdis.

But still the Miw rejoiced in him. And beyond, among the trees and beneath the towers, some Miw greater than all Miw rejoiced.

Welcome Smerdis. Welcome the First!

But I *failed* . . .

The rejoicing continued.

Far above the Mausoleum, on the ramparts of the citadel, the watchman had seen a man thrown to his death by a golden cat. He ran to ring the great alarm-bell.

21

Cam opened his eyes. Why was the sky below his feet? Rocks and fields above his head? Sharp spears sticking into him all over?

Something warned him to keep still, in spite of the pain.

He was caught in a tree, upside-down. Far above, on the city-wall, heads and spears were moving in busy groups.

Gingerly, he moved his left leg. It still worked, right down to the toes. He wriggled his fingers and arched his back, so vigorously he almost fell on to the rocks below.

His body was unbroken.

It took a long time to get to the ground. But he was whole, apart from bruises and a long cat-scratch on his cheek. He looked round for Smerdis.

Smerdis had not shared in the miracle. His head waggled loosely and his fur was roughed-up in a way you never see in life. Cam couldn't stroke it smooth, no matter how much he tried. He spent a long time, stroking or just sitting, before he realised what he must do. There would never be a third Seroster now. But there had been a third Seroster's cat, brave unto death like all the others. He deserved to lie in his own place.

Cam set off for the hidden stair that led to Seroster's Dwelling. Crying so much, he didn't even wonder how he knew it was there. But he easily found the entrance among the tumbled rocks, and climbed the narrow winding passage. He moved in total darkness, without even a free hand to touch the walls. But he seemed to know every step of the way.

In the Dwelling, nothing had changed. The two-handed sword still lay on the floor, where he had kicked it. The hawk still watched him with its bright eye. The chessmen had not moved.

When he laid the cat on the leather thongs of the third bed, an odd thing happened. It did not live again, but the terrible untidiness of death left it. Slowly its body curled, the fur smoothed to normal. After a while it looked just asleep like the other two cats.

Cam sat; got up and wandered about fingering things, and sat again. Nothing happened. There was nothing more *to* happen. The only thing to do was go.

Nobody saw the hunched and miserable figure make its way down the scree below the cliff. They had come out of the city and searched for the body and found nothing. Their worries were all inside the city now . . .

Nobody noticed, not even Cam in his misery, that he carried on his shoulder, like a pick or shovel, the sword of Seroster.

All over the city that night, cats crouched in hiding. Most went underground, into the slimy clefts, and were safe. The foolish, the old, the helpless, hid above-ground and were hunted down. The fury of that hunt passed all belief; for a cat had been seen to kill a man.

Night long, by flaring torches, the massacre went on. A sister in Well Street tried to save her kittens by hiding them in a bread-oven; they were thrown down the well and drowned. Old Crumple-tooth, sixteen years old and near-blind, was beaten to death on the floor of the Bleeding Wolf. Georges' life was only saved because he was too astounded to stop them. But afterwards, Georges' son cried all night and would not be comforted.

"Coward!" he screamed at his father. "Coward! Why didn't you save him?"

Georges bit his lip. A prudent man puts his profits first so long . . . but when his son calls him coward . . . Next day, Georges told his lads to pack their bags, and take the swords off the wall permanent. He began to look for a chance to do them at the Palace *real* harm.

There were fair deeds that night, as well as foul. Sir Henri sat till dawn outside the door of his locked room; the key on a string round his neck inside his armour, his moustached jaw resting on the hilt of his drawn sword. Ironhand sent three men for Castlemew early. Sir Henri did not raise his head; merely opened his eyes . . .

The three men went away without a word.

Ironhand returned in a rage, with six.

Sir Henri opened his eyes again. Ironhand saw his own death in them; smashed one of his followers to the floor with a single blow and went away, saying he had more to do than wait all night for a single cat . . . For Ironhand was foremost in the massacre of Brethren.

The Miw had vanished without trace, the moment Smerdis died. But once safe, they knew they could not abandon the Brethren. They sallied forth again, and Sehtek, and the Miw-lord Khufu discovered the power of the heb-Miw for themselves, and saved many. Sehtek, pale under the moon, seemed immune to crossbow-bolts. But the Lord Khufu was not so lucky.

By morning, fifty cats had died, and eight men lay cold upon the stones. No man hunts cats across the rooftops with impunity. Some were led on where rafters were weak; some where stone crumbled.

The Lord Khufu was the last to die. At dawn he hid, wounded and bleeding, high on the roofs in the centre of a great chimney-stack. The usurpers gathered, wondering if he were dead or not. Ironhand swore that if he still lived, he would be flayed alive, and his golden skin nailed to the church door. Ironhand called for men to climb and bring the hidden foe down.

No man answered; they had learnt their lesson. But Ironhand offered five gold pieces, then ten. Then the son of Ironhand, Ironhead, began to climb. Not for love of his father, for he had none, but for the gold. Two went with him, to share the reward.

The dying Khufu waited.

As the three men approached up the roof, slipping and slithering and beating upon the tiles with their swords to scare him out, he gathered himself for a last mousing.

Ironhead shouted to the Miw to show himself. Not because he thought the cat would understand, but to impress his father and the men behind, and keep up his own courage.

The Lord Khufu waited until Ironhead was but six feet away, then leapt most lovingly into his arms . . .

Cat and men rolled down the roof together, in an avalanche of tiles. Fell together to the cobbles, far below. Two more were killed by their falling bodies, and a sharp-edged roof-tile cut the crest from Ironhand's helm. So Khufu missed mousing his greatest foe by the width of a shaving.

Khufu blinked once, regretfully, and died. But men murmured that Ironhand had paid others to do what he feared to do himself. Sent his eldest son, pride of his line. That the brave cat had outfaced him and set him at nought. From that time, the fear of Ironhand began to decay in men's hearts. If a mere cat . . .

Khufu would be remembered.

If any remained to remember him. For no cat save Castlemew dared walk above-ground. Crossbowmen watched every catwalk.

Cats could survive in the sewers for a time, for there water dripped and there was prey of sorts. And narrow fissures that the smaller cats would worm down, to find rats and mice in the country around.

But cats need the sun; and there were too many of them. And five humans crouched in the sewers as well. For them, if they remained, there was no hope.

22

When Cam descended the stair he simply wanted to go away. But he soon came to forks in the path.

And there are never any signposts which simply say 'Away'. Every time he had to decide which way to turn he lost his temper; it was an intolerable burden. In the end he was just turning this way and that, without thinking.

He would go home. Pictures of his plump mother baking, his grey-haired father sitting at table, his brothers playing, filled his head like rosy clouds. But a cold wind of memory soon blew them away. It was his mother's nagging, his father's interest in nothing but money, his brothers' constant bickering that had driven him from home in the first place.

He missed the cat unbearably. The feel of its tail against his legs, the purring in the night. He had lost reward, his own buried money, his dream of buying a manor, the friendship of all cats and all men of the city. He had lost the chance to become Seroster. He remembered with bitter memory the two men who lay in the Dwelling, who were safe now from disgrace and hatred, poverty, rain and hunger. How happy to be dead with honour! How he *wished* to lie with them . . .

Such morbid thoughts, together with throwing himself on the ground in remorse, gazing at his own tragic reflection in wayside pools, leaning his fevered brow against the rough bark of trees and composing gloomy and noble poems in his head, occupied him till dark.

The most frightening thing was that he belonged nowhere.

Yet that had never bothered him before.

When, at last, night and aching legs and a rumbling belly brought him back to himself, he found he'd been wandering in circles. He was again within a short distance of Seroster's Stair. He moved along the cliff further (having suddenly lost all taste for sleeping with the dead) and then, worn out, wrapped himself in his cloak and fell asleep with his head on a stone pillow.

Three times he wakened, to see the moon caught in the branches of the dead tree overhead. Each time he'd dreamt that Smerdis was alive, and wriggling in under his cloak. He seemed to grope for a cat just departed. Its purring seemed to echo in his ears; its warmth and smell lingered inside the cloak. Once, looking along the cliff, he thought he saw a cat sitting watching him. But when he rubbed his eyes, it was gone.

These maunderings were brought to a sudden close by a shower of roof-tiles. He leapt for cover. Then something landed with a softer thump; a black-and-grey cat with an arrow right through it. He picked it up. It gave one faint mew and died, leaving a trickle of blood from its mouth down his hand.

More tiles. The city-wall above echoed with shouts. Two more dead cats. Cam hid his face; the cats were being massacred and it was his fault. Somehow, the Seroster would have saved them.

Then came a dead man, neck broken and a stupid smile on his face. Cam didn't wait for more; set off for home with a real determination now. He'd put ten miles between him and the accursed city before morning . . . ship . . . Marseilles . . .

But though the moon was up, mist had risen and filled every hollow. He was soon hopelessly lost.

Two days later, he was still within sight of the city. At first wildly, then coolly and calmly, and finally despairingly, he'd tried to get away. But it was always the same. As soon as he left the main road, the countryside turned against him. There was always a bramble-thicket where he wanted to pass. Or sounds of combat. Or he thought a cat was lurking in the undergrowth. He was growing mortally afraid of cats.

And the main road was alive, night and day, with little bands of armed men who fought frequently, at least as far as shouting threats and loosing arrows was concerned. One lot, from the city, he increasingly hated. The other lot, with their crude new cat-head banners, he increasingly expected to hate him. So, though he nearly starved, he didn't dare beg a crust from either.

He would have starved to death, crouched in some ditch, but for the food he found. Every so often, at dawn or dark, he'd find a rough packet containing a half-eaten bannock, or rasher of bacon.

At first, he thought the warring bands must have dropped them.

But they came too regularly. And, on the soft ground around, he sometimes found pawmarks. The food was never more than a cat could steal and carry away.

The cats were keeping him. Like a prisoner . . .

It drove him to one last wild desperate effort. One dusk he left the sword lying against a tree-trunk, and all night forced his way through brambles, up cliffs, wormed past the sounds of battle, entered thickets he was sure were full of cats, and found none. It was a clear starry night, and always he kept the Pole Star at his back.

By dawn, he found himself clear, alone in the red desert. Thirsty, starving, but free.

Until he saw the white horse. It looked bigger, standing clear on the red soil; its legs were white, free of the mud of the swamp. But it still looked like a king . . .

He walked towards it unafraid. Called to it, with some vague hope of getting a ride on its back . . .

It stood still as a statue, watching him, its head turned to one side.

Then it pawed the earth. And came at him.

Oh no, not *that* again, he thought. He stood quite still, with his eyes shut.

It hit him straight on . . .

When he came to his senses, he thought every bone in his body was broken. The horse had backed off, and stood watching him.

Then it came at him again.

Rage seized him; he drew the knife, his wrist curling back . . .

The horse didn't waver in its gallop . . .

He threw with all his strength . . .

The knife stuck to the ends of his fingers, like a toffee-apple at a fair . . .

The horse hit him again . . .

He could hardly walk at all now; but while he walked back towards the city, the hated creature left him alone. Only he was walking sideways, too, towards the white cliffs that bordered the valley.

The horse couldn't follow him up the near-vertical cliff . . . but of course it was too stupid to know that. Already he was eyeing the cliff, looking for footholds.

He saw the best place; a gully full of jutting holds; easy, even when you were bruised all over. As he was passing the foot of the gully, he made a sudden run for it, up the broken scree. The scree slid beneath his feet; it was like running up a treadmill. But the scree hampered the horse too; he could hear its panting and slithering above his own.

Then he was on the first footholds. Just in time. He felt the horse rear up behind him; felt its bared teeth nip his backside; saw its great hoofs flail to left and right of him. Then he was safe. The horse's whinny of rage echoed and trumpeted up the gully . . .

He climbed steadily, easily. And still the horse trumpeted its frustration. He laughed. Hard luck, horse . . .

Until a shower of tiny stones came bouncing from above . . .

He looked up.

Another white horse stood silhouetted in the top of the gully. White horse on white rock. It stamped, and another, bigger shower of stones came pelting down.

He looked down. There were three horses at the base of the cliff, now. Quiet, waiting.

Suddenly, he knew they would kill him, if he went on trying to get away.

When he got to the bottom, they stood aside to let him pass. Towards the city. They followed him quietly enough, even mouthing at the odd tuft of dried vegetation. But he knew he was being driven, like a sheep to market.

They left him at a tree-stump he seemed to recognise; the sword was lying against it . . .

Each day his will grew weaker. And it seemed to him the will of the sword grew stronger. It was the mightiest weapon he had ever seen. With steel rings round the hilt to guard the hands, and curling tines halfway down the blade to catch opponents' swords (a two-handed swordsman carries no shield). An ancient weapon, twin to the knife. A ridiculous weapon; nobody used two-handed swords any more . . .

But he still carried it cautiously on his shoulder, like a spade. For he didn't like to touch the black pitch handle, bound with silver wire, to get a better grip. For then, the visions returned, with greater violence; the sounds of battle, the smell of burning. A quick fierce energy flowed through his muscles . . .

And when he came back to himself, the ground would be littered with the trunks of trees, cut straight through. How could *his* muscles do such things?

Once more he tried leaving the sword behind . . . he should have learnt that lesson from the knife. After that, he carried it with no further protest. In fact, the next day he stopped hoping for anything. He sat with his back against a tree-trunk and wandered no more. All right, he thought, something awful is going to happen to me. The sooner it's over, the better.

Shafts of sunlight lit the glade; the first for days. He felt peaceful. And a golden cat came walking towards him; a cat with unusually large though graceful ears and a *very* sharp expression.

His friend from the swamp.

This is not *true*, he thought. The cat is *dead*. But this cat picked up a dead red leaf in its paw and, rearing up on its hindlegs, tapped the leaf from one paw to another, making it live and run. Cam almost saw mouse-eye and mouse-ear . . .

He buried his face in the cat's purring fur.

Sehtek slipped away, leaving them alone together. It never ceased to amaze her, the unfu way men continued to hope . . . even when hope was dead. The Miw never hoped; how can you hope when you *are*? She would leave him with Amon, to be happy a little longer.

23

The Miw sat packed, like a cluster of dim gold stars, in the belfry of ruined St Lawrence's Church.

It was now their only vantage-point above-ground; they had crept there by sewer, crack and crypt. It gave a wide view over the city, through its shattered bell-louvres. The bodies of men had been cleared from the streets; the bodies of cats still lay, prey to flies in the sunlight. All but the body of the Lord Khufu, hanged on the highest pinnacle of the Palace, by order of Ironhand.

"Hunt-men tonight?" sent Gristletongue.

"Hunt and be hunted is no-way," sent Sehtek, wearily. "Fifty-us-gone-Re. Few men. Always so . . . "

"Us-taken by surprise. Do better next-time!"

"Men will not venture high-place again – wear armour all-time. Can you bite through mail? Need catfriend."

"City-men make heb-Miw in Morville," offered Mut.

"Rat-filth," sent Nibblefur. "Big-mouth, small-sword. Sit, drink, talk, do-nothing. When beer-tuns run dry they go away. All belly-wind!"

"Our humans must go-them. We cannot-feed . . . "

"Why not fight with Miw-magic?" suggested Gristletongue.

What you-know of old Miw-magic?" Sehtek's question sent two loose tiles off the steeple, to crash on to the cobbles below.

Gristletongue shuffled. "Pass Mausoleum once – Smerdis give Miw-learning. Old-Miw wave tails – raise storm."

"Smerdis dead."

There was a very long silence, till Gristletongue, poised for instant flight, sent, "If no one think of anything better . . . "

"Who remembers Smerdis-sending?" sent Sehtek, with deadly restraint. Several of Smerdis's old pupils tried remembering. Their memories were blurred, useless. The only thing that came through clearly was the irreverent mouse . . .

"Let us just wave-tails," suggested Mut gently.

So the Miw, feeling utterly absurd, rose and began to wave their tails gently, in that confined space. Once they found a rhythm, it held a certain unpleasant excitement; backs began to twitch.

The air in the church below grew oppressive. Old Geoffrey turned to the priest. "I think it's coming on to thunder."

"Go-look," sent Sehtek to Mut.

"Blue-sky," reported Mut, from the broken louvre.

The Miw waved their tails on and on, growing tenser and tenser.

"Why wave-tail *that* way, stupid cat?" spat Sehtek. Gristletongue was imparting an upward flick to his tail, at the end of each completed wave.

"This how old-Miw did it!"

"Rat-filth!" sent Sehtek, unworthily; tiny sparks were crackling among her whiskers. But the rest were following Gristletongue's example. Seemed more *natural*.

A shining opacity grew in the air around the disc of Father Re; the hot wind changed direction, whistling shrilly round the steeple. Below, the four heroes broke out in a prickly sweat. People in the city began wishing there would be a storm, to clear the air.

"Small-cloud, big-as-paw," reported Mut.

"Don't look too hard – you'll make it disappear!"

Encouraged, the Miw waved their tails faster. Wave, flick, wave, flick. Below, old Geoffrey felt his head was going to burst.

But the cloud grew. Its shadow fell upon the city. Men looked up, began to quicken their pace homewards.

Tension in the belfry became so bad that tails actually *touched*. Fights broke out; paws flew. Yet still the tails flicked; and suddenly Sehtek could feel everything inside her furry mind. The curve of the land, the rocky knob of the city, the billowings of vapour, the shadow of the cloud and the swishing of tails all fitted together.

She *became* the cloud; felt its power tingling inside her own muscles. Gingerly she moved the cloud a little to the right, a little to the left.

She leapt onto the crumbling windowsill. Still the cloud grew. Now it was full of the sharp claws of lightning. Mousing grew in her mind. She looked at the pinnacle of the Palace, where the poor broken body of the Lord Khufu hung. One of the usurpers was strutting beneath it, on lookout duty. Smaller than a mouse . . . Slowly, carefully, Sehtek thought down a cloud-paw to touch the Palace.

The moment they touched, a lightning-bolt hit the pinnacle. A mass of stones burst from it, carrying down to burial for ever the body of Khufu. And the tiny figure of the sentry with it. A scream came thinly through the leaden air; and was lost in the thunder of a thousand cannons. Then rain was falling in buckets.

Sehtek purred.

"Do it again," sent Gristletongue.

She chose another pinnacle of the Palace.

"Go *on*!" urged Gristletongue suddenly . . . disharmoniously.

The lightning-bolt missed by miles; struck the spire of St Alban's.

"What aim for?" asked Nibblefur.

Sehtek dropped from the windowsill, and departed without a word.

"Ingratitude," sent Nibblefur. "All that effort . . . quite *drained* . . ."

Sir Henri was drinking steadily, and declaiming a poem to Castlemew.

> "Western wind, when shalt thou blow
> The small rain down can rain
> Christ, if my love were in mine arms
> And I in my bed again . . ."

Castlemew lay on his chest, purring as if her lungs would burst and softly kneading him with her paws.

Sir Henri lifted her down gently and went to refill his goblet at the huge wine-tun that now stood in the corner. Four varlets had staggered up three flights of steps with it; it saved precious drinking-time . . .

There was a flash of lightning, greenly illuminating the room. Stones and a body came hurtling past the window. Sir Henri peered up, then sighed in a bored way.

"Raining again. Why doesn't something *happen*? I wish, cat, they would find that man they call Sir Geoffrey of the Cats. A worthy blade . . . I could joust with him . . . lend him my spare armour . . ."

Castlemew splayed her ears very wide; then shook her head to get rid of the thundering image of charging horsemen and sparking clash of steel that Sir Henri had put there. Slowly, she blinked them both back to tranquillity.

She much preferred the western wind, herself.

The sentry hauled the city-gate open, and yawned. Warm, in the sun, and he'd been up all night hunting cats. Enjoyable, especially at the Bleeding Wolf. *That* had taken the smirk off the inn-keeper's face . . .

But he'd be glad to close the gate for the night and put his feet up.

The last two carts of the day were slowly winding up the hill. Less came than used to. They reckoned the men from Morville were turning them back. But not these two, which belonged to the miller of Beauly, and crept round within bowshot of the city-walls. At least there'd be fresh bread in the morning.

"Evening," he said to the miller, who was riding on the front cart. As he said it, a shadow fell across the white flour-bags.

"Strewth!" said the miller, peering up. "I don't believe it. Second time today!"

The sentry followed his gaze.

The sky was cut in half; one section still bright blue, and the other a towering cliff of dark-grey cloud that seemed to threaten to push the whole city over.

"Get that flour under cover quick." But he spoke too late, for the first great drops fell like pennies on to the white bags, and then the sky tipped buckets. The rain fell so solid it was hardly possible to breathe. A wave of water swept down the steep street to the gate, and then the street became a shallow brown river, each cobble making its own ripple, and the water bubbling round the horse's great hooves.

The miller used his whip savagely. The horse started forward too quickly, slipped and slithered back. The cart slewed across, blocking the gate.

The sentry stared up the street. It seemed to him that a second wave was coming after the first. A wave of cats, black, white, grey, brindled and gold, their fur gleaming like a seal's under the rain. Snarling toms and queens carrying kittens in their mouths, all running silently for the gate.

"Call out the guard!" shouted the sentry. "Close the gate!"

But, blocked by the cart, the gate would not close. And the guard, turned out and lashing everywhere with their swords, slipped and cursed and fell in a swamp of mud and flour from burst bags. The river of cats flowed over them.

All but one small kitten, that fell from its mother's mouth . . .

Outside the gate, the mother swerved, fell on her side, then turned. She called sharply to the kitten, which was feebly struggling to rise . . .

But the sentry placed himself between them.

She was brave; but she had four more kittens to care for. She hovered, one paw in the air, torn between love and prudence. The kitten miaowed pathetically. The sentry's sword flashed glinting above it . . .

Then the world turned pale fiery blue. The armoured sentry fell to the ground like a pile of blackened cooking-pots; there was a smell of roasting . . .

The mother-cat mewed again, and the kitten picked its way across the awful blackened thing to safety. No other guard moved.

Sehtek looked down from the distant belfry; purred . . .

Then a little straggle of city people, appearing from nowhere out of a side-street, ran wailing after the cats.

"Come back, come back, cats! Do not forsake us! Or it is the end of the city." So piteous was their grief that the guard stood back, embarrassed, to let them past.

But, oddly enough, once outside the gates, the mourners not only ceased to call upon the cats to return, but showed no desire to return themselves. They carried on down the hill after the cats as fast as their legs would carry them. Some were even seen to be carrying packs and swords . . .

They vanished in the direction of Morville. Ten men, one woman and two small boys. One boy was clean but tear-stained; the other incredibly dirty, with what appeared to be blood and feathers round his mouth . . .

"Stop tail-waving. All-away." And despite the sadness of that hour, the fifteen Miw who had chosen to stay purred.

Then they made their way, by crypt, crack and fissure, back underground.

Above, the clouds broke up and blew away. The soaked carts of half-ruined flour moved in. The guard, as they closed the gate and cleared away the unmentionable blackened thing that had been their mate, remarked upon the strangeness of the weather for the time of year.

24

Frederick the fishmonger was in a proper rage. For a day and a night he'd been trying to get into the city with two varlets, six donkeys and a load of fresh fish. The fish was no longer fresh, and neither was Fred. The varlets were yawning, making increasingly unhelpful suggestions, and demanding extra wages. The donkeys were kicking out at the least opportunity.

Frederick had arrived looking forward to a quick sale and a good long drink at the Bleeding Wolf. But suddenly, a mile short of the city, there was Georges himself, sword in hand instead of tankard.

"What . . . ?"

"It's a siege, like," said Georges, scratching the back of his red neck uncomfortably. "No more food goes into the city while that lot's in charge . . . "

"Look," said Fred reasonably, "you may have time to go playing soldiers, but I've got a living to make. Let me past like a good mate."

Georges shifted his over-sharpened sword to his other hand and scratched his neck again. "Like to oblige . . . can't make exceptions."

"But we've always been good mates . . . " said Frederick heartily, putting his hand on Georges' shoulder, while he weighed up the situation like a pound of herring. Could he make a rush for it?

But Georges had his three lads with him, and although their stupid cat-head banner was starting to dribble in the rain, they had a pale set look Frederick didn't fancy. And a handful of horsemen were lounging under a tree nearby.

"I'll make it worth your while . . . for old times' sake . . . ?"

"No," said Georges, "there's some things more important than money."

"Never thought to hear you say that! Well, I'll be on my way . . . "

He went back the way he'd come; as far as the first wood he came to. Then he doubled back up the other side, took prickly advantage of a sunken ditch, moving with infinite caution and . . .

Georges was waiting. "You cunning old cheat," he said admiringly.

"Aw, stop messing about, Georges. I've got a wife and kids . . ."

"So have I. And they've seen things I hope yours'll never see. Why don't you go and sell your fish in Morville an' give us both a break?"

"I'll do that. You're too crafty for me!"

Liar, thought Georges. You'll be back. And he was. The two bands of men played hide-and-seek for a day and night. Frederick tried going as far as Beauly, and creeping back round the city cliffs, but even there he was caught. He kept wondering how Georges could see so well in the dark . . .

The tenth time, Frederick spat on the ground.

"And the same to you, mate," said Georges. "We'll give you half-price for that fish, to feed our lads. It'll be rotten before you get it home again."

"All right! But there's a man in the city owes me money. Can I go and collect it?"

"Providing you take no fish. We'll even search your pockets . . ."

After selling his fish in Morville, and having a friendly chat with everybody and a thorough look round, Fred went empty-pocketed to the city and got his money: three gold pieces.

He didn't mention who'd owed him, when he got back to Georges . . .

It had been Little Paul; in exchange for exact details of just how many armed men there were in Morville; and how well they kept watch.

Paul thought the news well worth the money.

Something was scratching at Georges' shoulder. More and more urgently. He raised bleary eyes from his too-thin blanket. Hard, sleeping in the open fields, at forty . . .

The cat scrabbled him again. Its enormous green eyes reflected, blank and unearthly, the glow of the dying campfire. A misshapen, long-legged, thin-bodied Miw with ears like sails and a working nose that could smell out a load of half-rotten fish half-a-mile away downwind.

These cats were tyrants! They wouldn't let any food pass through to the city at all . . .

"Bugger off, cat! Don't you ever sleep?" Georges put his head back down on the damp grass.

But now a low drumming sound came out of the ground into his ear. He hadn't heard that sound since the Siege of Calais. He leapt up, suddenly sweating, shouting to the lads.

"Aw, give it a rest, Georges. We gotta sleep some time!"

"Wake up, blast you!" He was kicking them now. "They're coming for us. Out of the city. Hundreds of them. Galloping."

Everyone was on their feet now, listening to the terrible hooves.

"Run. Run like hell for Morville!"

They ran on shaking, leaden legs; the bile boiled in their stomachs, and spewed up bitter into their mouths. One of them kept dropping his sword and going back for it. Finally, Georges took him by the collar and dragged him along swordless.

The noise they made must have roused the dozing watchman on the churchtower. The bell began to toll frantically.

They beat the terrible hooves to the village; just. The unbarricaded open street was a mass of running men, trying to pull up their breeches and buckle on their swords, shouting at their wives over the wailing of terrified sleepy children. I *told* them, thought Georges, bitterly. I *warned* them. I told them to plant stakes, dig pitfalls. Why didn't they listen?

It was the priest that saved them; simply by lighting the candles in the church. In the terrifying darkness the great coloured windows shone dimly, promising safety.

Old Geoffrey shouting in the darkness, over and over again, a voice fit to wake the dead. "Children into church! Man the churchyard wall!"

Somehow, the terror of those hooves got everybody behind the wall as nothing else could.

The wall helped; seven foot high, and the churchyard behind was higher than the village street, raised by centuries of dead. There are worse places to fight than on the bodies of your grandfathers . . .

It was well the blacksmith had been busy. Great stands of pikes were stacked in the tower. Their wooden hafts came readily to the men's hands, for they were smoothed with years of harvesting; only the heads were new, black, long, and fell, like swords.

The women thrust their screaming children into the hands of the priest, and went to rejoin their men. For their muscles were hardened too, with the work of the fields. Two-tined hayforks they held, and tools for hedging and ditching. Every hand shook, but none lost its grip. They knew the works of Ironhand; death was better.

At the far end of the village, flame sprouted from thatch.

"Louis' pigsty," muttered one villager to another.

But it wasn't just the pigs screaming. The riders screamed too, as they swept in. Fire, and screaming and the thunder of hooves; that was their way. Enough to fill the village street with scurrying, panicking men, ripe for slaughter . . .

But nothing moved, in the village. Only the cats were there, crouched on the thatch, and if the wolf-riders caught a glint of their watching eyes, they thought nothing of it . . .

Still they galloped, to and fro; but there was no one to slaughter. Finally, they gathered in the dark of the square, between church and inn. Foul they looked, in the light from the burning, dressed from head to toe in rusty armour, scavenged on the battlefield by the murder of wounded men.

"Is this a village of the dead?" shouted Ironhand.

"It's going to be!" shouted old Geoffrey. "We shall not bury you – our fields need manure." A grim farmer's joke; there was a nervous titter from the villagers along the churchyard wall . . .

For the first time Ironhand noticed the lychgate blocked by the coffin-cart, and the dribbled cat-head banner sprouting from the lychgate roof.

And the handful of bowmen, in the churchtower.

"You are waiting by your own graves," he shouted. "That will save bother!"

But the wolf-riders sat uneasily. They saw the firelight touching the pike-heads; they did not like that iron hedge. They had come to kill, not die.

A pause.

Then Ironfinger, second son of Ironhand, laughed and called for a blazing torch, and thrust it into the thatch of the inn. The villagers watched agape as the place they had met all their lives vanished into the jaws of flame. They saw the Duke's head on the inn-sign blister and char; saw the black rafters emerge as great chunks of burning thatch whirled up into the sky like flocks of fiery birds. They saw the old diamond-leaded windows burst outwards and tinkle on the cobbles.

Then Ironfinger rode across the square, brandishing the torch aloft, as if he meant to ride right up to the lychgate and burn that too. His laughter, full of contempt, echoed off the walls of the church. He loomed, on his great horse, as high as a statue on a pedestal; a statue of black steel. His burning brand made the air dark. He could look over the wall, as he stood up in his stirrups, and see the villagers cowering behind. He had no face; only a great snout of steel.

Only old Geoffrey did not cower; as he had not cowered to greater men on Bosworth Field. He caught the eye of the young bowmen in the tower; knew they were trembling. Skilled they were, in the peaceful quiet of coppice and spinney; in the evening hunt for rabbit and hare they were deadly shots. But they only had bolts fit for the soft-pelted deer . . .

It all hung on the first volley. If that missed; or worse, if all the bolts hit and bounced off the rusty mail, then the last thread of nerve that held the village men in their places would snap.

Geoffrey raised his arm, then dropped it.

Streaks of thin fire hissed from the crossbow's twang. Five bolts hit the iron figure, and rattled off like sticks.

Ironfinger laughed again and raised his torch higher, reaching for the lychgate roof. Under his arm, the edges of his plate-armour moved apart, on their hinges of leather . . .

Georges kissed the head of his single arrow. The bodkin-head shaped to spin in the air and drill through steel. Then he drew his longbow and loosed without taking a breath.

Everyone heard the shrill wail, that could not possibly have come from a being so armoured and fell. Ironfinger's torch-arm dropped; the torch singed his horse's neck, making it rear. Then horse and man fell together, like the collapse of a blacksmith's shop.

The horse struggled to rise and free itself from the thing that wailed like a great metal baby. It heaved itself upright, and began to walk slowly along the churchyard wall, dragging the obscene crying thing behind it.

Then, whether from hate or to silence the wailing thing, one villager jabbed with his pike. Suddenly, they were all jabbing. Some leapt on to the wall-top, to get a better shot. Some, foolishly, leapt clean over the wall.

"Get back!" yelled Geoffrey. Too late; the rest of the wolfpack had charged. There was a frantic scramble. Most villagers got back in time, but not all.

Then the fight was on in earnest.

It would have gone worse, had not Ripfur launched his heb-Miw.

The villagers never saw them; the cats had been chosen for blackness. It only seemed to the villagers that for a moment a wolf-rider would grow an extra head with two pointed ears. Helms fell ringing on to the hard ground. Or a sword-thrust would fail halfway; the sword be dropped, while the rider would gallop wildly away, clutching his jaw. If any villager saw a pair of glowing green eyes, he shook his head and put it down to the confusion of battle.

Even the wolf-riders seldom knew what happened. A sudden unnerving weight on shoulders already heavy with armour; an agonising pain in the face . . . life is desperately confined, inside a helmet in battle . . .

So when Ripfur called the retreat, the heb-Miw slipped away unnoticed, except for one young tom, trodden dead unwittingly by a horse. By the end of the battle, he was no more than a flat black patch of fur in the dust.

It could still have gone badly, for the villagers had broken their line. But their fear was broken also; they had seen the mighty fall from the saddle and cry like a baby. Their blood, quiet so long round field and dooryard, was up, and their pikes were long and sharp.

The attack broke; riders galloping off in all directions, their voices booming wildly inside their helms.

The villagers stared down at another dead rider, and three dead friends. Old Geoffrey muttered, "I can use them now. Afraid, but not too afraid; brave, but not too brave."

It was more a bickering now. The riders stayed well back, cutting at the ends of the pikes with their swords. Until one ventured too close, and a lucky pike-thrust opened up an arm or a thigh. Then he would ride off howling. The crossbowmen used up all their bolts but, in the wavering firelight, killed no one. They dared not run out and retrieve their bolts, from the bloodstained earth. The wolf-riders rode up and down, arguing.

"Stalemate!" said Georges, streaming sweat from head to foot.

"Where did you get your bodkin?" asked Geoffrey. "Haven't seen one for thirty years!"

"I've had it for thirty years – used it to get the broken corks out of bottles. Got it at the Siege of Calais . . . "

"Why did I bother to ask?"

"D'you reckon they'll pack it in, soon? The lads are getting tired . . . "

"Pack it in? They've not *started* yet. If there'd been one *soldier* among them, they'd have done for us by now. If they set fire to all the houses they could *smoke* us out . . . "

25

The cat, wriggling frantically from under his cloak, wakened him. He sat up, rubbed his eyes, and stared in horror to the north. The sky was pink and pulsed like a heart. The little trees of the wilderness were reduced to thin black skeletons by the light. And the endless noise of clinking and quarrelling went on and on. He didn't know what it was, but he grew afraid.

He looked to the cat for comfort; but the cat's ears were down, and it was shivering too.

Something made him look behind. And there they sat, the golden cats, like a dim necklace of the goddess's gold beads. All looking at him.

"What do you want?" he shouted.

They did not move. Instinctively he reached for the handle of his dagger, wanting comfort. But the dagger fluttered, and he let go as if it was red-hot.

He fastened his cloak round his neck, and picked up his pack, thinking to plunge away into the darkness.

But the cats blocked the way into the darkness. And they were packed so close he didn't dare walk among them.

Well, walk round them, stupid!

He tried to; next minute he was walking towards the fire, and they had closed round him, herding him like a sheep . . . to the slaughter? He touched the sword he was still carrying like a spade over his shoulder. But the sword was worse than the dagger . . .

Just short of Morville, two wolf-riders spotted him. They were in an evil mood, having been left to guard the rear and missing all the fun, especially the village women. Hungry for any victim. They swung their horses and came in for the kill, in the deadliest way. Galloping abreast, ten yards apart, so they would pass on either side of him, striking from left and right in the same instant. No single foot-soldier can withstand such an attack. Bewildered, he will often make no stroke at all.

Cam saw his death. He gave one last cry . . . I am Cam . . . Then his hands closed round the sword.

And Cam was gone. A careless bystander might not have noticed the change; but the tall slight body crouched; went up on its toes; swayed, shifting its weight softly from foot to foot. And if the bystander had dared go closer, he would have seen that the eyes were no longer large-pupilled with fear, but slits, thin as a blade of grass.

The Seroster turned to face the riders, his mind a red delight. Everything was movement; the pulse of the fire, the black clouds of smoke rolling along the ground, the dawn-wind stroking the little trees, the rippling muscles of the two approaching horses. His own body began to sway from the hips, in harmony.

The riders had meant to approach exactly abreast; but one was timider, starting to lag. The Seroster turned his unwinking stare on that rider. The man, feeling it, hesitated more. Now he was two yards behind, and still dropping back. Enough . . .

Fifty yards, forty, thirty, twenty. The Seroster's mind was a whirl of red joy. The long, long sword curled back over his shoulder, like the lash of a tail. Then the world was all circles of sharp moving steel.

The two smaller circles hit nothing but air; slowed and lost all force.

At the end of the great circle, an explosion of blood.

One rider galloped on untouched, rocking wildly in the saddle, bemused. When he finally got control of his horse and turned, he saw his friend's horse galloping away riderless. And a hump on the grass . . .

The Seroster had turned. Waiting.

The wolf-rider grew afraid; hate and anger drained away, leaving him empty and shaking. What did he care about his mate? Let the fool lie there . . .

It was his misfortune that he was riding a white horse. The Seroster whistled . . . The horse whinnied gladly, and began to gallop towards the summons.

It would have been better for the rider if he had thrown himself from the saddle, risking a broken leg. It would have been better if he had broken his leg and crawled away. Instead, he gathered together his last poor rags of courage and made a stroke . . .

There was another explosion of blood.

Cam struggled back into wakefulness as if from a nightmare. He was riding a white horse; leading a brown. Holding before him, upright, the two-handed sword. His hands were sticky on the hilt; he could hardly move them, as if they were glued. When he tried to move his mouth, his eyebrows, they stretched stiffly, as if caked with something. He looked behind, wondering. Saw the two humps in the grass . . . looked abruptly ahead again.

This was the place of his dreams; the burning buildings, the fight before the churchyard wall. He closed his eyes again, trying desperately to wake up from this nightmare before it was too late.

The battle fell apart.

The villagers stood behind their wall and gaped; at a man riding a white horse, holding a two-handed sword aloft; and a whole squadron of golden cats walking with him. It was a figure they had never expected to see in their waking lives, but still they roared, louder and louder, "Seroster! Seroster! Seroster!"

Ironhand's men fell back. All they knew was that the newcomer was riding a horse that had belonged to one of their mates, and was leading another, and was covered in blood not his own. And the shouts of the village men were different; like the howl of wolves, or the roar of lion after prey.

And the solitary rider, when he drew rein, stared at Ironhand as if he were the only thing left in the world. And Ironhand's horse began to walk towards that rider. It bucked and struggled as Ironhand tried to rein it in. Ironhand had to dismount and drag the horse back into his ranks with a cruel and savage hand.

The Seroster's eyes never left Ironhand; but his voice cut through the cheering like a knife. "Pick up your crossbow-bolts!"

The villagers glanced uneasily; then leapt over the wall and picked up their bolts, where they lay embedded in the ground. When they had them all, they leapt back over the wall again, helped by many willing hands.

"Unblock the gate!" The burial-cart was dragged from the lychgate, and the Seroster rode through, and the gate was closed again. The golden cats turned and leapt for the unburnt thatch, rejoining their fellows of the heb-Miw. And the square was empty . . .

Georges stepped forward, his eyes crinkling. "Hey, I know you . . . you were the lad . . . "

The red mask of a face turned to him; again the blue eyes

narrowed to slits. Poor Georges gasped, his hand still half-extended for a handclasp. Then he turned aside muttering, "This beats anything I saw at the Siege of Calais."

Then the Seroster turned to Geoffrey. "Do not keep your bowmen in the tower; they will shoot better placed among the pikes . . ." Then he said, "Where is the Duke?"

The Duke was led forward, trembling. Once, he would have screamed and wept to see the red mask of this strange creature; but the Miw had had him since. Now he knew the importance of the way you held your tail, while the people watched . . . The Seroster went on his knees, and held out his red hands, and the Duke put his small white hands round them, and accepted the Seroster as his liegeman, in death and life, for ever.

Then the Seroster walked among the people, and they touched his bloody clothes and blessed him.

Ironhand's men seemed to be going. They were making a great noise riding round the village, breaking into houses and loading loot on to carts. Every so often they would ride back to the churchyard wall, brandishing someone's live squawking chicken. Then they would wring the chicken's neck, laughing, and hang the dead bird from their saddle-bow. Further off, the village cattle were being herded together, to be driven away. More houses were set alight, at the far end of the village . . .

There was an angry growl from the village men; some put one foot over the wall.

"Be still," said the Seroster. "You have your lives. All else can be repaid." Then he stood long, as if lost in thought, staring in the direction of Ironhand. Then he took Georges and Geoffrey on one side and said quietly, "They will attack soon. I leave you here. Only get your pikes to hold this wall, no matter what noise they hear behind. I take the bowmen with me."

Then he led the bowmen behind the church, where night still lingered in the shadow of the tower, and urns and angels glimmered white.

"Conceal yourselves among the tombs, and shoot as you can. Only do not shoot the wielder of the two-handed sword."

The bowmen faded from sight. Only the Seroster strode to the midst of the graves and carefully chose a flat tomb-top, and kicked the moss off it, where it was slippery. Then he stood, feet apart and legs braced, still as a statue as the sky began to pale. Only the great sword moved slightly between his hands, its point grinding gently on the rough stone.

Still he stood, while the thundering of hooves came again from the other side of the church, a great shouting and clashing, louder even than before. The sky flared pinker through the church windows, as more houses caught fire. The Seroster smiled . . .

It was well done, for villains. Well closed-up, quiet and fast, up through the narrow funnel of the Rue de la Vierge. They were grinning like fiends as they leapt the churchyard wall. In their mind's eye they were already galloping round the corner of the churchtower, to fall on the bewildered pikemen from behind. A most enjoyable massacre . . .

The Seroster's blade curled back, and the leader's horse galloped on empty-saddled.

Five more he hewed as they passed; the great sword swinging left to right in dread circles against the sky.

And it seemed as if the village dead had joined in the fight. For the graves were close-packed here, too tight for horsemen to turn. One horse fell as a grave-slab gave under its weight; others were caught in the iron grave-railings, and yet others in the dense briars that crisscrossed the tombs. Another horse put its hoof through a pitcher of dead flowers and went mad. And as the raiders swung their swords to hack and hew, they seemed to fight the marble angels, kings and prophets, so tangled were they with them. Shattered swords and marble heads and great showers of blue sparks flew through the air.

And once they were down, they were down; no getting up; horse threshed against horse; the rear-comers ran down those who wrestled to get to their feet. The more raiders that piled in, the worse their state grew, until there was only a great writhing tangle of toppling stone and shattered slab and black splintered hole and strangling black briars and trapped ankles and blaspheming despair. It was said that in their blindness, some raiders killed each other. And into that seething mass the crossbowmen shot and shot, and in the midst the Seroster still stood on his sure footing, and still the awful sword swung.

Now they sought to escape on foot, back over the wall. But the Seroster, leaping from tomb to tomb, pursued them till they died, in the narrow places full of ivy and inscriptions to the forgotten dead.

Not one escaped. Then the Seroster cried in a loud voice, "Wrecks, I gypped us some!" Or was it "Rex Aegyptus sum"?

"I am the King of Egypt!"

Beyond the church, the shouting died. Georges and old Geoffrey came running to see what had happened.

"Dear God!" swore Georges, and meant it. "Whatever led them to ride into a place like this? They must have been *mad*!" He looked at the Seroster, enquiringly. The Seroster looked back expressionlessly for a long time, then blinked, as if that was some kind of answer. "Untangle the horses from this place," he said, "before they break their legs. They at least have done you no harm, and will be your good friends. They too have suffered much . . ."

And he was the first among those who rescued the horses, speaking to them with great tenderness, when they shied at the bloody smell of him. And it was not the least of the miracles that day that although the horses were in sorry plight, blown, terrified, scratched with briars, even shot with crossbow-bolts, not one was hurt beyond mending. And not one had been cut by the terrible sword of Seroster. In fact the sound of his voice so pacified them that they were soon able to eat.

Ironhand let his men straggle back to the city any old how, some driving cattle, others breaking into lonely farms, all ill-tempered, weary, accusing each other. So lost in misery they looked neither before nor behind, despising the village men. And the Seroster followed them, with the weary bowmen . . .

Plundered cattle drifted back into Morville all the morning; and some riderless horses, with dead chickens tied to their saddle-bows. And though even the Seroster could not return dead chickens to life, every man got back his own, and the air was full of the smell of roasting.

But they got no sleep. All that day Geoffrey and Georges drove them on, to dig pits and flood ditches and hammer in well-pointed stakes. By nightfall, the end of every street blocked with a well-soaked cart, Morville was an impregnable fortress.

Only then were they allowed to fall asleep where they lay.

26

Cam was wakened by the sun, winking through the roof of a small pavilion. There were two patches in the roof, so it wasn't new. But the patches were well-sewn. He wasn't lying on the ground, but on a fine feather bed. The quill-ends of the feathers stuck into him gently. He wriggled his body against them to scratch himself; grasped one quill-end and pulled, and surveyed the small white goose-feather dreamily.

Above him were furs . . .

And all around, as far as his ears could hear, the pleasant hum of human busyness. Women talking; one laughed. The clang of a bucket and the swoosh of water thrown on grass. Further off, horses blowing down their nostrils and munching.

He felt well, just a little stiff; stretched again, luxuriously. He hadn't the faintest idea where he was. Casting back, he touched nasty memories. Riding a horse, humps in the grass, burning. Sticky hands, face caked with . . .

He looked at the hand that held the white feather. It was spotlessly clean, cleaner than he'd ever known it. Not even dirt under the fingernails where there'd *always* been dirt.

He suddenly remembered the golden cat, washing itself back to calmness after bloody battle . . . He was clean as a newborn babe. Felt remarkably like a newborn babe . . .

He was stark naked!

The women outside the tent laughed again.

He shot upright in a panic. "Hey!"

Instantly a greybeard face thrust its way through the tent-flap. A long-nosed face that opened its eyes very wide, blinked three times and vanished. "The Lord Seroster is awake!"

All the busy voices outside took up the cry. A vertical line of heads appeared through the tent-flap, from a silver-haired granny's at the top to a very dirty child's at the bottom. Cam grabbed the furs up to his shoulders. Unfortunately, that pulled them off the lower part of his body; he felt a cool draught blowing.

"Out!" he roared, grabbing more furs. The heads vanished instantly. The greybeard's reappeared.

"Clothes!" roared Cam, looking around the pavilion desperately. There was a rich wall-hanging, portraying harvesting, spread on the fresh green grass. There was the accursed sword, propped against a carved chair. There was a finely-carved table with a flask of yellow wine, and a chessboard laid ready. But not a stitch of clothing in sight.

"Instantly, lord!" The greybeard vanished; to be replaced by a new row of assorted heads, all gaping.

"Out!" Cam reached for the sword . . . The heads vanished in a twinkling and stayed away this time. But various voices, shrill with near-panic, told each other the Lord Seroster had awakened in an ill-mood and what did this forebode?

The greybeard reappeared, bearing parti-coloured clothes in green and yellow, of great splendour. And shoes with foolish upturned toes.

"I want *my* clothes!"

Greybeard dropped the clothes and fled. Consternation increased outside; so did the number of voices, mainly female. There seemed to be a whole army out there, wondering how the Seroster might be pacified. Did he want meat? Cooked or blood-raw? Did he require a fair virgin maid to appease his appetites? It made Cam feel like a strange and fell beast in a cage. He looked at the clothes, saw a clean white shirt lying among them. Nipped out of bed to snatch it up, before the fair virgin maid might appear.

She was thrust in, just as he was pulling the shirt over his head. But since her eyes were screwed up tight with terror, he managed to pull the shirt down and get back under the furs with no further loss of dignity.

"Sit down," he said to the virgin, crossly. She obeyed, and no doubt encouraged by such a modest request, dared to open her eyes. And immediately put a pigtail in her mouth. It was the merchant's daughter from the Mire.

"Oh, it's only *you*," she said. "Why does it always turn out to be you?" She sounded almost insultingly disappointed. "What do you want of me?"

"Glass of wine!" said Cam abruptly.

"Oh!" She sounded even more disappointed.

"What did you think? That I was going to *eat* you?"

She blushed to the roots of her hair. Cam realised she was got-up very fine, in a low-cut dress of cloth-of-gold.

"You always dress up like that?"

"I'm *supposed* to be the Seroster's first virgin," she said with spirit, thrusting the goblet at him so roughly that a dribble of wine ran down his shirt. "The Seroster *always* takes a virgin, when he wakens from red battle."

"*Really*!"Cam thrust his face into the goblet so violently that more wine dribbled down his shirt.

A violent whispered argument broke out, outside, about whether the Seroster should be disturbed even with requested clothes while he was enjoying the first virgin. And two loud male voices, demanding admittance on urgent business . . .

"Come in!" roared Cam, getting a grip on things. Two figures, one bulky, one small and wiry, blundered in, and fell over the first virgin, who had resumed her seat in a fit of sarcastic pique.

Georges, picking himself up with an apology to her, and a very old-fashioned look at Cam, launched into a tremendous oration on the placing of counterscarps, the clearing of fields of fire, the manufacture of caltrops and the digging of pitfalls, with a recommendation that two houses at the end of the village be pulled down to improve the line of fire towards the city . . .

Then Geoffrey launched in with his tally of horses in the camp, those spavined, likely to suffer from croup, the staggers or faults in their withers. And the need for an edict to stop young men-at-arms galloping through the camp using flowerpots and lines of wet washing as targets for lance and mace . . .

"Enough!" roared Cam, his head beginning to overflow like a blocked sewer. He was getting a taste for roaring, and the instant silence that came in its wake. But he didn't like the way neither man would look him in the eye. Their eyes wandered wildly all over the tent, and when he shouted they broke out in a white sweat . . . why was he frightening them so much?

Then two old crones outside began wondering in whispers whether the first virgin had been enough to slake the Seroster's appetite, or whether more should be sent for?

"I want my clothes," roared Cam. Strange, this giving orders to invisible beings through canvas. The greybeard immediately fell through the tent door, and Cam was relieved to see his own boots and jerkin, leather gleaming with dubbin and studs sanded till they shone like tiny silver mirrors.

But no breeches.

"*Where are my breeches?*"

"Lord – the women scrubbed all night . . . they could not remove the blood . . . " The old man had tears running down his bewhiskered cheeks.

"*Where are they?*"

The first virgin gave a most unladylike snort of laughter.

"Burnt, lord!" quavered the old man. "Here are new ones . . . "

"*Green and yellow!* Out, out, out!" Then he added, "Oh, you can stay," to the first virgin. "Only turn your back . . . " As he got dressed he asked, "How did you get into this?"

"I offered to be your first . . . victim."

"Why?"

"I was *bored*, hanging around the camp. I'm still bored . . . "

He reached for the sword, in mock anger.

"Cutting me in half won't prove anything . . . " she sneered.

"Oh, go and fetch me some breakfast."

"What do you eat?"

"A new-born babe, of course!"

There was a screech from the two old crones outside.

"No – bread and cheese," he added, hurriedly.

"You really *are* a tinker, aren't you?"

He thwacked at her cheeky departing bottom with a leather gauntlet.

Still, he kept her by him. So that in the gossip of the camp she became not just the first of many virgins, but the First Virgin proper, a rank never known before in that city.

She was the only one who treated him like a human being; who didn't gawp in terror whenever he spoke, or touch the hem of his tunic if he turned his back; who did not fawn or ask favours, or bring problems or lawsuits. When the pressure of eyes and voices got too great, he would look across at her, for her wry grin.

(By the next day, she had suitors of her own, seeking her ear, because she had his.)

But meanwhile he had Georges to satisfy. He had to inspect every inch of the defences. It was weird, hearing Georges say, "I have done as you told me yesterday, lord." Weird to realise that from the time when he grasped the Seroster's sword, he had lost a whole day of his life.

Georges obviously knew his stuff. Cam found fault with a few of the sharpened stakes, suggested only one house was pulled down instead of two, and by the end of the morning not only had Georges eating out of his hand, but had acquired a good working knowledge of siege-lore and the entire history of the Siege of Calais . . .

There was one bad moment, when Georges said, over-matey, "You're different today . . . more like the lad I used to know!"

Cam gently rested his hand on the hilt of the dagger. He stared at Georges, and as he stared, his eye-pupils changed from points to slits . . . Georges broke out in another sweat. Cam hated doing it, but the Seroster must be the Seroster . . . "I am different every day," said Cam. "What is that to you?"

Old Geoffrey was harder to convince, shrewder. First there was a forest of horses' legs to inspect; and horse-lore is far deeper than siege-lore. Cam just listened and nodded, and let Geoffrey carry out what he suggested.

"I have watched you ride," said old Geoffrey finally, "and cannot make out where you were taught . . . " Cam looked at the old horseman, with his pain-lined face and bowed legs. His hand closed round his dagger . . . his eyes changed again.

"Not anywhere you know, Geoffrey . . . "

Geoffrey flinched; it was cruel, but it had to be done.

They got back to the tent, to find a new crowd gathered; new problems. After a half-hour of the priest and Mayor, the waiting crowd outside had got much bigger.

Cam roared for two saddled horses and some cold food . . . He and the First Virgin rode out of Morville, the sentries respectfully pulling aside a section of barricade to let them pass.

"Now it will happen," whispered one old crone gleefully to the other. "Now he will *take* her. I have heard he will do it while riding, on the very back of his mount . . . "

It seemed heaven to Cam, to ride out into the blue dusk, alone except for the cat, and the increasingly expectant silence of the Virgin. He felt so parcelled-out between the demands of Georges and Geoffrey, the Duke and the priest and the Mayor and the people that he no longer belonged to himself at all.

They dismounted in view of the city, and sat under a tree. The First Virgin took his hand and played with the fingers. At first he was so tired he did not notice what she was doing. Until she said, "I can't believe this hand really killed twenty men . . . " Distressed, he clutched his dagger; more and more he was coming to depend on it . . .

When he came to himself, it was quite dark. The First Virgin lay heavily on his arm, asleep and in some disarray, so at first he feared he had done her some harm. But from the look on her face, it seemed she had attained her heart's desire at last, and was no longer virgin. Cam just felt empty and miserable. He wished he was back in the wilderness alone. Yes, his house in the Mire . . . the cats . . . The golden cat wormed up to him, purring, and he welcomed it.

But it sniffed appreciatively at his jerkin; from which, as the dew fell, a slight but unwelcome butcher's-shop smell was issuing.

Even the cat, he thought sadly, had its own axe to grind.

For a while he slept, and was back at his house in the Mire.

27

After the Miw departed, the city grew wretched. The old women went round shaking their heads and chanting 'Finis felicorum', blaming everything from the milk going sour to the drains getting blocked on the departure of the cats. Every time two knives got crossed, or a black crow flew over, it was an omen of evil. They yattered till sensible men could hardly hear themselves think.

But the sensible men did think. They saw that the usurpers, having searched and looted every empty house, were now starting to search and loot those still occupied. Taxes going up and trade going down. Respectable people robbed in the street in broad daylight. Any robbers that were caught and taken to the Palace were released, penniless, within the hour. And the pickpockets were swaggering in the street and saying they knew Little Paul personally. They added that changes were coming, and looked at the sensible men's belt-purses and daughters.

One night, Pierre the goldsmith bought the Captain of the Guard a lot of wine in the Seven Stars.

"Is the city-gate ever left unlocked at night by accident?"

"More than my neck's worth."

"I once knew a neglectful captain who left his gate unlocked. In the morning he found someone passing through had dropped a purse . . ."

"How big a purse?"

"Twenty crowns . . ."

"That was a little purse . . ."

"It was only a little gate. A bigger gate might have yielded . . . more."

"Not more than my neck's worth!"

But the size of that purse grew, on successive nights. By the time it had grown to a hundred crowns, the Captain admitted that things might grow very slack at the gate, on Sunday nights about midnight . . .

The Captain prepared carefully; told the guard that Sunday was his birthday, and there might be a little wine. Then he went to the apothecary and bought a great amount of dried poppy-juice. He broached the wine-cask in the guardroom, before the new guard went to man the walls.

"By God," said one guard, "gaffer's in a good mood. Perhaps Little Paul gave him a birthday-present?" Everyone fell about; a weak joke, but helped down by strong wine.

In ten minutes, they were snoring. The Captain drifted out and looked round nervously; but every cobbled street leading from the gate was damp and empty. He unlocked the postern. When he looked round again, Pierre and his family were hurrying across the cobbles with great bundles.

The Captain grew greedy. "People I let through, but not bundles. They're confiscated." He expected Pierre to argue, but he just shrugged and laid down his bundle. The Captain grew more uneasy. "You told no one?"

Pierre smiled, shook his head. They passed through, handing over their purse. Rubbing his hands together, the Captain went to close the gate . . .

"Do not bother to close the gate, friend!"

It was the apothecary and his family.

"You can't pass!" Then, nervously, "How much will you pay?"

"I will pay with silence, about the dried poppy-juice. Little Paul will never hear it from my lips."

The Captain let them pass. Then slammed the postern loud enough to be heard up in the Palace.

"Do not abuse good wood, brother!" It was the maker of wine-casks and his family. And a crowd gathering behind.

"We all saw you let out the apothecary," they murmured. "But if we leave the city, how can we tell Little Paul?"

The Captain looked round desperately.

"Do not disturb your guards, brother. They have *earned* their rest!"

There was a low ripple of laughter.

"You mustn't all leave! Little Paul will notice!"

"Better leave yourself, brother, before he does!"

Again, laughter. The Captain drew his sword, but it was knocked out of his hand with a bundle. Another large bundle knocked him flying into a corner, then half the city was streaming past to freedom.

The last three came and looked at the Captain. Big rough men, charcoal-burners. "We will take Pierre's bundles. He said he would leave them to collect."

The Captain waved his arm despairingly; he no longer felt capable of anything; the men carried great cudgels.

"*And* we'll take Pierre's purse . . . "

"He made a bargain . . . " said the Captain feebly.

"Go to Little Paul for justice, then . . . "

The sound of laughing faded down the road.

The Captain staggered away blindly, on to the darkness of the hillside, leaving the gate open behind him.

Cam was wakened by the cold nose of the cat, thrusting up under his jaw. He could tell by the lowering moon that it was late.

The cat rose and stretched, walked towards the horses. The cat miaowed, summoning.

Cam eased the First Virgin's head off his shoulder on to a soft tussock of grass. She looked rosy-cheeked, bucolic as a milkmaid. Snored gently. She would be safe enough here, in a clump of shrub, far from any road. He drew the edges of the cloak over her, then ran for his horse with a lightened heart. It was good to be alone with the cat, under the moon.

But the cat was already streaking off through the undergrowth, cutting wide circles, as if it, too, was glad to stretch its legs.

Following, he soon came near the city, lying blue and enchanted under the moon. No watchmen walked the walls. He galloped towards the black arch of the gate, the wind lifting his new-washed hair, and the harness creaking like a waking lullaby. No danger; the knife remained asleep in his belt. He felt no desire to touch the sword; tonight he would be Cam, and live by Cam's wits . . .

He was below the very walls when he saw the black figures surging out of the gateway.

There was no threat in the straggle. They were carrying bundles, looking back fearfully at the city. They came in great surging gouts, as if the city was bleeding to death.

He reined-up, awaited them. They halted, frightened white faces staring, while others piled up behind.

"Look at his cat . . . " cried one.

"Look at his sword . . . "

"The Seroster . . . "

"He's only a boy . . . " said one woman.

"*Are* you the Seroster?"
"I speak for him," said Cam, keeping his hands together on his saddle-bow and feeling a spiteful glee at the expense of the sword.
"It is the Seroster's squire!"
Cam did not argue.
"Where are you going?" he asked the people.
"To my sister's . . . "
"To Souillac . . . "
Most were silent, realising they didn't know where they were going.
"To Harcourt . . . "
"I wouldn't go to Harcourt," said Cam. "Harcourt is undefended. Little Paul will send Ironhand to fetch you back."
A flurry of panic . . .
"Morville is safe," said Cam. "My master, the Seroster, has built great works there . . . "
"I'm for Morville, then!" The crowd started to move.
"Wait!" A cat-like malice filled Cam. "My master will allow women and children into Morville freely; but men must pay a price."
"What price?"
"A sword, a shield, a spear? Or a great cudgel?"
Some held these aloft joyfully. Others said sullenly, "Where can we get a sword this time of night?"
"The city-gate is still open . . . if you arrive without a sword, my master the Seroster will undoubtedly cut you in half . . . "
The crowd broke up into a hundred arguing groups.
"Time passes," said Cam. "Dawn waits for no man. But the city-gate will be swinging in the wind for an hour yet."
Why was he enjoying being so cruel? Then he noticed that one of his hands, unbidden, had crept to the pommel of the sword . . .
Then women and children were moving on towards Morville; men moving back towards the gate, fear and stealth in them now.
The Seroster's heart sang with mirth.
"How can you be so cruel?" demanded the First Virgin from behind his shoulder. She was sitting her horse, a little bedraggled, but ready for anything.
Cam deliberately tightened his grip on the sword, so that his eyes looked at her through cat-slits. "I thought my nature *delighted* you, madam? Escort the women to Morville. I will see to you, in the dawn."

The First Virgin made an explosive female noise, wheeled her horse violently, and was gone down the road.

Cam rode on up to the gate. On the rocks below, he saw a hopeless, huddled figure.

"Come to cut me in half, Seroster?" asked the Captain bitterly. "It will save Little Paul a job in the morning."

"Have you got a sword?"

"I'm not fighting you . . . "

"The place for men with swords is Morville."

"They will mock me!"

"No man died of mockery."

"Damn you, you scheming ghoul!"

"Do not shout so, Captain. You will awake your own guard."

As they approached the gatehouse, others, who hadn't been in Pierre's plot, were finding the gate open and making their escape; children of the streets, thin beggars and orphans who scoured the night middens for food.

"Take them to Morville, Captain; see they are fed."

"What, these sewer-rats?"

"To regain this city, we shall need both sewers and rats. Go with the Captain, rats!"

The leading rat pushed his filthy hair back out of his eyes. "I know you, Seroster. I met you in the churchyard. I *was* you!"

"Ask what happened in *Morville* churchyard," said Cam. "Go and get your pasties, and hear what happened."

"Pasties, lads!" And they were gone, whooping, with the Captain grumbling behind.

The postern was still swinging in the dawn-breeze. Cam stepped through, and the cat followed. Bundles of rubbish were blowing round the cobbles. The cat sniffed at one, delightfully fishy.

Cam sighed. The whole city was asleep. It would be so easy to take it now, and so hard to storm the walls later . . . But good and evil were still mixed; too many men had still not chosen.

So he went to collect his own gold, from under the flagstone in the outhouse. There were pike-staves to buy . . .

28

The venture to Beauly did not go well. The little army drew up on the green bravely enough, behind the royal standard newly-sewn by the women of Morville. The villagers turned out to gawp, barking dogs and all. Unfortunately, they knew most of the perspiring pikemen only too well.

"What be you carrying that great pole for, Robert? A-poking wasp's nests?"

Too much laughing, even after the new royal herald had blown a fanfare and proclaimed the new Duke. He blew one very ill note . . . The new Duke spoke up well, but his voice was shrill with nervousness, and the breeze blew half his words away.

"What's the child going on about?"

A gang of youths at the back began shouting, "Speak up!" Halfway through, the Duke dissolved into tears. People clucked, said it was a shame to put the poor child through such an ordeal, then began drifting back to work.

The headman of the village lingered. "There, there, sire! We're on your side really. Only there's the harvest . . . "

Cam took him quietly aside. "You can't go on sitting on the fence. Little Paul won't stay in the city till he starves to death . . . you know they tried to burn Morville?"

"I reckon Morville asked for it . . ."

"I'm warning you . . . " Cam's hand strayed for comfort to the hilt of the sword, hanging from his saddle.

The man looked him straight in the eye. "So that's it? We do what you want, or you cut us in half? We've heard you're very fond of cutting people in half. Seems to me there isn't much to choose between you and that city lot. Neither of you seems to fancy making an honest living . . . "

"That's not what I meant . . . "

"Maybe not. You're young, and you've got a lot to learn. City quarrels are for city folk. Live and let live . . . "

"I only hope you're left to live . . ."
"Don't worry; we can fend for ourselves."

The army trailed on. It began to rain. Heads went down, and spirits. The Duke became rebellious . . .

"You must tour your villages now, sire. Show your face and claim their fealty." Cam kept his voice soothing. Inside, he felt like strangling the little brat.

"Why shouldn't the villagers come to me? They know I'm Duke!"

"They've also heard you're dead. They'll only believe what they see with their own eyes."

"Why did you pick a rainy day? I *told* you it was going to rain . . ."

Cam stared ahead, gritting his teeth and blinking the raindrops off his lashes. The new banner, so lovingly embroidered by the women of Morville, was starting to sag and bulge alarmingly, as the rain soaked it. The Duke began to cry again. Noiselessly; but the tears ran down his cheeks, mingling with the rain. Cam abruptly swung his horse away, towards the rear.

The pikemen were finding the new fifteen-foot pikes far heavier than their old hayforks. They no longer looked like soldiers. They looked like wet farmhands, walking pointlessly in the rain. Only a quarter of a mile out of Beauly, and they were already straggling.

"Geoffrey, try to stop the pikes straggling!"

But the horsemen took their role of shepherds too seriously. Began pricking the odd lagging pikemen with drawn swords. Quarrels broke out. Finally, three pikemen threw down their pikes and refused to pick them up.

Cam wasted a long time talking them out of it. His hand kept straying towards the sword . . . but no point in cutting your own men in half. He galloped back to the front; the motion sent water cascading down his back inside his jerkin; he noticed his studs were rusting . . .

A black mood descended. Why had he ever got involved with this stupid little army? Or the stupid city and all its stupid people? Or the stupid First Virgin, whose appetites kept him awake half the night?

Amon ran alongside, golden fur standing out with the rain in brandy-coloured spikes. The discord made his head ache. He remembered longingly the ordered march of the cats to the cliffs.

Sun and mirfu . . . He sought out his master's mind, but found only a thunderstorm there, of impenetrable darkness . . . What was this dark madness that came into men's minds, cutting them off from every living thing?

He wanted to pray-Re, but there were only ragged grey rain-clouds. Still, he sent his mind out as far as it would go. Not easy, when the rain made your hairs prickle, weighed down your ears and whiskers.

There was something inside that wood ahead. A great iron claw. Many horses, under the dry shelter of the trees. Many men, kill-hunger flickering like mirfu in their minds. A gloating, a waiting . . . like an iron cat waiting to pounce on this poor wet bickering straggling mouse . . .

Amon leapt on to Cam's saddle. Uttering a dire yowl, he dug his claws into the sodden green-and-yellow breeches.

"Blasted cat!"

Next minute Amon was flying on to his back, among the rain-sodden grass-clumps. He picked himself up; shaking each paw separately; shaking himself all over; desperately wanting to lick his shoulder to soothe the indignity he had suffered before all the host. Several of whom were sniggering, damply and sullenly, at his discomfiture.

An abomination of desolation swept over Amon. He saw these foolish creatures throwing down their pikes and running, all over that flat wide plain. Saw them hunted down, screaming, the sharp swords hacking, blood spurting. Saw bodies twisted in death and wolf-gnaw and eye-peck of crows, and the skull forever grinning beneath the rusted helm. The sag-breasted desolation of widows, villages burning . . .

From all round that broad bowl of valley, Miw-sends replied to him. Sehtek in the city; even, from far away in the cliffs above Harcourt, a small send from Ripfur.

"You-trouble? Send heb-Miw?"

"Pray-Re!" sent Amon, over and over. "Pray-Re!"

And from all over, sends ascended to the invisible Father. Feeble sends, even from Sehtek, because it is hard to pray-Re when he has hidden his face.

But, for a fleeting second, the clouds relented. A tiny gap, a single beam of sunlight travelling faster than a galloping horse, swept across the plain, and brushed across Amon's upturned face.

Leaving the picture of a hedgehog.

Amon shook his wet ears in bafflement. What had hedgehogs to do with it? Young-Miw always learnt a good lesson from hedgehog. Hedgehog seemed easy-meat; slow-foot, juicy, fat. But the moment you pounced, he turned into a ball – full of spikes. Then all you could do was keep on hurting your nose or walk away. You could wait all day for him to open up; but he was more stubborn than any Miw, even when you painfully rolled him over with your paw. Yet you knew that the moment you turned your back, he would be on his slow-foot, fat juicy way again. What help was hedgehog? Yet the Father had sent . . . Oh, sighed Amon softly, I wish I was back with my cat-host . . .

Another stray paw of Father Re swept across his back.

"You have not cat-host. You have man-host, Calisirian Amon!"

Amon's flanks heaved, with a sigh of disbelief. He could not direct men . . . *could* he?

Obey-Re! And in that second, all was made clear. The foolish men must make a hedgehog . . . but where, on this terrible flat plain? Man-walls? None. Except for a ruined farm ahead and a little to the right. Only two-foot walls, but a mound in the middle where a standard might be raised . . . but too far, too far . . . the terror behind the wood would not wait . . .

Then he saw it all; took a deep breath, and began to send with all his might.

Cam's horse suddenly bolted. He came awake with a start, clinging on for dear life, hauling on the reins. But the horse seemed to have gone mad. However he hauled, it kept on at a dead run for that wood ahead . . .

Georges peered after him through the drenching rain. "What the hell's he up to?" Then, "I don't much like the look of that wood!"

"I'll search it!" said old Geoffrey, gathering his horsemen, and galloping off. But he seemed to have misunderstood, for he did not gallop for the main wood, after Cam, but towards a small coppice far away to the right. Which took the horsemen clean out of danger . . .

So, they are my heb-Miw, thought Amon.

But Georges' unease of the wood grew. He edged away from it towards the low mounds of white rubble. How far off they seemed . . .

What did that matter?

But for some silly reason, he'd feel better when they reached them . . .

Meanwhile, Cam galloped on, helpless. Now the knife was twitching in his belt. Danger. Danger in the wood and he was being carried straight into it. He felt a terrible desire to touch the sword. But also a terrible stubbornness not to. The rain was releasing the hated butcher's-shop smell of his jerkin. He would not *kill*. The sword was evil; it must not possess his body again, or soon it would have his soul. The Seroster would live for ever, and Cam would cease to exist . . . And so he galloped on, helplessly . . .

Slowly Georges approached the mounds; yet ever they seemed to recede into the swathes of rain. Marching forever, getting no nearer. Sweat broke out on his face, mixing with the rain. And the wretched pikemen marched behind, oblivious to everything but aching legs and pike-bruised shoulders and the water running down their backs. And old Geoffrey's men got further and further away . . .

Cam reached the wood, stared in horror. A file of armoured horsemen was emerging in good, tight order; they seemed to go on forever. To one side rode a knight in full black armour; the crest on his shield a wolf rampant. Cam heard Sir Henri's voice boom from the helm. Saw the black arm lift.

"Right face, ho!"

This morning, Ironhand's men rode like soldiers, under Sir Henri's eye. And not just Ironhand's men . . . there must be two . . . three hundred . . .

"Halt, ho!"

The line was still; only the pennants fluttered. And across their front Cam rode, still struggling with his crazed horse.

The horsemen knew him; behind their visors, a sudden flutter of unease, as they remembered Morville. The Seroster appeared to be struggling with his horse; was it another of his tricks? . . .

"*Stand*, ho!" roared Sir Henri; and the fluttering ranks were still again, watching Cam's erratic, drunken, frightening progress.

Quarter of a mile away, Georges saw too; and knew he was a dead man. Unless they could reach the white mounds . . .

Cam reached the far end of Sir Henri's line. Sir Henri stared at him too, his soldier's mind alert for any trick . . . but what could one man do?

Sir Henri fixed his ranks with an eye of steel.

"Walk, ho!"

The ranks moved forward, edging past the dread Seroster, leaving him behind . . .

"Trot, ho!"

They gathered speed. Leaving Cam helpless in their wake, struggling with his horse in circles.

"Canter, ho!" The earth began to shake . . .

Georges heard them coming, like his death, as he reached the white mounds.

"Form circle!" roared Georges.

The pikemen were still only conscious of rain and pain. But they'd formed-circle so often that they could do it in their sleep. Grumbling, swearing, slipping across the white stones . . . Georges ran among them, lashing out with the flat of his sword at their soaking backsides. "Dig your pike-butts *in* . . . in . . . well in . . . "

The pikes rose slowly. It was then that they heard the thunder of hoofs; saw the shaking bobbing endless line of steel coming at them through the rain. Five hundred tons of flesh and steel.

Pikes began to shake and waver . . .

"Stand," roared Georges, "or you're dead men!"

"Gallop, ho!" roared Sir Henri. He held his line as if it was his own clenched fist, his mind a roaring red joy; all sadness forgotten; he was living once more before he died. He set his lance in rest, squinting through visor-slits, over the top of his great shield, aiming his point at the centre of the trembling pikemen. He was greater than human, and less. He would not have felt a wound. Neither mercy nor love nor age nor death mattered. He *was* . . . And all the charging line drew on his strength. They *were* him, invulnerable, invincible, flying, inhuman . . .

Far behind, still wildly circling, Cam watched his friends vanish behind that mass of charging steel. They would be swept away like a sandcastle . . . Georges, Geoffrey, the cat who trusted him . . .

With a groan, he gave up his being, touched the sword.

Immediately, the horse became obedient. The Seroster took one look and hurled the horse forward, lending it, too, the strength that flowed from the sword. He began to overtake. Ironhand felt him come, like a thundercloud's shadow over his shoulder. Ironhand's men too. But it only made them spur their horses faster . . .

The Seroster knew he could never reach them in time . . .

The pikemen stood. Their pike-points waved in wild circles; some wet themselves, and worse. Some whimpered, some cried to their God, some cried for their mothers. The Duke drew his dagger and bit his lip till the blood ran down his chin, as the earth thumped like a mighty heart.

"Hold, hold, hold!" yelled Georges. "Hold, my lovelies, and you'll see your homes again." He knew they wouldn't; but they'd be worse off if they ran. And the pikes were steadying now; the men knew it was too late to run. The steel wave breaking over them held them in their places. They huddled close because there was nowhere else in the world . . .

Then the golden cat stepped forth; daintily over the white stones, till he stood below the wavering pikes.

"I thank Thee, Father Re, for all things. For birth and life and death. All things are in Thy paw . . . "

Then he gathered himself, so his ears lay flat against his skull.

And he sent forth such a hate-sending as might have cracked the stones . . .

Sir Henri felt it; crouched deeper in his saddle, clenched his legs and came on. The rest of the horsemen felt it; it threw their minds into chaos, but still they rode.

The horses felt it, and for them there was no armour. Desperately they twisted away from the thing that was worse than their deaths. Withers banged against withers, haunch against haunch, as they fought madly to escape it. A gap appeared in the midst of them; widened. The steel wave broke and flowed round the hedgehog as if it was a rock in the midst of the sea. A crash, a leaping foam of broken pike and helm, plume and shield, then the wave was past, and the rock still stood, and the ring of pikes was not broken and there was a wrack of dazed and writhing horsemen crawling on the red soil.

But the ring was broken in one place. A black horse lay on the white mounds, kicking, two pikemen trapped beneath it.

Sir Henri had not flinched. And he was up on his feet, his sword flashing among the pikemen. One he killed; the standard-bearer he felled . . . Then the Seroster was on him.

Round and round they circled, blow matching blow, till they seemed enmeshed in circling showers of sparks. So well-matched were they, they seemed more like dancers or jugglers of steel and fire. So it seemed to the Duke, kneeling, watching them open-mouthed across the body of the standard-bearer . . .

Then there was a sickening thud. And the Seroster, sword back for another swing, stood staring at his opponent unconscious on the ground. And Georges standing over him, the sodden standard that had struck the blow still in his massive hands.

"That's settled his hash," said Georges.

"A coward's blow," said the Seroster, eyes thin as needles.

"I don't give two buggers," said Georges. "He was doing too much damage."

The standard-bearer groaned, and began crawling round on his hands and knees, nothing worse wrong with him than glazed eyes and a crushed helm. But for the pikeman . . . everyone kept their eyes averted from his oddly-sprawled limbs and oozing wounds.

Instead, everyone stared down at Sir Henri, who lay as still as an effigy on a tomb, his visor fallen back, his great beak of a nose sticking in the air, and his grey eyes wandering everywhere, as he slowly came back to his wits. Several pikes were raised to finish him.

"Stop!" said Seroster. "He is not cattle to be slaughtered."

"He killed my brother," said a pikeman, sullenly.

Sir Henri staggered to his feet, under his enormous weight of armour. A crimson sheet of blood streamed from his nose. His tongue licked it thirstily.

"Sir, you are a true knight," he said, and held out his mailed hand. The Seroster took it, without hesitation.

Then, before anyone could move, Sir Henri had gone, out through the ring of gaping pikemen.

"He killed my brother," said the pikeman again. "He killed my brother and you let him go. Who's going to feed my brother's bairns now?"

"He was a true knight," said Seroster.

"Curse all you true knights and your damned wars . . . " The pikeman spat upon the ground.

"They're coming again," said Georges. Then, in a bellow, "Stand to your arms."

But it was feeble stuff; the horsemen rode round in circles, hacking ineffectually. Then Geoffrey put in a nice tight charge, but the enemy fled, and it was wasted.

They stood around for an hour, watching Sir Henri vainly trying to rally his side. But they proved as sullen as the pikemen, and eventually rode away; followed by Sir Henri, raging and weeping at the shame and disgrace of it all.

"Shut up," shouted the villains. "What's the use of killing this lot? They've got nothing worth plundering anyway."

And to that, Sir Henri, swordless and horseless, could make no reply, since the villains took good care to steer clear of him, even when he possessed nothing more deadly than his bare hands.

It was time to press on; the richer by five horses, and the poorer by a dead man, slung across one saddle. Weary and bloodstained, they did not impress Harcourt.

"You ought to have seen what we did to the other lot . . . " shouted Georges defiantly.

"Show us, then!" jeered the villagers. Then they said they would acknowledge no ruler. And a few threw clods at their departing backs.

At least at Hadel, they clucked over the Duke and gave him a goblet of wine. And took the wounded into their houses and dressed their wounds.

But Hadel too refused to join in the war.

They dragged home. To the pikemen, it all seemed a great waste of time.

Amon trailed behind, so exhausted he could hardly move a paw. But as he went, he constantly thanked Father Re for his mercy. And dwelt upon the mad ingratitude of men . . .

29

Castle Morville was a sea of grumbles.

The amount the cats ate . . . Hundreds had fled the city. Thirty more, already living in Morville, had joined them. They took over the whole tithe-barn, settling to a parliament in the hayloft, and having kittens in every manger and stall, so it was impossible to get a horse inside. On sunny days they gathered on the roof, in such numbers it threatened to collapse.

Constantly hungry, they were under every meal-table, reaching up and digging their claws, in a friendly way, into people's thighs, hinting they would like a titbit. If anyone was so unfortunate as to drop a chop, it vanished instantly.

But it was stupid to grudge their food. For in them, more than barriers of sharpened stakes, lay the safety of the village. They might laze all day, when everyone else had far too much to do; but at night they faded across the dusky fields as far as the city, and nothing moved but what they knew.

For Cam's sake, they had divided themselves into divisions according to colour. The black heb-Miw, led by Ripfur and Tornear, defended the bailiwick of Harcourt. The black-and-whites quartered the ground round Beauly and the tabbies haunted Hadel Common. The point of greatest danger, the city-gate, was held by the greys who, when they bushed up their frizzy fur, seemed to absorb the moonlight itself, and were invisible at twenty yards. Which was as well, for great bonfires burnt nightly in front of the gate, and nervous crossbowmen shot at sight, and even one grey lost half his tail . . . Tortoiseshells, black Matagot, swift Miw, and even the whites (who had let their fur grow dirty in the cause of war, so they attracted no more attention than the greys) each had their station.

It had taken Amon several nights to get this arrangement into Cam's thick human skull. If only Cam would keep hold of the sword at all times, like a true Seroster . . . but Cam was stubborn, always wanting to work out things for himself, and ever more afraid of the sword. Had there ever been a more bothersome human?

So each evening, Cam found a cat of each colour in his tent, and round them the Miw had strewn a strange mixture of objects; a frond of bracken, a twig of willow, a dead frog, a turnip-leaf, an ear of blackened barley. Each object, in the mouth of a certain colour of cat, denoted a certain place. A frond of bracken, in the mouth of a grey, meant there was an enemy moving on the slopes below the city-gate. A twig of willow in the mouth of a black, meant there was something brewing in Harcourt Hollows . . .

Two nights after the Battle of Beauly, Cam had settled to his writing-table. There was always plenty to deal with. A list of broken weapons; a bill for pike-heads from a blacksmith who was threatening to make no more; a lawyer's complaint on behalf of a farmer, about stolen hens . . . lawyers seemed to flourish in peace or war . . . But Cam's quill paused often, in the flicker from the tallow-dips. Some evil was coming; he could feel it like a headache starting, inside his skull. So it was almost a relief when, at a prook from Amon, the grey cat asleep on his bed rose, stretched, and picked up a hazel-twig from High Wood, by the city-gate.

"How many?" asked Cam.

The grey cat scratched on the turf floor. Once, twice, thrice . . . it went on scratching, getting more frantic, till turf and soil flew everywhere.

"Peace, Mistlurker," said Cam. But the cat would not be comforted; its back remained arched; its tail lashed.

"Out in force." He sent a varlet to ring the alarm-bell. Bonfires were lit. Every man and woman stood to at the barricades, straining their eyes into the dark.

But soon a tabby tom rubbed against Cam's leg, with a blade of grass in his mouth.

"Hadel," said Cam bitterly. "They were so nearly our friends . . . have the women tear bandages and heat soup . . . there'll be orphans by morning."

"I have a niece in Hadel," said Geoffrey. "Can't we . . . "

"With half-trained men in the dark?"

Geoffrey nodded, in silent misery.

But it wasn't Hadel. A black cat ran in through the barricade, with blood on its coat.

"Harcourt."

"I wonder who Harcourt's throwing clods at now," said Geoffrey. But there was gladness in his voice, because of his niece.

As he spoke, the grim outline of the city began to loom ever more clearly out of the night. Every pinnacle, turret and spire stood clear.

"It cannot be dawn yet," cried a young boy.

"Harcourt is burning," said the Seroster. "We march . . . "

"To Harcourt?"

"To the city-gate. Catch them as they return. I think we can manage to hold the men together, with that much light in the sky."

Tabitha crouched terrified in the Harcourt gutter. A weight lay across her, so she could not move; a fat old woman. Even in her panic, Tabitha would not scrabble an innocent to free herself.

When she first fell, the woman had groaned and sighed; once opened her old blue eyes and talked to 'pussy' in delirium. But she had been silent a while now, and her breathing came and went oddly. There was the scent of blood everywhere. And the light from the burning houses reduced Tabitha's eyes to slits and still made them hurt. It was becoming so hot she feared she would have to scrabble the old face and arms in the end, to save herself. She spat, as a hot coal came drifting down and singed her fur.

The villagers were still running to and fro. They no longer knew where they were running to. Simply ran, as a mouse does before the cat gets tired of playing with it. Every time villagers ran past, there were fewer.

Tabitha had seen it all from the beginning. It was her duty to see all, send all to Ripfur. She couldn't lurk in safety in the bushes, and let half-brown kittens go into danger . . .

So she had seen the midnight arrival of Ironhand; heard his proclamation of Commonweal between the city and the village, in which all property was held in common. Seen the barrels of wine trundled out, and the black-visaged riders drinking to the new prosperity, while their hosts blinked sleepily, or gawped stupidly. Seen the eyeing of the village women; the increasing unease of the village men. Then a young girl had screamed. And the headman had tried to stab Ironhand with a knife. The blade, deflected by the hidden breastplate, had merely gashed Ironhand's face.

After that, the village began to burn, and things got very confused for Tabitha.

She began to faint with the heat; the world began to sway oddly and go away. There seemed to be a black-bearded priest striding down the village street. Very strange and powerful he looked, in his black robe, bearing aloft the cross from the church. He planted his legs like two roots; as if nothing on earth would move him. The remaining villagers crawled to him, clutching his legs. A ring of riders formed, full of curiosity and drunken laughter.

The priest raised his cross.

"Begone, spawn of Satan! Would you defile the eyes of Mother Church?"

"Show me Her eyes," said Ironhand, "and I will put them out. A blind church! Then we could sin in peace, without the risk of giving offence!"

He laughed at his own joke; no one else did.

"Go, or I will curse you!"

"Too late, priest. I was cursed in my mother's womb, by my father, who was not my father. Except he was my Father, because he was a *priest*!"

The priest began to intone in Latin; a curse so dreadful that Tabitha closed her ears.

But Ironhand merely snatched up a young girl who crouched at the priest's feet. The priest stopped chanting.

"Harm her," he said, "and I will *kill* you."

Ironhand tore the girl's dress . . .

The priest swung the cross at Ironhand. But the cross broke, on Ironhand's breastplate. Ironhand laughed.

"You learn, priest. Church is force, and force is church. And God would be the biggest bully of all; if he existed. God is not stopping me now, is he, priest?"

He felled the priest with one blow. Next second, Tabitha was streaking away into the blessed darkness.

"We made it!" gasped Georges. "But my legs remind me I am getting old."

Cam glanced again round the interior of High Wood, and was pleased. Everywhere, the moon shone through black branches, picking out glints of armour. The pikemen carried their pikes horizontally, so they would not catch in the twigs as they ran out to block the road to the gate. Further down, crossbowmen crouched, bows ready-wound to speed the first flight of bolts. Lower still, the horsemen waited, each with his gauntleted hand by his horse's muzzle, ready to block the least whinny of welcome as Ironhand's horses approached.

The great sword called to Cam, from where it hung on his saddle. Called urgently, knowing its hour was at hand. But he had left it untouched. He had planned this battle himself. No need for the lunatic sword.

Nothing could go wrong now . . .

"Geoffrey – is every man in position?"

Geoffrey was silent; only his booted feet shuffled uneasily on the wet leaves. "Everybody – except old Yves' lot . . ."

"Yves!" The word was a groan. The fat baker of Morville and his fat bakery-lads were the bane of the army. None was braver, none more willing. They even put in extra pike-drill. But they were huge, gross, from too much sampling of their own sweet-smelling handiwork. Sweat ran down their faces the moment they laid hand on a pike.

"I tried," whispered Georges. "But if I hurried them, they straggled. And if I closed them up, they lagged. I lost them in a coppice . . . I've sent four different men back, to tell them to go home . . ."

"And none of your four have returned," said Cam, wearily. He looked down towards Low Wood which lay further off, towards Morville. Across the open fields, now mercilessly clear in the moonlight.

No sign . . .

"Ironhand's coming."

They straggled abominably; some were drunk, held on their horses by their cronies. Helms hung from saddlebows . . .

"Come on, my beauties," crooned Georges. "One more minute and nothing can save you . . ."

As if they had heard his words, the head of the column halted. But only to quarrel about the ownership of a dead pig.

"Come *on*," crooned Georges.

But Cam had seen something quite appalling.

A line of fat pikemen emerging from Low Wood.

From the great gate, the alarm sounded immediately.

Ironhand swung his head, suddenly alert.

"Come on," shouted Georges.

The pikemen ran out, to block the road.

The crossbowmen shot, but the range was too great. Their bolts fell at Ironhand's feet.

Geoffrey held his men, for it was too soon to charge.

Ironhand had not lost his wits. He pointed right. "To Morville!" It was a great shout. He spurred away downhill; his villains following blindly.

And suddenly, Cam had no army. The pikemen, the bowmen, became a mass of husbands, each running for home, frantic for the safety of his own wife and bairns.

Ironhand laughed, and swerved his horse back again. "To the city!" And again the villains followed him like sheep. The city-gate swung open; Little Paul's crossbowmen lined the walls.

Too late old Geoffrey charged; even the tail of the villains was vanishing through the gate.

It clanged shut. Crossbow-bolts began to fly . . .

Too late, Cam reached for the all-knowing sword.

Not everyone in Harcourt was dead. Four families had sneaked into the fields before the trouble started. A man thrown down a well had swum all night. A buxom widow, attacked in her house by a solitary raider, had lashed out in desperation with a fire-iron, fainted, and come to in the dawn to find the man dead beside her, and her house the only one unburnt in the village. Eight children were recovered alive from beneath the bodies of their parents. During the morning, more straggled in, mainly women who had lost the power of speech.

The bearded priest had survived too; unwillingly.

"Why am I left?"

Cam drifted away from those staring eyes, to where some pikemen were digging a very large hole. One pikeman eased his aching back.

"I used to do nothing but dig in the fields; now I do nothing but dig graves . . ."

The priest continued difficult; he refused to say the burial-service.

"God is dead. My people prayed to him, and he didn't answer!"

"Maybe they prayed a bit late," said Cam. "When their houses were burning. Earlier, they were too busy throwing clods at their rightful Duke . . ."

"God is dead," said the priest. "Give me a sword . . ."

30

The priest got his sword, and wandered everywhere, holding it. He had no idea how to use it; a burly, heavy, clumsy man, who had always dropped things frequently. Three times he was caught by the guard, walking blindly towards the city, sword in hand, and brought back. He babbled constantly about killing and dying, so that people came to call him Father Death. He was thought mad; the children mocked him, if they weren't watched. And he made Cam feel intolerably guilty.

Everyone made Cam feel guilty, the way they watched expectantly. Waiting for his great plan to recapture the city . . .

As if it were that easy! Cam rode round the city daily, eyes searching every nook and cranny of the walls. But the first Seroster had built too well. Every weak point Cam noted, the first Seroster had seen all those years before, and defended with arrowslit, murder-hole, or a soul-searing height of wall. It was like trying to play chess against yourself. There was no way in, except the Seroster's own narrow stair.

And every day came a messenger with a missive from Sir Henri, written in antique curling hand on any tatty bit of parchment or old wine-bill, addressing him as the Lord Seroster, and challenging him to single-combat . . .

And the weather was unseasonably warm and damp. Moisture stood out on every rusty shield and breastplate. Food turned bad overnight and even clothes stored in chests gathered mildew. Men moved slowly and felt their heads were full of clouds.

One night, Cam sat on his bed and threw down his gauntlets in a temper. Immediately the greybeard hurried in and took them for dubbining. He was getting impossible; more a jailer than a servant.

Cam stretched out half-dressed, but sleep wouldn't come. Who could sleep with ten cats watching? The cats were expecting a miracle too. Hard luck, cats! Meanwhile, the sounds of their persistent licking and scratching offended his dozing ears.

Three times he got up and lit his tallow-dip and tried to work; three times he found he couldn't think straight. Three times he returned to bed in a worse temper.

When he finally slept, he wished he hadn't. He dreamt he was leading his whole army up Seroster's Stair, in the black of night. When he got to the top, he found he couldn't push up the stone trapdoor, because sentries were standing on top. And still, from behind, his men came following in total silence. And he dared not speak to halt them. They pressed in, tighter and tighter, till he couldn't move, couldn't breathe. Men began to choke to death, and still the crush grew worse.

Then he screamed. And with the scream the dawn came. The rest of his army stood revealed on the slopes below the city, and the rain of death fell from the walls, and they died.

Then, in his dream, Little Paul broke down into Seroster's Chamber. The dead hawk he pulled to a handful of feathers. The dead Serosters were tipped from their narrow beds, and crumbled to dust. Then the city died too. Houses fell and walls tumbled and only white pits remained, indistinguishable from the white rock that had been there from the beginning. And the golden body of his cat, and his own body, crumbled with the rest . . .

He woke in a sweat and lay for a long time, trying to convince himself it hadn't happened. The cry of the watchman round the camp was like the breath of life. Finally he got up, lit the light, and helped himself trembling to a drink of water. He was thankful for one thing. He knew now for certain that an attack up Seroster's Stair wouldn't work.

But he had an eerie feeling that somehow Little Paul had eavesdropped on his dream; that merely by dreaming it, he had placed everyone in terrible danger.

Little Paul *had* heard, in a way. In his room in the Palace, by the light of his own guttering candle, he lay face-down, unconscious, on top of a great, open, ancient book. In one hand, he still held a little wax figure, that he seemed to have half-melted by passing it through the candle-flame. The figure held a tiny two-handed sword, and a tuft of golden fur, obtained by unknown cruelties . . .

Three times, Paul had sipped from his little blue bottle and drawn near in dream to Cam's mind. Three times Cam had awakened and slipped away, like trout in the green shadows of a stream. Then Little Paul had drunk the whole bottle. And reached Cam's mind.

Now his own mind walked the caverns and cracks in the rock. Came to Seroster's Chamber, and grasped the magic of the Dead who dwelt there. Began to trace a path back to the surface, to find out where the hidden entrance lay.

But then, behind him, in his dream, came the soft padding of paws. No longer was his mind free to explore the tunnels at leisure. Now it ran hither and thither, like a terrified mouse, trapped by its own magic in the maze of tunnels. Ever the padding paws pursued. He knew it was the black-and-white cat that would be his death. Almost he saw the huge black back rippling, the red jaws.

Paul moaned and tossed, bound up in sleep as if by ropes. For two hours the drug held him. He was played with, died, and released to run again, a dozen times.

When he finally wakened, he knew he would never feel safe again. He had imagined himself secure on the rock of the city. Now he knew it was hollow, riven with cracks and pitted with caverns leading to the outside. Every day he had walked over the heads of a hundred lurking enemies.

He threw the great book on the floor; the empty blue bottle fell with it, tinkling. He grasped his quill and began to write letter after letter, with a shaking hand. He didn't stop all day . . .

At the same moment as Little Paul wakened, Amon also wakened, at the foot of Cam's bed. He stood and stretched, with a very satisfied air, as if he'd had a good night's hunting . . .

"What are you looking so bloody pleased about, cat?"

Amon just purred savagely, and closed his eyes in bliss.

The following night, Cam got no sleep at all. Every two minutes, it seemed, a cat was scrabbling at his shoulder. A tabby, holding a fern-leaf in her mouth. A black, holding a pebble from the stream that flowed through dead Harcourt. A Miw, with an ear of the long-stemmed barley.

A general attack? Or were they fleeing the city in despair?

But each cat only scratched in the dirt once.

Messengers. Messengers fleeing to every point of the compass. All night long the children of Morville wakened to the sounds of galloping hoofs; watched lanterns flaring light on their tent walls; heard hasty arguments, and advice shouted from the saddle.

"We can catch him at Three Pines . . ."

"He'll be working down the streambed . . ."

By morning, eight bedraggled men were sitting with their backs to the wall of the burnt Duke's Head with ropes chafing their wrists. It was agreed by all they weren't worth hanging. Not real villains. None had been armed, or offered any resistance. Riffraff who had always lived in the city. Snatch-purses; eternal drunks. Each had a single gold coin. And a letter, sealed with the late Duke's signet.

Georges threw the letters on Cam's table.

Cam looked at the first, and began to tremble.

It was addressed to the Bishop of Toulouse.

They were all addressed to the Bishop of Toulouse. Cam had once been put on trial by the Bishop for witchcraft. It had started innocently enough with a conjuring-trick involving three oranges and a jug of water. But some jealous rival had reported Cam. So he found himself before the Bishop's Court . . .

It had been hard enough to do the trick again, under the stare of all those cold monkish eyes; he couldn't stop his hands shaking. Harder still to show the Bishop how the trick worked. But he'd managed it. The Bishop had lost his deadly holy look, sneered with disappointment.

"A juggler . . . have him flogged and throw him out." Cam's back tingled with the memory . . .

Others hadn't been so lucky. The Bishop served his God by burning witches. Once, in Toulouse, he had burnt two thousand witches in one day. He had burnt so many, he was known as the Woodcutter's Friend.

Cam ripped open the letter, and stared at Paul's crazed handwriting. Had the fool gone *mad*? He was asking the Bishop for aid . . . there were good Christian men in the city, beset by a horde of warlocks and witches that roamed the walls night and day . . . led by the Devil in person . . . one Seroster, in the form of a man with the head of a cat . . .

It would have been laughable.

Except the Bishop would come. And not alone. He'd raise the whole of the south . . . a crusade . . . Dear God, the Bishop will come and burn us all. Little Paul included. Once he started . . .

"What's he up to, then?" asked Georges. "Getting frightened, is he? Seems to have frightened you, as well . . ."

Cam looked at the trusting beloved faces. Georges . . . old Geoffrey . . . the balding Captain . . . the cat. Once they knew the

Woodcutter's Friend was coming . . . He gave the letter silently to Georges.

"No use to me, mate. Can't read."

Geoffrey shook his head too. And the Captain.

Cam's head whirled. Should he tell them?

He looked at the cat; the cat looked at the sword.

Cam dropped his hand casually, so his little finger touched the sword.

The Seroster smiled; shrugged. "Little Paul has sent for help, to some ruffian in the south . . ."

"Who?"

"Does the name Red Eye mean anything to you?" The Seroster lied quite easily; his slitted eyes revealing nothing.

"Old Red Eye," said Georges. "Oh, we can deal with old Red Eye. Nasty man up a dark alley, mind. But I wouldn't mind meeting him again, in present company. A pleasure . . ."

"Are these all the letters?" asked Seroster. "Or did some messengers get through?"

"Two got away," said Geoffrey.

"It is important that they are caught on the way back," said Seroster. "See to it. I shall enjoy this Red Eye . . ."

Laughing, the meeting broke up.

The city clock chimed midnight, through the cold fog. And still Cam sat fully-dressed on his bed, trembling. The Seroster had saved him. But at a price. For as he touched the sword, Cam had seen again the Seroster's Chamber. And noticed, behind the beds where the Dead lay, another door.

Cam had to walk through that door. He knew. For all power had left the sword and dagger. All he got when he touched them was the vision of that low door. And the longer he sat, the worse he felt . . .

When it became unbearable, he called for his horse.

Found it saddled and waiting . . .

Found when he reached the barricades they were already drawn back.

And the horse knew where it was going. At a steady canter, though Cam could hardly see ten yards ahead.

And in the fog, the shadows of running cats passed, urging him on. It was all as easy as falling down into a slippery pit you are never going to climb out of again.

The horse stopped.

He had no idea where he was. But the cats pressed round him, until he reached Seroster's Stair. And on the dark and winding climb, he felt them passing, rubbing against his legs.

A dim light came in through the chamber's window. Dark blueness falling on to black. He groped for his tinder-box; the chamber sprang into yellow light, glinting on the yellow eye of the hawk.

His vision hadn't fooled him. The door was there, behind the Dead. And the Chamber was full of Miw, facing that door, hunched, eyes closed, almost as if they prayed.

He remembered the dying blacksmith's words.

"Mother – allow your servant to depart in peace."

The Mother.

He remembered the little girl in the city churchyard, with the gaudy gown and the parchment cat-mask . . .

He opened the door . . .

The room beyond was a relief; empty, in the light of his shaking candle. Except for paintings round the walls.

Red-skinned men, with long black hair and short white skirts. Riding in chariots, hunting geese; sitting on thrones while bare-breasted women played on the harp and danced . . .

It was the place of his dreams. But the painted dreams were cracked and fading; a flake of paint fell, fluttered to a floor of grey fur.

His foot skidded on the grey fur. It rolled into little balls that fled away in the draught, like mice.

Dust. How many centuries . . . ?

Across the room, another door. He was a long time undoing the handle.

Then he saw Her.

Arms outstretched in blessing. Cats and kittens clustered round her feet. Tall, breasts full, under the clinging gown. The face of a cat. Golden.

She seemed to smile; beckon. Then, when he did not come, she frowned with rage. Then she seemed to smile again; beckon. And so it went, the smiling and beckoning, frowning and threatening, until he had drawn so close he could smell the ancient dreadful smell of her brassy breath. And her eyes saw into his soul.

He couldn't breathe; reached out a hand, half to greet her, half to fend her off. By accident, he touched her.

Cold, like ice; and furry with the cold. And the fur slid away under his hand and fell to the furry floor. Stiff she was, like one dead . . .

A statue; the only life in her was the flicker of the candle he held in his own hand, and her fur was dust.

All went black.

When he came to himself, he was riding back through the dawn; with only his own cat for company, sniffing at fronds of dawn-damp bracken as if nothing at all had happened.

But clear in his mind was a plan to free the city.

He sent for Father Death.

"I have work for you, Father."

"With a sword?"

"The cross shall be your sword, Father . . ."

In the days that followed, the people of Morville despaired of Father Death. He shaved off his beard, and he shaved his hair like a monk, and he fasted until he grew like a skeleton. And went out into every scrap of sunshine, so his pale podgy face grew as brown as a woodman's. Then he shaved off his great eyebrows . . .

And when the sun wasn't shining, he took off the sewer-rats into the woods, and neither he nor they would say why. But some said they had heard them, late at night, singing strange songs . . .

When people grumbled to the Lord Seroster, he just smiled, and asked if the pack-train had returned from the armoury at Marseilles . . .

31

In the city, they heard them coming far off. The sentry summoned the officer. There was a light mist that morning, so they did not see them until they had climbed almost to the gate.

A young boy carrying a plain wooden cross. Then fourteen choirboys singing sweet and shrill, all in red cassocks, with huge bound psalters clasped in their arms. Then a red priest, gaunt and emaciated, with shaven monkish head and deepset staring eyes. A man not of this world . . .

Then eight sumpter-mules, heavy-laden.

"What do they want?" said the officer, awed. "Have they come to tell us the world is coming to an end?"

"We knew that already," said the sentry, and laughed. But the officer was looking at the laden sumpter-mules, and feeling hungry as usual.

"Let them in," he said. "Send for Little Paul."

It was an uncomfortable wait. Though the priest looked about to blow away with hunger, he refused a seat when it was brought. But stood staring at everything in a holy and disapproving manner. There was plenty to disapprove of. The streets had not been swept for months. The priest, as he paced up and down, seemed to dance a dance of holy disdain between the dead rats and bits of garbage.

The spectators were worse. They swore horribly, within earshot of the priest. Kept stroking the sumpter-mules in a light-fingered manner. The officer kept muttering to the sentries to keep the riffraff off, but the sentries were as light-fingered as the rest.

However, priest and choirboys were no fools. One carried a censer, full of burning incense, which he swung vigorously at anybody who lingered too long, so that one would-be thief got his jerkin set alight. Another choirboy was amazing liberal with sprinklings of holy water. In the last resort, the priest would lay his hands on any intruder's head and begin to bless him in Latin . . . No one got within thieving distance of the purple panniers . . .

The officer rubbed his muddy boots against the backs of his equally-muddy hose. "A cup of wine, Monsignor?"

The priest stared at him, far too long, before replying. "I am fasting in repentance for the murder of the Holy Innocents . . ." As he said 'Holy Innocents' he gave the riffraff a meaning look.

"A little bread, then?"

"My master, the Bishop of Toulouse, has ordered us to fast for the sins of this city . . ."

At the very mention of that name, the crowd drew back.

Then Little Paul came hurrying down, still buttoning up his best robe, and all his henchmen with him.

The priest stared at *him* far too long, so everyone began to shuffle; then handed over a long letter. The crowd watched keenly; no one could tamper with letters like Little Paul; he was famous for it. So he didn't open it. He inspected the wax seal, sniffed it, tapped it.

"This is veritably my old master's seal, unbroken." He broke it now. "And this is veritably my old master's writing – I know it well. He is coming to our aid with a great army . . ." There was a half-hearted burst of cheering. "But where are my own messengers?"

Again, the priest stared too long. "My lord Bishop . . . was not satisfied with their answers. He has kept them to . . . examine . . . further."

Little Paul shuddered visibly. This priest had every mannerism of the Bishop of Toulouse . . . the too-long stare . . . the same mad eyes that no longer cared for anything in this world. The same smell of soot and burning . . .

"What will you do now, Monsignor?" asked Little Paul, nervously.

"I will be the eyes of the Bishop," said the priest; and looked around far too long again. "And your . . . late messengers told us that there was a church in this city, that through foul neglect, had been allowed to fall into ruin . . . St Lawrence on the Wall. Is that not so?"

Little Paul swallowed. "Yes, Monsignor . . . unfortunately we . . ."

"We shall re-roof it, and found a choir-school there. I hope we shall have your support, my lord?"

"Yes . . . yes . . ."

"But because we know the people of this city are now very poor (though no doubt grown in piety with their poverty) it is not my master's intention to leave his choir-school without support . . . "

All eyes turned on the pannier-mules. The priest opened one pannier and plunged his hand in. Everyone held their breath. The priest produced a stout sealed bag, one of many in the pannier. It carried a blue cross, and the word 'Ierusalem'.

"Salt," said the priest. "Salt from the Holy Land. Salt from the Dead Sea. Where Lot's wife herself was turned to a pillar of salt for her *blasphemies.*" Again, he stared round hard, producing shuffles.

Everybody looked fed up. Salt was all right, but nothing like as good as gold or silver. Salt would buy everyday things like bread and cheese, but to be rich you'd need a shipful.

"I give you, Lord Paul, the first bag as a gift from my master."

"Our thanks," said Paul, gritting his teeth with chagrin. "Will you eat with us?"

"The work of God will not wait." The priest gestured, the choir formed up. "We will live in the unruined church, St Alban's on the Wall, with your permission?"

Little Paul nodded humbly. He, and all the crowd, were too dumbfounded to notice that the choir seemed to know its own way to St Alban's, without having to ask . . .

They processed, singing. Still the hangers-on hung on, fingering the panniers, till the priest turned and preached them an interminable sermon on the drearier sins of the flesh . . .

Once they had reached the priest's lodgings, they barred the door.

"Wait," said the priest.

Within minutes, there was a hammering. One of the usurper-patrols. "Now let's see what you've *really* got in those panniers . . ."

They threw out everything. But there was nothing but blue-crossed bags and holy books. They slashed the bags unmercifully, looking for coins hidden inside, strewing the floor with salt till it lay like snow. The only other thing they found was a coil of rope, black with age. But still worth a bit . . .

"Do not touch that, in the name of God!"

"Why not?" sneered the leader.

"It is a holy relic – the very rope that Judas Iscariot hanged himself with. It is fatal to touch it, with unconfessed sins on your soul. I must first shrive you . . . "

The villains dropped it, like a poisonous snake. "Let's have the money in your purse, then! We'll keep it safe for you, in Little Paul's treasury . . . "

The priest emptied a few copper coins out of his pouch. "Take them, with our forgiveness. We will pray for your souls!"

"It'll buy a drink!" said the leader, spitefully, and off they went.

"Idiot," said the priest, fingering his blackened rosary. Which was made of silver coins, dipped in pitch. Then he turned to the choirboys.

"Gather up every grain of salt." The boys brushed up the salt as best they could, using holy books and the hems of their cassocks, and their hands. One boy licked his hand experimentally.

"Urgh! This salt is saltier than salt."

Father Death laughed for the first time since the Harcourt Massacre.

"It is not salt, my little sewer-rat, but saltpetre from the armoury at Marseilles. And if we acquire every ounce of sulphur in this city, and char a lot of wood and scrape off the charcoal, and mix all three together, we shall have that new creature of the Devil, invented by the heathen Chinee, called . . . "

"Gunpowder!" chorused the sewer-rats, amazed.

32

As day followed day, the people of the city got used to the priest. If the raiders of Harcourt found something familiar about him, it was not a familiarity they cared to dwell on. It brought vague feelings of guilt. But then, they said to themselves, it is a priest's job to make men feel guilty even when they aren't . . . And, like reasonable men, they forgot the matter.

The priest made himself hard to ignore. He was up at all hours, in all weathers, preaching repentance before the Day of Wrath on every cobbled corner. But though he preached much about sin, he never preached about anybody's sins in particular. So Little Paul left him alone too.

Daily, he and the choir processed from St Alban's to St Lawrence's. Two of the boys pulled a cart; many usurper-patrols searched that cart, but all they found was rusty nails and wood, and hammers for mending the decayed roof of St Lawrence's.

People watched amazed, as man and boys swarmed over that shaky roof. "They're mad!" And that was everybody's verdict. The priest was a harmless mazeling, to be avoided.

He did other crazed things, like putting poor-boxes into both churches. They were broken into daily. The thieves found nothing. Still, when the priest began spending the odd silver coin, no one suspected his secret hoard. They only said, "*Someone's* got a bad conscience, putting money in the poor-box!"

Little Paul's spies reported that the priest bought only the most ordinary things: bread and cheese, rope and nails; and, above all things, medicinal sulphur from the few remaining apothecaries. But this became a joke, because when the priest was not going on about sin, he was going on about sulphur . . . How the burning of it in bedrooms killed bedbugs, and drove out evil dreams. How a good dose of it purged the body of ill-humours. He carried an old bottle around, of sulphur mixed with water into a foul-smelling paste, and offered it to anyone he talked to.

"Egad," said one wit, "from his love of sulphurous things, this priest would seem a follower of Satan as well as God."

It was a good laugh. But perhaps some people hearkened to the priest's sulphur-sermons. Because he had no sooner bought some in an apothecary's shop (and thanked God for it out loud) than the following night some thief came and stole the apothecary's whole supply.

For the sewer-rats had gone back to their old thieving tricks. By day they were well-scrubbed (with sulphur-soap) and clad in spotless red-and-white. But at night they donned old rags and crept round their old haunts; only now they haunted rooftops as well as sewers.

For, on that first night in the priest's lodging, they had visitors. Sehtek and her faithful band crept along the ledge and mewed at the window. Only ten remained. Hunger and cold and crossbow-bolts had claimed the rest. The survivors were lank and wet of coat, and some were wounded. They were glad to get in front of a roaring fire.

In return, they showed the sewer-rats all the secrets of the catwalks. Taught them to worm their way down the slimy gullies with messages.

By morning, Cam knew everything that had gone on in the city the previous day.

In spite of thinking the priest mad, Paul's spies kept a close watch on St Lawrence's. Their nosiness was a matter of habit, of their bread-and-butter, and, in the end, of their necks.

They saw many innocent things. The boys seemed fond of making fires, with the waste wood from the roof. Of charring sticks and then scraping the charcoal off to make a point. But what boys do not? Nobody noticed how the boys carefully collected the loose charcoal afterwards, and stored it in a dry place.

The spies also reported that the priest had taken mercy on two of the city's hideously-deformed lepers. He allowed them to sit all day, one each side of the door to St Lawrence's crypt, displaying their unmentionable sores and begging for alms. At night, they slept in the crypt. Only the priest dared go near, with bags of foodscraps.

Some of the foodbags contained well-mixed gunpowder, which was piled-up in the crypt beneath fallen stones.

The crypt lay deep in the foundations of the city-wall. (Both churches had been built on the city-wall in the beginning, to strengthen the city's defences with their towers.) Soon there was enough gunpowder to blow a great breach in the wall . . .

The spies noticed that the walls and roof of St Lawrence's were soon festooned with rope-ladders. How else could the pious labourers get up with slates and mortar? And occasionally, a rope-ladder travelled back in the cart to St Alban's, obviously in need of repair. Soon, there were so many ladders travelling to and fro that the spies lost count. They never realised there were now six rope-ladders stored permanently in St Alban's crypt, also deep in the foundations of the city-wall. It would have been possible to lower them right down to the boulder-strewn slope below the wall . . . if only the window in St Alban's crypt had not been so narrow, a mere arrowslit . . .

The spies knew that one choirboy stayed behind every day in St Alban's, to tend the lamps, and scour the brasswork. They did not notice he spent all his spare time in the crypt, gouging out the mortar of the stones round the arrowslit. After a week, that wall was so weak that one heave with a crowbar would have opened up a hole big enough to take six rope-ladders at once . . . Even if the spies had examined that wall, they'd have noticed nothing. For the gaping cracks had been filled up with mud.

The spies noticed one more thing the priest did. A group of abandoned houses stood close by St Lawrence's. The priest asked Little Paul's permission to scavenge those houses for usable wood for the church-roof. Often, as the priest worked on these houses, their floors and roofs would collapse, making a great fire-risk in the dry weather.

But the houses were like separate stone towers; the fallen wood would merely burn inside them, as safely as in a great chimney. Fire would not spread to the surrounding inhabited houses. So the spies just said, "That priest will break his neck one of these days," and left it at that.

After two weeks, the message was wormed-down to Cam: "We are ready."

33

Splosh.

"Uuurk!"

"What's up, Glum?"

"It's gone down inside me boot."

"Water?"

"No, it's soft, slimy and wriggling an' I can't get it out. Bring that lantern here."

"Cross over to us. I'm not coming back over that bit again."

"Blast you, Creeper. I'll make you sorry. Wait till I tell Little Paul . . . "

"Fat lot of notice he'll take of you, mate. If you had any friends left, you wouldn't be down here with us."

"Let me hold your shoulder while I get me boot off. Strewth, that's better."

"What was it?"

"I'm not asking. It's gone. I tell you, I'm right fed up wi' this sewer."

"You've only had half a day. We've had a week. How d'you think *we* feel?"

"If we knew what we were looking for . . . "

"Don't ask me, mate. Old High-and-Mighty just said to keep on going in the dark an' report *anything* we find. It's that or the dungeon, 'e said to me. So I chose this. At least you still get two meals a day, and a bit o' daylight. Once Paul puts you in a dungeon, it's sort of *final*. 'E's got a bad memory for folk 'e puts in dungeons . . . "

"Tell you what, though," said a third voice, out of the dark. "Whatever is down here, old Paul's scared to death of it. Yet 'e sort of *wants* it too. Dead queer 'e looks, eyes shining an' yet sweating an' shakin' all over. An' 'e can't wait to hear what we've found. 'E has you straight in ter see 'im, no matter who 'e's busy with or what your boots drop on 'is carpet . . . "

"Some reckons it's cats . . . "

"Cats!" shrieked Glum. "I'm *off*!"

"To the dungeon, mate? Anyway, we been down 'ere a week, and we ain't seen no cats. Not a bleeding trace."

Ten yards behind, Sehtek could not resist a short soft purr, though her whiskers dripped with slime. She dropped back down the passage to the others. Fenlurker sneezed discreetly, and wiped his nose with his paw.

"Stay much-longer, get cat-flu."

Sehtek splayed her ears grimly. "Must-follow. Even Notep did not know all tunnels . . . "

"Lead them into bad-air-place," sent Gristletongue viciously. "Even a cat cannot breathe there unless it creeps. Or echo-place."

"Men *know* about echoes . . . "

"Me-try," sent Gristletongue. "You heard me in echo-place? Even frighten myself."

"Sometimes you frighten me." But Sehtek considered. She shouldn't be wasting time down here. There was too much to watch above. "There is hatred of men in echo-place, must-admit. I-agree. We try-it."

So they slipped past the floundering men, who were watching nothing but their own feet. And, making little noises, began to draw them on.

"What's that?" shouted Glum.

"Quick, down here!" shouted Creeper.

And at length they came to the echo-place.

And there their lanterns revealed something the cats had never noticed in the dark. On a flat place, where the round sewer ended, was a huge crumbling painting of a cat-head. Perhaps it was only a trick of the flickering lanternlight. But the yawning jaws of the cat seemed to widen and widen, until they could have swallowed the whole human party.

And in the depths of its throat was a speck of daylight, the end of darkness . . .

"Idiot!" sent Sehtek. "You have led them to Sacred-place!" She lashed out. One solitary claw caught Gristletongue on the soft part of his nose, and embedded itself, and could not for some reason be withdrawn . . .

Gristletongue's screech excelled even his own boastings. The echo-place magnified it a hundredfold into such malice that even the other cats screeched with terror. These screeches too were magnified. Terrified by their own screeching, the cats could not stop. The noise grew and grew until men and cats together fled in a scrabbling, slithering, sprawling panic. They no longer cared what they trod in, fell in, near-drowned in. Anything to get away from that noise.

Sehtek got her wits back first. She shouldered Fenlurker into a side-tunnel.

"Fetch-help. They must-die now. Know Sacred-place!"

"No-need," sent Fenlurker. "He leads them to bad-air-place . . ."

They watched in awe as poor Gristletongue fled on, the frantic men pursuing. Finally, they caught a glimpse of him, by the light of their lanterns, and saw his real, quite ordinary size. Their fear turned to rage; they lashed at him with their swords. When he came to the bad-air-place, and had to crawl on his belly, they were on to him.

"Hold up the lantern," shouted Glum. "I'll finish him!"

High went the lantern; the flame changed colour. The sword missed Gristletongue by a whisker, sparked blue on the stones . . .

The dark filthy air turned to orange flame. The bang shook the city. A blast of hot air warmed Little Paul's face, as he waited eagerly by the sewer-cover. It carried the smell of brimstone and Hell.

But he was not so afraid as the blackened, half-blinded, gibbering wrecks who stumbled out minutes later, pursued by the most terrible cat-noise ever heard in that city.

Glum took one look at Little Paul and said, "Show me where your dungeon is!"

Then he fainted.

The rest listened in horror to the noise coming from the sewer. Nobody realised it was not cat-menace, but cat-terror. Gristletongue was still yowling when the reinforcements reached him. Misguided to the end, he had crawled back into the heart of the echo-place . . . Sehtek sniffed him gently, sighed with relief.

"Will-live. Recover in-time. But he deaf, blind, smell-nothing, whiskers-blown-off. Think he all-alone. Lead-him Morville, gently."

As the others closed round him, Gristletongue stopped yowling.

When they got him out into the daylight, beyond the city-wall, they found Sehtek had underestimated. He was bald all over as well, from the blast.

For him, new hero, the war was over. A Miw-tale would be told of him, to the kittens, forever.

For Paul, it was just beginning. He knew now that he walked over not just pits of enemies, but also over pits of fire, magic that could drive men mad.

But he would steal that magic somehow; he would drive other men down other sewers.

Meanwhile, he had a much easier job to do.

34

Sir Henri was writing another letter to the Seroster, challenging him again to single-combat. He was very drunk; his quill sprawled all over the paper like a frantic spider.

"Sir, as you are a Man of Honour, I beg you . . ."

The quill, impelled by all the longing of Sir Henri's drunken heart, ripped straight through the parchment, leaving a splatter of ink-splotches like a plague of flies. Sir Henri gathered up the sheet and tore it into shreds. The Seroster never replied anyway . . .

"No honour," roared Sir Henri, throwing another fine crystal goblet at the wall. "No honour, no valour, no courtesy . . ."

Castlemew shifted her front paws uneasily, as the shower of glass passed over her. She knew Little Paul read all Sir Henri's foolish letters to the Seroster, letters full of words like 'love' and 'honour' and 'esteem'. She also felt the hatred growing daily in Little Paul's heart . . . But still she surveyed Sir Henri's pale and working face with a stare of undying love. To her, he could do no wrong.

"The Seroster sets me at *naught*!" Sir Henri, running out of crystal-ware, threw a pewter pot instead. "A man cannot even *fight* in peace, these days!" The pewter hit the wall with an unsatisfying clunk, and bounced into the middle of the floor. Sir Henri gave a sigh that made the ends of his moustache vibrate, and sank down into a chair.

"What have I descended to?"

Now was the time, Castlemew knew, when rage gave way to despair. Now was the time to sidle in under the great metal elbow and sit on those hard steel knees, and purr her lord back into peace of mind.

Henri stroked her without really noticing she was there. At first his hand was rough with rage; but she bore it, and slowly it grew gentle. Finally, her lord grew calm enough to notice her.

"Hallo, Lady Castlemew, how did you get there?"

But just as they were settling peacefully, a scratching knock came at the door. Castlemew felt her lord's hand pause and stiffen.

"Come in, damn you!"

Little Paul crept in sideways like a crab; hunched, as if fearing a blow. Hunched because he was also carrying a great golden bottle of wine, and glasses that clinked. Sir Henri noticed the bottle. His voice grew slightly warmer.

"Put down your burden, friend!"

"It is Châteauneuf-du-Pape, from my own store. I brought it to console you."

"Open it then. It will console no one with its cork in."

Paul did not put it on the table by Henri. He turned away to a side-table in a dark corner – a table far too low for comfort. Castlemew twitched her whiskers, leapt from Sir Henri's knee and ran across to see what he was up to.

Little Paul stamped his foot at her, hissed with fury. "Sorry – I can't abide cats."

"No accounting for tastes," said his host amiably. "Come here, Castlemew." Castlemew could only obey. In any case, she had seen enough; Little Paul was slipping a white powder into one of the glasses.

She went and sat on the table by her lord.

The glass came, brimming to the top. Castlemew sniffed; it had an odd smell, but faint. No mere man would notice.

Castlemew began to rub herself against the rim of the glass, purring in apparent ecstasy.

"Look at her," said Sir Henri admiringly. "Proper little drunkard. Can't get enough of it."

Little Paul grinned sickly; it had not escaped his notice that the cat was working the goblet nearer and nearer the edge of the table . . .

"Go on, puss! Have a swig!" Sir Henri laughed, as if it was the biggest joke in the world. The glass teetered on the edge. Little Paul made a grab for it. Castlemew, feigning panic at the approach of his hand, gave a great leap and landed goblet and contents in Paul's lap.

"Oops, you frightened her." Sir Henri flapped a filthy napkin all over Paul's breeches, in an attempt to repair the damage.

"I'll pour another," said Paul, gritting his teeth. Again he slipped powder in.

Again Castlemew made straight for it.

"No, no, my lady puss," said her lord. "Fun is fun, but

Châteauneuf-du-Pape is also Châteauneuf-du-Pape." He lifted the goblet to drink . . .

Castlemew could only leap for his arm, and send the goblet spinning to the floor.

"By Great Harry!" roared Sir Henri. "You *wicked* puss. Out! Out!" Quivering with rage, he pointed to the open window. And to the windowsill in disgrace, poor Castlemew had to go.

She watched Paul poison a third drink. Desperate; helpless.

But Paul too was having his troubles. His breeches, where the first drink had soaked them, were turning a strange vivid green. In fact, a thin green foam was fizzing out all over them. And from Paul's winces, the foam was doing something equally dreadful to the skin beneath. Still, he came back bearing a third deadly goblet. But by now the spreading green colour was so marked that even Sir Henri noticed.

"By God, sir, your breeches are very fine. Black, with a bright green crutch? Quite the coxcomb, eh?"

Paul was limping, his face twisted with pain. "It is the latest fashion, sir!"

"By'r ladykin, is it really? Could've sworn they were all black when you came in. My eyes aren't what they were, though. But . . . they're sort of fizzin' . . . is that fashionable too? Fizzin' breeches?"

"I think," said Little Paul, pale as marble and closing his eyes against the agony, "that the dye must have been defective . . . "

But the agony was too great. Paul gave a leap and a screech and fled the room, dropping the last poisoned goblet in ruin as he went.

"God's wounds, the rushes are fizzin' too!" Sir Henri gazed at the floor in drunken bemusement. "What a strange fellow – didn't even bother to say goodbye. No courtesy any more . . . no valour . . . no chivalry . . . still, he's left half the bottle undrunk." Sir Henri picked up a badly-dented but safe pewter tankard from another part of the floor, and helped himself.

"He's right – a fine vintage. Must ask him for another bottle, once he's changed his breeches. Eh, Lady Castlemew?" And he chuckled to himself, good humour restored.

But it wasn't really a laughing matter. For in a deeper part of the Palace, Little Paul, as he tore the shreds of searing cloth off himself, knew for the first time, and for a certainty, who his real enemy had been, from the day when the scroll with the grocer's death-sentence had gone missing. What a fool he had been, peopling his dreams with great black panthers coming to destroy him . . . All the time, as the fortune-teller had foretold, his downfall was being brought on by a little old dingy black-and-white alley-cat.

He turned all his devious mind to the killing of Castlemew. Once she was dead, the prophecy could not come true . . .

But first he must get a wax impression of the key of Sir Henri's chamber.

35

The citadel was the eye of the city. The highest point of the Rock. Day or night, anything that moved could be seen, inside the city or out.

It had been built by the old craftsmen, of stupefying white blocks you couldn't force a dagger-point between. Thirty bowmen could hold it against thousands. In its vaults was a deep well. It had never been stormed.

Since the Beginning, watchmen had stood there. A trumpeter, ready to trumpet armed men to any point of defence.

Who held the citadel held the city.

"There is a little salley-port," said Cam, "leading direct from the citadel on to the city walls above my Chamber. We shall trick them into opening it."

"How d'you know it's still there?" objected Georges. "How do you know some clever bastard hasn't walled it up? Maybe the lock's rusted . . ."

"I *know*," said Cam, "because I am the Seroster." He touched the sword with the tip of his little finger. Inside, the Seroster stirred like a sleeping dog. For a second, he looked out through Cam's eyes.

"Lay off, Cam!" grunted Georges. "That gives me the bloody creeps."

Cam laughed, and sent the Seroster back to sleep. "Leave the citadel to me. I'll take twenty men. If twenty can't do it, two hundred won't."

All the shining young men wanted to go with Cam. If anyone was remembered in song, it would be those who stormed the citadel. They flocked round Cam, shouting, "Take *me*, take *me*!"

"I'll come, and keep an eye on you," said Georges.

"No," said Cam; because he loved him.

"Why not?" roared Georges.

"You're too *big*," lied Cam. "You'd get stuck and block the passage."

Georges gave him a thump that knocked him against the wall.

"I'll let the Seroster out . . . "

"Aaargh," roared Georges, and left.

Cam took those he didn't love. Who were small and sneaky, and especially the left-handed, for they would fare better against the right-handed defenders, on the spiral stairways.

When nineteen had been chosen, the Duke stepped forward.

"Take me. I am small and quick and left-handed, and it is *my* city and I am sick of being carted round like a piece of baggage."

There was a sudden hush; the Duke's words seemed to carry on the wind. From everywhere, people came running. Even the cats, mousehole-eyed. The Seroster heaved in Cam's mind, like a sleeper turning over in bed. The whole world seemed to press on Cam's mind.

He said patiently, to the Duke, "You must *live* for the people's sake. If you are killed, they have nothing left to fight for. That is *your* burden, which *you* must carry."

"How will you stop me going?"

"I will lock you in the wine-cellar, and throw away the key."

"*You* will?"

"I will put you in that room with my own two hands," said Cam.

"Try it," said the Duke.

And somehow, with all the people watching, there was nothing to do but chase him.

Except the Duke had been the Big Kitten. He was impossible; seemed to have learnt how to run up walls vertically; walk along bare, charred rafters; worm through a hole where only a cat could go. Like all cats, he feared no heights.

After half an hour, the Seroster gave up, panting. With the Duke sitting on the highest gable-end in Morville, shouting "Let me go, or I'll *jump*."

"He has made his point," said the Captain.

"He has earned his place," said old Geoffrey.

"He is the true son of his father," said all the people portentously, quite forgetting the old Duke had been rather corpulent, and always avoided heights.

"Very well," said Cam. When the Duke finally came down, he gave him the hiding of his life. Afterwards, the Duke turned up a tear-stained face. "But you can't stop me going!"

By nightfall, some people were making out he had actually flown from rooftop to rooftop . . . They cheered him wherever he appeared. He got a liking for being cheered, and kept walking through the camp demanding weapons.

But though he (and everyone else) looked high and low, no shining armour was to be had in so small a size. In the end, Geoffrey cut down a jerkin that a very small soldier could spare. It was black with dirt, its studs red with rust.

"I can't wear that," yelped the Duke. "It makes me look like a chimney sweep."

"There's no better way to look, on a night raid," said Geoffrey. "Harder to see is harder to kill." He laughed, and reaching up the chimney, brought down a handful of soot which he smeared on the Duke's cheeks. "Now you look a *real* raider."

The Duke stopped spluttering and kicking, and looked into the dull camp-mirror Geoffrey held up. Suddenly, he quite liked his dirty, dark and dangerous look. Geoffrey put his own long dagger into the Duke's hand.

"She's stopped a few in her time," he said, remembering. "Her name is Misericord, or Mercy-giver."

The Duke felt the rough coldness of the steel; it made him feel very real . . .

He went on feeling pleasantly real, as they set off for Beauly in the dusk. The party were strung-out, a hundred yards apart, flitting from wall to bush. There was a Miw for every man, and they scouted all sides. Bigger armies would be moving tonight, but this was the one that must not be seen.

The Duke had to work hard. Watching for the signal from in front, signalling up the man behind. He was quite alone as the moon came up, showing the ramparts of the city on his left. Watchmen silhouetted against the moon; more than usual. It seemed a miracle they didn't see him, as he crawled along ditches getting sharp twigs into his hands without making as much as a sigh.

Lonely. The only company the occasional Miw, grey in the moonlight, coming out of nowhere and whizzing past, as if on purpose to make him jump.

Life felt real, too, in Beauly Willows, where they waited for the moon to hide her face.

Each man made himself as comfortable as possible, squatting on a grass-tussock above the water. Each fetched out some little comfort, a leg of chicken or a hunk of bread, and chewed to calm his nerves. One shadowy figure passed the Duke a shrivelled apple that tasted of oil.

"Something to stop your belly rumbling." He didn't speak with that mixture of deference and pity the Duke was used to. He spoke as if to a mate. The apple tasted better than anything the Duke had ever eaten. He knew they were discussing him in low voices, wondering how the lad would do (because each man was wondering how he himself would do). But their voices were gentle.

The moon hid herself in time (as Seroster said she would). The Seroster found the entrance to his stair as easily as everyone said he would. Oh, to be calm like the Seroster, thought the Duke, as he tried to stop his knees shaking by pressing them together.

Man after man crossed to that black hole where the Seroster's mailed hand beckoned out of shadow. When it was the Duke's turn he placed his feet as carefully as a cat. The city-wall was directly overhead, and he could hear the nervous voices of the watchmen bickering, as if they were in the same room.

They climbed the stair in blackness. It was good it was so narrow; your elbows brushed against the rock in the dark, and made you feel secure.

But how the walls pressed in, with all the weight of rock above. Cracks and buried things that had fallen down them when the world was young, to crumble or rot, or dry thin as paper. Skulls lay side by side; one had been the head of a man who had danced and sung when the other was already a skull. Now they were skulls together, and no man could have told the difference.

Time meant nothing down here.

Time meant everything down here. Rock and time. And time was as hard as rock; and rock was as old as time.

The Seroster's Stair was not for mortal men.

In his Chamber, the Seroster lit a glim of candle, and stuck it in the ageless wine-bottle, by the ageless hawk. The candle flickered, and the hawk's eyes moved, watching.

The men sat where they could, in the narrow crooked spaces between things; careful to touch nothing. Most of all, they huddled away from the Dead. No man would look on them; and the Dead grew greater, from not being looked at . . . as the shadows thrown by the candle danced, the Dead seemed, to the averted eyes of the living, to rise and stretch and walk their Chamber again.

Cam went ahead, with a few men, posting them at every turn of the Stair, to pass messages. He reached the top with only the Duke and Amon, a slender length of cord, a coil of rope, and a rope-ladder. He put his thin shoulders against the trapdoor-slab and heaved gingerly. The Duke could hear the outlet of his breath . . .

The slab grated loudly, moved. A slit of blue night appeared and the green breath of the city's gardens blew in, to disturb the dust of centuries. Cam wedged the slab with his dagger-hilt, and listened.

"Hey, Horn, c'mere!"

Sentries on the wall-top.

"What yer want?"

"Heard a noise, down in this house – sort of hollow groan, like!"

Silence for three long breaths, while Horn looked down. Then he spat loudly, and his spit hit the paving-stones by the slab. "Fool! Four bare walls an' a bare floor . . . You drunk?"

"Well, it's scary, that house. Why don't no one live there?"

" 'Cos it's got no roof on, fool. Look, your job's to watch outside the wall. Don't let Ironhand catch you looking the wrong way."

"Think 'e'll be round?"

"Yeah. Twitchy as a dog wi' fleas. There's something stirring. Making all the High and Mighty nervous."

"Think they'll attack?"

"Naw. Pot-bellied townsmen . . . "

"That Seroster ain't no pot-bellied townsman . . . "

"Ain't no such person . . . "

Cam raised the slab higher. Peered out, cheek to ground. As he'd remembered, the house-walls were sheer and bare. One storey up, a line of holes where the floor-joists had slotted. A few stumps remained. And, another storey up, the stump of the great roof-beam jutted against the sky. If they could reach that roof-beam, and it would hold . . .

The night was still. Horn and friend, distantly bickering. Someone else, further off, sang a snatch of bawdy song. A message came down from the citadel.

So the salley-port was still in use . . .

He left the Duke to listen, returned to the Chamber. There, he found a dreadful silence; each of his men sat in frozen panic, not looking at the Dead. By the time they came to fight, they'd be useless . . .

There was only one thing to do; though he hated doing it. He went into the alcove; sat down on the third bed. Took off his sword-belt, while every man watched, out of the corner of his eye. Then he lay down. And Amon came and lay on his chest, curled up comfortably. And Cam lifted the poor dry body of his old friend Smerdis, and laid that on his chest too . .

Every man in the Chamber let out a deep sigh. They relaxed, dozed. Even Amon fell asleep. Leaving Cam alone, with the cold leather straps of the bed cutting into his back, and his cold thoughts blowing through his mind . . .

I am the Rock.

The cracks are my veins, and the green water is my blood, and the grass that blows in the city gardens is my hair. Through my bowels the rats are running and through my hair the night-wind is blowing. Somewhere in this city a child is being born, and I am that child. A robber and a harlot are conceiving; and I am that child too. I am the old man who is dying, and I am the bones that still live. I am everything, and I cannot bear it, but I must . . .

He dreamed.

He saw them coming, out of the storm-tossed ships that strewed the harbour of the fishing-port with the torn papyrus of their hulls, like golden blood.

But there were no houses yet.

He saw them marching, through the Mire. And the white horses were already there, and they greeted the golden cats, then ran for the joy of running.

He saw them marching across the red plain, the golden cats and the men in white kilts. The cats were bigger, then, and the men smaller. And the men bore a palanquin, holding the statue of a graceful woman; with the head of a cat.

He saw them assault the walls of the city. The walls were lower then, of timber only. He saw the cats leap up the walls, with ropes in their mouths. Smelt the old smell of burning. Heard shouting.

"Seroster! Seroster!"

Then saw the figure fall from the heights, in the moment of victory. And the voices mourned, "Seroster! Seroster!"

He wakened; sweating.

In the midst of the thickets beyond Hadel, Geoffrey stood to get his breath back, and watched the army he'd trained file past. They placed their feet carefully, snapped no twig. They didn't straggle or bicker. Every man saving his breath like a good soldier. Their pikes no longer got caught in bushes, or poked at the eyes of comrades. Shortened, of course, for street-fighting . . .

Aye, thought Geoffrey. They'll do.

Two miles south, Georges was less happy. As he watched his bigger army pass, he swore and ran his fingers through his hair. They would not stop chattering and stumbling and crashing about, or calling to each other in the dark.

It was lucky they were an army that was *meant* to be noticed. Especially that great contraption with its creaking wheels that would waken the dead . . .

Why does it always happen to me? All his mates would be killing themselves laughing . . .

At least he had the bowmen. They had a whole wagonload of arrows, and at least *they* knew what they were doing . . .

36

Father Death sat waiting alone, in the crypt of St Lawrence's.

The sewer-rats had gone, wending their hymns through the darkened streets. The watchmen on the walls, long accustomed to seeing Father Death trailing behind, simply assumed he was there and never looked to see.

Even the helpful lepers had gone; even lepers love life.

The only company Father Death had now was gunpowder. And a lit stump of candle, a long length of fuse, and an hourglass. He watched the last grains of sand trickle through the glass, turned it, and scratched another mark on the wall. He had already turned it four times since, at dusk, he'd seen the green cart with the red horse leave Morville for Hadel.

That had been the signal; he had set the glass in motion then. A similar glass was with Geoffrey and another with Georges (desperately hard to turn and read, by the glim of a dark lantern). Tonight, everything would run to the order of the three glasses.

He watched the sand trickling through. This time, when it ran its course, he would not turn it again. It would be time to go.

But he fretted about the fuse. A poor thing, a strand unravelled from an old rope, dipped in wet saltpetre and carefully dried. For a week he had fiddled with that fuse, testing it and timing it against the hourglass. Sometimes it burnt slow; sometimes as fast as a galloping horse; sometimes it went out altogether. He sighed, and shuffled his hands through his priest's robe. No more time for fiddling; it would have to do.

Time for a last look round the church, to make sure things were right. He climbed the stair to the nave; tugged at the rope-ladder that hung outside the glassless window, above the city cliff. The one he would have to climb, to escape over the roofs; this was no night to be caught in the streets by a usurper-patrol.

The ladder was firm, though it swung sickeningly under his hand.

Then he went to the window that overlooked High Wood, and listened. The noise came up, subtle but clear; chink of sword on shield; a twig snapping. The wood was full of soldiers; if it had been any fuller the trees would have bent outward.

As he turned away, the scent of the church came to him like a whisper. It might have lain neglected for years, prey to dogs and drunkards who could not control their bladders. But they had cleaned and scrubbed it, and now the older smells had come back; incense and candles and prayer. Father Death felt sad. There had been times in the last days, up on the roof pretending to mend it, when he had almost been convinced he *was* mending it . . . But St Lawrence's must die now. It was just that he realised he wasn't going to enjoy blowing it up after all.

Time to go, before he grew morbid.

Time indeed; when he got back to the crypt, the sand had stopped running in the hourglass. How long ago? Was he one minute late, or ten? He lit the fuse with shaking fingers, watched it burn. It seemed to go out; then burnt a foot in the twinkling of an eye. There was only twenty feet to burn, but the little glowing spark held him hypnotised, like a red snake's eye . . .

Suddenly he recalled the long climb ahead, up the ladder and across the rotten rafters in the dark. He grabbed the hourglass and fled.

He went up the ladder like a monkey; began to work his way across the roof, spread-eagled, groping for a foothold among the tiles with fingers and toes. Imagined the fuse burning, in the dark directly beneath him; the stacked bags of black powder. How ironic, to be slain by a device he had so lovingly made. He who lives by the sword shall die by the sword, he thought, and crawled faster.

Perhaps there was a God up there, after all, tired of being denied and cursed by Father Death. A God who was playing with him, as a cat plays with a mouse . . .

He crawled faster still. How many times had he asked out loud to die?

The roof sagged beneath him, like a comfortable feather bed. He sucked his breath in; he had strayed too far right in the dark, on to the rotten part. He could hear tiles breaking from their wooden plugs, quite near, falling to the church floor inside.

Desperately he wormed left to safety. The roof ceased to sag; the tiles stopped dropping. But by the time he'd reached the roof of the adjacent house, he was panting so hard he thought all the sentries on the wall must hear. It'd seemed so easy by daylight . . .

The burning fuse . . . he wriggled on. Then heard voices.

"I'd love to know what's going on in that bleedin' wood." Two watchmen stood, directly overlooking the next roof he'd have to cross. He crept behind a chimneystack; trapped. Not far enough away from the church. This house would blow up with it.

The voices came nearer.

"What's in the wood, mate? Every man that lot can raise, mate."

"There's something coming up the road . . . a house-on-wheels. Can't you hear it creaking?" The voice rose to a squeak.

"Battering-ram, that is. They're going for the gate . . ."

They were so enthralled that Father Death took courage, and began to work his way across the roof, almost at their feet.

"Boiling oil will set it alight. Sir Henri knows his stuff . . ." The relaxing note in the speaker's voice warned the priest. Halfway across, he froze into a black bundle.

"Quiet enough inside the town." The changed sound of their voices warned the priest they were looking straight at him. He didn't dare raise his head; the white blur of his face would give him away instantly. They must be staring straight over him, taking his dusty robe for a piece of rubbish, of which the city was so full. He was all right unless he moved. But if he didn't move soon . . .

Father Death pressed his face against the tiles and tried to pray. But all he could think of was the fuse burning below.

"What's that moving there?" asked one watchman sharply.

It's all up, thought Father Death.

"That whitish thing, on the chimneypot yonder? Hey – it's a cat! Haven't seen one for weeks."

The crank of a crossbow rattled softly. The priest looked up. There was Sehtek, displaying herself on a not-too-distant chimney. Somehow she had turned the sentries' gaze until their backs were almost to the priest. Father Death blessed her, and finished his journey to safety. Immediately, Sehtek vanished, just as the crossbow ceased to wind . . .

But Father Death was no sooner safe than he began to fret. Before, he had had visions of God making the fuse burn like a galloping horse. Now he had visions of God making the fuse go out. Perhaps, all the time he'd been terrified, the fuse had been dead, black, cold. What a Godly joke – worthy of the Deity who had done nothing to stop the Harcourt Massacre . . . Too many minutes had gone by. He groped for the hourglass in his robe. His hand came away with a handful of sand and broken glass.

There is only one way to deal with this God, he thought. I shall go back and relight the fuse and stand over it till it blows up. He started to crawl back, but he was exhausted now, clumsy. His foot slipped, kicking a tile down to fall in silence, then break with a great clatter in the street below.

The sentries turned and spotted him immediately. At this range they couldn't miss. But hopelessly Father Death crawled back towards his church.

Then his exhausted eyes saw the roof bulge upwards, like a pig's bladder blown up to play football with. The roof split in a hundred cracks.

Father Death knew no more.

Sir Henri stood astride the gate. This was the life! No more peace. Never understood peace. Too complicated! But when the trumpet sounds, everything's clear. Them and Us!

Though I often like Them as much as Us . . .

It's the fighting that matters!

He liked the tension running through the city. The men had stopped arguing, scrimshanking. Felt like soldiers. Or at least cornered rats who would *fight*. More rats than soldiers, with their ribs showing through their grimy rags and leather armour shining with sweat. Hungry rats now; food running short; well, they'd fight all the better. Some had lost their boots, but they'd all got their swords, by God!

Too much wall to defend; two miles. Seroster knows that. He'll make a false attack, to draw us all together in one place. Put in his real attack somewhere else. That was the trick of war; make your enemy put his men where they're no damned use!

Sir Henri grunted; I'm far too old a fox to fall for that. False attack would come from High Wood. Far too much noise down there!

Here they come!

Fires blossomed, each side of the wood. By their light, companies came marching out. Nine companies; ten; eleven. Moving smartly, twelve-foot pikes, glint of shield and helm. Thirteen; fourteen; fifteen, each taking its place before the gate. Must be the whole of Seroster's army. Waiting.

For the terrible grinding, groaning, grating noise climbing up past the wood, very slow. Battering-ram. Made by a real soldier, too! Green cowhides, to stop boiling pitch setting it alight.

A plan *this* simple? A crude frontal attack? Sir Henri felt a bitter disappointment. Surely the Seroster could've managed something more ingenious?

He summoned reinforcements; set men shoring-up the gate . . . the slow-moving ram wouldn't be in position for half-an-hour yet. He listened to the ratchets of his own crossbowmen, starting to wind-up all along the wall, like summer grasshoppers chirping in the cold autumn dark.

One or two dark flickering figures exposed themselves behind the ram . . .

There was a whirr of crossbow-bolts departing; a glint like rain in the firelight; one of the flickering figures fell and lay still, till they carried it away.

Slowly the ram came on. He could hear the panting of the oxen inside, the slithering of hoofs, the swearing of their drivers. His own boiling pitch was bubbling nicely; smelt sharp and tingling to his nostrils.

But oh what a *dull* opponent!

Then the ram glowed orange before his eyes; and behind it, the whole countryside as far as Morville. Little orange faces stared up at him, cowering, as the whole world reeled on its axis. He was shouting at the top of his voice, and not hearing a sound. Then a cloud of stones and small boulders fell and bounced around him.

The smell, like hell and brimstone . . . gunpowder . . . they'd used gunpowder . . . breached the wall by the old church. *Damn* gunpowder . . . Damn Seroster, for his sorcery.

God's wounds, they were inside the city already. Houses burning, the clink of fighting . . . witchcraft. Suddenly Sir Henri felt old. He could see nothing; the smoke from the burning houses blanketed the wall, making his eyes sting and water.

The Free Army turned as one man, and marched towards the breach.

He had been totally outwitted.

"Trumpeter, to me!"

He ran, coughing and stumbling.

Father Death came to, hanging over a fearful drop to the cobbles. Possibly, God had been gracious. His priestly robe was caught over a jagged rafter.

His arms and legs worked, though he could only see out of one eye. When he felt for the other, there was a clotted mass of hair and blood that he decided was best left alone.

The two watchmen had not been so lucky; must have been blown clean off the wall.

Further on, whole houses were already alight, turning the night into a bewildering mass of smoke and flame. Beyond that, into the city, he could hear the shrill shouts of battle, the clash of sword on shield. He made for the noise, grinning. It was so realistic, he could have sworn the whole Free Army had broken in.

But the streets below were quite empty. And on the rooftops sat the sewer-rats, beating on old pans with hammers for all they were worth, screaming their lungs out and still dropping burning rags down inside the walls of collapsed and empty houses. They were still wearing their ceremonial robes, which were filthy.

"Good lads. We've pulled the trick!" He pointed towards where Sir Henri's forces were pouring along the wall to defend the breach and clear the town.

"Time to go." Still beating on their pans and screaming, the ghost army of Father Death faded away along the catwalks.

Sir Henri reached the breach. The church had vanished, and the wall with it, for forty paces. The rubble lay on the cliff below, making a smooth ramp for the approaching army to ascend. They would be here any minute, through the smoke . . .

Sir Henri prepared to hold the breach with sixty men and a trumpeter. He thought it might be difficult. But he got his men to shout loudly together, and beat sword on shield. He had the poor trumpeter blowing continuous blasts . . .

Minutes flowed past; no enemy. Where was Seroster? What was he up to, behind the billowing smoke? All the time, reinforcements kept arriving. Sir Henri moved them into place, made them rest to get their breath back. A few more, and he could hold the breach forever . . .

But he grew increasingly uneasy. He heard the creaking of the ram start up again, back at the gatehouse. Ran back to the wall-top and peered through the smoke.

The Free Army was marching back towards the gate, and the ram was within twenty yards of the portcullis now. It would take hours to demolish the gate, of course.

Unless it, too, was full of gunpowder . . .

"Damn!" roared Sir Henri. "Damn, damn, damn!" Now he would have to cover both breach and gatehouse.

"Trumpeter, summon the rest of my men!" That would strip the wall, except for a few sentries, and the citadel. But he knew where the Seroster's army was now; had them all in plain view . . . They couldn't attack undefended parts of the wall while they were marching and counter-marching between breach and gate.

Stalemate . . .

37

Midnight. The deep-bellied bell of the market-clock chimed. Down the winding stair, through the very rock itself, the men in Seroster's Chamber heard it; jerked from uneasy sleep and peered anew into the shadows where the Dead lay. On the stair, others shifted uncomfortably from one aching buttock to another.

Crouched under the trapdoor, the Duke heard Cam counting softly under his breath. "One, two, three . . . "

Then came the great flash in the sky, the tremor through the Rock. Frightened voices shouted overheard.

"What is it, what is it?"

"They've blown in the gate."

"Too far right!"

"It's the gatehouse, I tell you."

"I can't see. They're inside the city. Listen!"

"C'mon! Quick, afore they get a foothold."

The retreating sound of running boots, then silence.

Cam threw back the trapdoor; there was no one to hear its soft thud. Red light was flickering on the walls high up; but the trapdoor lay in black shadow. Behind, on the stair, the message was passed. The attack gathered.

Then they heard the watchmen returning. Horn laying down the law.

"You'll stand fast. We don't know *what's* happening down there."

In the shadows, Cam shrugged. Now or never! He picked up Amon, walked across to the wall, and with a soft whisper, threw him vertically up it. The cat scrabbled frantically, almost as if he was trying to run on air, then vanished into an empty joist-hole.

So far, so good, thought Cam. The sentries, though near and noisy, had their attention elsewhere. Fire was gaining in the lower city, and fire draws all eyes.

Cam uncoiled his rope, threw a loop over the nearest joist-stump. Tested it; started to climb.

The stump broke, fell to the ground with a terrible clatter.

No one seemed to hear.

He tried another joist-stump; that broke too. All rotten.

"Horn, Horn, I did hear a noise in that bloody house, I tell you."

Footsteps above. Amon crouched into his joist-hole. Cam flung himself into the shadow of the fireplace; everyone held their breath.

"Orders from the citadel!" A new voice. "Take half your lot down to the gate, Horn. Leave the rest here wi' me." Arguments broke out about who should go.

From his chimney, Cam beckoned the Duke; out of his snug trapdoor into the red light of the open air. Frightened, not understanding, the Duke flew to him.

"Up on my shoulders!" It was Seroster speaking now. The red firelight flickered on eye-slits. No thought of disobeying. The Seroster's shoulders were thin, but sinewy, like iron bands moving. He walked to the wall, and threw the Duke up, as he had thrown the cat. The Duke clung on in a daze, feeling the rotten joist-stumps moving beneath his feet, thrusting fingers into cracks to stay upright.

"Catch this cord!" The thin loop came snaking up. The Duke let go with one hand to catch it, and nearly fell off the wall.

"Put it round your neck, and stand *still*!"

The Duke braced himself. The Seroster's whisper was like an iron rod, stiffening his spine. He felt the big cat emerge and start to climb him; all thirty pounds hanging on claws that pierced his jerkin and gouged his flesh. The Duke stood firm, biting his lip. At last, the cat reached his shoulder, and delicately, head sideways, picked up the cord in its mouth. Its furred ear touched the Duke's and fluttered. But it was purring, and its purr comforted the Duke, as Sehtek's had so long ago.

"Hang on tight," whispered the Seroster. "Now!" The Duke felt the cat gather itself, and leap. The kick of those huge hindlegs nearly threw him down to the black-flagged floor.

The cat hit the wall six feet above with frantically-scrabbling claws; hung there a second balanced on nothing, then leapt again. One paw dug into the great rafter-beam. Slowly, slowly, like an old man, the cat got itself on top and dropped the loop of cord round the rafter.

Below, the Seroster had tied a rope to the cord. Drew on one end, and the great rope swayed up past the Duke.

"Look – there's something moving in that house, now!" It was the plaintive voice of the same old sentry. The Duke could imagine every eye turned on that fatal rafter.

Amon did the only thing left. He shuffled awkwardly on the rafter . . .

"It's one of those blasted cats!"

Amon leapt straight across the roofless house, straight at the approaching voices. The Duke saw him, a fiery golden shape, spread-eagled against the black smoky sky, as if he was really flying. Every tuft of his fur, every separate plume of his tail was sparking out; he looked twice his real size.

Amon vanished. An awful scream of terror.

"My face. Get him off my face."

"Kill the thing." Swords clashed on stone. The screaming and shouting got more and more distant.

"Quick," said the Seroster again. Now there was a rope-ladder attached to the rope, tapping against the Duke's shoulder. "Climb. Hook the ladder over the beam."

Sweaty-palmed, the Duke started up. The rope hurt his hands, but nothing mattered now, except to get the ladder in place. And as he clung on, he felt the rope lifting him like a bird, under the tremendous pull of the Seroster's muscles.

With agonising clumsiness, he got the ladder over the rafter. Climbed up on to it, closing his eyes in triumph.

Then opened them quickly, as he heard a hostile shout.

The sentries were returning. One swung Amon by the hindlegs. The cat looked horribly dead. And now the sentries could see *him* sitting astride the rafter, as clearly as they'd seen the cat.

For a second, he sat paralysed. He had a choice. Below lay the trapdoor, the tunnel, safety. He could climb down and run away and never come back. But then, the attack would fail and the city, *his* city, would die and rot.

Or he could do what the cat had done. Leap at his enemy; attack and die. He would not last as long as the cat. Then he would be carried around in triumph, a dead, swinging trophy.

He chose; he leapt out at the enemy. Tried to think of a great battle-cry, but all that came out was a great stream of meaningless gibberish.

The sentries were flabbergasted. Cats were certainly enemies.

But a filthy babbling guttersnipe, waving a toy sword? In his dirty ragged jerkin, he could be the son of one of their mates . . .

They stepped aside, laughing; let him run clean through their ranks. And since he had shut his eyes in terror, his dagger failed to draw blood. He didn't even realise what was happening until, twenty yards on, he tripped over a pike and went sprawling.

There was a cruel shout of laughter.

The Duke picked himself up, amazed to find himself still alive. He headed back towards them, still babbling, waving his dagger.

"Give him a whack," said someone. "Cheeky little sod!" A sword came up and descended. Not with the sharp of the blade, but the flat. Not through the Duke's skull, but smartly across his backside.

It still hurt more than he could ever have imagined. He screeched, leapt smartly in the air. Then they were all whacking at him, and he was a sea of pain. But he managed to keep retreating down the wall, drawing them off from Seroster's house and the fatal ladder.

The sentries had seldom enjoyed themselves so much. But one or two of the old hands kept their wits and held back.

So that as the Seroster reached the top of the ladder, his two-handed sword still dangling useless down his back, six of them threw themselves on him.

They knew exactly what to do with fully-grown intruders . . .

There came a hammering on the salley-port of the citadel. The men inside opened the spy-hole cautiously, for there had been sounds of battle outside, till a moment ago.

Six men stood there, wearing the symbol of Ironhand.

"Open up, blast you. We've captured the Seroster. Shove him in the dungeon, till the Gaffer can have a bit o' fun wi' him . . ."

The keeper of the salley-port peered through his hole more intently. He certainly knew the first two men . . . they had been in and out of the salley-port all evening. They looked pale and strained, but that was battle. And the salley-port-keeper had survived the Battle of Morville. One of the few who knew what Seroster looked like. Now he saw him again; the ghost of a moustache, the lank black hair drooping over closed eyes, the thin body hanging down nerveless to the ground between two captors. His jerkin was thick with blood; his feet dragged across the paving-stones. All his war-like glory was gone. Another of Iron-hand's men brandished the famous two-handed sword . . .

It was enough. Bolts were dragged back, the door opened, and the limp figure of the Seroster carried through.

Sir Henri was baffled. Time passing, and nothing really happening. The battering-ram had been abandoned, black and stinking now, a mass of singed hides and cooling pitch. As full of crossbow-bolts as a pincushion. Perhaps one of its axles had broken . . .

The Free Army seemed to be countermarching itself into total exhaustion, without making any attack. It was beginning to look very ragged.

"Stalemate," said Sir Henri again. "As defender, I win." But he felt bitterly disappointed. He considered the Free Army. Were there no real men among them? Who *wanted* a fight? They'd comported themselves like a gossip of women . . .

The nearest company had broken into little chattering groups. Didn't look right, somehow, even in the dim light of the dying fires. Kept tucking their hair back under their helmets. *Touching* each other, in an unmanly way . . .

Then a shining helm fell off, and a cascade of golden hair fell down, and the awful truth became plain.

The whole vast army before him was an army of *women*.

Where were the men?

"Tricked, bedamned!" But Henri's mind still moved like lightning. The priest; the damned red priest. *He* had blown up St Lawrence's . . .

Where was he now?

"March on St Alban's," roared Sir Henri.

Father Death sat waiting, in St Alban's crypt. He needed no candle now. The arrowslit in the crypt had been enlarged to the size of a barn-door. Light from the burning houses streamed in.

No one had heard the masonry fall. Two sewer-rats had done it, covered by the sound of the explosion. They were invisible from the wall-top, even if any soldiers remained up there. Rope-ladders lay coiled ready . . .

All was ready, save one thing.

A hundred yards along the wall, the citadel reared its height, pinnacle on pinnacle, arrowslit on arrowslit. Every slit commanded the rough slopes up which the invaders must come. There might be thirty crossbowmen in there. While they remained, it was death to move on the city slopes.

Father Death stared out at the citadel; it had an evil look, like congealed pinnacles of flame. Perhaps the Seroster had already stormed it? There was no way of telling by looking. The Seroster's signal of success was three blasts on a hunting-horn . . . that had sounded all right in the calm of Morville. But now, amidst the general blasting of trumpets, the roar of flames and crash of buildings . . .

"I thought I heard it then, sir," said one sewer-rat. Father Death caught him cruelly by the shoulder.

"Are you *certain*, boy? No cheering lies – that won't help us." But inwardly he thought, Dear God, what shall I do?

God was playing cat-and-mouse with him again.

"I heard it, sir. I'm sure I heard it," said another.

Father Death rose, and threw down the rope-ladders, one by one.

"Into Thy hands, O Lord," he said bitterly, as a host of men broke from the scrub below, and began to climb the slope.

The keeper of the salley-port flung back his door. Two men dragged the Seroster across the threshold.

"Scum!" shouted the doorkeeper. He pulled up the Seroster's face by his hair and spat on it.

Perhaps his spittle had miraculous properties; for immediately the Seroster revived, catapulted from between his captors and butted the keeper in the stomach. He made a noise like a punctured bladder and collapsed, bearing down two more who stood behind. And the Seroster's other late captors began to lay about them with their swords; at everyone but the Seroster.

It was very confusing.

It's hard to be brave when you're confused. The defenders of the salley-port turned and ran. After that, they were never allowed to stop running. They ran upstairs and down, into chambers and out, screaming warnings and panicking everyone else. You need *time* to explain things, especially if you don't understand them yourself. You need *time* to stand and fight. But the moment the defenders tried to do either, there were dozens of young men with bright swords and enthusiastic faces determined to stop them.

The guard tried hiding in closets; behind sweet-perfumed ladies' dresses in great wardrobes. To no avail. The bright eager young men rousted them out, draped in velvet and furs. Even when they were being led to the dungeons, the guard complained it was *unfair* – nobody had told them what was going on.

It was an easy victory, with nobody killed. It would have been nastier if the citadel's crossbowmen had joined in. But they were Genoese mercenaries, and they hadn't been paid for months. Their leader said, "Don't look at me, breathing fire and thunder. What's there worth fighting for?" He lounged against a wall, picking bacon-rind out of his teeth with a splinter of wood, his crossbow unwound at his feet.

"*I'll* pay you," said Cam.

"I'll pay *you*," said the leader. "To show us the road out of here."

One room, high in the citadel, was empty save for large books, and small blue bottles. It had not been empty long; a good fire was burning, and the felt carpet-slippers lying tumbled were still warm. Very small slippers . . .

"Little Paul!" roared Cam.

But he was nowhere . . .

"I let no one past me," said the new guard at the salley-port, "except that woman with the baby, poor little thing . . . "

"*What* woman?"

The guard pointed. A hundred yards off, along the wall, a small cloaked figure, tenderly bearing a bundle, was descending to the street.

"Hey, missus," shouted the guard. "Have you seen Little Paul?"

The cloaked figure turned, and made a gesture of great obscenity. Then threw the baby off the wall. It landed with a sickening thud, as the figure took to its heels. Everyone ran to rescue the baby, except Cam, who watched thunderously as Little Paul vanished up a narrow alley.

The rescuers trailed back.

"It wasn't a baby; only a bundle of rags."

"But it *was* a baby! I saw its face, poor wizened little thing. I heard it cry. That's why I let her go."

Cam laid his hand on the guard's arm. "Do not fret, friend. You are only the latest he has deluded." Then he turned. "Where's your hunting-horn, Raoul? I must make the signal."

But Raoul's horn was cut clean in two – the only casualty they had suffered. They searched the citadel desperately for another.

Found, eventually, a small wretched cracked thing. Cam went up on a pinnacle facing St Alban's, and blew it with all his breath. But its note was cracked too. And it seemed to Cam that the great wind caused by the burning took the noise and whirled it up to the heavens, where it was lost. He blew and blew, but nothing stirred on the slopes below St Alban's. Where was Geoffrey? The Duke? Amon? Where was anybody? A desperate inertia seized him, but he blew on. He could hear the trumpets of Sir Henri drawing near; the old war-dog hadn't been fooled for long . . .

Then, at last, men were moving up the fateful slope. Climbing Father Death's ladders neatly and precisely. But too slow. And surely too late?

"Lord Seroster, we have found your cat." Cam could not see the messenger's face. But he knew the news was bad. He sped recklessly down the spiral stair, unseen tears scalding his face. It was too much. All his tricks had worked; but now it was all going wrong. Duke lost, cat dead, army come too late. Oh well, he thought bitterly, doubtless it is nearly time for the great Seroster to die for his people . . . Then I shall get some *peace*.

A ring of men stood with torches, on the wall. There should not be so many, thought Cam angrily; they are neglecting their duty.

Amon lay still. He had bled from a dozen cuts; one ear was half-severed; there was no sign of breathing. Yet one pale whisker lay curled awkwardly against the paving, and Cam thought it twitched. Or was it just the flicker of the torches?

Cam clutched the handle of his dagger for comfort . . . as they all looked at him, sorrowing.

The Seroster spoke, "When a cat has suffered much . . . been hurt and hated, and is full of sorrow, he draws near the little gate of death. Yet if he has not received a mortal wound, he has the choice, whether to go through or not. Amon . . . Amon?"

And the night and the firelit wall vanished. And Cam was walking down a dusty road, towards a wide blue river. Great trees lined the road, casting stripes across it. And through the stripes of light and dark walked Amon, without a backward glance.

Yet Cam knew it was Amon.

The trees fell behind. A great ship moored, at the riverbank. Full of men and supple women, cat-eyed. And they played on instruments, making a merry noise, and sang, rejoicing, "Come, we are going down to Bubastis!" And there were Miw, and among the Miw was Smerdis. And all rejoiced in Amon.

But no one looked at Cam.

And Amon set one foot on the gangplank, and the men and women stood back, making way, showing him honour. And Cam knew that Amon was beyond pain and hunger and fear. Happy . . .

"Come, Amon, we are going down to Bubastis!"

But in a great tearing agony, Cam shouted, "Amon. Wait for me!"

And halfway up the gangplank, the cat turned and looked at him. Sighed. And leapt into his arms again.

And Cam was back on the wall, in the fire and the dark.

And on the paving-stones, Amon stirred, and raised himself wearily.

"Thank you, Amon," said Cam. And he flung himself with joy back into the battle, for beyond the battle waited Bubastis, and there was nothing left to be afraid of.

The Duke came to himself, raised his head, and looked back along the wall. The fighting had stopped; the wall was empty, except for a huddle of dark silent shapes. The door to the citadel was shut. He dragged himself upright; he could hardly move. He looked for his knife, Misericord, but could not see it.

Then the citadel door opened, and a woman came out, carrying a bundle.

He heard the voice of the man who let her out; one of his friends. The citadel had fallen. He began to run towards it.

But the woman advanced on him steadily. Looked at him. And he knew it wasn't a woman, and he grew afraid . . .

The door of the citadel opened again. More of his friends, shouting. All safety . . .

But in between, the woman with a bundle . . .

In terror, the Duke turned and ran.

He turned and twisted through alleys; dived into doorways as horsemen galloped past, flinging mud and filth into his face. The night was full of shouting figures, who ignored him. Only the figure of the woman cruelly persisted, never gaining, never falling back.

The Duke got out of breath. More and more lonely and frightened; finally stopped looking where he was going.

Inevitably, he ended up staring at a blank brick wall. Cul-de-sac. And the thin following figure was blocking the end of the alley, peering in.

There is an end to courage; the Duke simply gave up. Cowered in the deepest doorway, with his arms round his knees and his head down. He'd been here before, helpless, awaiting the knife. No Sehtek this time . . .

There was a commanding prook! He looked up, unbelieving. Sehtek was peering down, three more Miw with her.

But the wall she stood on was broken and crumbling. Still, there was an old twisted lead drainpipe. Sehtek prooked again, this time a Miw-command. Climb!

His aching legs would hardly work; Sehtek very high and very far away. And he heard quick small footsteps in the alley below; and the drainpipe began to shake, as someone climbed up after him.

And above the Miw just sat, like cats round a mousehole.

The Duke tried to climb faster; his legs ached like rusty levers. The creature behind was gaining . . .

He reached the sagging guttering, began to crawl over it. His face was pressed against Sehtek's fur, now. Comforting.

A cruel hand came from behind, and clasped his ankle.

Desperately he crawled on up the roof; pulling not just his own weight, but the pursuer's. Why didn't Sehtek *do* something? Just sitting there, waiting . . .

The old lead of the guttering began to sag under his toes . . .

Then Sehtek reared up, like a heraldic beast. Her eyes flicked, like lightning waiting to strike.

And struck.

A scream. The hand on his ankle nearly let go; then tightened again.

Sehtek's paw descended again and again; it sounded like she was thumping on a hollow pumpkin. Another awful scream; the hand on his ankle let go. There was a thump on the cobbles below, and a wailing that did not cease.

But slowly it made off down the alley; limping.

Sehtek gave a short rough purr of . . . disappointment, like a cat when a mouse gets away. The Duke had an awful feeling she'd used him, like cheese in a mousetrap. But he still buried his face in her fur. She smelt of soot and rain, and her bones were sharp under her skin.

But it was still Sehtek, and she still purred like the sea, far away.

38

Sehtek led him across the roofs. Between three chimneystacks, the Miw waited. Seroster had not been the last to use his stair that night. Every cat of the city was back on his own rooftop.

It was from the roofs that the Duke watched the race for his city. Saw Geoffrey's men pouring out of St Alban's, blocking every street with carts and barrels; anything to stop Sir Henri's furious charge of horse, thundering and sparking up the narrow ways. The barricades grew . . .

Desperately Sir Henri fought below Seroster's House, to stop the Free Men completing their line.

But he failed, because Seroster leapt down from the citadel. For a last time, they met in single combat, their swords carving circles of blue sparks that lit the night and made all lesser men cower.

But again they were too well-matched. When the barricade of carts was complete, Seroster broke away and leapt over it.

"Come back," shouted Sir Henri.

"Later. I have a city to win."

"Damn the city!" shouted Sir Henri, weeping visibly.

A spiteful time followed, a time of low cunning. Men broke through the inside walls of houses, to get behind their enemies. Fought and died on narrow burning stairs, in roof-spaces amidst the sleepy startled starlings, and in the slime of cellars.

Ironhand, stupid to the last, sent men over the roofs. It was well he did not go himself, for the cats were waiting. And the sewer-rats and Father Death, who threw many a shrewd tile.

Sehtek, drawing the Miw into a circle, conjured her last storm. But friend and foe were packed too tight. Amon sent to her to stop it, and they had a private thunderstorm between themselves.

By dawn, Cam held the citadel and half the city; Sir Henri held the rest; and both in great discomfort.

* * *

Castlemew had spent a wretched night. The dreadful flash and shaking of the earth had completely unsettled her nerves. The persistent smell of burning kept them unsettled. So much shouting and running in the corridor; the smell of human fear coming in under the door kept her tense no matter how often she scratched or licked her tail.

And her dear lord was out there in danger. Her mood swung, between wild ecstasies in which he wielded his sword, terrible as an army with banners; and wild despairs in which she saw him lying dead, bloody and trampled. She felt utterly lonely, but she didn't go and seek him. He had no time for her, when he was fighting. She wasn't any kind of fighting cat.

And someone in the Palace was trying to kill her. When she ventured out on to the ledge, to avoid soiling her master's room, things dropped from above on to the place where she squatted; stones, pots. One had hurt her shoulder, so that she limped.

Worse, someone came and tried a key in the door, every so often. The key didn't fit; yet. So the someone crept away as silently as he had come.

She was not afraid; but very, very unhappy. It was a relief when pointed ears poked over the windowsill, silhouetted against the burning.

"Sehtek-send," sent Tornear. "Time you-go. Sehtek know-best."

He dropped down to the floor, and they touched noses. He had lost half his left ear, and his left-hand whiskers were reduced to stumps. He smelt of blood not his own, which he hadn't bothered to wash off. He was huge, and he trembled with something more frightening than fear. She sniffed his ear. "Who-did?"

Tornear sniffed at the patch of blood on his fur which was not cat-blood.

"He not-do again." He sniffed the food she'd been too nervous to eat, tucked in heartily. She felt for the memories in his mind, but they were all dark and fire and . . .

"Your lord fight-well. Pity not-catfriend." He turned to her dish of milk; he was a very noisy drinker. "Don't blame you stay-here. Good-eat." He finished the milk to the last dampness and sent, not unkindly, "Come-now. All-we on-roofs. Push-tile-down. Kill many."

"Not-come," she sent, low and wretched, but defiant.

"Why? Good-mouse. Not-danger. Not-much."

"Master need-me. Little-Paul poison – last-night."

"Sure not-come?" He was thoughtful, for him. "Sehtek-send."

"No."

"Farewell." It was not the usual farewell. It was what a cat sends to another cat that is dying.

Without him, it was lonelier than ever.

Somebody came and tried the key again. This time it very nearly turned . . .

Then Sehtek herself was on the windowsill, sparks still flying from her fur, from the lightning she had been conjuring.

"I-summon. Why not-obey?"

"Not-coming," sent Castlemew; the tiniest possible send.

"Not-coming? That is Kitten-think! At your age! Obey *me*!"

It was like a bolt of lightning.

"No," sent Castlemew, even quieter.

"Your master is cat-foe. Come."

Castlemew did not move. There was a long sulphurous silence, such as is only seen between cats.

Then Sehtek drew herself up.

> "You are no-cat
> Outcast
> As your master is outcast
> You shall call, and we will not-come
> You shall starve, and we will not-feed
> Your kittens shall be no-kittens
> Of this city."

A curse so terrible that Castlemew shut her eyes and wished to die.

When she opened them again, Sehtek was gone.

She fell into a daze of cold and loneliness. She did not hear the key finally turn, and the door open.

She had a last moment of life; to realise Little Paul stood there, to give a last spit, a last feeble upward slash of her paw.

Then the world was fading. And she was, very puzzlingly, walking along a dusty road to a great blue river.

As she entered the ship, she thought desperately, "Who will soothe him, now I am gone?"

Everything was going bravely, thought Sir Henri. He'd got the trick of beating those blasted pikemen. Pepper them with cross-bow-bolts, till one fell and the rest scattered. Then follow in with the sword, before they could get their pikes up again. He held the eastern wall, almost to the citadel. Once he had won the western, he could command the town. Fire a few more houses, and Seroster would have to surrender.

He was leading another successful foray, then he was struck by a cold thought. Was all well with Castlemew?

Stupid. Never think about anything in a battle, except the battle. Can't afford to. And here he was, fretting about an old alley-cat. Get hold of yourself, man. Gettin' old, that's your trouble . . .

But he couldn't get her out of his mind. Any minute, he'd make a mistake, get himself killed.

"Stand fast," he told his sweating rogues. "Need a drink." Men cheered as he walked along the wall. But his fear for Castlemew grew.

People looked at him strangely, out of the corner of their eyes, as he entered the Palace. They did not speak, but whispered behind their hands. He hurried upstairs. His door was open, though he still had the only key on his belt. In the dawn light, the room was empty and desolate. Her food was eaten, her milk drunk, but no sign of her. He called; she did not come.

He ran here and there, through the Palace. No one would admit to having seen her; but they wouldn't look him in the eye. He felt trapped in a spiderweb . . . Were they all in a plot against him?

"I must know all is well with her! Or I cannot fight!"

His shout made everyone turn and stare.

"She is well enough, lord," said a man in a sly voice.

Then somebody laughed.

He blundered on. Found himself at last in the great stable-yard. And there she was, hunched on an island of rotten food, on the edge of the great stinking midden, her fur tinged red in the first red light of the sun.

He laughed for joy. She had eaten all her food during the night and, growing hungry, was gorging herself on the midden.

"Oh, you fat old thief. Back to your alley-cat ways, the moment I turn my back." He reached for her.

His hand came away red; it was not the red of the morning sun.

Suddenly, for Sir Henri, there was red everywhere. He walked across to a group of watching men and said, "Sir, who has killed my friend?"

A man said, suddenly frightened, "Lord, I do not know."

Another sniggered in fear . . .

That was the end. Sir Henri drew his sword, faster than eye could follow. Four men lay dead, before the echoes of that snigger faded.

Only one man looked on Sir Henri's face after that, and lived.

They heard the uproar in the very citadel. Something was wrong with the enemy. They were falling back from the wall in panic; running wildly into the streets.

"A trick?" asked Geoffrey.

"Who could fake that screaming?" said Cam. Walking soft, they ventured along the wall and reached the Palace. No man shot at them. The stairway down was choked with dead. The throne-room a battlefield. A curtain blew in the wind, and there was silence.

The disturbance was in the town, now; it seemed to move, going up one still-shadowed street, and down the next.

"Hold the wall," said Cam. "I am going down."

He met only death. Death hung from windows; cowered in holes in the ground. Death looked utterly bewildered.

Finally, in a smoke-filled street, Cam saw a man walking as if drunk. His helm-plume was gone; his shield no more than wooden splinters round a handle. The feathers of crossbow-bolts stuck from him, so that it was a marvel he still walked upright. Blood bubbled from every leather joint.

A voice sobbed, but not with pain. Then the empty eyes beheld Cam.

"It was you who killed my friend . . . " But the sword was only raised slowly, and as slowly fell. Cam parried it easily.

"Sir Henri?"

The dying eyes recognised him. "Seroster. The only true knight . . . "

"Sir, lie down. I will fetch aid."

"No. I shall . . . end on my feet. Seroster? Bury her at my feet."

"Yes."

"Everything's gone to pot, Seroster. What's the point of it all, eh?"

Cam was silent.

"Only one point. Die fightin'." His eyes flickered; over Cam's shoulder. As if he saw some new enemy. Some one, or thing, of such dread aspect that even his iron spirit quailed . . .

Then all the fighting gladness flooded back. Cam flung himself aside just in time.

Sir Henri made a stroke, almost too fast for mortal eye to see; it would have killed any earthly opponent.

But there was no one there. And as Sir Henri's sword hit the cobbles with a sparking crash, and splintered to pieces, his soul left his body. It was an empty shell that fell to the cobbles.

The pikemen crept up, surprised to find the Seroster weeping.

"Bear his body to the citadel with honour . . . "

"He was an enemy."

"He has saved this city," said the Seroster. "And your life."

And the city was indeed saved. A horn-blast sounded, and looking up, Cam saw Father Death on the wall with archers.

Cam sighed. "You have your victory, Lady Castlemew."

Now came the dreadful time. Cam had never planned how to end his battle.

There was nothing left to do. Every tower and bastion was taken, and strongly held. There remained a milling mass of furious, frightened men, penned in the square by the gate. By another mass of men, even more furious.

There was going to be a massacre. The air stank with it, buzzed with it. The Free Army, and even those who hadn't fought for either side, were remembering every insult, threat and evil deed of those who stood trapped before them. They screamed with rage, so it was hard even for the Seroster to hold them.

And the usurpers, despairing of life, gave themselves up to hate, each vowing in his heart to take a city man down into death with him.

Even the Duke, up on the wall, felt it. He would rule a city of ruins, widows, orphans, prey to every raider who could scale the broken walls . . .

The sun only made it seem more dreadful. In the distance, Morville and Beauly dreamed in the autumn warmth. Near Harcourt, an old man was winter-ploughing, with two ancient horses that had somehow escaped being drafted into the war. Rooks hopped behind him in the furrows, their black feathers glinting like armour in the sun.

Outside was peace and freedom; inside, war and death . . .

A sharp prook. Sehtek was looking at him, commandingly.

The ghost of an idea stirred in his mind. Something to do with peace being outside, and death being inside . . .

The city-gate . . . barred and impenetrable . . . if only he could open the gate . . .

Sehtek called again, leapt down over the edge of the wall. There was a ledge, that led to the great curling gate-hinges . . . so thick and massive that a cat, or a boy, could climb down. Holding his breath so it hurt, he climbed after Sehtek.

Nobody noticed. Everyone was watching each other in that strange stillness that falls just before something really dreadful happens . . .

The gate was held by a wooden bar; well-greased but terribly heavy. Sehtek couldn't help. He moved the bar an inch, then another. Then his hand slipped and blood spurted between his fingers. Wet drops were dripping down his face, too. He didn't know if they were sweat or tears, and didn't care. The bar was giving . . .

It fell to the cobbles, with a rattle. The Duke looked round fearfully. There were a hundred men within dagger-throw who would cheerfully kill him if they knew who he was. A few looked . . . but only with annoyance, because he was distracting them from the deadly silence.

He seized one half of the gate. It groaned. Blue sky and peace flowed in through the crack. He heaved again, and the gate stood wide.

But nobody moved. Should he shout? Something grand, like 'Begone my city, foul carrion'?

Something warned him it would not do. So instead he shouted, "Come on, lads, freedom!" He shouted it over and over, till his voice cracked. Still nobody moved, but a lot began to stare, curiously. More and more curiously . . .

The Duke panicked; ran off through the gate.

That did it. Several ran after him, to see what he was up to. Others, seeing them running, followed blindly. Then, like the start of an avalanche, they were all running. Out of the city, past the blackened battering-ram, and away down the hill.

An ugly roar came from the Free Army. Some started forward in pursuit.

"Let them go!" shouted Cam, facing his own men with that dreaded sword.

"Stand fast!" roared Georges, leaping to join him. That day, his voice excelled itself, more than at the Siege of Calais. In fact, it cracked forever, and for the rest of his life he served his drinks in a hoarse whisper. But men gave him honour for that.

Only one more blow was struck that day. As the shattered army of the usurpers spilled down the slope, Father Death was watching from the gate-top. He saw Ironhand riding in the midst, saddlebags bulging with the things he had stolen. He was laughing, clearing a way through his late comrades with his sword.

"The wicked shall flourish as the green bay tree," said Father Death.

A fully-wound crossbow, dropped in battle, lay at his feet. It came most smoothly to his hand, and its bolt lay beside it . . .

He raised the bow . . .

Then he saw Ironhand's horse. The beast was flinching under the spurs; red foam already at its mouth. And Father Death saw the harlot that ran alongside, red hair streaming and a child on her arm. And a beggar beyond, mouth working with fear as he plied his crutch . . .

"I am not God," said Father Death. And laid the bow down.

Ironhand passed. Then his horse stumbled, on a rock in the road. Ironhand flew from its neck, and horse and harlot, beggar and cart passed over the spot where he had fallen, as innocently and heedlessly as water passes over a pebble in a stream.

And when they had all passed, Father Death looked again, and was satisfied. But he went to catch the poor horse, and used its saddlebags to feed the poor . . .

Back in the square, Cam stood looking at the still sword in his hands, with a sense of shock.

It was over; and he was still alive. And the cat beside him was alive, too.

Then he remembered the Bishop of Toulouse.

39

Cam started up from sleep, sweating.

But the Bishop of Toulouse was not standing over him; the fires were not lit; the people were not screaming . . .

Yet. But the Bishop was coming; Cam could feel him like the weight of a thundercloud, coming from the east.

And no one knew but him.

He tried to take comfort from the moonlight on the great walls round the city; the calls of the watchmen . . .

The Albigenses had had walls too. But they all died in the fires of Mother Church. Seven thousand . . .

He could warn the people to flee. But where to, in winter? Strangers everywhere? And the Bishop would hunt every stranger down who spoke the patois of the city.

Well, *he* could get away. No one would be looking for an Englishman.

He dressed; put on his old jerkin; packed his old pack. Crept down the Palace stairs like a thief. If anyone saw him now . . .

But who dared question the Lord Seroster? Indeed the door-keeper, roused from a doze as Cam softly pulled back the bolts, gave him a wild and sleepy salute. So easy . . .

He would creep out by the Seroster's Stair. Two dead men and a bronze statue couldn't stop him.

The cat joined him as he crossed the square . . .

Her face seemed still to move; but it was only the flickering taper. The bronze kittens still crouched at her feet, beneath the protecting arms. She too was only cold bronze; stood there because men had placed her there. The balls of grey dust still ran around like mice.

The voice did not come from the bronze.

It came from the middle of his own skull; clear and cold and hard as bronze.

They were not his thoughts.

And since they were inside his skull, there was no point to running away.

I HAVE PLACED THEM WITHIN YOUR PAW AND THEY ARE SCATTERED.

He fidgeted, resentful. Looked at the cat, crouched worshipping in the dust. It had licked most of the blood off its fur, but its ear was a horrible, pathetic mess. He pitied it, deeply . . .

THERE IS ONE THING REMAINING.

Say what you have to say, bronze idol. I am still going away.

I WILL PUT THIS BISHOP WITHIN YOUR PAW.

Oh yes? And all his army? And Mother Church? And Almighty God? He shuddered. This awful bronze thing had led him on. Was he damned already? How could any man fight against God?

What are you?

TO THE CATS I AM A CAT. TO THE TREES I AM A TREE. TO THE ROCKS I AM A ROCK.

But . . .

DID YOU THINK I WOULD BE LIKE A *MAN*?

There was a hint of mockery.

ROCKS WERE FIRST-BORN. TREE WAS SECONDBORN. CAT WAS THIRD-BORN. MAN WAS LASTBORN. ROCK, TREE, CAT ARE JOY TO ME.

The Bishop is the servant of Mother Church . . .

BY THEIR FRUITS YE SHALL KNOW THEM.

But . . .

WHAT IS THE FRUIT OF THIS BISHOP?

His mind filled with the fruits of the Bishop. They were unbearably hideous.

A pregnant woman, writhing at the stake in agony, dropped her first-born into the flames.

GIVE YOURSELF TO ME AND I WILL PUT THIS BISHOP WITHIN YOUR PAW.

Mutely, desperately, he shook his head. But the fruits of the Bishop kept flooding in. At last they ceased.

I SHOW YOU NOTHING BUT THE TRUTH.

Yes, he said, yes.

GIVE YOURSELF TO ME. I WILL NOT FIGHT FOR THIS BISHOP IN THE DAY OF BATTLE. I WILL PUT HIM WITHIN YOUR PAW.

Yes, he said, yes.

And immediately he was far above the red plain, looking through the eyes of an owl. And he saw the curving of the earth, and felt each breeze in his feathers, and he flew south and saw the armies gathering, and the ships in the harbour. And he wept and said how can we beat them when they have so many?

And then he saw a small spider spinning its web in a dead bush, thin strand after thin strand, so slow, so weak. And then a venomous wasp flew into a strand, and the strand broke but other strands held and the wasp writhed and the small spider ran to and fro still frantically spinning . . .

I WILL PUT THIS BISHOP WITHIN YOUR PAW.

And he was kneeling, sobbing in the dust. The cat was kneeling beside him. And he saw the greatness in the cat for the first time, and said humbly, "Forgive me, my lord."

The cat purred, and washed its mangled ear, delicately.

"I wish I knew what the hell is up," whispered Georges. "He's too forgiving for my liking. One minute we're trying to cut each other's throats, and the next they're helping us rebuild . . ."

They were watching the women of the city scrambling on the slopes below St Lawrence's, loading fallen stone on to carts. And the usurper-women worked with them. Already the wall was rising again.

"They have to live somewhere," said Geoffrey. "He's weeded out the worst . . ."

"And the harlots. I wonder what he wants wi' the harlots?"

"Nothing. This morning, old friend, I am Captain of Harlots. I must take them down to the Mire and let them go. And they are to ride in carts, like ladies. I am to get them there in good spirits, well-fed and watered . . ."

"And I am to cut ten thousand stakes, and take them to exactly where I've been shown, and hammer them in exactly as I have been shown . . . you can't talk to him any more, can you? His eyes are funny all the time . . ."

"I suppose a Seroster gets more like a Seroster all the time. D'you think he ever sleeps?"

"We'd better be off; he's watching us."

"Right," said Geoffrey. "An hour's rest. There's a well in the square."

The harlots, some fifty in number, helped each other down and stared around. The village lay under the white cliffs, on the way to the Mire. White ruins; only a few arches and towers still standing.

But on every arch and tower sat a black cat flecked with gold. The women looked at them fearfully.

"Sir, what are those cats?"

"They're what we call Matagot . . ."

"Will they attack us, sir?" The women huddled to him.

Geoffrey scratched his head, baffled. He knew these ruins a bit, and he'd never seen Matagot here before. But if the women wouldn't go and get water for themselves, that would be a great bother . . .

"Oh, you don't want to be scared of Matagots. They're not fighters. In fact," a sudden bright idea hit him, "they do say they're lucky. If you catch one, and keep it in a chest and feed it well, it'll lay a gold piece for you, every day . . . "

The leader of the harlots raised an eyebrow; and he had to laugh at the silliness of the idea. But the women laughed as well, and went to fetch their own water. Geoffrey settled back, tipped his hat over his eyes . . .

A sudden outcry among the women; he jumped up with a curse, reached for his sword. But they were pleased, not frightened. One was holding something up, and the rest were trying to get it off her.

"Sir, I stroked a black cat, and it got up and . . . " She held out her hand and there was a small gold coin.

"You want to go on looking," said Geoffrey. "You might find a Matagot's nest . . . "

The women laughed again. But went on searching. All the noon-break there were little screams, and stroking of cats, and the finding of tiny gold coins. Then there was a great uproar. All the women gathered in one place, and there were shouts of, "I can't quite reach," and, "Pull out that other stone."

Geoffrey went across.

"Sir, we have found a Matagot's nest." A kneeling woman held out her hands, and in them were ten tiny gold coins.

"Some have all the luck," said Geoffrey, baffled and envious. "Now, time to go."

"We wish to stay . . . "

"If you stay any longer, you'll be wandering around in the Mire all night. Gold won't help you then."

Grumbling, the women got back into the carts. But all the way down to the Mire, they talked of how they would find the place again . . .

Geoffrey was glad to tip them out.

"There's a good clear road there, mesdames. Keep right on till sunset and you'll be at the fishing-port."

"How shall we live, sir?"

"There's an army arriving any day . . ."

That cheered them; they set off with spirit. Vowing to return . . .

They'd be disappointed, thought Geoffrey, passing through the ruins going home.

There wasn't a Matagot in sight.

Amon summoned Ripfur to the city. But he would not come.

"You come-us," sent Ripfur, stubbornly, and would say no more.

Sighing, Amon trotted up the track towards the cliffs. He was surprised to be challenged by two black sentries in the ruins of Harcourt. Still, they bowed, stretching out their front legs politely, and sniffed noses.

"We-take you Lord Ripfur . . ."

They passed through the last fields. They had been savagely harvested, to feed the army. Desolate. And crisscrossed with faint cat-runs. They entered the first defile leading up to the crags. Amon followed the sentries sleepily; he'd been up all night. So it burst in upon him like a storm. A hate-send of jolting power from the left; another even heavier from the right. Then white owls swooping at him from every angle, talons brushing his tattered ear. He crouched, mind in chaos, as a heb-Miw of black cats pounced. And left him untouched. Then another, then another. It seemed to go on forever. He was so shattered by the end that, although not a whisker had been harmed, he had to sit and weakly lick himself.

"Welcome to our city, *brother*," sent Ripfur. "Come and see-king!" He was led through long underground runs where many small caves had been joined by vigorous scrabbling. Through nurseries lined with rabbit-fur and dry bracken, where queens nursed striving young. There were springs of cool water, where he was invited to drink. And a young black she-cat he seemed to remember offered him fresh mirfu . . . and there was laughter through all the host.

"Greet-king!" sent Ripfur sharply.

And there was old Splayfoot, rising stiffly from a bed of extra-fine fur and bracken. And they smelt noses with great respect.

"Seek our-help?" sent Splayfoot. "We will be Miw-friend. Hold cliffs as far as Mire. No-man-come-there."

Amon was a Miw known for his tact. But that morning, he excelled himself in diplomacy. It did not help to know that Ripfur and Tornear were torn by inner gales of mirth, and so was all the cat-host. But they parted in gladness. Except that at the end, Splayfoot sent, "Harcourt ours-now. Men not-come."

Trotting home, Amon wished sadly that the war was over.

Cats were becoming too like men.

"I don't like this," said the Captain. "Death in battle I've seen plenty of but . . . "

A row of graves had been dug on the edge of the Mire; dug by the truly evil among the usurpers; who deserved to die. Now they sat hunch-shouldered by those graves, and stared at the dead trees around. It must have been a pretty glade once; mature old trees, but dead now, killed by the Mire creeping round their roots . . . even the new-dug graves were filling up with water.

The men's legs and wrists were hobbled; they stared at the Captain without hope; the Captain found it unbearable . . .

"Go!" said the Seroster, glancing at the setting sun, so it glinted in the slits of his eyes.

And the Captain went, without a backward glance.

The doomed men watched Seroster now. He came and looked at each of them, and they shuddered at the strangeness of his eyes. Then he took down the great sword. Ran his finger down the edge. Frowned. Selected a dead tree . . .

The doomed watched; it was their last chance to watch anything . . .

The Seroster screamed, like a cat fighting on a roof. His sword swung . . .

A dead oak crashed in ruin, severed by one blow. The Seroster did not stop till it was a pile of chippings.

Yet still he felt the edge of his sword, with a frown, as if not satisfied.

Another tree fell; and another. The men felt every blow. As the dead branches leapt in the air, they felt their own limbs were being severed.

Some fainted.

Just as the sun touched the horizon, the Seroster turned to *them* . . .

But then a golden cat ran in; the chirping of its voice came clear; many thought it bore a message. The Seroster leapt on to his horse.

"Wait here, brothers," he said to the doomed. "I shall not be long . . ."

He rode away. Darkness fell. And the men slept and started awake in terror.

Creeper felt something fumbling at the rope that tied his wrists, and shrieked.

"Quiet, friend," whispered a voice. "Do not betray me . . ." And Creeper felt his bonds unloosed . . .

"Who are you?"

"One who has no love for the Seroster." There was a hint of laughter in the voice. "Here is a knife. Cut your friends loose quickly . . . *Seroster* will be back soon . . ."

Creeper found just enough courage to free his mates. As the last bonds fell off, they heard hoofbeats returning.

They fled into the Mire.

Heard the terrible hunting-cry of the Seroster, following.

They did not stop running, until they reached the bridge over the black ooze, and vanished into the fishing-port.

"Could've been worse" said Creeper, glancing back. "Do you know what those fools did? They didn't even rob our pockets. I've still got enough to get drunk on . . ."

"Lead me to the nearest alehouse," said Sharkey.

Cam had followed them all the way. He doubled up in the reeds, laughing.

40

They assembled on the quayside, a very great multitude. Some were carrying wooden crosses; many tarred torches, that should have been kept for later but were already burning. Here and there, a cross caught alight from a torch, which made the crowd roar with delight. The air was ragged with grey smoke and pale flame. The flames were so pale in the sunlight that sometimes a man walked into them without realising, till his clothes and hair caught alight. Then he would jump, or be thrown screaming, into the muddy harbour.

The crusaders were having fun. All the march from Toulouse, they had hunted cats. Shrivelled furry bodies hung from the bigger crosses, and they sometimes caught fire too. The crowd roared with endless pleasure, drunk on more than wine. They had set off in their best finery, but after a week on the road, it was soiled and stained.

The Bishop of Toulouse blessed them, standing high above them, in his palanquin. He told them they were already in Heaven; anyone who died on this crusade would go straight to the blessed realm. No need for painful years in Purgatory. But nobody need die; the witches and heretics were weak and few . . .

Once they reached the city, they might take all the heretic's goods. No heretic must prosper on this earth. Thus, some might have their minds turned to the true things of Heaven before the flames claimed them . . .

They roared approval. The Bishop sat down. He was a man blessedly short of speech; a man in a hurry; on fire for his God.

The captains of the Bishop's bodyguard did not like it. They were German Lansknecht. Georg Langenmantel and Georg Frundsberg. Some said they were twin-brothers. It was certainly hard to tell them apart in their mail-capes and fantastic winged helmets. Both had straggling, greying, blond beards, bony noses, rat-trap mouths and gimlet eyes. Being mercenaries, they believed in nothing but money. Certainly they had no belief in God; which was why they were still alive in their fiftieth year. Men of steel and leather and few words, they attended Mass once a week. Otherwise their Bishop would have had them burnt. They attended High Mass, thinking about chops for breakfast.

They hated crusaders. Would have much preferred another company of Lansknecht, bored as themselves. Crusaders were a menace, clogging the battlefield, fleeing at the first dying scream, or running so wild with religion they killed each other. The Georgs hoped that many would die or wander away, before the battle started. Meanwhile, they constantly counted their own thousand men, like shepherds count sheep; kept them tightly around the Bishop, for the safety of whose body they were responsible.

"Let us proceed," intoned the Bishop. "In the name of the Lord our God!"

The bobbing purple palanquin led the way up the winding street of the fishing-port. The crusaders followed. Most reached the top, though some hundreds stopped for a last drink. Three were killed in tavern-brawls; ten had their purses slit and were never seen again. Many more grew too drunk to march, and next morning crept off home, rather than face the Mire alone.

Nobody missed them.

The good citizens of the fishing-port had built a new bridge, in honour of the crusade. In only seven days. Unfortunately, they were quite unable to provide guides through the swamp. They were, alas, merely fishermen, and their faces were set towards the sea . . .

The Bishop chose ten at random, to be guides. These immediately turned pale with terror, and fell to their knees, unable to walk. The other fishermen began to back away. Soon, the whole town was curiously empty . . .

Georg Langenmantel looked dourly at Georg Frundsberg. "It does not bode well." He drew a hand across his throat.

But then the Bishop noticed some distant men, on the other side of the bridge, cutting reeds.

"God has sent us guides," he said, and led the way across.

But when they reached the place where the reeds were being cut, the reedcutters had vanished.

"God himself shall be our guide," said the Bishop.

God gave them a trying day. The crusaders broke up into smaller and smaller groups, to find their way as best they could through the tangled maze of reeds. They kept on meeting head-on, on the narrow paths, in the heat of the day, screaming insults and using whips as they forced their horses past each other. God had made more insects in that swamp than anyone had ever seen before, and He gave them a great feast on horse and man . . .

As the day wore on, many finely-saddled but riderless horses were seen, nervously keeping their distance. Bodies clad in gay reds and yellows far out among the reeds and ooze. Nobody went to find out how they had died. It was too hot, too panicky, too insect-ridden. The Lansknecht and their Bishop went on, marching by the sun, with timeless grey-faced patience. The Bishop kept them going, singing pilgrim psalms; he had a fine high old voice.

That night they camped in great discomfort, where they could lie on the narrow paths; neither drinking the swamp-water nor giving it to their horses. But many others did so.

In the middle of the night, the watch gave the alarm, at a great light in the sky behind.

Neither Georg doubted for a moment that it was the splendid new bridge burning . . .

"I will *speak* with those unchristian fisherfolk, when we return," said Georg Langenmantel.

"How do you know it is the fisherfolk? They say we are marching against a sorcerer . . ."

"It worries me more we might be marching against a soldier . . ."

They emerged from the reeds at sunset the day after, and made for the nearest of the scattered farms, to replenish their great sweating, half-empty waterskins; gathered round the well.

"Before you draw water," said Georg Frundsberg, "use your nose."

The Lansknecht drew back, gagging at the smell.

"A dead sheep?" asked Georg, "or a dead pig?" He turned to the Bishop. "There will be no clean water before the city, your grace. Though some fools will drink anything." A great number of crusaders were emerging from the Mire in ones and twos and forming an indignant huddle, well downwind of the Bishop . . .

"More than I expected," said George Langenmantel, disappointed. "Two-thirds will be here by morning."

"A pity. I do not think this Seroster is much soldier. He could have set fire to the reeds also, and killed us all."

"Perhaps he has a mother's care for us . . . ?"

"Perhaps he has another plan."

The Germans stood by their horses till dawn. Heard nothing except the drinking and yelling round the big uncontrolled bonfires of the crusaders' camp. The drunken shouts every time a few more stragglers joined them.

The Bishop prayed to his God all night. The march eventually began again, long after dawn or even sunrise; the Lansknecht in a tight group to the rear, and the vast labouring coils of red and yellow and dust that was the main army ahead.

This Seroster worries me, that he does not come . . . "

"Perhaps he is poor. Perhaps he needs all those crusaders' weapons and horses for his own men . . . Why should he carry them himself, when he can get those fools to carry them a few more miles?"

"Look, they are spreading out to look for water . . . "

"They might as well save their legs . . . "

"There will be fresh springs in those white cliffs. They cannot poison a spring . . . "

"Take ten men and a cart, if you like. You might find some amusement, but I will bet a crown you will not get water . . . "

The small party of Lansknecht started up a side-valley towards the cliffs. They almost had to wade through a scattered mass of crusaders. Men who had drunk water from the swamp, and were now squatting desperately behind every dead bush. Men who had drunk all their wine, and plodded along head down, or crawled, or lay on their elbows, hopelessly drunk.

"What can I give my horse to drink?" screeched one young man at Georg Frundsberg. "I have found three wells and each has a dead sheep down it."

"Every well before the city will have a dead sheep down it," said Georg, as if he was saying that swallows always return in May.

"What can I do?" shouted the young man, desperately scrabbling at the sleeve of Georg's blue-and-yellow doublet, in the way that would have caused the death of a sane man. Georg merely brushed his hand aside, looked with interest at his foundering horse. A thoroughbred.

"I will give you a gold piece for your horse . . . "

"I paid fifty for him!"

Georg glanced up at the buzzards that were already circling overhead. "By tonight, your horse will be worth nothing."

"All right," said the young man. Georg went to his own glistening, depleted waterbag, poured a little in his winged helmet and gave it to the horse.

"Give *me* some water!" shouted the young man. "I am more important than a horse!"

"The *horse* is *my* property," said Georg Frundsberg; with a look that sent the young man cold in spite of the heat. "If you would save your life, go home." He pointed towards the Mire.

Georg Frundsberg returned with a wagon of water; but his winged helm was gone; and he had nearly lost an eye.

"This Seroster is a sorcerer," he said calmly, as he took a spare helm from a wagon. "The owls attacked us and, nearer the cliffs, cats also. Ulrich fell off his horse and broke his neck."

"He was never a good rider. Cats, you say? The last sorcerer I dealt with used bears. In a forest. We caught him and cut off his head, just the same. But he gave us bother . . ."

"Those fools are talking about flying cats. It will be all over the camp tonight . . ."

"Do they fly?"

"Almost. I will not go back to those cliffs again."

"We have enough water. Also some new friends . . ."

He pointed west, where a massive dustcloud was rising. "A group of horse. I make them a thousand strong . . ."

Georg Frundsberg pulled his Galilean telescope from his saddlebag. It was large and clumsy, and frequently got in the way on campaign. But it, too, had been a cheap bargain, like the horse. He focused it.

"Led by a *soldier*. Cat-head banners. Most of the horses are white. Some on the fringe are riderless. I cannot see more for the dust . . ."

"There is another group to the east. Bigger."

"Will they attack?"

"Not us. But I do not think we shall have our crusader friends much longer . . ."

The western dustcloud closed over a mass of straggling crusaders.

"God rest their souls," intoned the Bishop. "They are in Paradise . . ."

"They are out of our way," said Georg Langenmantel. "That horse you bought was a good bargain, Georg."

More scattered crusaders vanished under the eastern dustcloud. The remnant could be seen through the telescope scattering wildly all over the plain, heading back to the Mire.

"This Seroster . . . handles his horse in the style of our old friend Jacob Empser . . . "

"What in Heaven would Empser be doing here?"

"Same as us. Doing his duty and getting rich . . . " It was an old Lansknecht joke.

"Empser would be troublesome . . . "

"Do not fret. There is too much dust to see anything clear."

The twin dustclouds attacked all the morning. They tidied up the crusaders wonderfully. Soon there were no more stragglers; only a tightly-massed group that clung on, half a mile behind the Lansknecht.

"Less than half of them left," said Georg Langenmantel.

"Good," said Georg Frundsberg.

The Lansknecht plodded grimly on; through the midday heat. Twice they had to stop for a violent dust-storm. After each storm had passed the group behind had got smaller.

"Do you get the impression," asked Georg Langenmantel carefully, "of a giant lioness leaping through the storm?"

"With sorcerers," said Georg Frundsberg, "you can expect such things."

But not all the stragglers were behind. They came across two crusaders locked in each other's arms. They might have been lovers, if they had not both still carried knives. Their blood had made only small puddles, before draining into the dry red dust. The waterskin they had been fighting over lay between them. It too was slashed, and already drained quite dry in the desert air.

"See," said Georg Langenmantel. "Why should this Seroster exert himself in the heat? Our unfortunate friends are doing his work for him."

"Better start looking for a place for the night. The sun will set early, behind those cliffs . . . "

"That little rocky hill . . . "

The night was worse. There was only room for the Bishop and the Lansknecht on the hill. Many crusaders tried to sneak through their lines for safety, as darkness closed in. Babbling of ghost-lions, and white horses with ghost-riders, and the Seroster, who turned into a werewolf after dark. Some, alas, would not take no for an answer. First they offered gold, and then, in their desperation, they offered violence . . .

Georg Langenmantel wiped his sword, and spat into the darkness. "I could hate that Seroster . . . "

"Because he is making you do his work for him?"

"Because he is not paying me. If I meet him, I will take my wages out of his hide."

Later in the night, there was a vast pounding of hooves that shook the hill to its roots. The Seroster had come at last; his leading horsemen carried torches that streamed banners of flame. The Lansknecht stood to arms; a hedgehog of steel pikes. But somehow in the dark, the Seroster avoided their little hill, and crashed through the crusaders' camp instead. They saw the campfires explode in clouds of sparks beneath the wild hooves. After that, no one came pleading to join the ranks of the Lansknecht. Only a few fading groans, and a sobbing that went on till dawn.

"That is the end of the crusade," said Georg Langenmantel.

"Strange," said Georg Frundsberg.

"What?"

"In the light of their torches . . . I thought all their horses were white, and no living man rode on their backs. Do you believe in the Devil, Georg?"

"Like I believe in God, Georg. Their handiwork always looked alike to me – dead children, burnt villages . . . How could I say if those white horses came from God or the Devil?"

"Give me some water, friend."

"I was saving it for my horse."

"Give it me. Your horse won't play chess with you – or keep your back warm, on a winter campaign."

Dawn revealed a few trampled bodies only . . .

"I start to feel I am dreaming," said Georg Frundsberg. "I have never known a battle in which there were so few bodies, alive or dead. How many of our enemy have we actually *seen*, Georg?"

"Not more than twenty or thirty . . . I keep on feeling I have imagined the whole thing . . . I never fought against a sorcerer before . . . "

They went on. All morning the Bishop sang psalms to his God. As he had sung them all night, also, they began to get on the Lansknecht's nerves . . .

"I do not think this will end well," said Georg Frundsberg. "If Empser has learnt witchcraft . . ."

"We should have knocked the Bishop on the head this morning, and taken him home while we still had enough water . . ."

"He would only have us burnt . . ."

They both glanced up at the old man they had served so long. Eyes shut, swaying to the motion of the palanquin, he was still chanting.

"He is not long for this world."

"I wonder what he expects in the next . . ."

"There will be many waiting with a grievance . . ."

"There will be many with a grievance against us . . ."

They kept marching. After all, it was early days. They had only lost Ulrich, who fell off his horse.

Cam shadowed the Lansknecht; sneaking up gullies, riding behind ridges. He could hardly keep his eyes open. His horse was worn out, too; the sixth he'd used in three days.

He was in despair. He had played every trick, and they'd worked. He'd won half a victory. The crusaders were streaming back to the port; except for the thousand or so who were tearing the ruined villages apart in search of gold; under the superior eye of the Matagot.

He was alone now, except for the cat; his handful of cavalry had ridden their mounts to a standstill. Ripfur's army were licking their wounds in the white crags, miles behind. Horse, too, was wearying, falling further behind every mile. Horse had suffered too much hurt, and was too far from home, and thirsty for the Mire.

The Goddess had been with him, leaping like a lioness through her dust-storms . . .

But upon the iron faith of the Bishop, and the iron disbelief of the Lansknecht, she'd had no effect. He listened to them now, distantly grunting their marching-dirge.

"Hut! Dich! Baur ich komm! Hut! Dich! Baur ich komm!"

Sometimes, when they got extra-weary, their voices fell to a simple counting.

"Ein! Zwei! Drei!" But they kept on coming. They did not have minds like other men, haunted houses of lust, terror, hate or despair. They worked for money, they knew their trade, and they had seen everything. Nothing but death would keep them from the city. They were as weary as him, thirsty, half-blinded by sand but,

"Hut! Dich! Baur ich komm!" And they had gunpowder-weapons. How would the men of the city stand up to gunpowder?

Would the men of the city even be where they were supposed to be? He would know soon. Here was the turn of the valley; a new view opening out.

"I knew it would end this way," said Georg Langenmantel. "I said to myself, we will come to a narrow place. And there will be pits dug and stakes planted. And we will have to charge uphill, and the pikemen will be closed up so . . . behind breastworks. And the crossbowmen will be placed so . . . with wagonloads of bolts. And there will be women and children on top of the cliffs, standing by great piles of stones they have been days gathering. Do you think the women will torment our wounded, afterwards? . . ."

"We came to burn them," said Georg Frundsberg. "What do you think?"

Langenmantel glanced behind, at the dustclouds where horses still reluctantly followed. "And as we fall back, Empser will put in a final charge . . ."

"Our venture is no longer profitable."

"I doubt our venture is any longer possible . . . but we have been paid."

"I have forced a worse place, at Württemberg. Those who survive will be rich . . ."

Langenmantel shrugged, and began to call out orders. The Lansknecht made up their fighting-formations swiftly, in spite of weariness. The gunpowder-weapons were set on stands. Aim was taken at the pikemen . . . Slow-matches were lit and ready. There was a brief flurry of interest as a single horseman rode past, and stood in front of the stakes; a two-handed sword in his hand . . .

"That does not look like Empser," said Georg Langenmantel.

"Empser will be with the cavalry," said Georg Frundsberg.

Behind them, standing high on his palanquin, the Bishop called for God's blessing on Christian arms . . .

Here it ends, thought Cam. Maybe I can blunt their first charge. But I will not last long . . . He was glad; it would be good to rest in the Seroster's Chamber.

He noticed the cat had joined him . . .

The armoured Lansknecht started up the slope, like a tight steel tortoise, shield to shield, pike to pike. They had the calm look of time-served craftsmen, in spite of their parti-coloured hose and fantastic helmets . . . Cam scrabbled his feet, for a good grip. But the sword had no life in it; it lay for the first time in his hands like a lump of pig-iron. The gunpowder-weapons fired, balls flew . . .

Then a shadow fell, across the advancing Lansknecht. Cam glanced over his shoulder.

The sky was half blue, and half a towering mass of cloud, that looked like it was going to push the world over. And, sitting on the cliff like a pattern of gold beads in the Goddess's necklace . . .

Lovingly, Sehtek brought a cloud-paw down.

The air turned black, blue, black, blue, black, blue. In front of the advancing Lansknecht, rocks split and flew; dead trees burst into flame. And as they hesitated, the rain hit them. In a second, the dry slope they climbed turned to mud, a leaping torrent. They waded, fell sprawling, rolled down, their visors full of water and their lungs full of smoke. Struggled to their feet and fell again, rolled on top of each other.

The rain doused every slow-match for the gunpowder-weapons; turned the gunpowder itself into mud, so that it too spewed away downhill.

And still the rain fell. While, above, the men of the city stood dry-clad, in sunlight . . .

Bemused, the Lansknecht backed away, leaving the Bishop standing in his palanquin, alone. His mitre fell off; his splendid robes clung to him darkly, till he looked a sodden scarecrow. The lightning fell on him alone now, rending the rocks at his very feet. His palanquin-bearers turned and ran . . .

But the Bishop prayed on, unharmed.

"This is business beyond us, brother," said Georg Langenmantel.

"I am glad to be a simple soldier only," said Georg Frundsberg.

At last, the rain stopped.

The Bishop ceased praying, looked at his Lansknecht. "Advance! Do your duty! Or you will burn!"

"There is no wood in this place," said Georg Langenmantel, "except . . ." He looked at the massed stakes of the city men. "I would make peace with this sorcerer, lord. He seems merciful. He has killed few yet."

Silently, the Bishop made a gesture to his late followers; that made Amon shudder. Then he stepped from the smouldering wreck of his palanquin and, supporting himself with his crozier, strode towards the army of the city.

And again the lightning played about him; but he was not consumed, except in prayer. He picked his way, with tortoise-like care, through a gap in the stakes, and walked on alone towards the city. The ranks parted, awestruck, to let him through.

Now a white rag was brandished on a stick, by Georg Frundsberg.

"Parley! Parley!"

Cam walked down; they all stared at each other with great curiosity. Cam had never seen Lansknecht before. Georg Langenmantel and Georg Frundsberg had never seen a living sorcerer.

"Has your worship any use, by chance, for a company of Lansknecht?"

The Bishop walked on; the witch-army fell behind. A few witch-brats followed, staring, thumbs in mouths. Something small and gentle and long-forgotten moved in the Bishop's heart. But he thrust it from him. Sorcery! Drove them off with wild swings of his crozier, and the sign of the cross. Then they put their tongues out, and pulled down their eyes at him in a dreadful way, and finally threw stones . . . revealing their true nature . . . snares of the Devil.

He walked slowly, sensing he was coming to an end. But the silence was pleasant, the sough of the wind, the warmth of the sun on his back. He remembered being a boy.

More Devil's tricks!

The Bishop broke into one of his favourite psalms.

> "The Wicked plots against the Righteous
> And gnashes his teeth at him
> But the Lord laughs at the Wicked
> For He sees that his day is coming
> The Wicked draw the sword and bend their bows
> To slay them that walk uprightly
> Their sword shall enter their own heart
> And their bows shall be broken.
> They vanish – like smoke they vanish away . . ."

At the very thought of smoke and burning, the Bishop's body seemed to acquire a new life, and he strode on manfully.

Everything became faint and far; it was long since he had eaten. So he was glad to see a little stream gurgling across the path, soft grass. And lying on the grass, a half-eaten bannock . . .

He knelt, praising God.

Then asked himself who had put the bannock there, in this accursed land . . .

Two golden cats watched, a little further upstream.

He was on his feet in an instant; staggered on.

"Unfu," sent Sehtek. "What-do?"

"Less-strength than-kitten," sent Khephren.

"Follow . . . "

The Bishop came to the city; it took a long time to climb to the gate. Every ten yards he had to halt and say a psalm. Sehtek and Khephren waited below, politely.

The gate was barred. Women on the gate-top watched him idly. But much more their eyes were turned down the valley. The Bishop hammered on the gate with his crozier. "Open in the name of God!" The third time, they heard. The postern opened; a stout woman stood there. "What you want?"

"Witch! This city is judged. It will be better for Sodom and Gomorrah . . . "

"What's 'e want, Yvette? 'As 'e come from the battle?" There were two women now, staring. The Bishop realised his mitre was gone, his crozier broken, his vestments turned dull brown by the rain and dust of the road.

"Repent! Before the flames . . . "

"Don't let 'im in, Yvette. 'E don't look right in the 'ead."

The Bishop tried to push in. The stout woman sent him sprawling and slammed the postern.

He got up eventually, hammered again. The women's heads appeared on the rampart above.

"Go away, you old fool. Or . . . " She held up something dark and menacing against the sky. The Bishop thought of the Blessed Martyrs.

A lukewarm deluge descended, soaking him. His twitching nostrils told him it was nothing death-bearing . . .

He continued to demand admittance. More deluges. Finally, half-blinded, he turned.

There were not two yellow devils watching now, but hundreds. He grasped the form his martyrdom would take . . .

They led him away beyond the city, up into the white cliffs. A narrow ravine, where no man ever came, with a distant view of the city. They hemmed him in close, a great multitude . . .

"Into thy hands, O Lord, I commend my spirit." When he had finished praying, he opened his eyes.

They were all gone. Except one, sat far off, and it was washing itself. It was black, with gold-flecked fur and eyes.

Then the Bishop understood the Lord had delivered him. There was even a dry little cave, and a clear spring, and dry bracken for a bed. And a half-eaten bannock . . .

The Bishop remembered the ravens, that fed the prophet Elijah . . . St Antony, who dwelt in a desert and was tormented by demons in animal form . . . St Jerome, who in the Wilderness sanctified the lion to be a child of God. He bit into the bannock hungrily, wondering how he might sanctify the evil black cat . . .

"He stay," sent Nofret the Matagot, with a wild glint of glee at the success of her scheme. Not for nothing had she dwelt weeks in the crypt of St Alban's, and listened to the pious sermons Father Death had preached on the prophet Elijah, and St Antony and St Jerome . . .

41

Cam sat by the fire in the Fleur-de-Lys warming the soles of his boots, which still contained five gold pieces each.

It had passed like a dream, the triumphal days. Hiring the Lansknecht, for the time it took to get them back to the fishing-port. The city men, noticing their fearsome weapons, had paid up willingly for that. And the Lansknecht had cheerfully marched at the head of the army, mail-shirts open to the waist, and helms hung from pikes and arquebuses.

"Hut! Dich! Hier ich komm!" But it had a merry lilt now. They drove the remaining crusaders before them. And there were old dead to bury. Not many, but some. The Lansknecht buried as they went. All Cam saw were the little groups of long mounds. But still he shuddered.

They rousted out the fools still digging for Matagot's gold, in every ruined village they passed. A lost army in themselves, that had pulled the villages apart, dug great pits, found in all less than a hundred gold pieces and killed each other for them.

The great pits were used to bury the dead.

And the way through the Mire, returning, had been so obvious . . . How had anyone ever got lost? The burnt bridge had not been rebuilt. But the Lansknecht gathered great bundles of reeds as they marched, and cast them into the black ooze, and the whole army passed over, though wet-foot and uneasy.

But before then they had seen the black palls of smoke hanging over the port. That was more than any bridge burning . . .

In the port, screaming women ran for protection from the rampaging crusaders. Bodies and fighting in the streets. The Mayor of the port ran up, to seek deliverance.

"Kneel to your rightful lord," thundered Cam, revealing the Duke riding behind, pale-faced at the carnage. The Mayor, catching sight of the cat-head banner, groaned aloud, "Shall we *never* have done with cats?"

The odd thing was, Cam hadn't even realised the port belonged to the city, until that instant. Then he realised his hand was on the dagger . . .

It was finding the Fleur-de-Lys that had put him in a good mood. The landlord, running out as they passed, had bade the great lords welcome. His apron still had the hole in it that the knife had made so long ago.

All the others were upstairs, washing. There was wine at his elbow, and a good smell of roasting. Better still, his old pack was packed, ready by the door. And in spite of the greybeard's urging, he'd refused to change. He sat waiting for his guests in his old black jerkin with the rusty studs.

When dinner was over, Cam said, "I have a last tale for you. A last tale, and a last toast!"

Their faces grew troubled, as they looked at his pack lying by the door.

He clapped his hands. The shipmen were led in, red-faced and uneasy in such company. The first shuffled forward. "Sir, I am an honest man. Yet I bring a tale no man will believe."

Cam thought back over the months. "Shipman, I know how you feel."

"Sir, it concerns a nun who was carried off by the Devil."

Georges snorted; Geoffrey buried his face in his wine. The shipmen exchanged despairing looks. "Sir, this is a true tale, and my friend is here to bear witness. Two days since, as we lay at this quayside, a nun came, a pretty red-cheeked mother abbess. It was clear she was a lady of great piety, for she was constantly looking over her shoulder and crossing herself. We saw the colour of her money. So my friend here undertook to carry her across to Afric, our next port o' call. She was going to enlighten the benighted, she said.

"Well, you never saw a nun wi' such luggage. Four heavy trunks, seven leather bundles and a wicker basket. My friend Marples here says something about laying up treasure in Heaven, in a friendly way, an' she gives him a look from under her wimple that'd make a basking-shark turn tail. An' the weight of those bundles . . . there were some jokes about the burden of poverty, I can tell you!

"She embarked at sunset, but we had to wait till dawn for the tide. She was very insistent that we pull up the gangplank and draw out a good way from the shore. Though she couldn't swim an' was mortally afeared o' the water. Anyway, we broached a keg to celebrate, an' slept like babes till dawn. An' I'm just as glad we did, 'cos on the morrow, all over the new-scrubbed decks an' the furled sails an' even in the crow's-nest were the black pawmarks o' cats. Except there ain't been no cats in this town for six months – an evil name cats has in these parts, sir, the townsfolk drove them all out."

And the shipman gazed uneasily at the Miw, who were perched on every chairback and sideboard, cracking chop-bones.

"An' when we went to bestir the lady abbess, there weren't no sign o' her. We waited three days, but she never showed. Then we opened her bags an' they were full of *pennies*, sir, besides gold, an' many papers from your city, an' little blue bottles . . ."

"Paul," said Cam. "Drowned." And everyone stared aghast at the Miw. Who calmly went on cracking chop-bones.

All dead now, thought Cam. Ironhand, Sir Henri, Paul. All over, and I am alive. He blinked, as a prisoner who is let out of a dungeon; and dismissed the shipmen with good reward.

He raised his glass. "Friends. A toast. Then I must be on my way . . ."

But the landlord had come in silently, and put a sweet-smelling bowl at his elbow. So sweet that Cam picked out a chestnut gingerly, and cracked it with the hilt of his dagger, and offered it to the First Virgin.

Then realised what he had done . . .

"*Landlord*! Who ordered you to bring chestnuts?" The landlord shuffled.

"You always has chestnuts, sir. They goes wi' the knife . . ."

"Always? I've only been here once before. It was the blacksmith had chestnuts . . ."

"Aye, the Seroster . . ."

"You mean the *blacksmith* was the Seroster?"

"Aye – a poor lost soul, living beyond his time; always trying to get away, you see. But he never got far beyond this port. The knife brought him back . . . till he sold it to you."

"He tricked me . . ."

"Serosters are always tricked. Who'd *choose* to be Seroster?"

Cam leapt to his feet. "That mother is a trickster . . ."

"All gods are tricksters," said Georges heavily. "None of us know what we are doing. You were lucky. You understand more than most."

They all looked at him, in the flickering candlelight.

"Stay," said the First Virgin. "I am with child."

"Stay," said the Duke. "I am too young."

"My job is running an inn," said Georges.

"I am getting old," said Geoffrey.

All the familiar faces . . .

"Damn the knife!" Cam shouted. He threw it down on the table.

But it flew the length of the room, embedded itself in the mantle.

"I am *Cam*," he shouted. "Cam of Cambridge." And walked to the door.

"The knife will fetch you back," said the inn-keeper. "Till you are too old to walk . . . "

"How old was the blacksmith?"

"My great-grandfather knew him; he was not young then."

"Very well. The knife goes *with* me." He plucked it from the fireplace. Again they watched him; their pleading faces made a dungeon.

"I have done my work. All your enemies are dead!"

"There are always new enemies," said Georges.

Cam paused on the doorstep. Amon stood there. And Cam remembered the wide blue river, and the ship. The cat had been faithful beyond death. He couldn't leave it now. He picked it up in his arms and said softly, "Come, Amon. Every road leads to Bubastis."

Then he was gone, running lightly down the cobbled street, under the new stars.

"We'll wait," said Georges.